THE CERBERUS AFFAIR

CHARLOTTE VALENTINE

For my mother and father, who inspired me to believe that anything was possible.

You were the wind beneath my wings.

Heart pounding, hands shaking, her eyes straining to focus, she watched the scene unfold in slow motion. She struggled to stay conscious. She had to make a decision, and she had to get it right. For both of them.

Then a voice. 'Catherine. Please. Do it.' The words were barely audible over the pain ripping through her head. She forced herself to turn in their direction as she tried to hold the gun steady in her hand.

She saw a pair of eyes and she knew. Just as she'd known when she first looked into them. They jolted her into consciousness now and told her the choice she must make. She steadied her hand and directed her aim.

She took a deep breath, closed her eyes and fired.

The sound of the shot, the force of the gun's recoil and the throbbing pain in her head were the perfect storm that finally overwhelmed her.

As she sank into oblivion, another face and another fateful day flashed into her mind. The face that had made her go back.

And the day when all this began.

PROLOGUE

HIM

He watched as she sank to the floor, her body a crumpled heap. Please God she had not lost consciousness from the force of the blow. He needed her now more than ever. This couldn't be the end, not like this. Not when they'd barely begun.

He saw her eyes flicker open and stare into his. Those beautiful, intelligent eyes, now full of confusion. He saw the glint of the gun in her trembling hand. Somehow, he got the words out. 'Catherine. Please. Do it.'

He looked into her eyes again and willed her to make the right choice. He told himself she would. As she took aim, he closed his eyes.

And waited for the shot.

HER

CHAPTER ONE

The day Adam died was the day Catherine decided to change her life.

She woke early that morning after a restless night. In the half-light she rummaged for her phone on the bedside table and deleted the now unnecessary alarm. It was barely 7 a.m. and there was still an hour until the daily ritual of getting her son Will out of teenage first gear. She craved more sleep, but knew it was pointless to try while her head continued to perform its mental somersaults.

She sat up in bed, deciding to distract herself with the morning headlines before she threw on a tracksuit. She opened her Google news app then caught her breath at the words that flashed up on the screen.

JUNIOR HEALTH MINISTER FOUND DEAD

Her phone shook in her hand as she stared at the photograph underneath the headline.

Adam.

This couldn't be true. She could hear her heart beating,

pounding to escape the confines of her chest cavity. Her blood pumped faster. She lost her grip on the phone; as it hit the floor she sank back into her pillow, waiting for her heart rate to slow down.

What had happened? It was only a month ago she'd seen him and Lizzie in London. He couldn't be dead.

She took a deep breath, leaned down, and picked up her phone. It had landed screen up, and Adam's eyes stared into hers.

Tightness gripped her throat and tears blurred her vision as she forced herself to read the words beneath the photograph.

Junior Health Minister Adam Wentworth, 53, has been discovered dead in his London home. He was considered a rising star in the Government and a potential future party leader, despite being a late-comer to the political arena. Insiders claim the Prime Minister had an especially high regard for Mr Wentworth who was being widely tipped for promotion to a senior Cabinet position in the upcoming reshuffle.

No details have yet been released about the cause of his sudden and unexpected death although sources indicate it is not being treated as suspicious. Mr Wentworth leaves behind a wife Elizabeth, and daughter Clara, 22.

A statement from the Prime Minister is expected shortly.

Fifty-three, her age too. Her thoughts rewound to her first week at Oxford. She'd felt like a fish out of water as her strong northern accent stood out among the clipped public-school voices. Everybody else seemed to already know some-one. She knew nobody; then Adam and Lizzie came along, and they all hit it off instantly. She and Lizzie became best friends, and Adam and Lizzie had fallen in love before the end of the first term.

Catherine had always been a little in love with him too, although she never told anybody, including him. She doubted he even suspected. He was the man she always compared others to, and nobody ever came close to measuring up. Despite her feelings for him she knew he and Lizzie were perfect for each other. She loved them both dearly, and she'd been bridesmaid at their wedding in Oxford the summer they'd all graduated.

She couldn't believe she'd never see him again, nor imagine what Lizzie was going through. She had to speak to her.

She half-expected the call to go straight to voicemail, but her friend answered on the third ring.

'Catherine. Thank God. I so need to talk to you. I've been wanting to call but there's been no time since I... found him. There are so many people here.'

Lizzie's calmness startled her. She'd expected distraught and inconsolable but instead her tone was flat and emotionless. Apart from one stumble, it was almost business-like.

She stammered, 'Lizzie, I...I'm so sorry. I can't believe it, and I can't imagine what you're going through. But you know I'm here for you. I'll help you through this, every step of the way.'

'I want him back, Catherine. I...I never got to say...' Lizzie's voice trailed off.

'I know.' Catherine shivered at her own response – she'd been denied the chance to say goodbye too.

Then Lizzie started to cry. Low, breathless whimpers, like a confused wounded animal, unable to understand why everything hurt.

Each sob pierced Catherine to her core. She felt paralysed and made inadequate by her own grief, but she had to take care of this special woman. 'Lizzie, I'll get there as soon as I can. And I'll take care of everything. Whatever you need. Anything at all.'

'What I need is for you to tell me how he died.'

Catherine caught her breath as she heard the flatness back in Lizzie's voice. The crying had stopped as abruptly as it had begun.

'What have the doctors said?'

'What I knew they'd say. Natural causes, unforeseen heart attack. They'll blame it on stress, but they're wrong.' Lizzie's voice lowered to a whisper. 'Something's not right about all this. I don't know what, but there's something.' Catherine frowned at her phone screen. She had to get to London quickly. Her friend needed her; this reaction was all wrong. Hopefully Clara would be home soon to take charge until she could be there herself.

'Is Clara on her way from Durham? You should ask your doctor to give you something to help you rest till she arrives.'

'She's on the train. And I don't need my doctor, Catherine. I need you to understand and believe me. You'll think I sound crazy because Adam's gone, but I'm not. He didn't die of natural causes. I think someone did this. Someone who knew exactly what they were doing.'

Catherine bit down on her lip. What the hell was Lizzie talking about? 'Look, I'm going to get there as soon as I can. I know nothing must make any sense at the moment, but what you're suggesting...'

'I'm more than suggesting. I'm certain of it. Adam was murdered.'

Catherine's stomach lurched at the words. Where was all this coming from? Her friend was in a seriously bad state and she needed to find some way of calming her down before her daughter came home and heard the same accusations. She thought for a moment, looking for the right words. 'Lizzie, you're in shock, you're bound to be. I understand, and I'll get there as soon as I can. But your priority now is to look after yourself and Clara, so please stop torturing yourself like this. I know it's impossible to believe Adam's gone, but if anything looked remotely suspicious the police would already be on to it, and so would the Government. You need to rest as much as you can until Clara's back, and give in to your grief. Talk to your doctor about how you're feeling. He can help.'

'He can't help with this. The police are still here but I doubt they'd believe anything I said even if I told them, which I won't. I can't talk about it to anybody but you. I know this isn't how you expected me to be or what you expected to hear, but this isn't shock speaking, Catherine, it's me. It's Adam too, in a way; you'll understand that when I tell you more, but I can't now. Some more officials have arrived. Please get here as soon as you can. I need your help. You're the only one I can trust to find out what's going on.'

'Lizzie. I...' She didn't get the chance to finish the sentence.

'I'm sorry you saw the news before I could tell you. And one more thing before I go. Check your emails.

CHAPTER TWO

Catherine sat at her kitchen table and picked up her mug. She must have made coffee after her conversation with Lizzie, but she couldn't remember doing it. She took a sip and almost spat it out. It was lukewarm and tasted bitter. How long had she been sitting here? She pressed the palms of her hands hard against her head, trying to force out the image of a lifeless, unseeing Adam. She couldn't comprehend the thought of him being dead. And even less Lizzie's whispered suggestion he'd been murdered.

Tears and guilt welled up as she recalled her last conversation with him a month ago. The weekend she'd spent with him and Lizzie had been dominated by her issues. They'd given her all the time she needed to talk through her plans for after Will left for university and she'd opened up about her personal and professional frustrations to the two people who knew her best.

Despite the pressures Adam must have been under – more than she'd realised, it seemed now – he'd done everything he could to encourage her to make the changes she was considering.

'You should get yourself back to London, Catherine. In today's political climate we need minds like yours on our doorstep to challenge us, and you were one of the best investigative journalists the Guardian ever had. You're so obviously bored with what you're doing now. You're underutilised and frankly wasting your talents up there in the frozen north.'

She smiled at his description, but he was right. She had let herself get into a rut. Each day seemed to flow indistinguishably into the next and too often she felt she operated on virtual autopilot, defined by tasks and routine.

She loved the small North of England town where she lived, and it had given Will a wonderful childhood. It was gentle, friendly and relaxed and her parents had been happy they were there. They'd been the reason she moved there after Will came along, but there wasn't the fast-paced excitement she'd always loved about city life. More and more she missed her old life in London, but how practical was it for her to go back?

She'd given Adam a sceptical look. 'I'd love to think I could get back on the paper, but I can't expect to pick up where I left off. Any successes and reputation I had were a long time ago. I'm a bit scared to be honest. I'd be starting out all over again and I'd need one hell of a killer story hook to even get through the door. And I'm so out of the loop these days.'

'Stop finding reasons not to do it. Being scared isn't your style, and with your intelligence and talent it's the last thing you should be. I'll think about some issues you could get your teeth into. I'm very much in the loop.' He paused, looking directly at her. 'Probably too many loops as it happens.'

She raised her eyebrows as he looked away, his hands fidgeting as if he was about to tell her something but wondering if he should. He frowned and started to speak. 'I...'

'Lunch is ready you guys. Stop putting the world to rights

and come through.' They both turned in the direction of Lizzie's voice.

Catherine touched his arm as they stood. 'What were you going to say, Adam?'

He smiled the same boyish smile that had charmed her the first time they met at Oxford. 'It can wait till another time, but the boss won't, so let's go and eat.' They linked arms as they walked through to the kitchen. 'But if you're looking for an angle for a story, you might want to think about genetics. It's controversial stuff and the research is moving fast these days. Some interesting developments are about to hit, I think. Lots of competing vested interests so it's right up your street. I'll send you some links to get you started.'

Now he was gone, and she regretted she hadn't pushed him further to tell her if something was troubling him. They'd never got another time, and she wondered what he might have told her if they had.

Ironically, during the night she'd been planning another weekend visit to tell him and Lizzie the decisions she'd reached about her future. Or the ones she thought she'd reached. She'd lain awake for hours going over things. But then this was about more than just work. Something else was missing from her life. Or someone. And she'd decided to do something about that too.

This morning her night-time preoccupations seemed ridiculous in light of Adam's death and what Lizzie had to face. Her plans would have to wait. This news had thrown her totally off balance, and she had to pull herself together. She needed a clear head to be of any use to Lizzie.

And she had to take care of Will. He was always her priority. She glanced at her watch and decided to leave him to sleep in before she told him the news. He'd be devastated.

Adam was the closest thing he'd had to a father figure in his life.

She moved to make herself a fresh drink, hoping caffeine would kickstart her system, and suddenly remembered Lizzie's final words. She fired up her laptop to check her emails, but there was nothing from Adam or Lizzie, or anything relevant to this morning's events. Until she opened her spam file. She could never resist looking before deleting all the unsolicited garbage, something which had always amused Adam. And then she saw it, among the discount codes and unwanted product offers, an email address and message subject that had to be from him. Only the three of them knew that in-joke from their student days.

Timed at 5 a.m. this might be the last email he ever sent. It felt ghoulish, but she knew she had to open it. She took a deep breath, clicked on the message and began to read. Before she reached the end, her early morning shock had been replaced with a calm resolve.

Adam had believed he might be in danger. He'd hinted at it when she last saw him, and she hadn't paid enough attention, but now she would. He'd made her decision for her. He'd given her an investigation and a story, as he'd promised. It just wasn't the story she'd hoped for or wanted to write.

But he'd thought his life was at risk, so she had no choice. She had to go back and find out why.

CHAPTER THREE

Clayton Mortimer hit the snooze button on his phone as Guns N' Roses rocked him awake at 6.30 a.m. Maybe he should consider changing his alarm track. His daughter insisted it showed his age, but they were his favourite band and they never allowed him to oversleep. Although today he almost wished they had. All work and no play were grinding him down. A whole weekend of sleep sounded appealing, but he couldn't afford that indulgence. Perhaps he should at least give himself a night off.

Maybe he should be a bit more like his best friend David. He never looked ground down. They'd talked on the phone last night, a rare departure from their usual four-word texts. Or rather David had talked, and Clayton had listened. His friend loved to regale him with his latest female conquest, occasionally in overly lurid detail for Clayton's tastes, although he usually detected a heavy degree of exaggeration. But David was basically one of the good guys. His wife had hurt him badly, and Clayton suspected he used the bravura act as his protective armour against being hurt again.

'You work too hard mate. You need a night off. Find yourself a new woman.' Typical David. Always thought sex was the answer to everything.

'That's easier said than done. Between work and making sure Becca's okay I've hardly got much time to go looking. Anyway, getting involved with someone isn't on the radar at the moment. I think I'll leave the search for the perfect woman to you.'

'If I find one, I'll ask if she has a hot friend.'

'You never know. Keep me posted. And I'd better grab some sleep. Early lecture tomorrow. I'll message you in a couple of days about that night off. We'll go for a few beers.'

When he hit call end Clayton smiled. David always made him smile. They were unlikely friends in many ways and so different. His best friend was a born joker, which had helped him cope with his marriage break-up, and he teased Clayton for being so intense. Which he was. Life had made him that way. He doubted any girlfriend who was David's type would have a friend who'd be his. Not that he was sure he even had a type; these days he rarely gave the prospect of romantic entanglement any thought.

But occasionally, for a brief moment, he'd have the strange feeling that somewhere out there someone was waiting for him. A unique woman who'd show up one day who he'd be unable to resist, and she'd blast through all his defences. His emotions wished she would, but his intellect told him otherwise. He didn't need the complications. So, he dismissed it as ridiculous and unscientific, told himself to get a grip and buried the stupid notion again. He had way too much to occupy him to dwell on idle fantasies.

Guns N' Roses blasted him alert again. He switched off the snooze button and walked to the shower, catching sight of himself in the mirror. Six foot two and naturally slim, he kept himself in reasonable shape by swimming twice a week in the university pool. At fifty-four he supposed he should consider upping that to three times, to keep his still passably defined abs.

Ten minutes later he emerged from the shower, his mop of dark wavy hair still damp. Between haircuts it became untameable, but he told himself it made him look professorial.

'My mate, the mad Professor.' He smiled as he thought how David liked to wind him up with that introduction. But he figured all Professors needed a little madness. It was almost an occupational prerequisite.

He fired up his laptop to check over his lecture notes as his coffee brewed. He always found something reassuringly calming about the rhythmic gurgle and drip of the filter machine. It was part of his morning ritual, followed by an early check-in on Becca.

'Hi Dad.' She answered on the third ring and, as usual, he heard laughter in her voice at the predictability of his timing. He loved the sound of her voice and her laugh. And he was predictable where she was concerned.

'Hi Becks. Everything ok? Is Tim there?' Damn, why did he always ask that? He sounded like an obsessive father.

'Yes Dad, he's here. He says hi. How are you? Early lecture today?'

'Yep, and a day of tutorials. How about you?'

'We're about to head to the library. First lecture's not until 12. So how are your admiring female students? You do realise they've all got the hots for you, don't you?'

'Stop it Becks! I'm sure they all think I'm borderline decrepit. And a bastard when I'm marking their essays. Anyway, how are you? Everything ok?' He asked the same question every day. He couldn't help himself.

'I'm absolutely fine Dad. Got an A for my first Shakespeare essay so I'm feeling good.'

Clayton smiled with pride. She was a great kid. They'd

come through some difficult times together and he never stopped being amazed at her toughness. Nothing fazed her. She had a rare combination of gentleness and total generosity of spirit, mixed with an unshakeable strength, qualities that he'd only ever seen before in his mother.

'Well done. Told you you're a candidate for a first!'

'It's early days Dad and I've a long way to go yet. It might be beginner's luck. So, are we meeting up this weekend? Lunch on Sunday?'

'I'd love to. I need to work most of the weekend, but a few hours off would be good. You have a great day today okay? I'll call you tomorrow. Message if you need me.'

'You too Dad. Love you loads. Speak tomorrow.'

Clayton hit call end and breathed in with relief, as he always did when he spoke with her. Relief at not hearing the words he always dreaded would come someday. That she'd done something clumsy, dropped something, stumbled, lost her balance. Something she'd make a joke about, not realising its possible significance. But he would. And the thought was unbearable. He could live with a ticking clock inside himself. He didn't know how he'd live with that same clock ticking inside her.

He forced himself to focus on skim-reading his lecture notes. No point in dwelling on what-ifs. He was a scientist, and he only knew one way of dealing with a problem. Find the solution. He'd head to the lab tonight.

Nights off would have to wait.

CHAPTER FOUR

Clayton looked out at the rows of bemused faces in the lecture theatre. He grinned as they snapped their laptop lids closed in virtual unison. This section of the course always taxed all but the most gifted students. The Human Genome Project sounded cool, clever and cutting edge but, in reality, it was a complex subject which most struggled to get their heads round. A thirteen-year global scientific mission that had set out to sequence human DNA and map out the genetic code. The greatest achievement in genetics since Gregor Mendel discovered its fundamentals in the 1860s. An Austrian monk with none of the technology available to twenty-first century scientists, and an inspiration to Darwin, he could never have foreseen where his early work experimenting with pea plants would lead.

Today, the sheer scale of the genome surprised Clayton's students. He watched their faces as they tried to visualise the three billion paired strands of DNA packed tightly into their chromosomes and containing over twenty thousand genes that made them unique individuals. He'd struggled to imagine it himself when he'd first got into its complexities, but he'd been determined to build on the pioneering work of the Genome Project's scientists. And now here he was, London's senior Professor of Human Genetics and one of the country's most acknowledged experts.

He hoped his mother would have been proud of what he'd achieved, and of what he still dreamed of achieving. The breakthrough he needed to make. His eyes moistened at the thought of her. That gentle but strong woman, still in his mind daily, still willing him on.

'Professor?'

He turned with enquiring eyes to meet those of Susie, always alive with intelligence. He considered her one of the most gifted students he'd ever taught, and he forecast a bright future for her.

'Susie. Hi. Thanks for not crashing out in the lecture. I spotted a few who did.'

'No, I'm fascinated by it. Now I see the enormity of your subject I can't wait to learn more. I loved how you helped us visualise our DNA.'

He smiled. He always concluded this particular lecture by telling them that the DNA tightly coiled in any human being's cells, if stretched out, would be about twice the diameter of the Solar System. 'I guess that description does tend to grab the attention. The human body is a remarkable piece of engineering.'

'Is it ever, and our DNA underpins everything doesn't it? I've thought about your offer to join your research team, and I'd love to be a part of this. I wonder if we could fix a time to go through some details?'

'I'd be delighted to. You'd be a great addition to the team. But it means a huge time commitment. Research is addictive, trust me. You need to be sure.'

'I am sure. And I want to help.'

'Then come and find me in the lab around 8.00 tonight.

I'll be working and we can talk. We're making some exciting progress, but I need to add brain power to the team urgently.'

'It's a date Professor. See you later.'

As Susie bounded out of the lecture theatre with all the physical exuberance of youth, he caught himself remembering when he'd always moved at that pace without thinking about it. Now he took nothing for granted. He was fit for a man of his age, but how long would it last? He told himself to dismiss the thought. No news was good news.

He turned to pick up his papers and his tutorial file fell out of his hand. He froze for a second before bending to pick it up. Please God don't let it be starting. Not yet. He took a deep breath and told himself to stop over-reacting. It was probably nothing. He should take a walk, clear his head and grab a Starbucks before his tutorial group.

Fifteen minutes later he sat in his favourite area of the park. Apart from the occasional passing dog walker he could almost guarantee himself solitude here at this time of day, and he wanted an hour of quiet time. He needed to think logically as he'd been trained to do and not jump to premature conclusions. So he'd dropped a file, big deal. It happened to people every day. No point having a panic attack about it. Except he wasn't like other people. He was on borrowed time, and sometimes a small part of him wished he didn't know it.

A part that wished he'd never opened his mother's letter.

CHAPTER FIVE

Telling Will was the toughest thing Catherine had ever had to do. Feeling his pain was like reading about Adam's death herself all over again. She held both his hands tightly as his face crumpled before tears came. He'd done that ever since he was a baby, as if he was processing an event, deciding if he should cry. She pulled him to her, trying to absorb the pain, wanting him to hurt less.

'I'm so sorry sweetheart. I know how important he was to you. And he loved you very much. Cling on to that. And your happy memories of him.'

His tear-stained face looked up at her. 'He was like a Dad to me,' he said breathlessly between sobs.

'I know. And he thought of you as the son he and Lizzie never had.'

'What happened exactly?'

'I don't know all the details yet, but it sounds like a sudden heart attack.' As she spoke, she tried to block out Lizzie's sinister suggestion, and the email she'd just read. 'Lizzie found him first thing this morning.'

'I can't imagine him dead.' He buried his head into her shoulder, and she clutched him to her again.

'I know. Death is so final, and we never expect it to happen to the people we love. It just stops everything else in its tracks. But he was so proud of you and thrilled about you getting into medical school. Thank goodness he knew that before he died. And in his way, he'll be by your side all through it, spurring you on.'

He looked up and they exchanged faint smiles at their shared memory of a man they'd both loved.

'How are Lizzie and Clara? Was Clara there?'

'No, but she's on her way back now. And Lizzie's in shock. I'm going to go down and see her tomorrow if that's OK with you.'

'Can I come with you?'

She faltered before she replied. She couldn't risk exposing Will to a situation she didn't understand herself yet. She took his hand. 'I think I should make this first visit myself. Lizzie won't want you to see her looking and feeling the way she's bound to be tomorrow. Do you mind? I'll only stay one night, and I'll call Nina to tell her about Adam and ask about you going to stay with her and Jack.'

'Of course, I understand. And I'll see Lizzie at the...the funeral. I hate that word.'

'Everybody does.'

'When will it be?'

She'd anticipated his question, but she had no answer. 'Too early to know yet. They take a lot of time to arrange and I suppose because of his position there'll be some government involvement, which will complicate everything. I'll know more after tomorrow.'

She glanced at the kitchen clock. 'We'd better call the surgery and tell them you won't be going in today.

In preparation for Cambridge he was spending his

summer shadowing their GP, who said he was a natural. Will was loving every minute of it.

'Actually Mum, would you call them while I get changed, but only to tell them I'm going to be late, and explain why? Dr Roberts has some interesting cases lined up for today and I'd like to sit in on them. Do you think Adam would mind?'

She looked at his earnest expression and squeezed him to her.

'I think he'd be even more impressed with you than he was already.'

As he scraped his chair back and ran up the stairs, she smiled in spite of everything. Will never did anything slowly or quietly, and something about the normality of that helped. He'd been a challenge growing up, but what joy he'd brought her. She was proud of the man he was becoming since he'd at last emerged from what she'd christened his three-year teenage Neanderthal grunting stage.

She would never regret a single moment of the time she'd devoted to him, although she sometimes wondered if she'd lived too much of her life through him. Maybe all mothers did that, especially when they were single parents. For so long her pleasure in life had come almost exclusively from seeing him happy.

She thought again about her conversation with Adam about her life in London when her career had been at its peak.

She'd made the move North to be near her parents when she'd adopted Will. Both had been huge decisions. At thirty-five she'd been content to be manless, but she couldn't contemplate the prospect of being childless. The desire to be a mother had burned deep inside her. It had started as a flickering flame she tried to ignore until it threatened to scorch her insides. The day she first held her new son that burning desire had been replaced by a love so powerful it overwhelmed her and she vowed to be the best parent to him she could be. London and her career could take a backseat. Her parents had been thrilled to have them both on their doorstep and they had doted on Will. She'd paid the bills with regular freelancing work for the local papers supplementing her savings, lived relatively frugally, and given Will the best life she knew how to.

As soon as he left for the surgery, she booked the earliest train she could for the following morning. Lizzie and Clara needed private mother and daughter time today. Then she called her best friend Nina.

They'd been kindred spirits ever since they collided in the school playground thirteen years earlier; both proud owners of five-year-old boys trying unsuccessfully to look tough on their first day. Will and Jack became best friends and so did they. They navigated motherhood, kept each other sane through the childhood tantrums and dramas, and rode the rollercoaster of puberty, teenage monosyllabic communication and raging hormones together.

They were always there for each other, and Nina's was the shoulder she needed to cry on now.

CHAPTER SIX

As Catherine walked towards their usual table in their favourite café, Nina stood with outstretched arms, and she fell into them. She clung on, listening to her own heaving sobs, reluctant to let go. She half-imagined that if she stayed cocooned in the safety of her friend's hug the events of today would go away.

Nina stroked her head gently. 'Let it all out Catherine. I know how much he meant to you. I'm so, so sorry.'

When the sobs had exhausted her until she had nothing else to give, Nina pushed her into the waiting chair.

Catherine looked at her through eyes swollen and half-shut. 'I must look like a heavyweight boxer who got the crap kicked out of him. The guy who should've stayed down.' She looked around the café, relieved to see it was empty apart from the waitress keeping her distance behind the counter. 'What must poor Monica think? I'll need to apologise to her.'

Nina gave her a faint smile. 'No need, I pre-warned her what to expect. And yes, I've seen you look better. But my God this is a shock.'

Catherine tried to smile back. Even her cheeks hurt from

crying. 'Thank you for being here. You're the only one I can let go in front of. I still can't believe this has happened.'

Nina took her hands across the table. 'Neither can I, and where else would I be?

I know you're going to be there for Lizzie through all this and she'll need you. So will Clara and Will. But I want you to know that I'm here for you every step of the way. Never forget that. You've done so much to help me, especially this year.' Her gaze dropped to her left hand as she automatically touched her empty ring finger. 'Funny how I still do that, expecting to twirl my ring, but at least the indent's starting to fade. Sorry, hardly a big deal compared to today. I hope Lizzie's rings will be some comfort to her. She and Adam were such a happy couple.'

They looked at each other. Catherine sensed they were both recalling the day, three months earlier, when Nina's messy and acrimonious divorce had become final.

She had burst into the café that morning, her face glowing, and waved the lawyer's letter at Catherine like a victory flag.

'It's here, thank God. I'm finally free of him. It's official.'

Catherine had hugged her. She noticed a few men glancing in their direction and suspected she wasn't the attraction. Her friend had been constantly exhausted for the past two years but today she looked like she'd stepped off the catwalk.

'I think single life agrees with you, Nina. You look five years younger.'

'I feel it. This is like waking up from a nightmare and switching the lights on. I'm so relieved. And so grateful to you. I would never have got through this without you. You and Jack kept me going. We must celebrate soon. With champagne of course.' She winked. 'Say farewell to the bastard in style.'

The bastard was Daniel. Nina's ex, who had suddenly and unceremoniously packed his bags one night and left to move in with his secretary. To Catherine, it was predictable; she'd always thought he was a loser. Charming and good-looking, but still a loser.

'So how is the walking cliché? Checking how much money he's got left presumably. I'm guessing Lucy's no cheap date. Serves him right.'

'Jack says they're always arguing about money. Seems she spends a fortune on Botox and fillers. Always having stuff either pumped in or sucked out.'

'She's worried his wandering eye will wander again I suppose, and it's only a matter of time until it does. Daniel isn't quite wired for monogamy, is he?'

Nina grinned. 'You always did have him figured out. He's so disorganised she'll clean him out if he's not careful. Not that I give a toss now I've got my settlement. So, our night outs on me. I want to thank you properly.'

'No thanks required. That's what best friends are for and I'm thrilled the nightmare's over for you.' Catherine couldn't be more pleased for Nina. Yet for some reason her voice sounded strangely hollow and detached even to her, and not her own. It was an uncomfortable feeling she tried to ignore. This was Nina's moment.

'Are you OK Catherine? You suddenly seem miles away.'

'Sorry, just thinking about something I need to do this afternoon.'

'No, I'm sorry for not asking how you are. No problems are there? You're never very good at sharing your stuff. You just seem to deal with it.'

Catherine forced a smile. 'Everything's fine. The usual stuff. Got a short article to finish and a few other things to tick off today's list, so I can't stay as long as I'd like, but I'm looking forward to our night out.'

'You and your lists. I know what I'm doing when I get home, signing up for Tinder. Did I tell you Sandra's met someone off it? A bloke called Eric. Pretty hot she says. Think she's a bit smitten.'

Catherine grinned. 'Never thought I'd hear the words hot and Eric in the same sentence. Are you sure she's not making it up?'

Nina laughed. 'Think you're forgetting Eric Cantona. Actually, this guy sounds really nice. You'll meet him soon anyway. I want to start entertaining again so I thought I'd invite them to lunch. You must bring Will. Jack hasn't seen him for a while.'

Catherine smiled at Nina's infectious laugh and energy. 'Sounds great. Tell me when.'

'Of course, I might have an Eric of my own by then. How cool would that be? I'd better start looking.'

Catherine had read about Tinder. Apparently, lots of people were into it and online dating. She didn't especially like the sound of it, but it occurred to her that nobody ever asked if she used it. Why did that bother her all of a sudden? What was wrong with her today? She wondered if Eric really was hot, then wondered if she'd even know hot if it jumped up and bit her.

Nina's voice cut across her thoughts. 'You're doing it again, fading out on me. What's wrong? I can tell something is.'

'Sorry. Guess my head's a bit all over the place today.'

'No, it's more than that. I may not be the smart one here, but I can tell when something's not right. Look, let's move outside and make the most of the sun. I'll order us more drinks, and you're going nowhere until you tell me what's going on.'

As they sat at a quiet corner table Nina beckoned the

waiter, ordered two cappuccinos and waited for her friend to talk.

Playing nervously with her hair, Catherine took a deep breath before she spoke. 'I'm not sure where to start.'

'The hair twirling and the look on your face tell me you'd better start somewhere. I've never seen you like this. What is it?'

Catherine hesitated then said, 'I feel guilty we're talking about me when this is such a big day for you. I'm thrilled that you're looking great and you're excited about moving forward, I truly am. But when we were talking, I had some weird reaction, which I don't understand. I felt... never mind. Ignore it, please. It's stupid.'

'Nice try but no deal. Tell me. I'll decide if it's stupid or not.'

'OK so I suddenly felt flat. Envious too, I think. Of you, of Sandra, of everybody who's moving on in some way. Awful thing to say after what you've been through. Maybe it's all the talk about Tinder and meeting people. I realise nobody ever asks me if I've been on these dating sites or met anybody. Why the hell not?'

Nina gave her a questioning look. Catherine stared down at her hands and fidgeted with her napkin as she tried to find the right words. Her friend knew her too well. Maybe she did need to talk about how she felt. Perhaps opening up to Nina would help her to understand this herself.

'I suppose the truth is I'm bored with my life here. Apart from Will and you there's not enough here for me now, especially since I lost Mum and Dad. And work's pretty dull these days. Nothing exciting ever seems to happen for me to write about and I miss London and my work on the paper so much. I don't think I fit in here anymore, and maybe I never did.'

She paused and looked up at Nina. She realised her friend had never seen her like this. She didn't do emotional outbursts, she always liked to be in control, but today she felt disconnected, as if she was drifting off course. They weren't feelings she was used to. 'I've no idea why all this is coming out now and I'm sorry. Today's about you, not me.'

Tears welled up in her as Nina squeezed her hand. 'Bloody hell, Catherine. I did say start somewhere but I didn't expect that. It sounds like this needed to come out though, so stop apologising. I'm glad you're finally telling me. So, is this about meeting somebody, or more about the job and this place? Or have you met someone already? Is that what's caused this? You've never mentioned anybody to me.'

'Because there isn't anybody. There hasn't been anybody all the time I've lived here. And not that many when I lived in London either. There's never been anyone special, and maybe that's part of my problem. I feel everything's passing me by somehow.' She shrugged her shoulders. 'Hell, I don't know. Life's got a bit screwed up I suppose. Maybe I'm screwed up.' Her hand shook as she reached in her bag for a cigarette. She struggled to light it. 'See. Even my bloody lighter's screwed up. And I'm sure I'm not making any sense at all.'

'Slow down, Catherine. You're the least screwed up person I know, but you look like you're about to explode.' Nina took the cigarette from her, lit it and handed it back. 'I think I'd better have one of these myself. Now take a time-out and drink your coffee please.'

Catherine hadn't noticed the coffee arrive, but she needed it. She took a big gulp too quickly and winced as it burned its way down her throat. She looked at Nina. 'I guess you're shocked at all this.'

'No. Surprised to hear it all suddenly come out like that, but not shocked. I've never thought you and a small town like this were a fit, but you gave the impression you were comfort-able enough with it, so I didn't say anything. And you always said that, compared to London, being here was like living the dream.'

Catherine smiled. 'It felt it, for a while. When Will was little and Mum and Dad were around, but it doesn't now, at least not for me. I feel more like I'm stuck in a middle-aged nightmare I can't wake up from to be honest.' She looked at Nina who started giggling.

'And that sounds more like you talking, thank God. I thought you were totally losing it for a moment back there. So, how long have you felt like this?'

'A while I suppose. But I guess I got good at hiding it from everybody, including myself. I really don't know quite why it's come tumbling out today. Sorry.'

'Stop saying that. And it doesn't matter a sod why. But you need to face up to it. I'm not surprised you miss London. I've always thought you were a city girl at heart. And from what you told me about the career you had there I always suspected you'd wind up back in London eventually. It sounds like now's the time. You have to go for it, Catherine. You can't go on feeling like this.'

'But it's such a huge decision and I have Will to think about. He's the main reason I moved up here and he loves it.'

Nina reached for her hand. 'Listen, he'll be fine. Will's a tough kid and you've done a brilliant job with him. Trust me, he wants you to be happy.'

'Maybe the fact he's off to university soon has partly triggered all this off. I've been so preoccupied with his exams that I never stopped to imagine life without him here.'

'You must be so proud of him making it to med school, especially Cambridge. I always knew he'd do well.'

'I am. We had a few anxious moments during his exams, but he's worked so hard and everyone's convinced he'll get the grades. He deserves this. He's always wanted it and he'll

make a great doctor.' She smiled. 'And when we're a couple of
wild old ladies we'll have our own private medic.'

Nina grinned. 'We might keep him busy. But it's time to
stop worrying about him and focus on you. If you moved
back to London would you try for a job on the same paper
again?'

'Hopefully, but it wouldn't be easy. I'm older and I've been
out of the mainstream a long time. But I'd definitely write.
Freelance stuff if necessary and I might take a crack at a novel
at last.'

'At least with Will heading south you're a free agent. Not
like you've got a relationship or a marriage to worry about.'
Nina threw her hands up as she saw Catherine's expression.
'God I'm sorry. Bloody insensitive of me after what you said
earlier.'

Catherine gave her a weak smile. 'Don't worry about it.'
But her friend's tone had been so matter-of-fact, and it hurt.
She'd always been too busy for romantic entanglements and it
had never bothered her before, but it did now. 'You're right, I
don't have anybody, and I regret I've missed out on that. I've
never had that whole butterflies-every-time-you-look-at-the-
guy feeling I hear other women talk about. I've always
dismissed it as pretty stupid to be honest, but I suppose I'd
still like to feel that about someone. At least once.' She
shrugged her shoulders in resignation. 'But maybe I've left it
too late.'

'Of course it's not too late, but it's strange you've never
brought this up before today. In fact, we've never talked
about you and men at all, which is weird since we've talked
about pretty much everything else. I suppose I've always
assumed it might be a bit of a sore point or you weren't
interested.'

'Which I'm sure is the impression I've given. I've always
convinced myself I wasn't interested. Too busy with every-

thing else. Plus, nobody's ever come along who got me remotely fired up. I thought there might be someone once, but he fell totally in love with somebody else, so it never became anything.' She paused as her Oxford days flashed in front of her, then she grinned at her next thought. 'I suppose people here assume I'm gay, do they?'

Nina spluttered on her drink. 'I doubt it and I've certainly never heard anybody suggest it. I think they've assumed the same as me. That you're the independent type who copes fine on her own, that the serious man thing never happened for you and that you're not bothered about it. But I can see that you are, and I wish you'd told me before. This must have been festering for ages Catherine. Yet you've organised and navigated the rest of us through all sorts of crap, especially me, and none of us knew you were feeling any of this.'

'Hardly your fault. I've never brought it up have I? And you're right, the man thing never bothered me before. But for some reason it does now. That and this feeling of being stuck in some mindless groove professionally when I'm craving challenging work.'

'Then it's time you did something about both. Go back to London. Be where you want to be, doing what you want to do. And I bet your Mr Perfect's there too.'

Catherine smiled. 'One thing at a time. There's the small matter of a job and somewhere to live first.'

Nina's phone pinged. 'Shit. Text from the lawyer. Some urgent paper for me to sign about the house.'

'Go and do it. I'm going to stay a little longer and have a think.'

'I hate leaving you. Will you be OK?'

Catherine smiled as she gave her a hug. 'I'll be fine. I feel better than I have in ages. Telling you all this has helped so much. And the fact I've admitted it to myself. Now I have to figure out how to deal with it.'

Nina hugged her back. 'You will. You've got your determined look on your face.'

As she searched in her bag for her car keys and started
walking to the door she turned back to Catherine. 'And
remember, you're the priority now. Tell yourself what you've
always told Will. Follow your dream, make it happen. This is
your time, so follow yours.'

Catherine sat back and lit another cigarette. Her hand
was steady on the lighter. She felt back in control. She knew
what she wanted, and she needed to make it happen.

The sound of Nina's voice giving their order jolted her back
into the present. For a brief few moments she'd escaped the
reality of Adam's death but here she was, facing it again. And
wishing she hadn't been so desperate for things to change.

'I got more than I bargained for when I said I wanted a
challenge, huh? I guess calm and uneventful weren't so bad
after all.'

'Stop it. You could hardly have foreseen this. Not the
challenge you wanted I know, but Lizzie couldn't have a
better person to deal with everything's that's going to hit her.
And then you're going to get your plan back on track.'

Catherine smiled at the irony in Nina's innocent words. If
only her friend knew how big a challenge she might face once
she got to London tomorrow.

She didn't even know herself.

CHAPTER SEVEN

Clayton left the temporary sanctuary of his park bench to head back to work, his head full of images of the mother he'd loved. It had been ten years since her death, but the memories remained vivid. Every day her final words played in his head. Words that led him to the letter which had shattered his assumed future.

Nothing had ever been the same since. It had changed the entire course of his life and work.

He'd been summoned back to Sydney and spent the entire flight praying to God that he'd make it in time. A God he didn't believe existed, but his mother did. He hoped her God would come through for her and get him there before the end.

The end. He could barely comprehend he was saying those words to himself or imagine life without the strong but gentle woman who had always been there for him. As overhead reading lights dimmed and his fellow passengers settled down to sleep themselves through to Sydney, his eyes prickled from the threat of tears at the thought of what was to come. The most painful goodbye he could ever imagine himself having to make. He had to make it in time. He needed to be holding her hand at the end. He couldn't imagine how he'd cope if her God didn't give him the chance to do that.

And he was a man who always coped. A scientist, an empiricist, a man who'd taught himself to bury his emotions and give his intellect free rein. Nothing and nobody ever got in the way of that. With two exceptions. His daughter and his mother. The usual pang of guilt at not including his wife shot through him. But Angela had never penetrated his soul like they both did. No woman ever had.

He smiled through the sadness as he thought about Becca. At eight she was already so like her grandmother. Uncannily so, especially as they had no genetic connection.

Clayton had guessed he was adopted way before his mother told him on his tenth birthday. Their physical differences had become impossible to ignore. She was so diminutive that by the time he was nine he towered above her. And he bore no similarity either to the father he'd only seen in photographs. But he never pushed her to tell him. She'd do it in her own time, and eventually she did. At least the little she knew. That his birth mother had been young and had disappeared from the hospital within hours of giving birth. She'd vanished without a trace after registering with a false name. It was as if she never existed. And to Clayton she didn't. He never thought about her. He had the only mother he ever needed. And now he was about to lose her and every part of him hurt.

He had no recollection of falling asleep, but he woke up to the simultaneous sounds of breakfast activity in the galley and the cockpit announcement that they were an hour from Sydney. For a moment he told himself he'd had a bad dream and his mother would be waiting for him with the car and her beloved Labrador Rupert, but then reality hit him again. He wondered how often bereaved people woke up in denial and were forced to relive their grief.

Three hours later he was greeted at his mother's door by her lodger and good friend Marjorie and an elderly, arthritic Labrador. As Clayton bent to stroke him, Rupert's half-hearted tail wagging finally cracked the composure he'd desperately clung onto since he left London. He and Marjorie hugged each other for mutual solace until she finally spoke through her tears.

'Clayton I'm so sorry. This all happened so quickly. But thank God you're here. The doctor thought we were losing her earlier, but she's been finding the strength from somewhere to hang on till you arrived.'

'That's my mother. She's never let me down, has she? Not ever. God Marjorie, how will I cope without her?'

'Because you will. Because you're as strong as she is. Because that's how she raised you. And because Becca needs you.'

'I need to go to her. Before....' He didn't want to say the words.

Marjorie gripped his hand. 'I know. And it won't be long now the doctor said. Go. Make the most of whatever time you have with her. I've said my goodbyes. This is your time. She needs you.'

Five minutes later he sat at his mother's bedside, gently stroking her hand. She looked and felt like a delicate porcelain doll. He wanted to squeeze her hand and hug her but was frightened she'd break. She was shrinking and diminishing in front of him, and he felt he was in suspended animation, as if he was about to fall from a skyscraper. And he had no idea what the ground would feel like when he hit it.

Her breathing was steady and soft. Please God let the end be peaceful for her at least. Rupert was scratching at the door, wanting to come in. When the time came, he would let him. Losing her would be hard on him too. The thought of those sad brown Labrador eyes brought tears to Clayton's. Then his mother opened hers. She smiled the angelic smile he loved as she looked at him and raised her free hand to touch his face. He moved nearer so she could.

'My darling boy. I knew you were here. I sensed it.'

The weakness of her voice shocked him. He'd never heard his mother sound so tired. 'Oh Mum.' He couldn't find any more words.

'Clayton, listen. Don't be sad. Be strong. I've had a wonderful life, because of you. Miss me like I'll miss you, mourn for me for a while, but move on with your life.' She paused, breathless from the effort of speaking, then grasped his hand. He tried to will some of his body's strength into hers. 'Go back to London as soon as you can. Your life is there now. And you have your work. And our beautiful Becca.'

'She wanted to come Mum, but I thought. I mean...'

'I know. She had such a wonderful holiday here and that's how you wanted her to remember me. Not the way Marjorie told you I look now.' She smiled the half smile he knew so well. 'I heard her on the phone. She thought I couldn't, but I did.' Her flickering smile brought a glow back to her face. He knew he would never forget that smile.

'This has all happened so fast Mum. It feels like only yesterday we had that brilliant farewell dinner in the city before Becca and I flew back.'

'Maybe it's better for these things to be fast. So your memories are of the happy times like that night. Not of the end. Not this part.' Her voice faltered and he took both her hands in his. They were trembling as she grew weaker, and pain ripped through him.

Rupert's scratching was more frantic, and he was beginning to whimper. Maybe he sensed the end was near.

'You need to let him in Clayton. He'll have all the paint off that door.'

'Are you sure? I'm worried he might leap up and hurt you.'

'Nothing can hurt me now. Only leaving you. And I need to see him. I want both my boys here. Please.'

Clayton opened the door and somehow Rupert used his arthritic legs to climb on to the bed and rest his head on her chest. As her hand gently stroked him, she took Clayton's hand in the other.

'There are some things I need to tell you sweetheart.' Her voice was a weak whisper.

'Please don't worry about practical things Mum. We'll sort everything out when...when we need to. Please rest. I don't want you worrying about the house and stuff like that. I'll deal with it.'

'The house will be yours, but I told Marjorie she can stay on. And she'll look after Rupert. You know how much she loves him.'

'Of course she must stay, this is her home. And she's been such a wonderful friend to you. Now rest Mum. Please.'

She took some short, shallow breaths and he stroked her hand. It trembled against his as he watched her strain with the effort of trying to speak. 'Would you pour me some water please sweetheart. I'm so thirsty.'

He emptied the last of the water jug into a glass and held it while she sipped. 'I'll go and top this up, Mum.'

She put her hand out to stop him and it shook with the effort. 'No, stay here, please. I need to tell you something before it's too late.' She patted his arm and he felt her hand tremble as she started to speak again. He wanted her to stop, to conserve the last of her strength, but the agitation in her voice told him he must let her continue. 'And I need you to promise me something.'

'Mum you know I would promise you anything. What is it?'

Her voice dropped to a whisper. 'To forgive me.'

He squeezed her hand gently. 'Mum how could there be anything I need to forgive you for?'

He put his arms round her. God how he loved this woman. Pain tore at his insides at the thought of losing her.

As they clung to each other she whispered into his neck, constantly catching her breath between stuttered words. 'Your other mother. Some information. I wrote it down. A letter. In my desk. Your name on it. Should have told you before. Was scared. Love you so much. You're my boy.'

His other mother. He couldn't care less. This was his mother, in front of him, slipping away. He clung on to her. Willing her not to leave.

'It doesn't matter Mum. You're my mother. I love you. Don't leave me. Please.'

But he heard her gasp her last breath. It was over. She was gone.

He continued to hold her. He'd expected more time. He'd wanted more time. This had happened too quickly. He felt himself absorb the last of her maternal strength. Even in death she was giving him what he needed so he could deal with losing her. He didn't want to let go of her but knew he must tell Marjorie and then call Becca. He turned to see Rupert's puzzled brown eyes. As the Labrador moved to lick his mistress's now still hand, willing her to stroke him one more time, he let out a howl.

And Clayton started to sob.

CHAPTER EIGHT

Clayton sat at his mother's desk, with Rupert curled up beside him. Since his mother had gone, her dog had followed him everywhere. They were partners in grief. He'd found the envelope addressed to him yesterday but had put it straight back. It was too soon to open it and he still didn't want to. What could it possibly contain that he'd care about? The woman who gave birth to him was an irrelevance. He'd lost his real mother. But he knew he'd have to read it eventually. It had obviously been important to her that he did.

It would be handwritten of course. Somehow the technological revolution had completely bypassed his mother. He smiled thinking how often he'd tried to navigate her through the menu of the smartphone he'd bought her.

'I don't like this screen touching business Clayton. Why doesn't it have proper buttons? And the letters are so small. How can I possibly type a message on this?' And she never could. He'd eventually given up trying to decipher the gobbledegook which always made Becca giggle and told his mother they'd better stick to voice calls. Now he caught himself wondering how often these silly, almost trivial, memories would hit him out of nowhere and remind him of what he'd lost. He couldn't imagine a day when they wouldn't. But she was right. He had his work to focus on, and Becca. Nothing else mattered.

Yet as he prepared himself to read the letter, an image came into his head, one he couldn't make out. Yet he recognised this strange feeling. It had happened once before, on the plane as he'd drifted into sleep. He'd put it down to stress or a silly dream and forgotten it. It was a feeling that someone important was out there who he was destined to connect with. A woman. A special woman. But as quickly as the image had appeared, it was gone. He guessed it was grief making his mind play tricks on him.

The letter was dated two months earlier. Had his mother known then how little time she had left? She must have found out just before he and Becca had made their last trip. How typical of his mother to keep it to herself and not let it spoil her granddaughter's visit. He thought of Becca now. She'd been devastated when he called with the news, but then that strength her Grandmother had taught her shone through. She was more concerned about him than herself, wanting him to get home as soon as he could. He smiled at the thought that his mother would never entirely be gone while Becca was around. Then he started to read.

My Dearest Boy

If you're reading this, it's because I've gone. The doctors tell me it will be soon and it's the hardest thing to bear. Not my illness or death, my faith will sustain me through both, but the thought of no longer seeing you in this life. But what joy you've brought me for more than 50 years and how I will miss you. My wonderful son. Never ever forget how much I have loved you from the first time I saw you.

By the time you read this I hope I will already have had the chance to apologise to you for what I'm about to tell you and I ask for your forgiveness again now. I should have told you this sooner, I know that, but I was never brave enough. I couldn't bear for anything to spoil the wonderful life we had together. But now I know I must before it's too late. And I cannot go to my God without being honest with you.

He put the letter down, took off his reading glasses and wiped his tears. This was tough. Sitting at her desk alongside her dog, and reading her words, it was as if she was still here. Three days ago, she had been. He looked out through the French doors at her terrace and garden, where she had sat so recently. Marjorie had told him yesterday.

'We sat there with Rupert only two days ago and talked. Then she got too weak to go downstairs. But she enjoyed that last evening on the terrace.' Marjorie's voice had broken with emotion. 'She wanted to watch the sunset looking at the oak tree. And your old tree house. She told me all about when you built it. She was so proud of how you were able to do almost anything you set your mind on Clayton. And how she panicked the day you fell out of it.' Clayton had smiled at the memory as Marjorie spoke. He hadn't fallen out of that tree by accident at all, he'd controlled the fall, but for some reason his eight-year-old self never told his mother. He was surprised she'd still remembered it after all these years. And he wished now he'd told her.

He got up from the desk and Rupert staggered to his feet. 'Let's take a break Rupe. We both need some air.' As they wandered slowly around the garden at the Labrador's pace Clayton wondered what the rest of the letter would hold. What was the big secret his mother had been too scared to tell him? Was his birth mother still alive? He wondered what he'd do if she was. Was he expected to find her? To see her?

Go through the charade of playing the long-lost son? What would his mother have wanted? What would Becca want? Too many questions. He was a scientist. He needed data. He turned back to the house. He had to finish reading the letter.

It's true that when I adopted you, I knew virtually nothing about your birth mother. That's how things were back then. Everything done in secret. I was told she'd been young and scared and was presumed to have given a false name. But I did learn one thing that I've never told anybody till now. That there had been two baby boys. You and your twin. The agency had no idea what happened to him. And I know I should have told you, but I didn't know how. I wondered if she'd kept him. And if she did how could I tell you that? That she took one baby and left the other. But I've thanked God every day that she did. Because I got to keep you.

His hands shook as he read that line. A twin he'd known nothing about. So, his birth mother had had a choice. And she didn't choose him. Where was he supposed to go with that? What the hell sort of woman had she been? Where was his twin now? He forced himself to read on. Maybe his mother would give him some answers.

I never thought about your birth mother or your twin brother again. Until five years ago. A letter arrived from the agency out of the blue, enclosing a letter from her to me. There was something she thought I should know. She was ill, suffering from something called Huntington's Disease. I'd never heard of it but apparently it affected her movements and coordination. She wanted to check you were ok because apparently it can run in families. She didn't tell me anything else about herself and she didn't mention your twin. I asked the agency to tell her I was so sorry to hear her news but that everything was fine with you. I hoped that would at least put her mind at rest.

Clayton did a double-take. Huntington's Disease. A shiver ran through him. Please God let this not be true. The thought of it made his insides churn. His mother had totally underestimated its seriousness and its effects. He was no expert in genetic diseases, but as a molecular biologist he understood enough to know how devastating the symptoms of this one could be. Gradual loss of brain function and body coordination. Jerky, uncontrolled dance-like movements. Currently incurable and still with limited treatment options.

His gaze dropped automatically to his legs. He imagined they were shaking but they were rock steady. But the disease could hit him any time if he'd inherited the mutated gene that caused it.

Dear God. Becca. If he had the faulty gene there was at least a fifty per cent chance she had it too. And that prospect made his insides churn more. How would he tell her? His hand tightened on the letter. He forced himself to read on.

I planned on telling you Clayton, but you were physically ok, always so strong, so I assumed it hadn't affected you. And it would have opened up the past again, so I decided not to. And her letter didn't say anything about seeing you and it gave me no indication of where she was. I thought all that might upset you and I couldn't deal with that and didn't want to put you through unnecessary pain.

But now I have to leave you. And it seems wrong to take this secret with me. I cannot be at peace if I do. I have no right to keep you from maybe finding her if you want to. And your twin. And maybe Becca should know her true heritage.

I feel I'm leaving you with a burden. But you've become such a strong man. The man I'm so proud to call my son. You will know what to do. I only hope you will understand my reasons for not telling you before and will forgive me.

Never forget how very much I love you. I always will. And I'll always be watching over you.

Mum x

Clayton felt dizzy as he put the letter down. Part of him wished he'd never found it. Now his mind was in turmoil. Grief, love, anger and fear rushed at him, at random. He had no idea what to think. He needed to leave Sydney and process all this. He needed to be home, like his mother had told him. And instantly he knew he forgave her for not telling him all this sooner.

But as he put the letter in his pocket, he thought about his birth mother. And knew instantly he could never forgive her for the legacies she'd left him.

The legacy of not wanting him; of choosing his brother over him. The legacy of being denied a relationship with his twin whose existence he hadn't even been aware of until now. And the legacy of a potentially devastating genetic disease.

And worst of all, a genetic legacy that could affect Becca. He would never, ever, forgive this unknown woman for that.

CHAPTER NINE

Catherine slumped further into her seat, her body weak and aching with tiredness after two nights without sleep.

She fixed her gaze on the train track, forcing herself to stay awake, but it reminded her that the comfort and familiarity of her northern home were receding behind her as the train sped her south. She looked away, wondering how much uncomfortable strangeness they would be replaced with in less than three hours. If only she could stay in high speed locomotive limbo and never have to find out.

But as Adam had told her, running scared and issue avoidance weren't her style. That's why he'd trusted her, and she didn't intend to let him down. Whatever she found; she'd face.

She reached into her bag for the water she'd bought at the station and gulped it down, willing it to energise her. Then she woke up her sleeping phone, opened her gallery and scrolled down to last year's Christmas album. She'd already ignored Adam's first instruction to delete his email. She'd wiped it from her inbox, but not before she'd opened it on her mobile mail app, screenshot it and filed it in an unlikely place. Then she'd added fingerprint authentication to her phone's security.

She hit the first of the several screens his message filled and read it for what seemed like the tenth time. With each successive read she was more determined to discover the truth.

POPEYE & OLIVE

> *From popeye121*
> *To catherinepreston249@quickmail.com*

My Dearest Catherine

> *Before you read this please make sure you have nobody looking over your shoulder. I know that sounds as weird as hell but trust me. And after you've read it, delete it. You should only act on it if something happens to me. Which I now fear it could, which is why I have to tell you all this.*

> *Yes, I can almost hear you saying it. 'What the hell is this Adam? A Mission Impossible script?'*

> *Truth is it feels like it, but it's all too real. I can't tell you everything in this email, but I can tell you some of it. What you do with this knowledge if the time comes will be up to you, but you're the only person I know I can trust with it, apart from Lizzie of course. But if something does happen, she'll have too much else to cope with to deal with this, and she'll need you.*

> *You're probably wondering why I'm not telling you this in a phone call. The answer is I daren't risk exposing you. My phones could be bugged and heading to a payphone at this hour would just create even more suspicion. I already think my movements are being monitored but I'm pretty certain this email's safe. Nobody knows it exists, or the device I'm using, and once I hit send it won't exist anymore. I'll delete it. And get rid of the device. Luckily I know you can never*

resist checking your spam, and I know you'll figure out the Popeye reference straightaway. Those were happy days, weren't they? I wish the three of us were back there.

But this is now, and things aren't good. I've recently stumbled across some things I almost wish I hadn't. Some pretty powerful people obviously wish I hadn't too. I think there's some serious corruption inside our Government, at least within the Health Department. I can't say what level of seniority it extends to, but I can tell you that the financial stakes are high, and I think at least one of the major Pharmaceuticals is involved, possibly more. I believe public funds are being misappropriated, and that some key potential research developments are being manipulated and possibly derailed.

I still need to join up the dots before I can go official with any accusations, but a couple of veiled threats I've just received convince me I'm on to something.

I've said nothing about it to Lizzie, but I know she thinks something's going on. I've never been good at hiding anything from her. She has some documents for you, to be opened if anything happens to me, which I've told her concern things you need to know as the principal Executor of my will and nothing for her to worry about now. I'm not sure she believed me. If anything does happen, you should open them and do whatever you think fit. This is a lot to ask and I'm not giving you much to go on, and what there is may be just the tip of the iceberg. But I hope you'll find a way to finish what I've started - if you need to, and if you agree there's something in all this. If you do, be careful. You'll probably need some help but I've no idea who to tell you to trust apart from Lizzie. Maybe one of your contacts at the paper. I hear good things about the new Editor. But don't trust ANYBODY involved with health or the pharmaceuticals. Tell Lizzie I only kept this from her to protect her. And tell her how much I love her.

I hope I'll get to figure out how to deal with it this myself, but I need a contingency plan. And you're it. You're the only one it can be. And I'm sorry this must all sound so cryptic but if anybody can do this it's you. I probably should have talked to you about it when we saw *you. I almost did, and I think maybe you sensed something, but I thought I could control it myself then.*

Nearly 5am. Early start today. Must shower. Not feeling too great now. Hope it'll wake me up. Remember to delete this. Hope you never have to handle any of this. You have no idea how much I hope I see you soon.

Ever your friend.

A.

PS Before I hit send. Have to say it again. Trust nobody. Not even my

Each time she read it, that unfinished PS brought tears to her eyes. Who was he referring to? He'd obviously just found the strength to hit send before he collapsed. Whatever killed him had been sudden, and the email made her feel she'd been with him, if only virtually, at the moment of his death. She hoped the remote electronic connection with her had helped him feel less alone.

As they always did, the nicknames took Catherine back to memories of their Oxford days, the three of them exploring the city in their first week as newbies in awe of its dreaming spires. Sitting in their bohemian, randomly furnished, living room in the two-up two-down they'd rented in Jericho in their final year, talking into the early hours. Their triumphant group hug, sharing tears of relief, the day they learned they'd all graduated, she and Adam with Firsts, Lizzie with an Upper Second. Those had been such happy days. And the silly names she'd given the two of them had stuck. Adam the fitness freak with his bulging biceps had been Popeye by the end of Freshers' Week and Lizzie his perfect Olive Oyl - tall, lanky and with a shock of jet-black hair that refused to be anything but straight.

Now she was trying to understand his death. It still felt

unreal and she wished it was, but she had to uncover the truth, however difficult that proved and however long it took.

She exited her gallery and tucked her phone back in her bag. The action prompted two questions she was surprised hadn't struck her before. If Adam had hit send only moments before he died, he couldn't have deleted the email. She threw her head back, annoyed with herself for being so slow. Of course, he didn't. Lizzie had told her to check her mail, so she must have seen it and recognised the nickname straight away.

And that's what had either prompted or confirmed her friend's suspicions. She'd read, then deleted, Adam's message. Otherwise the police would have seen it, asked her for the documents he'd referred to and the investigation would now be in their hands. Had Lizzie also taken care of the device Adam referred to? Catherine hoped it was safe; she needed to see what else it contained.

She also hoped her logic was right; if it wasn't, her name was out there as the email recipient. And she and Lizzie were in danger.

CHAPTER TEN

In her half-asleep limbo, random thoughts of London flooded Catherine's mind. Autumnal days, rediscovering the city on foot. Exploring the bookshops she'd always loved and discovering new ones. And as dusk became darkness, standing by the Thames, watching the city's lights dance in rhythm with the water's currents. Until another image rose from its depths. A man. A face. Smiling at her with his eyes and his mouth. But the image was out of focus. He started to speak but she was jolted awake by another voice before she could see him clearly or hear what he was saying.

'...now approaching London Euston where the train will terminate.'

She reached in her bag for the bottle of water, dehydrated from the warmth of the train. She'd dozed through the last two stops and her eyes felt sticky and heavy-lidded from the unfulfilled desire for sleep. She tried to recall the face she'd seen, and couldn't, but she was certain it wasn't Adam's.

She stood for a moment outside Lizzie's house. In a tree-lined street at the smart end of Muswell Hill, five minutes from the bustling Broadway, it was classic double fronted Victorian, in distinctive red brick, with twin gables like isosceles triangles.

She'd always loved its welcoming cosiness. Richly patterned walls and fabrics showcased its carefully preserved period features and three ageing leather chesterfields were grouped around the tiled original fireplace which threw out a homely glow. Adam had loved this house, and she struggled to comprehend that he wouldn't be there to welcome her on the other side of the imposing panelled and stained-glass door.

Before she reached it, the door swung open. She dropped her bag and ran towards the pale, tear-stained face that appeared.

'Oh Lizzie.'

They gripped each other in silence. Lizzie spoke first, her voice shaking and gulping through tears.

'What am I going to do? How am I going to live without him?'

Catherine stood back, holding her friend's shoulders and looked into her face. The features she knew so well were etched with pain and bewilderment. Grief had shrunk this woman she'd loved since her teens for her warm-hearted strength and vibrancy.

'I wish I could give you an answer to that, but God knows I can't. But I'm going to help you through it. Every step of the way.'

Lizzie smiled a weak smile. 'I couldn't ask for a better friend. Let's get you in and have tea.'

Catherine turned and picked up her bag. 'You sit down. I'll make it.'

'Not a chance. I had enough of that yesterday. I wanted to scream at them at all. I've lost my husband, not my ability to use a domestic appliance. Let me be me, Catherine. You're the one person I can do that with.'

She smiled as she followed Lizzie to the kitchen. Her friend's strength was battling with the grief that threatened to overwhelm it, but it was still there.

Between them, they'd get through this.

They were sitting on opposite Chesterfields, still drinking tea. They'd talked about Clara, about Will and about each other. But they hadn't yet talked about the nature of Adam's death. Unspoken questions hovered above them like aircraft caught in a holding pattern.

'We need to talk about it, Lizzie,' Catherine said at last. 'We can't put it off any longer. And we're going to have to open the documents he left.'

Lizzie stared down at her hands. 'I know.'

Catherine asked as gently as she could. 'You sent the email, didn't you?'

Lizzie looked up and nodded. 'I knew you'd figure it out.'

'It was the only logical explanation for why the police didn't see the open screen. But how? Was he...?'

'Yes.' Lizzie looked at her with glazed eyes, as if she couldn't make the connection between herself and the grim task she'd been forced to perform. 'It was horrible, but I knew I had to do it. For him. Even though it meant...'

'I understand. Take your time. Try to tell me everything that happened. I need to know. And it might help you deal with it.'

'I woke up and he wasn't there. I didn't check the time, but it felt like the middle of the night. Suddenly I felt worried about him. He'd been acting strangely for a while, on and off. Jumpy, looking preoccupied, not like Adam at all.' She paused and gave Catherine a questioning look. 'Didn't you pick up on something when you stayed last time?'

Her stomach flipped with that pang of guilt she'd felt

yesterday - that she hadn't pressed him more to tell her what was troubling him.

'Only once. Just before you called us through for Sunday lunch. As if he wanted to share something with me. But he didn't, and the moment passed. I should have pushed him, and I didn't. I can't tell you how much I regret that. I'm so sorry.'

'Don't be. I asked him several times, and he shrugged it off. But in the last few days it got worse. Checking his phone all the time, then disappearing into his office and closing the door. Making calls I assume he didn't want me to hear. He never worried what I heard usually. So, something changed. I began to wonder if...well, you can guess what.'

'Not Adam, Lizzie. I'd stake my life on that. He wasn't interested in anybody else. It has to have been work related.'

'That's what I told myself. And now I'm certain it was. But when I walked into his office and saw him...I...'

'It's ok. Take your time. I know how tough this must be. Remember how much he loved you. You were everything to him from the first moment he saw you. You and I both know that.'

Lizzie shrugged. 'I always thought I did, but I started to question it. And when I walked in and saw him slumped backwards, with his hand resting motionless on top of an iPad I'd never seen before, and didn't even know he had, I had to check the screen. I ...needed to know.' She started to sob.' I can't believe I doubted him, even for a split second.'

'I understand. But he was definitely...'

'Dead? Yes. I've seen death often enough before to know.'

'So how did you...'

'I went into mental auto-pilot. The email was still open. I scrolled up and saw it

was to you. Once I read it, I knew I had to hit send and then delete it. Then I hugged him. Over and over. Apologising for doubting him. Screaming it, hoping he'd hear it. Knowing he couldn't. Then I forced myself to calm down and made the 999 call.'

Catherine moved to sit beside her and hugged her into her shoulder. Lizzie's head flopped, as if the effort of recounting those early morning events had drained it of all strength.

'You did the right thing. Exactly what Adam would have wanted.'

'I keep telling myself that but...having to move his hand...and lean over him to touch send. I keep seeing it in my head. It'll haunt me forever.'

'Those images will fade. But we have to make sure they count for something and finish what he started.' She paused. 'Or at least I do. You've got yourself and Clara to concentrate on.'

'It's a lot he's left you with Catherine. You know how much he trusted your intellect and judgment, but you have to decide if you want to do this. You must put yourself and Will first. This could be dangerous. Maybe I was wrong to say nothing to the police. Maybe we should just hand everything over to them.'

Catherine shook her head. 'I thought that when we spoke yesterday, because I assumed you were talking through grief. Then I read Adam's email. I did still wonder about us speaking to the authorities, but now we've talked, and I'm here, where it happened, I feel it. There's something. And I have to try to find out what.'

'But...'

'No buts. I have to do this. For him, and for you. I assume you've said nothing to Clara? She can't know any of this Lizzie.'

'No. I chose my words carefully yesterday when she got back.'

'Good. We'll have to be very careful whenever she's around, and if we talk

on the phone. Where is she by the way?'

'Went for a walk with one of her friends. She should be back anytime soon.'

'Then I should probably take those documents from you now. And...I have to

ask...'

Lizzie stood up. 'I know, the iPad. It's safe. I hid it while I was waiting for the

police and medics to arrive.'

Catherine got to her feet and wrapped her arms round her friend. 'Adam would

be so proud of you. So am I, Mrs Wentworth.' She saw the slight blush on Lizzie's cheeks. After all these years that still happened when she was paid a compliment. 'Now let's get these things into my bag before Clara arrives back. I'll take them home with me tomorrow. Better everything's out of this house.'

'You are sure about this? It's still an option to tell the police.'

'I know, and maybe we're crazy not to, but I'm being guided by Adam. He told me to trust nobody but you, but he forgot the only other person I can trust. Him. So, for now, we do this his way.'

CHAPTER ELEVEN

Clayton blinked at the screen and rubbed his eyes before comparing the two printouts again. It had been a long day followed by several hours in the lab and he needed to be certain he wasn't jumping to conclusions. His years of research had taught him to be wary of false dawns.

He poured another black coffee from the ageing filter machine as he waited for Susie. He had a feeling she would be punctual. Scientists generally were. It was in their DNA. He smiled at the appropriateness of the thought as the door opened and she breezed in. He glanced at the clock. Spot on 8pm.

'Hi Prof. What are you smiling at? Had a Eureka moment?'

'Just smiling at how punctual we scientists always like to be. I guess we're wired that way.' He watched her bounding towards him in her usual combination of worn jeans and university sweatshirt. Outfit choosing would never make Susie late. He'd never seen her wear anything else, whatever the occasion. She was definitely work driven. 'Grab yourself a mug of our indifferent coffee and come take a look.'

She pulled a face as she took her first sip of the filter machine's now lukewarm offering. 'I remember the first time I drank this coffee the night we agreed I'd join the team. Don't you think we've earned a new one?'

'I guess it is pretty bad. Tell you what. If this data is as promising as it looks, I'll hit Amazon and buy us a new one. Deal?'

She high-fived him. 'Deal. Now please tell me all about this.'

As always, her energy and enthusiasm for the project impressed him. Despite her relative youth and inexperience, she was as committed as any of his team to finding the break-through that he continued to think they were tantalisingly close to.

Not that any of them knew how much he personally had vested in that breakthrough. He sometimes wondered if they might guess. After all, apart from the time he spent with his daughter, his life revolved almost exclusively around his teaching and his research. Didn't they wonder why he appeared to have nothing else in his life?

'Penny for them Professor.'

'Sorry. Idle thoughts. Not like me.'

'You looked like you were miles away all of a sudden. Is everything ok?'

He smiled. As well as being smart she was a nice young woman. He was pleased he'd introduced her to his daughter, and they'd become friends. She and Becca had really hit it off and had the occasional night out. He wondered how often he was the topic of conversation when they were together.

'Everything's fine, but it's been a tiring week. Suppose you all think I'm a crazy workaholic.'

'No, not crazy, driven. And totally committed to making the breakthrough that would help so many people. We all have such respect for you and we're happy to do whatever it takes to help you.'

The earnestness in her voice tempted him to tell her the truth, but he didn't. Even though so many times in the past ten years he'd felt alone with his secret. Alone in knowing he had the Huntington's time bomb within him and, worse, knowing that he might have unwittingly condemned Becca to it too. He'd got himself tested as soon as he returned from Sydney and the result had been as he'd feared. He had the Huntington's mutation, and the waiting game had begun. A game of hoping daily the symptoms wouldn't start. He still hadn't told Becca or had her tested. He kept a close eye on her and prayed to his mother's God that she'd beaten the odds and escaped it.

How often he'd wished he had someone to share his secret with. A special person, who would understand, support him and not judge or recoil from him because of it. But that person had never shown up, so he dealt with it in his own way, in the only way he knew how, through his work. And the hope that eventually he'd be smart enough and lucky enough to make the discovery that would be a genetic game-changer. A hope that he'd nurtured every day since his mother's letter had turned his world upside down.

'I appreciate everything you and the rest of the team do Susie. And I'm convinced the answer is close. I know we're on the right track.'

'With the gene silencing?'

'Yes. A few research teams are close on that one, but it only takes us so far. Now we need to push the boundaries much further. Gene editing is the Holy Grail. That's what I was looking at when you came in. Some theoretical results from the model we developed. It's given me some thoughts about where we go next.' He paused and wondered how much he should tell her.

'Further into the Brave New World? Everybody says gene editing is still a long way in the future. Isn't it?'

'We've all told ourselves it is, but if we want to eventually eradicate the horror of Huntington's and the other hereditary diseases then editing is where we have to keep pushing.' He gulped the last of his drink. God, he was tired. He gripped the coffee mug as he looked at her. 'I know we can get there. We have to.'

The force of his grip on the mug almost broke it. His knuckles were white. Boy did he need to de-stress a bit. He saw her glance down at the obvious tension in his hand. He'd better reassure her he wasn't morphing into a mad scientist.

'Sorry. I get a bit carried away I suppose. Been at this a long time and I've got a lot of myself invested in it.' She smiled and nodded at him. If she and the rest of the team only knew how much of himself was invested in this.

'I understand. I've only been involved for a few months, but I feel invested too. We all do. You inspire that in us. And anyway, we all want to be able to dine out one day saying we worked for a Nobel Prize winner. We're convinced you'll be one.'

Clayton smiled. 'Then we'll definitely buy a new coffee machine. Maybe one each.' He paused and looked away.

'Professor?'

He turned back and saw her enquiring look. Dammit, he could trust this girl.

'Actually Susie, it might be closer than we think. I've been running some new computer simulations and I'm almost certain I've hit on a new approach that might work. Hence why I'm a bit preoccupied. This could have all sorts of consequences.'

'Are you talking editing? Seriously?'

'Yes I am. Editing out a potentially inheritable genetic

mutation so it can't be passed on. I don't believe I'm actually saying those words.'

She looked taken aback by his bombshell. 'Holy crap. That would be the ultimate game-changer. Although...' She paused.

'Exactly. Although is the word. People will accuse me of playing God. The ethicists will have a field day and be into the whole designer baby debate, which isn't what this is about, but I suppose opinions will differ about when intervention's right and when it isn't. I'm treading a delicate path here, which is why I'm always careful about how much I say.'

'I can see that, but if you can eradicate these horrible diseases you have to go for it. Nobody could not want that surely.'

'I don't know. Some people will say we're interfering with nature. Going against God's plan.'

'I can't imagine why God would want human beings condemned to a life struggling with something we find ourselves able to prevent. Why would anybody think he would?'

'I guess some people do. Divine will and all that. But I'm a scientist. I have to leave the ethics to others. The politics and the economics too.'

'Yes. I'm realising what the impact of this would be eventually. Issues about who could afford it and who couldn't. I suppose it would change the whole nature of the pharmaceuticals business too.'

'It would. Eventually there'd be no need for any treatment drugs. Their whole profit model would change.'

'Clayton.' It was the first time she'd used his first name. 'This is dynamite. The fact you're potentially so close to something.'

'I know. Which is why I have to ask you to say nothing to anybody. This is so sensitive.'

'I understand that, and I won't. I'm pleased you told me though. You can't carry this around on your own. I'm flattered that you trust me with it, which you can. Totally.'

He nodded at her and smiled. He'd been right to trust her.

CHAPTER TWELVE

Two hours later Clayton told Susie to go after she'd rejected three calls from a boyfriend. He admired her commitment to the work, but it shouldn't dominate her life the way it dominated his. As he sorted out his papers before heading home, he thought back to the evening in February when they'd talked about her joining the team. He smiled as he recalled how she had bounded into the lab with her usual energy, wearing her customary outfit, and how they'd talked for hours. He'd expected her to have done her research and she had. She knew the right questions to ask. She had a seemingly inexhaustible desire for knowledge. And she'd insisted he go right back to the beginning. She wanted to know everything.

'What made you decide to move into genetics in the first place? And why the focus on Huntington's?'

He'd chosen his words carefully, as he always did when asked this question. He told the truth, but he left out the personal aspect of it. 'It was ten years ago. I wanted a new challenge and I stumbled across an article about Huntington's, referring to it as the cruellest disease known to man. I read how its sufferers have been stigmatised over the years and I wanted to try and do something about it.'

'And that was soon after the Genome Project had finished, right?'

'Yes, and Genetics was big news in the scientific community. The Genome teams had laid the groundwork for us to dig deeper into the genetic roots of diseases like HD and look at treatment options. Not that I'd be content to stop at treatment options. I want to go further. Find a way of eradicating the mutated gene. Or at least stop it taking hold and causing symptoms.'

'If I've understood what I've read correctly, in Huntington's the mutated gene tells the body to produce a protein variation that causes the damage. Am I right?'

'Absolutely right. Genetic instructions are all about the recipes for proteins, and sometimes the recipe is wrong. In this case the recipe for the huntingtin protein in the brain. Not to be confused with George Huntington, the doctor who first described the disease symptoms. Hence its name.'

'Yes. The spellings confused me for a while. Quite a coincidence. But when you talk about the recipe going wrong it all sounds so simple. But it's not is it?'

'There's the irony Susie. At some level it should be simple. We now know precisely the root cause, and we should be able to fix it. That's why some scientists call it the most curable, but incurable, brain disorder. How to deliver a cure keeps eluding us, so we have to work harder, smarter and faster.' He smiled at her. 'It's also why I need people like you.'

'I'm in if the offer still stands. Now please give me tons of stuff I can read before I start.'

He remembered how she'd staggered out of his lab that night with almost half her body weight in reading material.

'Focus on learning everything you can about trinucleotide repeat expansion.' he'd told her.

She'd given him a questioning look, then grinned. 'I think I'll start by making sure I can spell it.'

He'd smiled back. 'Sorry. Triple repeats for short, but we geneticists love giving things fancy names. It's basically how the genetic mutation of the DNA that causes Huntington's repeats itself. Put simply, the more triple repeats, the more the likelihood of increasingly worse symptoms, so we need to stop those repeats. Like I need to stop talking and let you go home. Enjoy your homework.'

Typical of the Susie he now knew so well, she'd appeared early next morning having read and absorbed everything he'd given her. He couldn't have wished for a better addition to his team.

It was approaching 2 a.m. as he drove home, desperate for some sleep, but more positive than ever before about the night's encouraging developments. He sat at traffic lights and dared to imagine he could at last be close to the break-through that had eluded him for so long. Close to figuring out how to control the triple expansion he'd discussed with Susie, and tantalisingly close to being able to switch the mutated gene off and render it powerless.

But he was too tired to give it any further thought tonight. As the lights turned to green, he told himself to switch off and enjoy his drive home. He loved London at this time of night when he encountered so little traffic. Maybe the only other people out were mad scientists like him.

He smiled at that thought, and hoped his madness was about to pay dividends.

CHAPTER THIRTEEN

Catherine dropped her bag in the hallway, sat at her kitchen table and laid out the contents of the package Adam had wanted her to have. There'd been no opportunity for more than a cursory review in London, before Clara got home, but now she had three hours alone before Will would be back from the Medical Centre. Time to take a closer look and see what they told her.

She'd risked looking at the iPad on the train back but learned nothing. Adam had barely used it; it was empty apart from the account he'd emailed her from, which had nothing in the inbox or outbox. His message to her still sat in the deleted file. It was no surprise Lizzie had forgotten it would stay there for a few days before disappearing automatically, so she hit clear and got rid of it. She considered deleting the entire account as Adam had intended to do but decided to keep it. There was an outside chance something might arrive in the inbox, although she doubted it. If nothing did in the next week, she'd shut it down.

Before she looked at the documents, she picked up her

phone to call Lizzie and tell her she was home. This was going to be another difficult day as Adam's doctor was expecting to receive the post-mortem results and she knew Lizzie was dreading taking the call. Catherine paused and frowned, wondering if and how that call might affect the direction she was taking. She hoped the news would come soon.

She scrolled down her favourites to Lizzie's number and realised the one question she hadn't asked yesterday. How had she missed the obvious? Lizzie answered immediately.

'Hi. Back home?'

'Yes. You OK? Sorry. Stupid question.'

'I'm better for seeing you. I don't feel quite so alone with this now.'

'You're not, you know that. Is there any news from the doctor?'

'Not yet. But he did say it could be late afternoon. I'm dreading the call, but we need to know. How are you doing?'

'I'm fine, looking forward to seeing Will. I have another question for you, and I can't believe I didn't ask yesterday. Adam's personal phone. Where is it?'

'I thought about that this morning after you left. Think I was afraid to deal with it yesterday. I've been looking for it, but I can't find it.'

'I have to ask...What was he wearing when...'

'His dressing gown, it was so early. He often kept his phone in the pocket, but the police and the paramedics didn't say they found it. And I don't remember seeing it on the desk. It's certainly not there now. I've looked. Only his government mobile's there.'

'You've checked the desk drawers? Charger?'

'Both. And nothing.'

'Have you called it?'

'No, and I daren't Catherine. I couldn't bear listening to his voicemail greeting.'

'I'm sorry. Insensitive of me. Let me try it and see if it rings. Listen out for it. I'll put you on hold.' Moments later she resumed their call. 'Nothing. Network message saying it's not available.'

'Do you think…?' The voice trailed off.

'I think it's a distinct possibility that someone's taken it, checked it and disabled it, which doesn't help us. I'd like to have looked at it, but it's another indication that we're right to be suspicious.'

'And the documents? Did you look at those on the train?'

'No, it was too risky, the compartment was crammed. I'm about to take a look now. You get as much rest as you can. I'll call you later.'

She laid out the various papers on the kitchen table. At first glance she was faced with a random selection of departmental emails and memos; minutes of meetings; new drug reports and financial spreadsheets, but once she got them into some sort of order, she began to see patterns within the apparent randomness.

Most of the minutes concerned meetings of Pharmaceutical Advisory Boards with Health Service doctors and managers in attendance. Several had paragraphs blanked out, and, in two cases, a missing page. Certain names kept reappearing, often simply as initials.

She turned her attention to the spreadsheets, high level summaries of government health spending with several entries red circled, she assumed by Adam.

She could see massive sums were being paid to the Pharmaceuticals, which she expected. She knew from her online research that NHS spending on drugs was heading towards an annual £20 billion. But what shocked her was the frequency and extent of the money flowing back in the opposite direction, to the NHS, categorised as Services and Advisory fees. It was no surprise to her that NHS officials were called upon to advise Pharmaceutical boards, but she was surprised at the apparent scale of it. She wondered how many people knew its full extent. NHS accounting systems were understandably complex and focused at local and regional levels, so who saw the details behind these aggregate numbers? Adam had talked about 'the tip of the iceberg'. Were there more of these payments that she wasn't even seeing?

Why had this never been investigated? At best there was scope here for lack of impartiality in official decision making and, worse case, scope for corruption.

She rubbed her eyes, tired from focusing on numbers. She had more questions than answers, and she was going to need help with this. She knew where she had to go to get it; the one place that would give her investigation a legitimate cover and the resources it required.

Her phone rang; it was Lizzie, and the conversation was brief. The post-mortem had confirmed the probable cause of Adam's death as sudden cardiac arrest, an electrical failure within his heart that couldn't have been predicted and which had hit him without any prior warning. It was as they'd both expected. The authorities had deemed he died of natural causes. Nothing was suspicious, no further investigation was planned, and the case was closed. Tomorrow's headlines would report it as a promising career cut tragically short. And Catherine was no further forward.

She looked at her watch. Will was due back any minute and she would devote this evening to him. They wouldn't have many more nights together in this house.

Tomorrow she'd do what she'd told Lizzie she would. She'd write her sales pitch to the new Editor of The Guardian.

She was back in the investigative journalism business.

CHAPTER FOURTEEN

In between helping Will prepare and pack for university, she'd finished her presentation, and convinced the initially reluctant executive assistant to the Guardian's editor to give her an hour of her boss's time. It was scheduled for ten days' time, a week after Adam's funeral. She wished it was sooner, but it seemed her past reputation had at least got her through the door.

But today it was time to load up her old VW Golf with Will's belongings and drive to Cambridge. Nina and Jack arrived to help and wave them off. As she backed the car out of her driveway, she saw Will staring at the For Sale sign and read his mind. Life was never going to be the same again.

She forced thoughts of the funeral and her investigation to the back of her mind as they unpacked the car, allowing herself to be thrilled at her son's obvious excitement about his new life.

His room was small and furnished with the bare essentials, but he loved it. They took a selfie of themselves grinning and pointing at his name on the door, and once they unpacked his bags and the shelves were almost filled with his books and photographs, it started to look like home. Pride of place went to the new MacBook Catherine had bought him and to the bright red Beats Pill speaker that was his going away gift from Nina and Jack.

They explored the college and checked the notice boards for the events of Freshers' week. Over drinks in the Pembroke Café, Will's excitement about all the Clubs and Societies he planned to look at spilled out of him, but it was tempered with an unspoken recognition from both of them that it would soon be time to say their goodbyes. Over the years they'd talked about this moment, and now it was imminent. Catherine knew it would be as tough as she'd always imagined.

They arrived back at his room as his next-door neighbour emerged and introduced himself as Troy, a six-foot-tall American from Chicago, at Cambridge on a scholarship to study Engineering. Within minutes Catherine could see he and Will would become good friends. They were already deciding on a time to head for the bar later. She felt a strange combination of sadness and relief, knowing this was her cue to leave, but confident that her son would be fine.

Back in her car, she watched him walk away before he turned to give her a final wave. She pressed her head against the steering wheel and sat, motionless, contemplating past, present and future. Will was here, she'd done the job she'd set out to do eighteen years ago, and now she had a funeral to face. A funeral to mark a death that had happened way earlier than it should. Then she had an investigation to resume.

An investigation she'd been temporarily forced to suspend. She had no idea where it would lead, but it was about to begin. She lifted her head, looked in the mirror, and watched herself take a deep breath. Then she gave the key a firm, decisive turn in the ignition and started the engine.

CHAPTER FIFTEEN

'That must have been tough, driving away from Will, and then straight to London for the funeral. I want to hear everything about it but then you must take some time out for yourself. You look exhausted.'

Catherine forced a weak smile. She badly needed to sleep and recharge her batteries before she rehearsed her Guardian presentation until it was word perfect. Her investigation needed the resources the paper could provide, and she couldn't afford to put a foot wrong.

Nina had insisted she drove straight to her for a meal before going home to an empty house, and Catherine was pleased she had. She needed a few hours recovery time with her best friend. 'I'm not sure the word's been invented to describe how I feel, Nina. Let's say I've had better weeks.'

Nina took her hand. 'I know. And you did brilliantly to get Will settled so quickly. He looked great in the pics you sent of him in his new room. Jack can't wait to go down and see him. But he must've been disappointed he couldn't go to the funeral with you.'

Catherine nodded. 'He was desperate to be there, but

Freshers' week is a big deal and I couldn't let him miss it. It's a rite of passage. I knew what Adam's opinion would have been and Lizzie agreed. So, I told him to stay.'

'Are you up to telling me about the funeral, and how Lizzie and Clara were? If you want to wait, I understand. It must still feel so raw.'

'It does, but it'll help to tell you about it. It was a beautiful service, typical Lizzie. Adam would have loved it. Understated. No fanfare.'

'And not religious?'

'Extremely un-religious, just how he would've wanted it. Not a hymn or a prayer book in sight. His coffin came in to R.E.M.'s Losing My Religion and he left to ELO's Mr Blue Sky. The government powers that be had a shit fit about those choices, but Lizzie stuck to her guns. They were his two favourite bands.'

Nina laughed. 'That sounds like Lizzie, good for her. She obviously did him proud. And how were she and Clara? It must have been an ordeal for them.'

'They held it together. Lizzie was incredible, as always. They both were, but they let it all out after everybody left. They needed to.'

'They must still be in shock. He was so young and fit. Not someone you'd expect to have a heart attack. But all the news reports said at least it all happened quickly for him. That must be some comfort to Lizzie.'

Catherine shrugged her shoulders and wished she could tell her the truth about what she and Lizzie suspected. She and Nina had always been open with each other, but she was on her own with this one. She could only talk through her plan, and not divulge that the circumstances of Adam's death had been the final catalyst for her permanent return to London.

'I hope in time it will be. And, of course, I'll be there to help her.'

'And to start your new life.' Nina looked down at her hands. 'I'm excited for you although I can't believe you're going in a week. Life... won't be the same around here.'

'I guess we're both making new starts. I know everything's going to work out well for you and you deserve it to. And this move's the right thing for me, for lots of reasons, but it's a scary prospect, trying to pick up where I left off. And it'll be hard leaving you. I don't want to think about that part.' She blinked away tears as she tried to imagine a new life where she didn't talk to, or see, Nina almost every day. 'You've become such a special friend to me, and I'll miss you more than I can begin to tell you.' 'I'll miss you too, but you're going to be a huge success. And you're hardly going to the moon. We'll message and video chat all the time, and I'll expect a guest room to be permanently ready for me. Even when you're rich and famous and all loved up with Mr Perfect.'

Catherine smiled. Nina had her future all mapped out, and she wished it was that simple. 'I think Mr Perfect will have to wait a while. Anyway, he's taken this long to show up, doesn't look like he's in a hurry to find me.'

'He's out there somewhere, and you'll find each other. I'm convinced of it. Don't worry about anything here. I'll keep an eye on your house, and it sounds like it's going to sell pretty fast. But there's one more thing we need to do before you go.'

Catherine raised her eyebrows. 'And what would that be?'

'A shopping trip to get you kitted out and fit for purpose. I'm not letting you loose in the big city with your current wardrobe. Not for work or play. I'm taking you in hand. And a day off from thinking about everything will do you good, so no arguing. Deal?

A pang of guilt hit her stomach as she realised how much

the prospect appealed, but maybe a day trying not to think about Adam, and the task he'd set her, would energise her and give her some perspective to move forward.

She high-fived Nina and smiled. 'Deal. What would I do without you?'

CHAPTER SIXTEEN

Catherine arrived at King's Cross Station and joined the throng of commuters snaking their way across the concourse. Her senses were assaulted by the noise and the frenetic buzz that were the hallmarks of a London working day. This used to be her life, and it was about to be again, but momentarily it fazed her. Part of her felt like a small-town girl a long way from the familiarities of home.

As she navigated the crowds, she saw her reflection in a shop window. Nina had decreed which outfit she should wear to 'walk the walk with the rest of those city slickers' as she'd put it, and Catherine was confident she'd made the right choice. Slim black pencil skirt, crisp white shirt, grey linen jacket and black court shoes.

She took a deep breath. She was dressed for the part, but now she needed to talk the talk too. Investigative journalism was all about confidence and chutzpah, risk-taking and edge. In the past she'd always had those in spades, and she needed to ooze them again today.

Her future in this city depended on the next couple of hours in the distinctive glass building in front of her, home to the paper that had been dubbed 'Britain's non-conformist conscience.' She'd spent months wanting to be part of that conscience again, for her own sake, but now this was about more than re-launching her career. It was for Adam, and his family. His death had been senseless and if it had also been deliberate, despite what the post-mortem and brief official investigation had concluded, she'd never forgive whoever was behind it. But she could make it count for something, by finishing what he'd started and exposing those responsible.

For that she needed the protection that the weight and gravitas of the paper would give her. The three-hour train journey the previous night had been the perfect opportunity to hone her thoughts and her presentation, and she knew it was good; now she had to deliver it. She could do this, and she must. Failure was not an option. This was for Adam.

She smiled at the young man holding the conference room door open for her as he shot her a reassuring conspiratorial wink. They'd talked briefly while she'd been waiting. She learned he was George, with a degree in Biochemistry from Newcastle, a strong Geordie accent and a sense of humour to match. Witty and smart, he confessed he was a fan of her past work, which he'd researched. She knew success today would earn her the right to her own researcher and she couldn't imagine a better candidate.

He introduced her to the Editor and his deputy, then left, and Catherine launched straight into her pitch. Thirty minutes later she at last paused for breath. Neither of the two men facing her had interrupted, and as she sat back in her seat and invited their questions, she tried to read their reactions. But their inscrutable expressions told her nothing. Had she done enough? She waited for one of them to break the silence.

'Wow, Catherine. That was one helluva pitch. And, given your relationship with Adam Wentworth, it must have been damned tough to deliver.' At last, the Editor had spoken. She'd done her research on him. Sam Saunders, mid-forties, a New Yorker with a Harvard MBA and a reputation for straight-talking. If he was positive, she was virtually hired. 'You have a potentially dynamite story here. Looking at some of these numbers this could be a real shit-storm for this government. So much for them being elected on a clean-up politics agenda. No question there's a case to answer here, but...'

She threw him a questioning look. 'But?'

'It's a hell of a leap from that to the murder of a government minister. The autopsy doesn't indicate anything, and clearly the Met see nothing suspicious.'

'Sam, I get that this could look like desperation from the grieving widow and her best friend, but trust me, it isn't. Too many things don't quite add up, and remember how well I knew Adam. He wouldn't have left this information for me if he hadn't believed he was at risk. Nobody knows that apart from his wife and you guys, and I'd like to keep it that way.' She paused for a moment then added, 'Although at the moment I doubt anybody would suspect me of being involved or of being a threat. I've been out of the investigation business for so long.'

'Understood. Everything we discuss today stays in this room, and I suggest we get everything his wife gave you out of your possession, and into our safe, pronto. Let's have our guys clean your hard drive too, make sure there's no trace of that email or today's presentation. I'm not sure I'm buying the whole murder conspiracy theory, but we don't want any leaks, or any trail linking you personally Catherine. Could be risky.'

'You can say that again, Sam.' Catherine recognised the

voice of the man who'd so far sat in silence next to Sam. Peter Johnson, Deputy Editor. He'd been with the paper over forty years. She'd never worked closely with him but had butted up against him a few times in the past, and sensed he never liked her, 'This whole thing's risky, in all sorts of ways, and we'd better be damn sure of our facts before we put anything out there.' He paused, directing an icy gaze at Catherine, 'And I'm not sure I appreciate the two of us being dragged into some of your more dramatic suspicions either. Puts all our reputations at risk, and God knows what else.'

Catherine said instantly before Sam could comment, 'I'm sorry you feel that way Peter. That was never my intention. Nor do I think it's an issue.'

'Well you seem convinced your friend got himself bumped off because of what he suspected. And now we're in on it. How the fuck is that not an issue in your opinion?'

'Because Adam was one man. And as it happens an extremely good man and one of my dearest friends. But easy to target. This situation is entirely different. You have the protection of a major national newspaper corporation. And in any case, nobody knows you've heard this.'

'But we've only got your word for that haven't we?'

'Peter, I can assure you I thought long and hard before sharing this with you. Adam warned me to be careful who I trusted. My first instinct was to go this alone and believe me it would have been my preference. But this is too big for me to handle without some extra resource and expertise and that's the reason I'm here. That and the fact I believed this newspaper was about getting to the truth. Obviously, you don't agree.' She pushed her seat back and began gathering her papers up.

Sam raised his hands and looked at both of them in turn. 'Time out guys. Catherine, stay where you are. And Peter, this is a story we can't ignore. If the information pans out, we're talking about a misappropriation of health funds and potentially a level of government corruption that this paper has a responsibility to expose. A few of what you guys call backhanders are one thing, we all figure that goes on, but this looks like a whole new ballpark and I have no intention of backing off.' He paused, looking at Catherine directly, 'I know you think there's more to this than numbers, Catherine, but for now we confine ourselves to those. Unless you can convince me otherwise, this paper can't get involved in wild conspiracy theories. Now, I suggest we adjourn for the day and regroup first thing tomorrow morning.' He stood and looked directly at them both in turn, 'You two should go kiss and make up over a drink. I want us at one on this. Then rest and settle into your hotel tonight Catherine. The serious work starts tomorrow. And by the way, you're hired.'

As he swept out of the room Catherine looked at Peter. His expression told her he found the idea of spending any more time with her a totally unappealing prospect and she tried not to laugh. To his credit he clearly read her mind and stifled a half grin. Maybe they could make this work after all.

'You heard what the man said, Catherine. I'm not comfortable with this but I'll give you the benefit of the doubt and hear you out. Let's go and grab a Starbucks. Call it an advance on your expense account.'

CHAPTER SEVENTEEN

Two hours later Catherine walked back into her hotel. It was typically tourist and indistinguishable from its neighbours, with garish décor and a permanently 'Out of Order' lift, but thankfully it was budget-friendly. She wondered if she'd ever progress to the luxury that existed a mere ten minutes away. That was one of the things she'd always loved about London. How basic morphed into opulence in one tube stop.

She felt tired, but relieved, after her meeting. At least she was hired, and Sam was on board to the need to investigate the scale of potential financial manipulation she'd presented, even if he wasn't convinced there was more to this. The time she spent with Peter had left them feeling more comfortable with each other. He still had concerns about the riskiness of her project but was prepared to give her time to convince him. His very scepticism made her sense she could trust him, and she needed that. She didn't know how many other people she could.

Telling herself she should eat, she picked up a laminated card that had seen better days and looked through the limited and uninspiring room service menu for the least complicated option, one that even this hotel's kitchen couldn't screw up. With a roast beef salad and a tub of vanilla Häagen-Dazs ordered, she opened the room safe and took out the originals of Adam's papers. They'd be secure in the newspaper's safe from tomorrow, along with the copies she'd already left with Sam. She was relieved she was no longer alone with what they contained.

She stared at the documents spread out on the hotel bed. Words and numbers were suddenly an unreadable jumble as tears blurred her vision. A sea of data that she remained convinced had cost Adam his life, Clara her father, and Lizzie her soulmate.

A familiar pang rose up inside her, and she tried to suppress it. That realisation again of something that she'd never found herself, a good man of her own. She told herself not to go there, this wasn't the time, but the feeling refused to go away.

A feeling that he was here, in this city, close by, and he was about to turn her world even more upside down. And, as a knock on the door announced her food had arrived, a feeling that Adam would have liked him.

Thirty minutes later she cleared away the half-eaten roast beef salad and empty Häagen Dazs carton, made herself coffee and settled back on the bed. Sam was right, she needed to recharge her batteries for tomorrow.

As she contemplated what the morning might bring, she noticed one of the spreadsheets had fallen off the bed and was face down on the floor. As she reached down to pick it up, she saw something else, something she hadn't noticed before; faint pencil scribblings on the back of one of the spreadsheets. It looked like random doodling, but she recognised Adam's writing. A word followed by three questions:

CERBERUS. Who? What? Where?

Cerberus. She remembered the word from her childhood love of Greek mythology but googled it to check her recall was correct. A monstrous three-headed dog, the guardian of the underworld. What the hell did a mythical creature have to do with all this? The name made Catherine uneasy. Without pausing to think she picked up her phone, took a shot of that spreadsheet's details and filed it to her photo gallery.

Then she ripped the original into the smallest pieces she could and buried them within the salad remnants in the waste bin.

CHAPTER EIGHTEEN

Catherine and George were sitting in his favourite wine bar which he'd dubbed their second office. He'd jumped at the chance to be her wingman when Sam had agreed she needed a resource to help her analyse and investigate Adam's data, and she already loved working with him. In two days, they'd become firm friends and he'd proved himself to be as smart and committed as she'd thought when they first met. She'd also learned that being the only son of a successful businessman had given him a taste for the finer things in life, including good wine. It seemed to disconcert him that he hadn't yet converted her to its virtues and that she continued to shun it in favour of still water.

'Nothing like a glass of a decent chilled Chablis to focus the mind Catherine. You don't know what you're missing.'

'We didn't all grow up with a silver spoon in our mouth you know, or in your case a crystal glass.'

He held his hands up in mock horror. 'OK. Don't start with the working-class speech again. I get it.'

She grinned at his expression, but her voice was serious. 'I'm so pleased you're working with me on this George. I only wish we were getting a bit further with these documents.' She tightened her grip on her glass. She knew she had an important story to tell, but so far only enough to make a case for an independent inquiry into pharmaceutical company payments to government health officials, and to flag potentially compromised impartiality.

They didn't have any other evidence of criminal wrongdoing, but she'd shared with George her conviction that there was more to this and that Adam's death was somehow linked. He'd read her copy of Adam's email, although she hadn't told him about the mysterious Cerberus, and she was no nearer to any answers about who or what it referred to. She still felt she should keep the name to herself for now.

George interrupted her thoughts. 'So, where do we go from here?'

'For now we print our evidence of payments to these so-called independent health officials and I write the best article I can. In reality they're acting as pharmaceutical consultants and that must suggest potential conflicts of interest. But we don't have evidence of anything more do we? Other than my instinct that something doesn't feel right.'

'No, we don't, but I trust your instincts. If you think there's more to all this, then I suspect there is too.'

Catherine smiled at him despite her frustration at their slow progress, touched at his earnest expression and how much he believed in her.

'Did you come up with anything else connecting the particular pharmaceutical companies that keep coming up?'

'Sorry Boss. Nada. Certainly nothing connecting the three that feature the most in Adam's papers. These guys run bloody tight ships of course. Their new drug trials are kept so under wraps it's incredible. They use alpha-numeric code names and none of their employees talk. They've all got a shitload of investment riding on this new stuff and they're getting some pretty big slugs of public cash to help fund some of their research.'

Catherine interrupted him. 'Which is an issue in itself. The taxpayers get a double hit. We contribute to the research, then we pay extortionate costs for the new drugs. I'm not sure that model's entirely fair.'

'Maybe not, but that's how it's evolved. And when it comes to health treatment, I guess it's a seller's market. A lot of the research seems to be aimed at genetics incidentally. I figured that out piecing together extracts from the board minutes Adam left you.'

Catherine threw him a sharp glance. 'Genetics?'

'Yes. It's a hot area at the moment. Lots going on I hear, but all pretty secret squirrel stuff. You look surprised.'

'Because it reminds me of a conversation I had with Adam a month before he died. He told me genetics was an area I should look into if I wanted to find an interesting angle for an article to pitch. Gave me some introductory stuff to look at before we met up next, but...'

'But, of course, you never did.' His voice softened, 'I know how tough this must be for you.'

'It is, but I'm OK. And I think we should pursue this genetics link. Only a hunch but it's too much of a coincidence, and we don't have much else to go on. And Adam seemed so preoccupied with something the day he brought the subject up. I'll forward you the stuff he sent me to read, and I'll take a closer look at it too. Meanwhile I guess we focus on the scale of these numbers. It must be a continual balancing act for these companies between revenue kicking in from drugs that make it to market, and money at risk in new trials. If they get that balance wrong, they're screwed.'

'Big time. We're not talking small change here. The pharmaceuticals financial analyst I met with from J P Morgan Chase told me that researching and trialling a new drug and bringing it to market can hit two billion dollars plus.'

Catherine almost choked on her water. 'Shit. That's enough to keep a few CEOs awake at night. Maybe enough to tempt the more unscrupulous ones into some financial sleight of hand? I'm sure that's what Adam suspected.' She looked down at her hands. 'I feel I'm letting him down by not making more headway with this. I wish he'd been able to give me something more to go on before... well...you know what I'm saying.'

George touched her hand. 'Catherine, I know how much he meant to you and I know how much this means to you, but you can't beat yourself up because we haven't yet cracked whatever's out there to be cracked, and I can't believe Adam would want that. He'd know you'd give him your best, and you're doing exactly that. If there's more out there to find, you'll find it.'

She clasped her hand over his. 'We'll find it. We're a team now, right? The Mulder and Scully of modern journalism. The truth is out there, kiddo.'

He laughed. 'Loved The X Files. Always quite fancied myself as Mulder. Trouble is, Sam's not going to give us too much longer to figure stuff out, is he?'

'I doubt it. He's anxious to see at least something in print soon. He doesn't want to risk another paper picking up on this and beating us to it. He's still new here remember and he wants to make his mark.'

'Didn't get chance to tell you,' George said quickly, 'I heard some rumblings earlier today that a major expenses-type scandal is expected to break soon. So, either someone's on to us, or somebody else is already on to this.'

Before she could answer, her phone rang. Sam's name flashed up on her screen, as if on cue, and she answered on the second ring. He bypassed the pleasantries.

'Catherine, I need to know where you're at. Now. Word on the street is that others have got wind of this and I need you ready to go to press pronto. Have something on my desk first thing tomorrow please. We run it past the legal boys then we hit the presses. I don't want the competition stealing this from under our noses. They got the MP's expenses scandal; I'm not losing this one to them as well. I'm guessing you're with George and I can imagine the look you're giving him right now, but don't even think about arguing. The time frame's not negotiable.'

'I understand your concerns Sam. We've heard the same rumours. That's why we're here reviewing where to go with this.'

'Where we go is public with what you've got so far. Nothing new presumably?'

She looked at George and rolled her eyes as she replied, trying to mask her exasperation at Sam's clipped New York delivery. Surely he realised that nobody wished she had something new more than she did. 'No, nothing new yet, at least nothing concrete. But I'm certain we can force an official independent inquiry and that's how I'll write my piece. Beyond that, everything's potential connections and our suspicions, but there is more to all this Sam. I'm convinced of it.'

'You may be right Catherine, but if there's more behind all this, the guys responsible are damned good at concealing it. I know you want the truth about what happened to your friend, and so do I, but we have a responsibility to the taxpayers on this. It's their money being fooled around with. And we have a responsibility to this paper's reputation. We can't lose this story. Major on the whole conflict of interest and impartiality thing, the scale of the numbers, and let's force at least force that inquiry. Write the thing and I'll see you tomorrow.'

CHAPTER NINETEEN

Catherine stared at her phone for another second after it went dead. She met George's questioning look.

'I take it from the lack of hello or goodbye that we got our arses kicked. How long did he give us?'

'Till tomorrow morning.'

'Shit. He must be nervous someone's going to beat us to it.'

'He is, and I wonder how somebody else could have got hold of this. We've been so careful.'

'A hundred per cent careful, but I guess you've got no choice but to go with what we've got. And we can keep investigating after we've got your piece out there.'

'I guess at least this'll shake the tree, and we see what falls out of it. But I wonder if Sam's appetite for this will change, once we've got something in print. He'll want to move onto some other issue, he's that type of guy. Meanwhile we might only have exposed the tip of the iceberg.'

'But you won't leave it at that, will you? I can tell by the look in your eye. And your grip on that glass. Any tighter and it'll shatter,' George grinned at her.

'No, I won't let it happen. I'll go solo on this if I have to. They may take you off me, though.'

'Bollocks. Not happening. Me Mulder, you Scully remember?'

Catherine grinned. 'We are starting to sound like a couple of conspiracy theorists, except we haven't figured out what the conspiracy is yet.'

'So, we keep digging.' He clicked his fingers in front of her face. 'Catherine? Where are you?'

'Sorry. I'm thinking about this possible leak. Isn't it all a bit convenient when we're so close to going public with something? Because of it we're going to end up rushing out some watered-down version of our suspicions.'

'I'm not sure where you're going with this, and it's hardly watered down. We're getting an important issue out there and under some objective scrutiny at least.'

'I know. But what if we're right and this is about way more than numbers and there's a much bigger cover-up going on? Maybe whoever's behind it wants the music to stop here so they can deal with the fallout from this but deflect us from digging into the real story.'

'So, they leak this themselves to try and make this the end of the story?'

'Exactly,' said Catherine. 'A bit like a plea bargain. Take a knuckle-rapping for the lesser offence and avoid being hammered for the bigger one.'

'Wow. That would be Machiavellian.'

'Maybe, but credible yes?'

'Only one way to find out. We keep looking. Finish what we've started,' George held out his hand to her.

Catherine reached across the table to clasp it again. 'Yes, but let's agree on one thing. We have to careful. If Adam was killed because he stumbled onto something, then whoever arranged that won't hesitate to stop us. They need to be convinced we're letting this go. From here on we keep everything to ourselves.'

'Deal. I can do convincing.'

'Right, I'd better head back to the hotel and write a convincing piece with what we've got. I'll call to talk you through it later.' She smiled at him as she got up to leave. 'Enjoy the rest of your Chablis. And George?'

'Yes?'

'Thanks for believing in me.'

By 11.30 that night she'd written and honed her piece. She hoped Sam would be happy with it. She and George had talked through it on the new mobiles Sam had arranged for them both, which they were confident were secure. Although her article didn't go as far as she'd hoped it might, it still packed a punch.

Now it was done, she paced the room, restless and dissatisfied, despite George's attempts at lifting her spirits. The article brought her no closer to solving the mystery of Adam's death. She told herself she should contemplate the possibility that he'd been wrong in his suspicions, that he'd seen more here than existed, but she couldn't. He had to have believed he was on to something, to get her involved like this. She owed it to him to uncover the truth.

She needed sleep but first she needed some air. Maybe a walk and some late-night window shopping would calm her down. She threw on a tracksuit top and grabbed her personal mobile. She checked her notifications as she took the four flights of stairs that she now knew so well. She'd missed an earlier text message from Nina.

'Hiya C.
How's life in the fast lane?

Let me know how the meeting went.
Spotted Mr Perfect yet?
Msg me when you can.
Miss u loads. N x'

Catherine smiled. She missed her friend and badly wanted a catch-up chat, but it was almost midnight, so she shot back a message.

'Hi. Meeting went great thanks.
I'm in!!! Search for Mr Perfect on temporary hold.
Haven't spotted him in a crowd yet.
Maybe he's hiding!
Hope all ok with you.
Call you soon. C x'

As she stepped out into the night air, she imagined Nina smiling at her continued refusal to use text speak. Everybody else did, but not her. She loved words too much.

The walk energised her, but she felt too cold to stay out more than fifteen minutes. Back in the room she made a mug of hot tea, got ready for bed and set her phone alarm. She wanted to be in the office before Sam arrived in the morning, with time to read her piece over one more time.

Her phone pinged with another message from Nina, and she smiled. Nina always had that effect.

'Don't kill me.
I decided to start your search for
the perfect man myself.
Whacked you on Tinder.
Used a couple of the photos
we took on our shopping trip.
Well you'll never get around to it.

Right swiped on this bloke and - guess what –
he matched you back!!
Hot...or what???
And he's in London!!!! Nxx
PS At least look at him & tell me what you think.
Told you that dress I picked for you would work.'

Despite everything, Catherine had to smile; her friend was incorrigible. Within seconds an image and some words popped up on her screen.

She was surprised to find herself so instantly attracted to a face in a photograph. A strong, angular face framed by dark brown, almost black, wavy hair, it belonged to Max, fifty-four. Clutching her phone, she sank back into the pillow. If he'd liked her, maybe it really wasn't too late for her to find someone. This man had just shown up at the wrong time.

She messaged Nina back.

'You are too much, but I love you to bits!
And yes, he looks pretty good!
Pity the timing's off,
but I guess there's hope for me yet!
But for now, you'd better delete my profile.
Early meeting tomorrow at the paper.
I just wrote my first piece for the Ed to review,
so wish me luck and I'll call you at the weekend.
Sleep well if you can drag yourself off Tinder. Cxxx

She fell asleep within minutes, wondering what tomorrow might bring from her meeting with Sam, hoping he'd like her piece. But it wasn't his face she saw when she closed her eyes.

It was the face in the photograph.

CHAPTER TWENTY

A cacophony of notification sounds from her phone jolted Catherine awake. The lilt of her alarm tone and an assortment of message pings competed with each other like a discordant dawn chorus. Barely awake, she grabbed it, flipped the case open and was assaulted by alerts. Early morning news was rarely good news and she immediately panicked about Will.

She sighed with relief that there was nothing concerning her son, but Sam's name jumped out all over the place. He'd been trying to contact her by voice, email and messenger app for the last fifteen minutes. How had she missed them all? But then she'd obviously plunged into an overdue deep sleep.

She opened Sam's text message, hoping he was simply moving the meeting time.

'Wake up for Christ's sake.
Check your news app
and get straight to the office.
We need to talk.
Bring the sidekick.'

His voice message was equally terse. What the hell was going on? Before she could get to the newsfeed a message from George flashed up and she caught the first line.

'Fuck. Have you seen it?
Call me. We're screwed.'

She flicked to the breaking news and did a double-take, as she had on the morning she'd seen the Adam newsflash. Like then, she had a fleeting moment of denial, telling herself she wasn't seeing this. But she was. The morning's headline.

PUBLIC HEALTH OFFICIALS PAID BY MAJOR DRUGS COMPANIES INQUIRY DEMANDED

Virtually the exact headline she'd drafted to present to Sam, but under someone else's by-line. Followed by a detailed piece about compromised impartiality and criticism of the Government's clean and transparent politics agenda that had featured so strongly in their election manifesto. Everything she'd included in her article. She'd been beaten to the punch, lost the story and very possibly her return to top journalism. This had been her passport back, and somehow, she'd blown it.

Worse, she'd let Adam down. He'd entrusted all this to her, and he and Lizzie had both believed in her. She lay back on the bed, put her phone to silent and allowed herself the self-indulgence of tears.

Ten minutes later she'd cried out her anger and frustration.

Exhausted, she stared at the ceiling, focusing on the slightly melted and discoloured plastic lime green light fitting. Another hotel homage to 1960s decor. This place so needed a major revamp; like she did too. Horrible circumstances had brought her back to London and the relaunch of her career that Adam had so wanted for her, but she'd fallen at the first hurdle.

Here she was, alone in a cheap hotel room with a shitty light fitting, crying as her investigation and career relaunch lay in tatters. Maybe she should pack her bag, check out of this Godforsaken place, jump on the first train north and face the music with everybody later. She and Lizzie should tell the authorities their concerns maybe. Take a risk on letting the experts handle this. Clearly, she wasn't up to it.

Her phone vibrated with another message alert and she wanted to throw it at the wall. She wished it would leave her alone. No doubt another Sam chase up. She almost couldn't be bothered looking, but force of habit compelled her to. It was Will.

'Hi Mum. Cambridge is so great.
Loving it.
Thank u for helping me get here.
Ur the best. Loads to tell u.
How's London?
Bet ur rocking it.
Love. Will xxxx'

She sat upright on the bed and read his words again. Rocking it. Her son had such belief in her. And what the hell had she been doing for the last ten minutes? Feeling sorry for herself, considering quitting. Well dammit, her son wasn't a quitter, and neither was she. She'd come here to do a job and it wasn't over yet. It was only beginning. Someone had derailed her story and she needed to find out who. She wouldn't let Adam and Lizzie down.

If her theory about this leak was right, it only served to reinforce Adam's suspicions and she had to keep going, finish what he'd started and be the person he'd trusted her to be. She glanced back at Will's message on her phone. She wasn't about to let her son down either.

She got up and flipped the kettle switch on. She needed a caffeine hit and she needed to think.

Fortified from a two-sachet mug of the room tray's weak coffee, which she suspected was way past its use-by date, she called Sam's number and left a voicemail. She apologised for missing his messages, but not for the leak. She wouldn't let either herself or George take the rap for that. She told him they'd be in his office within the hour.

Then she called George who answered immediately.

'Catherine I'm sorry. One day. One more bloody day and we would've had this. This story should be under your name.'

'I know, I'm sorry too, for both of us. But I'm not giving up. If anything, this makes me more determined to get to the bottom of what's going on and what happened to Adam, which I'm certain is more than the diluted version they've printed, good though it is. I'm not prepared to let this end here.'

'Me neither. You know I'm with you. So, what's the deal with Sam?'

'I left him a voicemail. Said we'd be there within the hour.'

'No problem. Not looking forward to it though. I suppose he's gone ballistic.'

'I should imagine he has, but we haven't spoken yet. And George?'

'Yep?'

'In the meeting follow my lead, OK? Trust me.'

'You got it boss. See you in sixty.'

Catherine took a shower and got ready at warp speed. It was too cold to do anything else. She'd decided how to handle Sam. It could backfire on her, but it was her only option if she wanted to stay in the game. She grabbed her bag, phone and laptop and as she opened the room door to leave, she looked back and made another decision. Today she'd start looking for somewhere to live. She'd had it with the cheap hotel gig. She was a Londoner now, and she needed somewhere to call home.

She found George nursing a Starbuck's outside Sam's office. Through the closed door she could hear him on the phone, shouting at someone. George stood to give her a conspiratorial hug of support as Sam flung the door open and barked at them to come in. Catherine took a deep breath. She needed to keep her cool and salvage something from all this. She didn't need Sam Saunders as an enemy.

Once again, he bypassed the pleasantries.

'So, this is a monumental fuck up of the first order. How did they get this out there so quickly and where did they get so much information from? Did you two leave something lying around somewhere? Bloody Brits. Every night's amateur night.'

He barely paused for breath and Catherine sat impassively through his rant. Better to let him blow himself out before she reacted.

He gave her a challenging look. 'Well?'

'Well what Sam? What the hell do you expect me to say? You've summoned us here like two naughty school kids called to the Headmaster's study for messing around in the science lab. George and I did not leak this. We were committed to this story.'

'Yes, but...' He tried to interrupt but she didn't let him.

'Whoever they got hold of this from, it wasn't either of us. But it's happened, and maybe I should've seen it coming. So, if you're on a witch hunt, I suggest you start somewhere else. Somebody on your staff must've let something slip, and when you find out who please tell me. In the meantime, you might like to consider how George and I are feeling, which is shit to be honest.'

'Catherine look, I...' Sam tried again but she held her hand up and stopped him.

'And you might want to read the article as I wrote it. I finished it last night and as soon as we're done here, I'll email it to your inbox. No need for secrecy now is there? It's better than the one that hit the presses this morning; but then for me this is personal, as you very well know. Theirs was OK, but I'm convinced they've rushed out a watered-down version of the truth. I don't suppose my version will ever see the light of day now.'

She sat back in her seat, arms folded in defiance, hoping she hadn't pushed it too far. Sam hesitated, as if he wanted to be sure she was finished before he spoke. When he did his earlier aggression had gone. 'Catherine, I'm sorry, I'm being an insensitive bastard. I know how much you had invested in this. I promise you I'll look into the leak and if I find out it's one of our people, God help them. But this isn't over for you, or for the paper. We may have lost the early initiative, but as far as I'm concerned you guys are still on the story. I need someone following up on the independent inquiry, which we can assume will now happen, and I'd sooner it was you two.'

She smiled. She'd been right about him. He might be tough, but he was one of the good guys. 'I appreciate every-thing you've said Sam, but for me this is over. George is more than capable of handling the coverage you need from here on. He deserves the opportunity and you should let him run with it. If I'm going to rebuild my reputation, I need a big story of my own, and I need time to look for one.' She turned to George. 'Are you good with that?'

He was staring at her in shock. 'Good with it? You bet I am. It would be one hell of an opportunity for me. I can't believe you're handing this over.'

'I can't believe she is either.' Sam sounded equally shocked. 'And what the hell are you going to live on till you find the big scoop...fresh air? This city doesn't exactly come cheap.'

'I've got a few stories and articles I'm confident would sell fairly quickly, and I'm sure I can pick up some freelance stuff. That and some savings should tide me over while I figure things out. And I might start writing the novel that's buzzing around in my head. I'll be fine Sam.'

'I don't doubt it, but here's a proposal. I'll pay you a small retainer, renewable monthly, until you've sorted something more permanent. We'll book it as editorial consultancy advice. You help George when he needs it, and if I need back up or cover on any other projects, you're it. Meanwhile you work on your own stuff and you give me first dibs on anything big you decide to run with. Deal?' He stood in front of her and held out his hand.

Catherine stood up and shook his hand, relief flooding through her. She couldn't have hoped for a better outcome, and this positioned her where she needed to be to take her plan forward.

'Deal, and thank you Sam.'

'Now you two get the hell out of here and plan George's piece for tomorrow.' He grinned. 'I need to start interviewing suspects.'

They smiled back as they walked to the door. 'Are you sure we can't stick around for that? Maybe read them their rights?' Catherine couldn't resist.

'Go. Before I change my mind about that retainer. I'll let you know what I think of the piece you had lined up for this morning. Let's see if George can't still use some of it. And start thinking about some new ideas and email me.'

She gave him a smile and a thumbs up, but he'd already begun punching numbers into his phone.

They headed for the nearest café which was conveniently empty. They found a table and George spoke first. 'You're full of surprises. I hadn't expected that, but it was smart. Hope I played along ok?'

'Word perfect Mulder. I'm exactly where I want to be.'

'With everyone thinking you're officially off the story.'

She nodded. 'Exactly. I can appear to fade into the background while I dig deeper into Adam's suspicions.'

'And you don't really think someone off the paper leaked this do you?'

'No, I don't. Now I need to find out who did.'

'So where are you planning to start?'

'Good question Mr Reporter. Are we on or off the record? Either way I have absolutely no idea where to start.'

CHAPTER TWENTY-ONE

The university security guard reluctantly glanced up from Angry Birds to call good morning to the tall, jeans-clad man muttering into his phone as he headed for the exit. He wished these bloody people would stick to the rules about signing in and out during non-core hours but most of them couldn't be bothered. Arrogant intellectual bastards, thinking they were a cut above. He was fed up with the sneering response he usually got when he reminded them, so he'd given up. Like he could be bothered anyway.

And this bloke couldn't even be arsed to reply to a simple greeting. Just pulled his baseball cap lower and ignored the words. John didn't recognise him. He considered challenging the rude sod, but he'd lose too many seconds in his game and he didn't really give a toss. So he went back to his phone and launched a few more birds.

The man in the baseball cap glanced back briefly once he was the other side of the glass doors. The overweight, out-of-shape guy on the desk was focused on his phone again.

Some stupid mindless game or a porn site probably. He knew the type. He'd met enough of them. Thought the uniform made them important. Same as the screws had in Wandsworth.

He glanced at his watch. He'd barely make it in time. Why they'd had to call him up twice God knows. Easy for them in their smart offices, with their unlimited taxi budgets and their high-heeled assistants sorting their schedules out. Now he'd need to really leg it to the Tube station.

As he got to the corner he stopped. Had he cleared the computer search history when he'd finished? Shit, he couldn't remember. Their bloody phone call had distracted him. Damn, he never made stupid mistakes like that. If he went back now, the guard he'd probably pissed off might challenge him. Sod it. He'd have to gamble on Mr Smart-Arse Professor not noticing. Or if he did, assuming it was one of his poncey students. He raised his collar against the cold and headed for the underground.

Clayton flicked on the lab's bank of overhead fluorescent lights; they spluttered into life in random fashion as he hit the on keys of his two desktop computers. Then he selected a capsule at random for the new Nespresso machine. It seemed unnecessarily complicated and time-consuming to him with its multi-coloured array of capsule choices, but Susie and the team had told him this was the coolest machine out there and he had to admit it made good coffee.

He could certainly use an injection of caffeine. He'd woken up at stupid o'clock, his mind racing with ideas, and he wanted a couple of hours of lab time before any of the team arrived and before his first tutorial, a weekly session with a struggling student. He and his colleagues had decided they'd reached the end of the line with this guy and now it was up to Clayton to deliver the bad news. It was the only part of his job he hated.

As he waited for his coffee, he hit Google on the computer he kept for his exclusive use. His daily routine was to go straight to the morning headlines, but today an item flashed up in the search history that he didn't recognise. It wasn't one he'd done, and, in any case, he was always meticulous about clearing his search history. This was a financial analysis site, not his thing. Who'd been using this machine and what for? None of his team ever touched it. He clicked on the search item and among the list of choices he could see the specific site last visited. Financial Ratios of the Top 5 Pharmaceuticals. Viewed at 6am. Who the hell would have been in the lab then? He'd arrived here himself at 6.30 so must have almost run into them. He found that thought uncomfortable.

Thankfully all the research was tightly password protected and backed up securely and further protected inside the university servers. Nevertheless, he'd call by Security later and check if they had a record of who'd been in the lab then and he'd speak to each member of the team. There was probably an innocent explanation. Maybe one of them had forgotten something last night, come in early and inadvertently logged into his personal machine. No harm done. Probably stress and long hours were making him paranoid.

He hit his Google newsfeed. By coincidence the pharmaceuticals had made today's headlines. The article he read screamed potential conflict of interest and demanded an inquiry into Government health officials being paid for advising pharmaceutical boards. It sounded like the usual journalistic witch-hunt to him. He'd been called in as an academic adviser to several boards himself and never felt himself conflicted. Not that he'd ever accepted payment, he was just happy to contribute to the roll-out of effective treatments, but it was typical of the press to want to see demons where there weren't any.

He took time to glance down the list of specific companies named and was pleased to see that ABZ Pharmaceuticals wasn't listed. They were the major sponsors of his research. A successful multinational, although not one of the biggest, he'd been drawn to them by their ethical approach to business and their willingness to give him freedom to push the boundaries, even if it meant progress was slower. If this story about the companies who were listed had any credence at all it was further proof his assessment of ABZ had been sound.

He glanced at the clock, surprised and annoyed to realise he'd been here an hour and made zero work progress. He opened his documents and clicked on his Conferences folder. He wasn't remotely in the mood to prepare yet another presentation, but he'd signed up to be a keynote speaker at a Genetics symposium in less than a week. He'd come under pressure from the university Vice Chancellor and the CEO of ABZ to do it and both had made it clear that refusing wasn't an option.

He knew it was an opportunity for both institutions and for him, but he hated these events. The perfectionist in him always spent more time preparing for them than he could afford to spend away from his research. Although nobody else knew, his apparent confidence at the podium masked the nerves that wracked him whenever he spoke to a large audience of strange faces. He was dreading this one especially.

As the biggest gathering of global genetics experts and interested parties to date, expectations of him would be high.

He'd almost finished preparing his talk, an overview of the latest thinking on gene editing. He knew some of his views would be controversial and that he couldn't give much away about his personal research. He needed to be more certain about its latest direction and progress before he broadcast it, and he had to be especially sensitive to ABZ's concerns about confidentiality. All the Pharmaceuticals were known for their corporate paranoia about secrecy. Not surprising given their massive investments in research and development. Teams like his wouldn't exist without their sponsorship.

An hour later, after one final detailed review, he felt confident his pitch would appeal to the mix of academics, corporate representatives and scientific journalists he'd be presenting to. It lacked a few attachments, but he'd delegate those to Susie. She'd been delighted when he invited her to attend along with the rest of his team. He just had time to call her and discuss exactly what he needed before heading to his office for the tutorial he was dreading.

She sounded out of breath when she answered.

'Hi Professor. Been for my morning run and I struggled a bit. I blame your daughter. We've had a couple of late ones recently. She's tough to keep up with.'

Clayton smiled, more delighted than most parents would be that his daughter could work hard and party hard. It was reassuringly normal. Maybe she could beat the Huntington's odds.

'I hope she isn't leading a key member of my team astray. And I'm afraid I have another job for you.'

'No problem. Is it your presentation?'

'Yep. I need some decent graphics for a couple of new sections. Your forté. Would you take a crack at them and have something for me to see tomorrow morning?'

'Sure. Email me the content and I'll come up with something. You know I love doing stuff like that. It'll be cool when my dad sees some of my work up on screen.'

'Your father's coming to the conference?'

'Yes. Didn't I tell you?'

'No. I thought his field was Cardiology?'

'It is, but he's also an adviser to Galen Pharmaceuticals

and they've invited him to be a delegate at the conference.' She grinned. 'He jumped at the chance knowing my boss is one of the key speakers.'

'Then I hope I don't disappoint him. Thanks for agreeing to do this Susie. Message or email me if you've got any questions OK? I'll see you in the morning.'

As he rang off Clayton thought back to the article he'd read earlier. Galen were one of the firms cited for offering questionable perks and incentives to health officials.

He wondered why he hadn't picked up on Susie's father's connection with them before.

CHAPTER TWENTY-TWO

Catherine left George with every intention of heading back to her hotel but changed her mind halfway down the steps of the Tube station. Since she'd been back in London, she'd hardly seen any of it. She decided to take the pressure off herself for a few hours and get her head straight. Walking would do her good, so she'd take some time out to play tourist, rediscover places she hadn't seen for too long and maybe discover some new ones. London had changed a lot in the years she'd been away. Parts of it were unrecognisable to her and a change of scene might help her to process the morning's events and plan her next move.

First, she needed a change of outfit. She turned back to the King's Cross concourse and its array of shops. Half an hour later she was dressed for action, top to toe in black Nike apart from the gold trainers she'd been unable to resist. Not too financially responsible given her newly unemployed status, but as she'd better learn to enjoy walking everywhere, she told herself they were an investment as much as a fashion statement. She couldn't keep topping up the Travelcard and tapping the Uber app.

As she walked to the underground, she decided she'd head for the river. She loved the Thames and its iconic bridges which had always played such a major part in this city's life. She emerged at Monument station, adjusted to the unusually sunny day, then walked onto London Bridge. She stopped halfway across to take in the view in both directions. Standing here, on the river's oldest crossing point, her spirits lifted. This stretch of water had always been the lifeblood of London and she felt it telling her that this was once again her home.

Her walking tour took her to Tower Bridge and back. She decided she would build a weekly river walk into her schedule. The Thames's natural energy had always inspired her, and she promised herself she would come back here to write someday.

Her only stop was in Southwark Cathedral, where she made another promise, this time to Adam, that she'd keep going until she finished what he'd started. When she emerged from the Cathedral, the riverside restaurants and cafés were beginning to fill up with a cosmopolitan mix of tourists and City workers anxious to make the most of a rare sunny lunchtime.

She found herself a quiet table in a small pizzeria. She needed to call Lizzie and arrange to see her. She was surprised her friend hadn't contacted her. By now she'd probably seen today's headline and be wondering what the hell was going on. Catherine wasn't looking forward to the conversation, which she knew she'd been putting off all morning. She decided she'd eat first, then make the call.

It was late afternoon when she arrived at Lizzie's. Dusk hung in the air waiting to descend, the temperature had plummeted, and a light drizzle had started to fall, its drops illuminated like glitter by the street lamps. Lights began to appear in house windows and curtains were being drawn in anticipation of a cold night.

She'd called Lizzie from the pizzeria to check she'd be home and gauge her reaction to the leaked article, and hoped she'd imagined the flat hollowness of her friend's voice.

Lizzie opened the door within seconds of her ringing the bell. 'Catherine, you must be freezing. Kettle's on. Come and warm up by the fire.'

It was typical Lizzie. Despite what she was going through it was instinctive for her to care, and to put others first. Catherine put her arms round her, hating how frail her normally toned and worked out body had become in a matter of weeks.

Lizzie returned the hug, then took a step back. 'Please don't trot out the same crap as everybody else. I should eat more. I need to look after myself. It makes me want to scream when I hear it. Come through for some tea.'

Catherine followed her down the ornate hallway. 'I could use some of that. And you'll eat more when you feel like it, I understand that. But I'll be keeping an eye on you, that's what best friends do. Right now, though, I'm happy to plonk down on a squidgy sofa and watch you make the tea. It'll be a relief to take these trainers off for a while to be honest. They're new and I seem to have walked for miles in them today.'

'I noticed them, very cool. Clara will love them. Since when were you into running shoes and all things Nike?'

'Since I decided my finances won't run to regular public transport much longer. Not after this morning anyway.' She paused before looking directly at her friend. 'Lizzie let's get to the point of why I called you and stop skirting around it.

We need to talk about the article. I'm so sorry, I feel I've let you down. Let me explain.'

Lizzie left the kettle to boil, came to join her friend by the fire and took her hand.

'Stop it. You haven't let anybody down. The story leaked, but at least it's out there flagging some of what Adam was concerned about. I'm only sorry it didn't go out under your name. What happened?'

'A screw up. Not the most illustrious start to my journalistic return, but that doesn't matter. I'm more concerned about how you are. I thought you'd be upset.'

Lizzie twirled her wedding ring on her finger as she spoke. 'After losing Adam I don't think anything else can ever upset me again. Not now I know what true desolation feels like. Whatever else life throws at me I'll deal with.'

Before Catherine could comment Lizzie got up and busied herself preparing the tea.

'Lizzie....' Her friend held her hands up.

'I'm fine Catherine. Let's have tea and talk about some nice stuff before we get back to the article and the investigation, please. Leave all the awfulness for a bit. I want to hear about how Will's doing and about your plans.'

Catherine knew Lizzie well enough not to argue. It would take time for the light to return to her friend's eyes but her innate strength and intelligence would get her through this, and she had to do it her way. She didn't even realise she was smiling until Lizzie threw her a questioning look.

'What are you smiling at?'

'The force to be reckoned with that is Mrs Lizzie Wentworth. I can't help but be worried about you and I know how difficult this is going to be for a long time yet. But I also know how strong you are.'

'I'm trying to be. I still keep having these moments when I've almost folded and given in. Times when I want to curl up and die. But then I see his face and I feel he's right here alongside me, and I know he'll help me get through this.'

'You had an incredible relationship. I know it's been cut horribly short, but my God Lizzie, what a thing to have had.'

'I could never find anybody else like him as long as I live. I wouldn't ever want to try I don't think. But you need to find someone Catherine. For some reason I've been thinking a lot about that since Adam died. It's your turn and you deserve it. I'm desperate to know what happened to Adam, but this investigation can't dominate your life for ever. That wouldn't be fair, and he wouldn't want that. Maybe we have to set a time limit on this, then live with the outcome. Allow you to get on with your life. There has to be a perfect man for you out there.'

'Maybe, although this is hardly the time to go looking for him, so that's a conversation for another day. I want to tell you about Will, then we're getting back to the investigation. No time limits, I'm seeing this through to the end. And now it's your turn not to argue.'

Fortified and warmed through with hot tea and two slices of chocolate cake from the local upmarket bakery, she brought Lizzie up to date with Will's start at Cambridge. There had been no opportunity to talk about it when she'd been here for the funeral and now Lizzie wanted to know every detail. She'd always regarded herself as his adopted aunt and she loved him deeply.

When Catherine had finished, she saw Lizzie smiling with pride. Some more light had returned to her eyes. 'Sounds like he's loving it and taking it all in his stride. Medicine's a tough course and Cambridge is about as tough as it gets. You must be so proud of him. I am, and Adam always was too. He would have loved hearing all this.'

'I know, and I kept thinking of the three of us when I was settling Will in. Remember Freshers' week at Oxford? I felt so out of my depth until you two showed up.'

'I think we all got each other through those early days. They were such happy ones, but we needed each other. Will's different, he has a whole level of confidence that we didn't. You've given him that and he's going to make a huge success of his life.'

'I hope so. And talking of successes how's Clara? She coped wonderfully at the funeral, but this must be so difficult for her.'

'It is, and I've been particularly worried about her this past week to be honest. She seems to be going through the angry phase of grief now. She's angry with everything I think.'

'I guess that's normal and she was so close to her dad. She worshipped him.'

'Now she's angry with him for leaving her, and angry with me for some reason. Hopefully you'll see her before you leave. She went back to Durham after the funeral but she's home again for a few days. I think she found it difficult to settle back there.'

'She'll sort herself out Lizzie, but it'll take time. Talking of which, I should think about leaving soon. But before I do, we need to talk about my plans after this morning's surprise.'

'So how do you think the story got leaked?'

'I don't know. I have a theory which might sound a bit crazy, but for now I want you to know that I'm determined to keep investigating. Not through the paper, under my own steam. Unofficially I can still access some of their resources, but officially I'm off the story, and unemployed, which probably helps me to fly under the radar a bit. I'm still convinced there's something way bigger going on here than anybody thinks, and I'm determined to find out. And if it somehow cost Adam his life, I...'

She was interrupted by a voice, 'If it isn't the ace reporter. Why don't you let it drop for Christ's sake?'

Neither of them had heard the door open: Clara was leaning against the doorway. Catherine barely recognised the normally pretty girl's twisted smile and she involuntarily flinched from eyes that flashed with anger. Clara walked towards her, swaying as if she was drunk, and her body language screamed aggression as Catherine stood up.

'Clara. I know you're upset. I realise how tough this is for you.' She stepped closer to give her a hug, but the younger woman held her hands up in a gesture of defiance and backed away.

'You don't know anything, and I wish you'd stop encouraging my mother with this stupid suspicious crap. I heard her talking to you on the phone, so I know what you're doing. Leave it alone. Dad's gone, and you going off on some investigative ego trip and playing Miss Marple in Nikes isn't going to bring him back.'

'Clara please.' Lizzie spoke softly. 'Catherine's only trying to help. I'm the one who asked her to look into this.'

'Yes, and the whole thing's ridiculous. She should've told you to drop it, not encourage you with this stupid idea. He had a heart attack. Deal with it and move on. I'm going to my room for a lie down. I'm going out again tonight so don't cook for me.'

As she turned away towards the stairs Catherine looked round and caught the hurt look on Lizzie's face. She needed to say something to diffuse the awkwardness she knew her friend felt about her daughter's outburst.

'She didn't mean to be cruel Lizzie. She's not herself at the moment.'

'The fact she's drunk doesn't help. I've no idea when that started or who she's mixing with these days. And she refuses to tell me who she's going out with tonight, but I've got a feeling it's a new man. That worries me because she's so vulnerable at the moment but what can I do?'

'You keep an eye on her, but you let her work it out in her own way.'

'She shouldn't have been so sharp with you though. She's being unfair and I'm sorry.'

'Forget it. Please. It's grief talking, not the Clara we know. But I think it might be a good idea to downplay our suspicions, let her think we've dropped them.'

She felt strangely relieved when Lizzie nodded her agreement. For some reason she also felt the less Clara knew the better.

CHAPTER TWENTY-THREE

Catherine leaned back in her seat in the taxi Lizzie had insisted on ordering. She'd been about to refuse the offer, but a combination of the exhaustion that had crept up on her and the sound of the wind howling had persuaded her to give in gracefully. Walking up Lizzie's path, hugging herself into her jacket, convinced her she'd been right to accept, and she sank into the cab's warmth with a grateful final wave to her friend.

She closed her eyes and reflected on her day. She'd lost her exclusive, become unemployed, blown a fortune on impractical trainers, and had an unpleasant encounter with her best friend's daughter.

At least her private time with Lizzie had reassured her that her friend was slowly coming to terms with things, but the exchange with Clara, and the younger woman's aggressive demeanour, had left her feeling uneasy. Adam's death had been devastating for his daughter, but, worse still, it had produced a Clara that Catherine didn't recognise. She wondered if Lizzie was right, and it was the influence of a new man, in which case the sooner she worked him out of her system the better.

As the cab turned into the bright lights of the Broadway her spirits lifted briefly at the sight of a few early Christmas displays and festive menu offerings in the shop and restaurant windows. London would soon be gearing up for the festivities. She'd always been a huge fan of Christmas, especially since Will had come along, and she loved making it magical for him. She couldn't imagine how she'd focus on it this year, but she'd better talk to him about how he wanted to spend it.

As if he'd read her mind the taxi driver turned to her as they stopped at a red light.

'You starting to think about Christmas, love? Starts earlier every year. Gets more bloody expensive too. Always have to rein the wife in a bit. Spends a fortune if I don't. I blame all this online shopping malarkey.'

Catherine smiled at the reassuring normality of his question after her strangely disconnected day. 'It seems to be coming around quicker than usual this year. I haven't done anything yet. Suppose I need to start thinking about it.'

'My missus is already on to it. Started her Christmas present drawer. Then the tree goes up first of December, like clockwork. Bloody lights normally blow on Christmas Eve she has 'em on so much.'

'In a minute you'll be telling me she puts the sprouts on then too.'

'Pretty much, but there's still always a panic on the day. Big family we've got, and they all come to us.'

The lights changed before she replied. The driver cursed and sounded his horn at a couple who ran across as red and amber turned to green. Through the windscreen she saw Clara's startled eyes looking straight into hers, until her companion took her hand and pulled her to the pavement. Catherine couldn't see much of the man. He was tall, his face obscured by a baseball cap pulled low. She turned as the cab pulled away from the lights, but they'd disappeared into the night.

The driver cursed again. 'Bloody pedestrians. Always rushing about this time of year. Heads up their arses most of 'em. Sorry about the language love. But who'd be a cabbie at Christmas?'

It was more a statement than a question, and Catherine smiled her agreement, her mind still on Clara. She'd sensed discomfort and anger in that startled look. The girl clearly wished Catherine hadn't seen her.

Her thoughts were interrupted by her mobile ringing. Lizzie's name flashed up.

'Hi. Everything OK?'

'Yes. I'm pleased we got a chance to talk. I wish Clara hadn't been so horrible to you though. Please forgive her. Adam's death has hit her so badly.'

The startled guilty look on Clara's face minutes earlier flashed back into Catherine's mind but she decided to say nothing to Lizzie. Her friend didn't need anything else to deal with at the moment.

'I know, and she'll come through this in time. We're all still coming to terms with it. And she's so young. It's rough on her.'

'Thank you for being so understanding. How's the cab ride? Bet you're pleased I suggested it now. What a night, I'm glad I'm inside.'

'I know, it's awful. And thanks for treating me to the taxi. Should be back at the hotel in about twenty minutes. Bath and an early night I think.' She crossed her fingers as she spoke. The hotel's heating and hot water systems were sporadic at best and she guessed they'd struggle to cope with the sudden dip in temperature.

'The other reason I'm calling is to tell you something. It may not be significant, but I thought you should know. I decided to check a second private email address Adam had. Only Clara and I knew about it. He used it for our private family stuff and anything he didn't want the office to see. He knew security monitored his other email accounts.'

'Of course.' Catherine wondered how Adam had kept track of so many email addresses. Another consequence of managing a public and private persona. 'So, what did you find?'

'Information on a major genetics conference next week, here in London. It seems he'd planned on going, although not in his official capacity. I'm not sure what that all means. I know he had an interest in this, but I'm surprised he could afford the time.'

Catherine caught her breath. Genetics, again, for the second time in two days. Had she been sitting on a clue from Adam ever since their last conversation? Why hadn't she paid more attention to it until George brought it up yesterday?

'Catherine, you still there?'

'Yes, sorry, genetics struck a chord. Adam suggested it was an area I should look into when I last stayed with you both. I never got round to it, but I will now. I need to explore anything that could be a link to what happened. It's a hot topic at the moment, and I guess the scientist in Adam would take a particular interest, but, like you, I'm surprised at him taking time out to go himself. Why wouldn't he send someone else? Or wait for the conference report to come out and read that?'

'I know. It seems odd to me too, which is why I thought I should tell you about it. I'm still logged into his account. I can forward the details to you. There's a whole schedule attached, and a link to a website.'

'Yes, I'd like to see it, but don't email the whole thing.

Send me the link on another mobile number I'll give you, a more secure phone. God, I'm sounding paranoid.'

'After what's happened, how can we not be paranoid? We're a long way from those innocent heady days at Oxford. What the hell's happened to us, Catherine? How did we get to this? Maybe Clara's right and we are being ridiculous.'

The startled girl she'd just seen flashed back into Catherine's mind. 'And maybe she's wrong, and we aren't. Send me the conference link and I'll check it out. It sounds like something I should try and get to myself. I'll call you from the other number as soon as I'm out of the cab. No need to reply, just add it to your contacts.'

'OK, I'll wait to hear from you. Keep warm.'

'I'll try. Back at the hotel. Speak to you soon.'

As she rummaged through her purse for some change to tip the driver, he stopped her.

'Not necessary love. Save your money. Pleasure to drive you.'

She noticed his quick glance up at her hotel as he spoke. Yet another letter in the illuminated sign had gone out since last night, which added to its shabbiness. He obviously assumed its residents couldn't afford tips.

She smiled as she handed him some coins. 'This place isn't as bad as it looks, really. Please, take this. Put it towards all that online Christmas shopping and have a very Merry Christmas. With lights I hope.'

He laughed. 'You too treacle. Happy Christmas. Be good.'

She gave him a wave as she climbed out and ran towards the hotel door, embarrassed the tip hadn't been more, and hoping he hadn't noticed the gold trainers.

Thirty minutes later she huddled up in bed wearing two sweaters. The bedroom radiator's dial refused to move from its lowest setting, the bathroom towel rail had given up completely, and she'd abandoned the idea of a bath.

A second mug of hot tea warmed her up and as she sipped it and crunched her way through that day's complimentary pack of biscuits, she clicked on the link to the

conference details Lizzie had sent. Only days away, with a theme of *Towards the Next Breakthrough*, it was being billed as a major global event in the field of genetic research and development. A quick glance at the range of speakers told her it had attracted the top academics and researchers from the world's premier universities and would cover some cutting-edge developments.

Genetics wasn't a subject she knew much about. Like most people her understanding went no further than a superficial awareness of DNA's importance, and how it determined eye colour. Beyond that, what these experts were proposing to discuss sounded futuristic and slightly scary to her. Progress mattered, but at what cost? Did the world really want to put cloning and genetic engineering in the hands of a select few? But she would go along to this and learn more about it instead of pre-judging. It had clearly been important to Adam and she wanted to know if there'd been more to his interest than scientific curiosity.

She scrolled quickly through the schedule of speakers and topics to the list of sponsors which read like a *Who's Who?* of pharmaceutical companies and academic institutions. The three names at the top of the list were in bold type, signalling them as the primary sponsors. She recognised them straightaway as the same three pharmaceutical giants that had dominated Adam's spreadsheets.

She'd call George in the morning to figure out how they could both attend but now she needed sleep. A wave of tiredness had hit her, and she started to scroll back through to the conference home screen via two pages of speaker profiles. She paused as one thumbnail photo caught her eye. She moved her cursor, clicked on the image and did a double take.

She'd seen that face before. She opened the messenger app on her phone and checked her recent message thread with Nina. Then she looked back at the photo on the conference page. It was a more professional shot, but her recall was correct.

She was staring straight into the eyes of Max.

CHAPTER TWENTY-FOUR

The name was different, but it was definitely his face. What the hell was this guy playing at?

She read the brief biographical summary beneath the photo. Clayton Mortimer, fifty-four. Brought up in Australia, with a first degree in Biology from Sydney University, he'd moved to London to study for his PhD in Immunology and stayed. He'd been a latecomer to the genetics field ten years ago, but had since had a meteoric rise to fame, becoming London University's Senior Professor of Genetics and a world-renowned authority on genetic diseases.

Presumably the name change made it easier to assume an alter ego and have his Tinder fun, but it seemed high risk for someone in such a prestigious position. Maybe he got a kick out of living dangerously, or maybe he adopted the Max persona when he needed a break from work pressures. There were lots of maybes, but she was too exhausted to think about them. She took one last look at the two photos. Clearly, the same man, and yet something was subtly different between the two shots. Her eyes refused to stay open to figure out what, and she fell asleep before she could turn the laptop off.

She was in a strange windowless room. The overhead fluorescent lights almost burned her eyes when she looked at them. Banks of computers lined one wall. As she stumbled around, trying to find a way out, she kept colliding with men in white coats, but they walked straight through her as if she was invisible. She called out to them, but they didn't respond. Why couldn't they see or hear her? This place and these people made her uneasy. She needed to escape. She didn't feel safe. Then one of the men turned in her direction and she saw his face. He looked familiar but she didn't know why. Another man turned to talk to him. He had the same face. Her eyes darted around the room. Suddenly she could see all of them and they all had the same face. She looked for the door again but couldn't see it. She started to back into the corner. The white coats with identical faces were all walking towards her now. She was trapped. Her legs gave way beneath her....

Catherine woke up startled by the sound of her phone ringing. Groggy and disoriented, she couldn't remember where she'd put it. She looked in the direction of the sound, but it had stopped. Her head ached, her mouth felt like parchment, and the two sweaters she'd fallen asleep in were heavy and uncomfortable. She knew she'd been dreaming, and she couldn't remember what about, but it had left her feeling disturbed. She needed some tea to wake her up and wash the uneasiness away. She sat up and saw her laptop about to hit the floor. She must have kicked it to the edge of the bed during the night, and as she rescued it, she remembered the face in her dream. Clayton AKA Max.

The missed call was from George. Revived by the tea she hit his number. She needed him to get them into this conference. She wanted to do what Adam couldn't, but now she had to admit she was going to check Clayton Mortimer out too.

George answered instantly. 'How's it going? I left you alone yesterday, but I wanted to check you're OK.'

'As in, how's life as a member of the unemployed, I suppose? Actually, I'm pleased you've checked in on me. I had a full day yesterday and I've got a few things to tell you. How's life in the fast lane?'

'Very funny. I met with Sam again briefly yesterday afternoon. Can't say his mood had improved.'

'I guess he's smarting about our story being hijacked, but I think his bark's worse than his bite. He made a very fair offer to me.'

'I know. And I get that he's pissed about the article, but you're the one with the personal connection which makes it all much worse for you. You've got a lot of yourself invested in this.'

'Which is why I have to keep going with it however many dead ends I hit. I saw Lizzie yesterday by the way.'

'How's she doing?'

'Amazingly well under the circumstances, but worried about what she's got me into. Her daughter's giving her a hard time, wants us to drop it and move on, but then she's struggling to cope herself I think, which is another worry for Lizzie. Anyway, let's not talk more now, let's meet. I've got a lead we should follow up.'

'Me too. Usual place in thirty?'

'Give me an hour. We unemployed older people take more time to get ourselves in gear.'

'A likely story, but you got it. Laters.'

George ordered cappuccinos and croissants while Catherine opened the conference website on her laptop.

He smiled. 'So, what's the news? Where are Mulder and Scully heading next?'

'To this, if you can make it happen. We're a bit last-minute so we'll have more chance if you organise it through the paper.' She turned the screen in his direction, and he nodded.

'It's already done. That's the other reason I called you. To tell you about this.'

'You're kidding me.'

'Nope. The Science Editor planned to go but he's been called away on family issues. Sam asked me to step in and cover it, and as soon as I saw the subject matter, I jumped at it. After yesterday's conversation we have to be there. And it looks like quite an event. I touched on genetics at uni, but only scratched the surface. I'd love to know more about it.'

'Of course, your Biochemistry degree. Do you ever regret not taking that further?'

'Hell no, I'd had enough after three years. Science runs in our family, so I kind of automatically fell into it, but I was never cut out to be one of those clever lab researcher types. Should have done journalism in the first place. I find the whole genetics thing fascinating though, even if some of it is quite scary stuff.'

'I don't know much about the science behind genetics, but I'm interested to learn. Plus, we'll get to see all our pharmaceutical friends in the same room. Assuming I can come with you?'

'Natch. Got us both on the list. So how did you hear about it?'

'Lizzie stumbled across it on Adam's private email. Apparently he'd been planning to go, unofficially it seems. It may have nothing to do with what's happened, but genetics keeps coming up, one way or another.'

'And neither of us believes in coincidences, do we?'

'Not in this case, no. Did you see the list of sponsors?'

'I certainly did. The top three are the same names that keep coming up in Adam's paperwork. I'll try and find out which of the research teams they're each sponsoring and make sure we catch those presentations.'

'Good idea. Would you also see what you can find out about this guy Clayton Mortimer? He's a presenter.'

George clicked on his profile. 'What's the particular interest in him?'

Catherine felt herself blushing at his question and hoped he hadn't noticed.

'I've got a feeling about him. Call it woman's intuition.'

He raised his eyebrows. 'Woman's intuition? Wouldn't have anything to do with him being tall, dark and handsome would it?'

She had a horrible feeling she was blushing again. 'Stop it. I agree he's an attractive man, but I assure you that has nothing whatever to do with my interest in him. He seems to be researching some cutting-edge stuff I'd like to hear about.'

George raised his hands in mock horror. 'Methinks the lady doth protest too much. It would hardly be a crime if you did fancy him a bit. It is the way the world works you know. Maybe you'll get two bangs for your buck at this thing.'

'Thank you, Mr Matchmaker. You could've put that a bit better. Now can we focus on business please?'

'If you insist. I'll be watching you checking him out though, you can bank on that. The blushing tells me everything.'

Catherine decided not to protest any further. Her mind was elsewhere. This conference couldn't come around quickly enough, for more reasons than she cared to admit.

CHAPTER TWENTY-FIVE

'Let me introduce you to each other. Prof this is my father, Dr Richard Cameron. Dad, meet my mentor and boss, Dr Clayton Mortimer.'

Clayton turned to shake hands with the tall smart-suited man next to Susie and smiled. He'd lost count of how much smiling and handshaking he'd done in the last hour as he'd dutifully worked the room. He hated the forced smiling and the glad-handing at these events. His stomach was performing its usual somersaults ahead of his presentation, still an hour from starting. Another hour for his nerves to become even more frayed. Why the hell did he agree to do these things? Now Susie's father had said something to him, and he'd missed most of it. The guy had probably already labelled him the stereotypical absent-minded professor.

'I'm sorry Richard, I was miles away for a moment. Slightly preoccupied with my pitch.' He turned and smiled at Susie as he spoke. 'I have to say your daughter's been a great help with it. She's been a superb addition to my team. You must be proud of her.'

The other man's face was expressionless as he said, 'I've always been disappointed she didn't follow me into the medical profession, but then Susie's always been determined to do things her way.'

It wasn't the fatherly reaction Clayton had expected and he avoided eye contact with Susie who he sensed would be disappointed at her father's lack of enthusiasm for her work. He tried to keep his own tone light. 'I have one of those determined daughters myself. Mine's more into Shakespeare than science though, so she's definitely not following in Dad's footsteps. Determination is a good quality though and your daughter's makes her perfect for research. She never wants to give up. I have to virtually throw her out of the lab sometimes.'

He threw a Susie a friendly glance. She was smiling, but it seemed forced, and her eyes appeared duller than usual. He wondered if she was used to put-downs from her father, who said,

'So, Professor Mortimer, are you unveiling the next big thing today? The rumour mill has it your research is heading into some interesting territory. You'd better be careful of the pro-lifers if you're thinking of rattling their cages. I've spotted a few of them here. God knows how they muscle in on these things.'

Clayton felt himself bristling at this man's tone, but he told himself not to rise to the bait for Susie's sake. 'They're entitled to their views Richard. I understand their concerns and I have a degree of sympathy with them actually. Genetics goes right to the core of what makes us unique human beings and I realise a lot of people are wary of us interfering.' He hoped he hadn't said too much. Something about Richard Cameron irritated and bothered him. He was arrogant and supercilious, totally the opposite of his daughter, but it was more than that. He seemed to know more than Clayton felt comfortable with about the latest direction of his work. Or was the man hazarding guesses and fishing?

He was relieved when Richard's attention was caught by a powerful-looking man who tapped him on the shoulder. Clayton recognised him as one of the primary conference sponsors. Susie's father clearly knew him well and, with a curt goodbye to her and Clayton, went to join him and his corporate entourage. It occurred to Clayton he hadn't taken time to introduce his daughter to any of them.

As he watched Richard walk away it also occurred to him that their paths had crossed before. He couldn't recall where, but he had a strong suspicion he hadn't liked the man then either.

He turned to Susie to ask if she was OK, but her eyes were focused on the other side of the room. He followed their direction and smiled. She was checking out a young man who had walked in. Then he noticed the woman he'd walked in with. Tall, blonde and pretty, her face was animated with laughter as she talked to her young male companion. Clayton couldn't take his eyes off her. He felt drawn to her like metal to a magnet and as he stared at her the nervous knot in his stomach that had been there all morning was replaced by an entirely different sensation.

Then she looked round, her eyes met his, and his mind went blank. He heard Susie telling him it was time to set up for his presentation and he realised he no longer had any idea what his opening line was.

Catherine couldn't resist teasing George as they walked into the crowded room. 'So now who should be blushing? I saw you checking out the brunette across the room.'

'Touché, you got me. She looks a bit like an unmade bed but she's kind of cute too.'

Catherine laughed. 'If she's smart enough to be here she'd probably kill you for both those descriptions.'

'Maybe, but what a way to go. I have to find a way of talking to her before the day's out.'

She gave him a mock frown. 'Can we focus on the matter in hand first please?'

'Sure thing, although my motives aren't entirely dishonourable. You might want to focus on who she's with.'

Catherine followed his gaze back towards the brunette. And then she saw him. Clayton Mortimer. And staring straight at her. She tried to look away but couldn't unlock her gaze. She heard George talking to her, but nothing that he said registered.

'Catherine.' She finally turned towards George and blushed at his grin. 'So much for your protestations lady. You fancy him.'

His words brought her back to reality. What was she thinking? She was here for Adam, not Clayton Mortimer. But she couldn't deny she'd felt inexplicably drawn to him at first sight. Then she remembered his Max alter ego and told herself she shouldn't go there. Not that he'd given her any hint that he recognised her from her photo, and she didn't want to admit how much that disappointed her.

Strangely though, when she'd stared back at him, she hadn't seen the same arrogant confidence she recalled from his Tinder profile. Obviously, he'd perfected the knack of separating his online and real-life personas.

She turned to George, trying to project an indifference she didn't feel. 'He's good looking I grant you, but I'm more interested in what he has to say. Let's grab some coffee and circulate before the presentations start.'

'If you can drink it with those butterflies in your stomach.'

She pulled a face at him as they walked towards the refreshment bar, but he was right. Her insides were churning in reaction to those few short seconds when she'd met Clayton Mortimer's gaze. But it didn't feel like butterflies, it felt like the whole zoo.

CHAPTER TWENTY-SIX

Clayton took a deep breath and scanned the sea of faces in front of him as he walked to the podium. He couldn't see her, but he sensed her, and the thought of her watching and judging him excited and unnerved him in equal measure.

He spotted Richard in the corporate VIP seats, still wearing his arrogant self-important smile and turning to say something which made his power-suited friend laugh. Clayton was determined to remember where he'd seen that smug face before. It would come back to him, things always did.

Catherine sat transfixed, oblivious to George and everybody else as she watched Clayton glance round the room, telling herself to dismiss the thought that perhaps he was looking for her. Her eyes followed the direction of his until he stopped and stared at a tall distinguished man who she recognised from the programme as one of the major sponsors. But it was the man next to him who was occupying Clayton's attention, and now hers too. As she took a closer look his face was familiar to her, but she had no idea why.

She looked back at Clayton as he clicked the device which brought his first graphic up on screen. She sensed his nerves and wished she could take his hand and reassure him. Where had that thought come from? She didn't even know him, but again she felt a magnetic pull between them.

She sensed he was uncomfortable with presenting, but once the words flowed his initial shakiness disappeared and he was a man in complete command of his subject. His brief as opening speaker was to give an overview of the latest thinking in relation to gene therapy, gene silencing and gene editing, presumably for the benefit of the non-scientists like her. He had an easy style and the ability to demystify the complexity of the science.

Catherine was fascinated. She'd had no idea until now of the progress he and others were making to find treatments and cures for the devastating consequences of genetic diseases. When he moved on to his personal mission - to eventually find a way of editing out genetic mutations in order to eradicate genetic diseases entirely, not merely treat them or slow their progress - his passion and drive were infectious. He acknowledged that viable and safely deliverable gene editing might be years away, but this was clearly his life's work. She got the impression it was also personal, and she wondered why.

As if reading her mind, he turned away from the graphic he'd been explaining, and his eyes met hers. Instinctively she found herself nodding her reassurance to him. He paused to give her the faintest of grateful smiles and held her gaze briefly before clicking on his next visual.

She looked around the room. Everyone was focused on what he was saying, and she noticed how the women especially were watching him. She clearly wasn't the only one who found him an imposing and attractive man. But she wondered who had smiled at her. Was it Clayton the scientist, or Max the online player?

She bit her lip and wished she'd seen the Clayton version first.

Clayton felt himself relax after a few minutes into his pitch. The audience appeared to be with him, at least so far, although he knew how some of the journalists would react when he moved on to the issue of gene editing. The ones who wanted to sensationalise the work he and his colleagues were doing by reducing it to scare stories about genetic engineering, designer babies for the rich and the exaggerated spectre of human mutations. He got that it all made for good copy, but it angered and frustrated him. More importantly, it belittled his work.

At least the pro-lifers demonstrating outside were genuine in their opinions, even though he disagreed with them and wished he could change their minds. The irony of their position constantly baffled him. Why would they not understand that he was as pro-life as they were, but pro-quality life.

He paused as he finished his section on gene silencing, his nerves returning as he clicked on his first gene editing graphic. He intended to keep his words general today. Part of him wanted to scream out his recent progress, but it was out of the question and way too early to hint at a potential breakthrough. He couldn't even be sure he had one, and if he did the ramifications were enormous. It would open a Pandora's box of consequences he could barely imagine. The future would become a very different place.

He looked around the audience, wondering where the journalists were sitting, but his attention was drawn towards the centre of the room. There she was, staring right at him with those intelligent eyes. What was it about this woman?

He had no idea who she was, yet he felt he knew her. She nodded and smiled at him, as if sensing he needed approval. He hoped she noticed the faint smile of thanks he tried to communicate back to her before she glanced away.

'You're smitten. I think he is too. I saw those smiles earlier.' Catherine turned to see George grinning at her.

'I am no such thing, and I'm sure he's got far more important things to think about. I found his talk fascinating and he's an impressive guy. End of. Stop trying to play Cupid.'

'I don't believe you for one second.' He was still grinning as they got up from their seats.

Clayton had ended his presentation to a burst of applause. As she watched him walk off the stage to be high-fived by his smiling assistant, she decided she had to meet him. George was looking in the same direction, clearly captivated by the professor's young colleague.

'You can talk. Would you stop staring at her for a moment please and focus on the reason we came here?'

He held his hands up. 'Guilty, but I can't help the fact she's cute. And her boss is exactly your type I'd have thought. Tall, good looking, mega smart, clearly at the top of his game from what we heard. We need to engineer a meeting.'

'Pun intended presumably given his subject matter. And yes, he's mega smart but I'll bet he's mega married too.'

'You're the investigative journalist so it won't take you long to find out. Anyway, now we've seen him in action what's happened to that gut feeling you had about him? Changed your mind?'

'No, I haven't. Adam had a reason for wanting to attend this. I've no idea why, but I think this guy is somehow connected to that.'

'Except that the company sponsoring his research is ABZ. That name didn't even come up on Adam's spreadsheets.'

'I know, they're one of the few who didn't feature at all. Any theories? What do we know about them?'

'They're one of the smaller global pharmaceuticals. Relatively young company, progressive and forward-thinking management team by all accounts. Maybe they haven't felt the need for external advisers. They don't attract a lot of press coverage, but the venture capitalists seem to love them. They launched several of the early gene therapy drugs but nothing new or ground-breaking recently. Maybe your professor's got more up his sleeve than he's letting on and there are big things in the pipeline.'

Catherine looked over at the corporate VIP area and spotted Clayton straight away. Although he had his back to her, his height and slightly unruly wavy hair made him impossible to miss. She turned to George. 'Only one way to find out. We go and introduce ourselves.'

As they walked across the room Catherine noticed the two men Clayton was in conversation with. It was an animated exchange and she gestured to George to slow down. 'Who are the two guys he's talking with?'

'The tall guy on the right's Paul Naylor, CEO of Galen Pharmaceuticals.'

'One of the major sponsors here.'

'Yes, they're number one in the business at the moment. Naylor took the helm about three years ago and the share price has rocketed ever since. The general consensus is he has the Midas touch. Galen are rumoured to have some important new launches imminent and the City boys love that.'

'And they were the most prominent name on Adam's spreadsheets. Any idea who the guy with him is?'

George shook his head. 'Sorry, no. Why such an interest in him?'

'Because I'm certain I've seen him before, but I can't think where.'

'Maybe it'll help if you see him close up and hear him talk, and he may recognise you too. Time to gate-crash their conversation.'

'I think that's your job. I'm here unofficially remember.' She glanced at her watch. 'We don't have long till the next session starts and I can see some other press heading in their direction.'

'Don't worry, I'm on it.' He gave her his conspiratorial wink. 'Time to work some George magic on the cute assistant.'

CHAPTER TWENTY-SEVEN

Ten minutes later Catherine found herself face to face with Clayton Mortimer. The George magic had worked, and he was deep in conversation with the cute assistant who'd they'd learned was Susie, an undergraduate member of Clayton's research team. Catherine liked her immediately. Bright and quick- witted, with an effervescent enthusiasm that reminded her of herself at that age, she was clearly as smitten with George as he was with her.

Before Susie could introduce them to Clayton, he was waylaid by a woman Catherine recognised as Science Correspondent for The Economist. Instead she found herself shaking hands with Paul Naylor. A fast-talking Canadian who radiated power and energy and oozed effortless charm, his eyes constantly worked the room, and after thanking her and George for their interest and attendance he made his excuses and left. He would be chairing a group discussion later and Catherine shot George a look. He nodded his agreement. They needed to attend that session.

The man he'd been talking with was about to follow him until Susie grabbed his arm. 'Dad hold on a sec. Meet George

Bishop and Catherine Preston. George is covering the conference for The Guardian. Guys, this is Richard Cameron. He's a cardiologist and a consultant with Galen. And my father, obviously.'

Despite Susie's enthusiasm, her father shrugged her hand away. He barely glanced at them both as he focused instead on a group Paul Naylor had joined, and his tone was dismissive. 'I'm sure we can rely on your publication for an unbiased view of events young man. Now you must excuse me. Susie, call your mother soon please. You know how agitated she gets.'

As he walked away, Catherine was even more convinced she'd seen him before, but she was certain she'd never spoken to him. If she had she doubted she would have liked him any more then than she did now. She was relieved he'd barely glanced at her and showed no sign of recognising her.

'So, Ms Preston. What brings you to a genetics conference?'

She turned at the sound of Clayton's voice and noticed the departing Economist journalist turning back and giving him an admiring glance. Wondering how to reply she was relieved when Susie gave her extra thinking time by effecting introductions.

'Catherine, George, meet my boss, Dr Clayton Mortimer. I've explained you're reporting on the conference, George.'

Clayton smiled his easy smile and shook George's hand. 'I hope you'll give me at least a reasonable review. Off the record, I'm way more at home in a lecture theatre or my laboratory than being centre stage at these things. I hope it wasn't too obvious.'

George grinned. 'Not in the slightest, and it will be a more than reasonable review I can assure you. We were both fascinated weren't we Catherine?'

She heard the teasing in his voice. She still hadn't spoken, let alone responded to Clayton's question about her reason for being here. She held out her hand to shake his and felt a shiver run through her body as skin met skin. She wondered if he felt it too. She noticed he didn't wear a ring and hoped he hadn't seen her glance at his hand to check.

'I'm pleased to meet you Dr Mortimer and I found your presentation absorbing. I had no idea such advances were being made. This is a whole new field for me. I came along to support George, and I'm pleased I did.'

He gave her a questioning look. 'Are you a journalist too? And please, call me Clayton. I can never quite deal with the whole Dr thing.'

'I am, but I'm freelance. I prefer the freedom it gives me.'

'And what areas do you write about? Sorry, I'm firing questions at you. Born researcher, I'm afraid.'

She smiled and almost wished she could tell him the truth about why she was there. He had something about him, something that made her want to open up to him, and it scared her. It wasn't a feeling she was used to.

'I'm between assignments, but your talk has given me some ideas. You don't need me to tell you how huge the issues are around your research. I want to catch some of the other presentations before deciding on an angle for an article. I should go, and I'm sure you need to circulate.'

'I probably should, but please, take my card. I hope you'll call me if you decide to write your article. I'd like to help.' He reached into his pocket then pressed a card into her hand. He tilted his head towards George and Susie. 'I think you may have a challenge dragging your colleague away for the next session though.'

She turned to see George and Susie giggling as they both tapped away at their phone screens. Exchanging numbers, she assumed. Hopefully with that part of his mission accomplished she could prise him away. As if on cue he turned in her direction and she tapped her watch face.

'We should let Clayton and Susie circulate, and I need to make some calls before we head to the next presentation.' She glanced at Clayton and Susie in turn. 'Lovely to meet you both and thank you for taking some time out for us. Maybe we'll bump into each other later.' She rushed her words as she began edging towards the exit, hoping George would follow.

She wanted some air and some time to think Clayton Mortimer out of her head, but before she got to the door she was compelled to turn and look at him again.

Clayton watched her leave, hoping she'd turn around one more time, and as she reached the door she did. She paused as if making a decision then walked back towards him. He felt like a teenager faced with his first crush as she approached. He took a few steps towards her but before he could speak, she put her hand to his ear and whispered to him. 'One more thing Professor. Say hi to Max from me, will you? And don't worry. Your secret's safe with me.' Then she turned away, half ran to the door again without giving him a chance to respond and was gone.

Motionless with shock, he watched her leave. What the hell had that been about and how did she know Max? Dammit, he'd always known the guy was a risk. He'd known it for ten years. A risk he might one day pay a price for taking.

He hoped that price wasn't Catherine Preston.

CHAPTER TWENTY-EIGHT

Clayton had returned from Australia a changed man after his mother's death.

Her dying words and the revelations in her letter had played on a constant loop in his head for days and he couldn't turn the volume down. He knew his life would never be the same again, but he also knew how he had to spend whatever was left of it.

He'd thought the flight home from Sydney would never end. He envied his fellow passengers as, after dinner, and almost in unison, seats were reclined, TV screens folded back, and overhead lights switched off in collective preparation for high-altitude sleep.

He wished he could join them, but he was too preoccupied, and he didn't want to risk waking up and having to deal with the events of the past week again. At least in the confined virtual reality of life at 35,000 feet he could almost convince himself his mother hadn't died, that he'd never read her letter, and that both he and his daughter weren't at high risk of gestating a crippling disease within their DNA.

Becca had been on his mind constantly. When they spoke

on the phone, she captivated him as always, with her infectious enthusiasm about everything and her determination to try and make him feel better.

'Everything will be alright Daddy. It's horrible that Gran's gone but you've still got me. I'm going to look after you now. Tiger's going to help me. He's promised.'

Tiger. The tiny ginger kitten who'd appeared from nowhere in Clayton's garden a month before he was called to his mother's bedside. Becca had fallen in love with him instantly and soon they were inseparable. Clayton smiled at the memory of the two of them snuggled under her Hello Kitty duvet the night they'd found him. The vet had pronounced the four-week-old kitten undersized and in need of food and TLC, but otherwise fit and healthy. He'd laughed with Clayton as Becca had danced with delight hugging the newly christened Tiger. It was clear to both men that Tiger had hit the feline jackpot.

Now Clayton thanked his mother's God that Tiger had chosen their garden to wander into. Becca was showing the emotional resilience and strength that were becoming her trademarks, but he knew how upset she was about losing her grandmother. Her new best friend was a welcome diversion.

As the plane taxied towards the terminal, he switched his phone back on, knowing there'd be a message from her. There it was, from David's number, saying she couldn't wait to see him. His friend had insisted on collecting him from the airport and bringing Becca to welcome him back. As he read her message, he imagined her continually asking David how much longer it would be till her dad walked out of the arrivals door. As a typical eight-year-old his daughter didn't do patience, but then today neither did he. He prayed for a short line at passport control and a minimal wait at baggage reclaim. As the pilot expertly navigated the 747 towards its stand Clayton replied to the text, telling her he couldn't wait to see her and promising to update them on his progress through arrivals.

The long walk from the gate after he disembarked gave him time to readjust to ground level reality. Thoughts of his now uncertain future were replaying in his head again. A week ago he'd expected to be returning as a grieving son, but his grief had been usurped by anger at his biological mother, curiosity about his unknown twin and, above all, by his horror and fear of the devastating condition he might be programmed to inherit.

He'd forced himself to research as much as he could about Huntington's Disease, and it made for grim reading and viewing. He watched footage of sufferers at various stages, with their bewildered expressions and jerky, uncontrolled movements. He stared in horror at their faces and at the fear and incomprehension in their eyes. When all the faces suddenly became Becca's, he couldn't bear to watch more.

Instead he formulated a plan. He was a scientist, trained to research and analyse data. A scientist who took a problem and tested potential solutions until one of them worked. He would never be faced with a bigger problem than this or need to find a solution more than he did now. Before he left Australia, he stood at his mother's graveside and made a vow to her.

'Maybe your God put me in this position for a reason Mum. I wish he hadn't, but now it's happened I have to do something about it. Something to help all those frightened faces, but especially to help Becca. I'll make it my life's work to find a way to beat this disease, I promise you.'

Now, back in London, he had to deliver on that promise. There were people he needed to talk to, genetics courses he needed to take, another PhD he needed to research. It would be tough going and he had no idea when this disease might start to take hold of his body and mind, but he was determined to try.

He'd make a start tomorrow. For today though, only one thing mattered. To be reunited with his beloved daughter and to find the strength to make sure he gave nothing away about any of this. Nobody must know what he knew. Until he learned more about what he was dealing with everything should continue as normal. He took some deep breaths to relax himself as he reached the baggage carousel and sighed with relief that the belt had started to move.

He punched the air when his bag appeared within minutes. He grabbed it and called David's number, knowing his friend would let Becca answer. Her giggles and squeals of delight were still ringing in his ears five minutes later as he emerged from customs into the packed arrivals' hall. Within seconds she ran into his arms. Looking up as he hugged her, he smiled his thanks at David. Then he stepped back from the hug and looked at his beautiful daughter. Nothing had changed. She was still the happy healthy Becca he'd left. Now he had to keep her that way.

As she clutched his hand and the three of them walked towards the exit it felt good to be home, and he knew exactly what he had to do.

He had to find a way to make this alright.

CHAPTER TWENTY-NINE

The next morning, with a protesting Becca safely deposited at school, he could plan his next moves. She'd wanted to spend another day with him and Tiger and simultaneously avoid a maths test. He was tempted to give in and indulge them both, but he knew it would amount to issue denial, and he couldn't afford that.

The previous evening, as wonderful as it was being back with her, had also been fraught. He tried to control it, but every time she was childishly clumsy his heart skipped a beat. He couldn't imagine going through her entire adolescence waiting for the alarm to ring on the ticking clock that might be lurking within her DNA. And if it was, then it lurked within his too. A minute part of their respective complex genetic code which could have such devastating conse-quences. If they were in this, they were in it together. He had to face it and do whatever he could, for himself and for her. He had two days compassionate leave left and he needed to make the most of them.

After the school run, he called his university colleague and friend Malcolm, a genetics expert who had worked on the

Human Genome project. At fifteen years his senior, he had also been a valued mentor and guide since Clayton's appointment as the university's youngest ever professor of microbiology.

Malcolm was the one exception he'd made to his plan to keep the Huntington's problem to himself. He trusted him completely, and he needed his help and expertise. He had called him from Sydney within hours of reading his mother's letter and they agreed to meet as soon as he got back to London.

When he arrived at the café near Russell Square Malcolm was waiting. He stood immediately and clasped both of Clayton's hands.

'I am so sorry my dear friend. I know how much your mother meant to you. Such a wonderful person. I wish I'd met her more often.'

Clayton smiled. As a nervous traveller his mother had been an infrequent visitor to London but had met Malcolm when she came over to celebrate her son's appointment as a professor. He had always sensed she was a little smitten with his colleague, a lifelong confirmed bachelor, but had never remarked on it 'And she liked you. More than she cared to admit I think.'

A blushing Malcolm laughed nervously. 'Now you tell me.'

It occurred to Clayton that the university gossips who dismissed his friend as gay were way off base. He suspected he was shy around women. Perhaps that had appealed to his mother's nurturing instinct. He regretted there hadn't been more opportunities for them to meet.

'Then the least I can do is treat you to breakfast, and I'm definitely in need of a large Americano. Still recovering from the jetlag. God it's a long way.'

'Especially with so much on your mind. I hope now you're back I can help.'

As Malcolm sat down, Clayton glanced at the stack of files on the table, before heading to the counter. There was obviously a lot to learn about the world of genetics and Huntington's specifically. He knew his mentor would come prepared.

When he returned to their table, Malcolm was flicking through the first file and followed Clayton's gaze to the pile in front of him. 'I can tell what you're thinking. Yes, this is a massive subject and with so much of it we're still at the learning stages. I wish I could tell you we weren't.'

Clayton frowned, 'And my knowledge of it is still so general. I need to learn everything about it.'

Malcolm raised his hand. 'One step at a time. As I told you on the phone, we've had a test available for Huntington's since 1993 and we should organise one for you as soon as we can, then at least we know what we're dealing with. A lot of people in your position would choose not to take it, but I know you're not one of them.'

'No, although I can see why denial would be appealing. But I guess that's what being a scientist does for you. We're trained to confront, analyse and solve, aren't we? And that's how I need to approach this. To be as involved as possible.' He could see Malcom was about to say something, but he continued, 'Don't try to talk me out of it or tell me to slow down Malcolm. I can't, and I don't know any other way of dealing with this. I won't let it have power over me, and I certainly won't stand by and watch it take over Becca. Not without a fight.'

'Then let's do the test straightaway. At least you already know the odds.'

Clayton nodded. 'Fifty-fifty that I've got the mutation, festering away. But why no symptoms?'

'Yes, those are the odds. The faulty gene that produces Huntington's is a dominant one, and it only takes one affected parent to pass it on. If you have the mutation, the test will help us figure out why you have no symptoms yet. To put it simply, the age when they start, and the severity of them, is determined by how many repeats of the faulty DNA sequence you develop. In Huntington's disease three of the four nucleotide bases on a particular DNA strand keep repeating. Cytosine, adenine and guanine. Hence the term triple repeats. And we refer to them as letters. CAG. Sorry, I get a bit carried away with the science.'

Clayton smiled as his friend blushed. Malcolm was always intense about his subject, and his shyness was endearing. 'No. I need to understand it. So, basically this is all about three letters in a sequence going rogue?'

'I guess you could put it like that.'

'Which makes it all sound so simple.'

'Ironically, in some ways it is simple. Or at least the cause is. The problem is the consequences of those letters going rogue, and we have no idea how to fix that or stop it happening. But the good news is you may be at a low level of those repeats, so there's a chance you may never develop symptoms. The fact you haven't so far is a good sign.'

'But it doesn't mean I never will, does it?'

'I'm afraid it doesn't. I wish I could give you a different answer Clayton.'

'What about Becca? What are her chances? Don't sugar coat it Malcolm. I need to know what we're dealing with.'

Malcolm paused, his face reddening again, as he looked down at the table and shifted uncomfortably in his seat. Every gesture told Clayton his friend knew he wouldn't like his answer. 'Unfortunately, she's the potential victim of the worst possible combination as a daughter inheriting the faulty gene from her father. Typically, in that situation, the daughter's repeats level is higher. We don't yet know why, but our clinical studies suggest it.'

'Shit. So she could end up with a worse outcome than me? Bottom line Malcolm, please.'

Malcolm looked him in the eye, swallowed, and said, 'It's highly possible. In fact, if you test positive, then it's probable.'

'And if I don't, she's in the clear? She can't inherit it from her biological grandmother?'

'No. Only from you. It can't skip a generation.'

'So, can we rush the test through? How long do the results normally take?'

'Several weeks generally. It depends on lab time. But not in your case. The sooner we know the better.'

'I'm grateful Malcolm. You've always been such a good friend.'

'At the moment I wish I was a friend with more positive things to say.'

'It is what it is. Or whatever it turns out to be. So, tell me about where the latest research is on treatments and cures.'

'In its infancy I'm afraid. The best we can hope for in the short term is to produce better treatments to help the symptoms. A cure for any of the genetic diseases is still a long way off. That involves finding a way of silencing the mutated gene, which is our challenge.'

'And what about eradicating mutations completely? Preventing them from being passed on at all?'

'Now you're talking gene editing which most people see as in the realms of science fiction. The stuff of movies. Most of them would like to keep it that way too. They see designer babies and monsters, which is nonsense. But try telling the man in the street that who thinks we geneticists are all mad Frankenstein types. Blame Hollywood.'

'I hear you. And I have another favour to ask. I want to be a part of this work Malcolm. I need to be involved in the research. Especially if I have this, but even if I don't. The hell of living with the prospect that I might has been enough to make me want to join the fight against it.'

'Clayton I can think of nothing I'd like more than to have you join my research team. And to see you build a team of your own. You know my respect for your intellect and capability. But you're talking about a huge commitment. It would mean taking a temporary step back in status. And if you really want your academic future to be in genetics you have to look at doing another PhD. It's a long haul even for someone of your ability.'

'What's the story with current research funding?'

'A walk in the park for someone with your background and academic reputation. Genetics is hot stuff at the moment. Pharmaceuticals would be falling over themselves to sponsor you.'

'Then let me fix up an appointment to talk to the Dean. I want to do this. Hell, I could hardly be more motivated. Like I said, brushing up against this and knowing how the fear feels makes me want to be part of eradicating it for others.'

Malcolm grinned at him. 'OK, you've convinced me. The Dean will be a pushover.'

'I hope. And one more question. This identical twin my mother's letter mentioned. Presumably his odds are the same as mine?'

'Exactly the same. If you're identical twins, then so is your DNA. If you're positive, he's positive. If he's been living with your birth mother, then he must know the risks. Are you planning on tracing him? And her?'

'My initial reaction was not to do that. I feel no connection with them whatsoever. Or at least I thought I didn't. Now maybe I need to. And I suppose I'm a little curious about them if I'm honest. I don't want to be, but I am.'

'You should think about it. Your twin especially. Apart from anything else there could be some great research benefits in studying your joint DNA. That's not an opportunity that comes our way very often. Identical twins are so rare.'

'Could our levels of triple repeats be different?'

'Yes. We've come across a few instances of that. We assume environment plays a part, but we don't know for sure and we don't know how. It would be another avenue of research if you can track him down, but it's a big decision and I can see how you might need to think about it.'

Clayton shook his head. 'Not anymore, the decision's clear. We need him, so now I have to find him, and the sooner the better.'

Malcolm nodded. 'I'll help any way I can. Ready to head back?'

Clayton barely heard the question. He was already planning his search.

CHAPTER THIRTY

Clayton realised how little he had to go on in the search for his mysterious sibling. He didn't even know which hemisphere to look in. He was in unknown territory and tracking his twin down would take time; time he didn't have. Yet finding him was an imperative.

Not that he could care less about playing reunited happy families with the guy - whoever and whatever he turned out to be - but he needed him. He knew how valuable a pair of identical twins could be to genetic research.

And as he'd told Malcolm, part of him was curious. As one half of a matching pair he wanted to see the other half, his biological doppelganger. But this went beyond curiosity. Somewhere inside himself, where he'd tried to bury it since he read his mother's letter, a gnawing question kept stubbornly resurfacing. Why had his birth mother chosen his twin over him? Why had she left him behind? Maybe being face to face with his mirror image would help him deal with the sore which had festered ever since his mother's revelations.

Malcolm was typically true to his word. He organised a

blood sample and got the Huntington's diagnostic test underway as soon as they were back at the university. With that and a meeting with the Dean organised for the following week, it was time to begin the search for his brother.

Fortunately, the private investigator he decided to commission proved fast and effective. Short, slightly overweight and in his mid-forties, Bob wasn't the cheapest of the three he interviewed, but his success rate on similarly difficult cases was impressive. Clayton suspected those results owed a lot to Bob's apparent willingness to bypass the rules when necessary. He didn't choose to know the details, and nor did he care. He was the client, a man in a hurry, and he wanted the job done.

Two months and several cash payments later, it was. He sat in the West End pub where he and Bob held their update sessions for the final time, staring at a folder containing everything he needed. A name, an address, a life history and a photograph. A photograph he should have been prepared for, and thought he was, but which freaked him out as soon as opened the folder and looked at it. He found himself staring straight into his own face.

Even Bob, who'd bragged he was unshockable, kept commuting between the photograph and the real man opposite. 'Bloody hell mate. I've had a few surprises in my time. Met all sorts being in my line, including a few sets of twins. But never like you two. I mean, you guys are beyond identical... like...you're the same person. It's unbelievable.'

Clayton smiled. Bob had a habit of saying the same thing at least three different ways, but he was right. He could scarcely believe it himself. Three months ago, he'd thought the only photographs of this face were his. Now he was seeing his reflection for the first time without a mirror and trying to absorb the information he'd received about the other man who owned his face.

He slid an envelope containing his final cash payment across the table to Bob, thanked him for his help, then walked out of the pub into the normality of a busy Friday night in Central London. He felt isolated and remote from the smiling carefree faces that emerged from the city's bars and restaurants and the crowds who walked past him. He wondered if he would ever be normal and so apparently care-free again. He hailed a cab and jumped in the back. As he leaned back in his seat and closed his eyes, he tried to imagine how it would feel to be face-to-face with the man in the photograph, seeing his own reflection in the flesh, but he couldn't. It all felt too unreal and he was desperate to be back in the familiarity of his apartment. He needed some sleep before he planned his next move.

A few restless hours later, he decided further attempts at sleep were futile. Armed with a pot of coffee, he started to read the investigator's report in more detail than he'd been in the mood to do last night, when his first sight of the photo-graph had left him reeling. Bob had told him his twin was called Max, that he had been living in London since the age of three and was about to be released from prison where he'd spent the last five years for aggravated burglary. It wasn't the first time Max had served at Her Majesty's Pleasure.

Clayton settled down and prepared himself to find out what had led his brother into a life of crime. By the time he'd finished reading he no longer envied the man who had been chosen over him as a baby. Five pages were all it took for the festering sore of his biological mother's rejection to be cured. It was cauterised by the images of his beloved adoptive mother which flooded his brain and his senses. He thanked her God again that she had found him and given him the best life a mother could.

Max had not been so fortunate. Their birth mother, Linda Winterbottom, had been a mess. Bob unearthed no information about their biological father but discovered that Linda had left Sydney for Queensland with her baby son and taken refuge with an old school friend working on the outskirts of Cairns. When Max was three, she met a British backpacker who she followed on his return to England. His interest in her and her son was short-lived, but she survived on her wits and a willingness to make whatever money she could by whatever means she could. Max spent his infancy in a succession of cheap rooms where his mother took her turn to babysit her fellow tenants' children on the nights she wasn't selling her ample assets.

As Clayton read on, he remembered the warmth and security of his own childhood and tried to envisage how life must have been for his twin on the opposite side of the world, witness to a succession of nameless, faceless men.

By the time Max was eight he was out of control. He played truant from school so often that Linda gave up taking him. As Bob put it, Max simply dropped out of the system, and temporarily disappeared from the authorities' radar. For the next few years he educated himself, unfortunately following a personal curriculum destined to land him in trouble. He became an expert pickpocket and small-time thief and wasn't afraid to use his increasingly impressive physique and his fists to get what he wanted. He and his mother moved from one shabby set of rooms to another.

According to neighbours Bob had met, Max went from hating their lifestyle to deciding it suited him. He liked living on his wits, answerable to no one. Whenever the law, or a local gang whose turf he intruded on, threatened to catch up with him, he persuaded his mother they should move on. She had no idea how to control him, instead choosing to turn a blind eye to how he came by the cash he would occasionally pass over to her for her spasmodic trips to the supermarket.

His luck held until he was fourteen, when he was caught on CCTV breaking into an off-licence, raiding the till and beating up the owner to within an inch of his life. His first experience of incarceration, in a young offenders' institute, was to be the first of many. Bob's report of offences and institutions ran to two pages. There wasn't much Max hadn't done, short of murder.

Clayton could hardly comprehend the difference in their lives. He looked up from the report to glance at the portrait of Becca on the wall. How lucky he was to have such a wonderful daughter. On that too it appeared Max hadn't been so fortunate. Bob had found no evidence of him having children. It was clear there had been plenty of women in his life, several of whom had been at the receiving end of his fists, which had landed him in trouble more than once, including his most recent brush with the law. A liaison with a married woman – one of Max's apparent specialities – had turned unpleasant. Her husband had spotted the bruises Max had inflicted despite, as the court heard, his wife's attempts to disguise them. The affair had been an expensive indulgence for Max who was currently serving another three years in Wormwood Scrubs, now virtually his home from home.

During his latest incarceration their mother had ended her life with a rusty knife to both her wrists. Clayton read those words with mixed emotions as he looked again at the date. It had happened a year ago. On the one hand he felt nothing, on the other he felt guilty that he didn't. Whatever she had done wrong in her life, she had given birth to him. Surely he should feel something for her? Perhaps his emotions were now so overloaded he had no space to feel anything. At least if he met Max, he might discover more about how her condition had affected her at the end. He could only assume it had contributed to her desire to end her life. He shuddered at the thought of the same thing happening to him, or worse, to Becca.

He stared again at Max's estimated release date at the end of the report. Three months from now, provided he behaved himself. Clayton had better try and make sure he did. He needed his brother back in the outside world. He grabbed some paper from his desk. It was time to compose a letter, introducing himself to his brother. He had no idea if Max even knew of his existence. Had their biological mother told him? Before he started writing he called Bob's number. He needed advice on how to arrange a prison visit.

The sooner he made contact with his twin the better.

Clayton Mortimer. Max sat in his cell and looked at the name on the letter again. This was a bolt out of the blue. He'd known he had a brother somewhere. His sad excuse for a mother had told him on what turned out to be her last visit to him. Not that he could have cared less at the time but thinking about him now made Max's face contort. The guy wrote like a right smart arse. University type, probably totally up himself. The bastard had even managed to land himself a posh name. Mortimer. Sounded all upmarket and clever, same as his letter did. And what had he got stuffed with? Winterbottom. OK, so the Max part was cool, and girls had always liked it. He gave the woman some credit for choosing that. But why had she never changed their stupid surname? Didn't it occur to her that the kids at school would take the piss?

Not that it had taken him long to knock that on the head. When the school bully did a chant calling him some kind of a stupid arse once too often, Max snapped. Even now he enjoyed thinking back to how he'd nearly put the guy through a classroom window. He smirked remembering how easily he'd got away with it. Everybody had believed him - angelic looking Max, with his cute face and hair - over that fat piece of shit.

Oh yeah. Max had fixed him good and proper. And anybody else who'd tried to mess with him since. Nobody ever tried twice. He'd learned more that day than on all his other days at school.

He looked at the second letter the screws had brought him that morning. From the idiot woman who'd landed him in here. What a mistake she'd turned out to be, and she hadn't even been that hot. Now she said she missed him and wanted to see him. But then she'd enjoyed Max's particular brand of sex. Like so many women had over the years. They tried to pretend they didn't, but secretly they were gagging for what he gave them that their boring vanilla husbands didn't. But this one had turned out to be real trouble and he'd had to teach her a lesson. He felt himself getting aroused thinking back to it. He reckoned she'd been turned on by him hurting her too. But then she'd blabbed about it to her tosser of a husband. He flung her letter in the bin. Like he cared that she missed him now, that was her problem. She'd got what was coming to her, and he definitely wasn't going there again. Bloody women, stupid and selfish all of them. They all needed teaching a lesson, like his mother had.

Of course, she'd ended up paying for the shit life she'd given him. Struck down by a weird disease he'd never heard of. Trust her to have something with a stupid name. Some kind of dancing mania, her arms and legs all over the bloody place. And forgetting things all the time, even more than she always had. In the last five years, every time he'd seen her, which he made sure was as infrequently as possible, she was crying. Saying she was sorry she hadn't given him a better life. Sorry she hadn't told him about his brother sooner. That this thing she'd got was God paying his debts. Blah blah blah. Max hadn't given a toss.

She'd given him some garbled story that he might have the same thing. How he could have inherited it from her, and he should be checked out. He'd laughed at her. Screw tests, he was as fit as a fiddle. He decided he'd cross the jerky arms and legs bridge if he ever got to it, then never gave it another thought. Max lived for the moment and he planned to continue making most moments revolve around him.

Now he didn't have his mother getting in his way, the bloody brother had shown up out of nowhere and wanted to meet him. Saying he'd only recently found out about him and there were things they should talk about. Some crap about wanting to help him when he got out of this place. What the hell was that about? The guy was obviously some sort of do-gooder.

Max looked round his cell. It wasn't bad as cells went; he'd been in worse. And over the years he'd figured out how to blag himself a few creature comforts. He'd almost be sad to leave.

But now he had something to look forward to when he did. He'd play along with brother dearest and take whatever he was offering, the guy owed him. Lucky bastard got the better deal, being abandoned by their waste of space mother. Now it was payback time.

Max sneered again. He'd find a way of settling the score.

CHAPTER THIRTY-ONE

George caught up with Catherine as she raced through the foyer of the conference venue and finally took a deep breath of fresh air outside. He grabbed her arm.

'Christ Catherine, what was all that about? You ran off like a bat out of hell. What happened in there?'

'Nothing. I needed some air.' She looked at him. She felt stupid and she knew he didn't believe her. She didn't even believe herself.

'Was it about Adam? Were you thinking about him?'

Adam. Now she felt guilty as well as stupid. Guilty because she'd barely thought about him the entire day. Too blindsided by Mr Professor and his smiling charm. Guilty because George was concerned about her and she didn't deserve it.

'I don't know what I was thinking to be honest.' That was true. She couldn't believe she'd blurted out that stuff about Max to Clayton. It had felt good at the time, but now she wished she hadn't done it.

'We need to get you away from here for a while. Let's find

somewhere quiet for a drink and a chat. We can come back later. Paul Naylor isn't presenting until this afternoon.'

'But you can't afford to miss anything. What about your article?'

'Sod it, I'll wing it. Anyway, I've got Susie's number, she can fill me in on anything I miss. Good excuse to call her.'

Catherine smiled. 'I could tell how much you liked her, I did too. Lovely personality, fun I think.' She gave him a playful nudge. 'And seriously smart. She'll give you a run for your money.' She linked her arm in his. 'I feel better already. Fresh air and space have helped. Lead on and let's go for that drink.'

They walked for ten minutes until they found a quiet pub. It was early and they had the place to themselves. As she waited for him to bring their drinks over to the table, she told herself to dismiss Clayton Mortimer from her mind. She couldn't allow stupid thoughts about him to interfere with what she needed to do. She turned her attention to Richard Cameron again. What was his connection to Adam?

'Deep in thought as per.' George put a glass of water in front of her and sat down. 'Drink, you need it. You've been through a lot recently Catherine. Dealing with Adam's death and propping up Lizzie. Not to mention the emotion of sorting your son out. You need to ease up on yourself a bit and take some time out for you.'

Catherine barely heard him. She slammed her glass down and gave him a triumphant look. 'Of course. I remember. It was at their house. I'm surprised it took so long to come back to me, but there was so much happening that day.'

'Whose house and what day? Whatever you remember, it obviously feels important. That glass barely survived it.'

'Adam and Lizzie's. That's where I saw him. Susie's Dad, Richard Cameron. I knew it would come back to me. He was at Adam's funeral.'

'I'm not sure I see anything too strange about that. He's a highly-rated senior medic and an adviser to the biggest of the pharmaceutical giants. He and Adam could have had several reasons to cross paths.'

'I understand that. But Lizzie kept the reception at the house small and private. She didn't want an official event. Only family and people she knew well, plus a small group from Adam's department who she invited as a courtesy. They pretty much stayed in the background keeping themselves to themselves, and now I remember he stood alongside them most of the time, so he seemed part of the group. Lizzie made a point of introducing me to everybody she knew who came along for Adam, but I didn't meet Richard Cameron. That's why it took me a while to remember, but I know he was there.'

'I guess we should check him out then. I'm still not convinced it'll turn out to be significant but I'm learning never to underestimate your instincts.'

She smiled at him. 'They're not infallible, but I do have a feeling about this guy.'

'Your gut feelings are always worth pursuing. After you asked me to work with you, I checked you out with a few people and everybody who worked with you in the past were unanimous about one thing. If Catherine Preston believes there's more to something - however unlikely to everybody else - she's usually right. Quote unquote.'

'So, what else did they say? Polite enough to repeat?'

'That you never, ever give up when you feel strongly about something. I admire that in you Catherine. So, let's run with this for a bit. Can you remember anything else about him?'

'No, and that's the point. Why be there, if only to fade into the background? Not his usual style I'm sure. We saw that today, he's an arrogant type, definitely not someone Adam would have taken to at all. And earlier it seemed he hadn't recognised me but now I realise he must have done. He's smart and he's in a profession that's all about observation and I was fairly centre stage at the funeral, so I don't see how he could've missed me. And he couldn't get away from us fast enough when Susie introduced us earlier could he? The question is why?'

'I admit it's strange he didn't refer to Adam when...yes... he must have seen you at the funeral. But today he was in a hurry to get back to Paul Naylor's side so I'm not sure you should read too much into him rushing off.'

'You might be right, but I'll talk to Lizzie about him and see what she knows about his connection with Adam.'

George nodded. 'For the record I didn't like him any more than you did by the way. How different from him his daughter is. So much for the apple not falling far from the tree.'

'It did in this case. She's lovely.' She gave him a playful nudge in the ribs. 'You are so smitten.'

'Stop teasing me about her. Let's stick with her Dad. You talk to Lizzie and I'll see how we can keep tabs on him.' He winked at her. 'Which may not be exactly a hardship.'

'You mean through Susie. I don't like the idea of us using her George. It's bad enough seeing the dismissive way her father treats her. I don't want us doing that. I like her too much.'

'I know, and I won't. I like her a lot too and I wouldn't want to do anything to threaten getting to know her better. But if I can arrange to see her, and pick her up at her house, who knows? I might notice something he says or does or see something lying around which connects him to Adam. Or I'll straight out ask him.'

Catherine frowned down at her cup. 'You know, hearing that makes me wonder. Am I seeing demons everywhere that don't exist?'

He shook his head. 'I don't think that's your style Catherine. You're tired, but I'm certain you're not prone to imagining things. If you think we should look into this guy more closely, then whether I'm convinced or not doesn't matter. We should do it.'

'You're right, I am tired, and I guess I'm frustrated about whether we're ever going to make real headway with this crazy mission Adam's sent us on. Maybe there's nothing sinister to find and I'm clutching at straws. It's not as if we have anything concrete, do we? This whole thing is based on coincidences and our instincts.'

'Apart from a dead junior minister. Doesn't get more concrete than that. Plus, we now have the incident at your hot professor's lab that Susie mentioned.'

CHAPTER THIRTY-TWO

Catherine looked up in surprise. 'What incident at his lab? I didn't hear her say anything about that.'

'I guess you were talking with the professor when she mentioned it. I had no chance to tell you before we got into the Richard Cameron discussion.'

'Tell me now then.'

'It happened just before the conference. Suspected unauthorised access to Clayton's computer, and some lab papers moved about, but they never got to the bottom of it. Eventually he dismissed it as one of the researchers being careless. Seems he didn't want to make a big deal out of it and start a witch hunt. That's the type of guy he is apparently. According to Susie his team love him, and it sounds like they'd walk over hot coals for him, her included. She said all the female researchers have a bit of a crush on him too.' He grinned. 'You might have some competition.'

Catherine raised her hand to dismiss his last remark. 'I'm not interested in whether there is or isn't competition for his attention, but I am interested in the incident. I know it could be nothing, but all these could be nothings are starting to mount up into a possible something in my opinion. I can't believe I'd started to doubt myself. We have to stay on this.'

George nodded. 'So where do we go from here?'

'We see if there have been any other similar incidents in genetic research labs.' She was already typing into her search bar, then looked back at him. 'Bingo. A lab fire near Edinburgh, last year.'

'And? What caused it?'

'According to this report the police investigation was inconclusive. But we should look into it ourselves. See if we can find any connection with the incident at Clayton Mortimer's lab.'

'I'm on it. I'll track down whatever CCTV footage I can on the areas around both installations at the time of the incidents.'

'Let's do that as soon as possible. And you follow up with Susie and try to get inside the Cameron house. It may be a long shot, but you never know. I have a feeling about her father.'

'Then consider it done.' He glanced at his watch. 'If we're going to catch Naylor's pitch we should start heading back. Are you feeling up to it?'

'Of course. I'm interested to hear what he has to say.'

'By all accounts he's bloody impressive. Where he and Galen lead, others seem to follow, but he always seems to be ahead of the game. Guess he's smarter than the rest.'

As he motioned for Catherine to walk ahead of him towards the door, she turned to him, 'Maybe, or lucky. But perhaps he has another advantage.'

As he held the door open for her, he gave her a questioning look. 'Like what?'

'Like early access to information that others don't have.'

· · ·

Paul Naylor turned out to be as impressive as they'd anticipated. An accomplished presenter, he radiated the same intellect and confidence he'd displayed in their short introduction
earlier. His talk reinforced to Catherine the sheer scale of
investment being made into research by the pharmaceutical
community, and especially by Galen. The cost of bringing a
single new drug from inception in a scientist's mind to
market, was mind boggling, as was the lead time until any
drug started to pay for itself. Failure, or the decision to back
the wrong research direction, could clearly be catastrophic.
She didn't imagine that Galen's CEO left much to chance or
tolerated failure.

She looked round at his audience. Virtually the entire
room, including his competitors, appeared riveted by his
every word, and by him. No wonder George had referred to
him as The Great God Naylor; he was a pharmaceutical deity.
Then she spotted Clayton, his expression inscrutable as he
stared at the podium. The two men's presentations could not
have been more different. Where the academic had inspired
with his passion for the new frontiers of gene silencing and
editing, the slick businessman talking now was all about
investment and revenue from successful treatment drugs.

As the presentation drew to a close, to rapturous
applause, Clayton turned in her direction. She looked away
and slumped down in her seat. She didn't want him to see her
or make eye contact with him.

Before the applause died down, she grabbed George.
'Let's get out of here ahead of the crowd.'

George took her arm and navigated their exit. They were
outside within minutes. He turned to her with a concerned
expression. 'Second time today Catherine. I hope you're not
sickening for something. We should get you home straightaway. Let's grab a taxi before everybody else tries to. We can
talk as we're driving back.'

Catherine sank with relief on to the back seat of the cab he bundled her into. 'I'm fine, George, don't worry. Nothing a good night's sleep won't sort out.'

'Make sure you have one, Doctor's orders. What did you think of Paul Naylor? Got to give it to the guy; he definitely packs a punch. The audience loved him.'

'Don't you mean his disciples? They lapped up every word. He's certainly impressive.'

George nodded. 'As were the levels of research funding he talked about. No wonder the universities love him.'

Catherine recalled the look she'd seen on Clayton Mortimer's face. There was one university man who didn't seem to be a fan. 'I'm still digesting the numbers he referred to. Even though we've talked about pharmaceutical financials before, seeing them on a big screen drives the scale of them home even more. Obviously, money is knowledge and knowledge is power in this industry. That's clarified something for me.'

'Tell me.'

She gazed out of the cab window at the crowds of faceless people they were passing as she chose her words. 'I know I've been a bit all over the place today, and I'm sorry. For some reason I've been having the odd moment of doubt about all this recently, but not anymore. I'm convinced there's something going on here, maybe a lot more than we thought. That instinct you keep teasing me about tells me it could be a hell of a lot more sinister.'

George paused for a moment before he spoke. 'I feel the same way. Sinister as in worth killing for.'

She turned from the window and looked straight at him. 'Very definitely worth killing for. And more than once.'

CHAPTER THIRTY-THREE

Catherine didn't expect to sleep well that night but was thankful she did. She woke up relieved to have had some respite from the rollercoaster she'd been riding since Adam's death. Sleep hadn't changed the facts, but it made her stronger to face them.

The sleep-induced calm was short-lived when she unthinkingly answered a call from an unknown number. She heard the unmistakable Australian accent and her temporary equilibrium disappeared.

'Hi Catherine. It's Clayton Mortimer. We met yesterday at the conference. I hope you don't mind me calling. Your friend George gave Susie your number for me.'

Why the hell hadn't George warned her? Now she'd been wrong-footed and was convinced that whatever she said next would sound stupid. She took a deep breath and tried to be cool and collected.

'Of course I don't mind. It gives me a chance to tell you how much I enjoyed your presentation. You introduced me to a whole new world and your research sounds fascinating.'

'Thank you. I'm not convinced everybody else there would agree, but you're nice to say it. Did you catch some of the other sessions?'

So, he hadn't seen her. 'We caught Paul Naylor's pitch. I found him a little slick, but he is impressive.'

'I agree, and he's obviously a great businessman. He and I approach this from different perspectives though.'

'Business success and the greater good aren't always the same, are they? Although he did talk about some interesting treatments they have in the pipeline. Galen clearly fund a ton of research.'

'They do, and they make a shitload of money from treatment drugs, but I'm trying to work towards more permanent solutions. I'll be interested to see how your colleague covers all this in his article.' He paused. 'But I didn't call to talk about work.'

She caught her breath, waiting for him to confront her about her Max remark. She had no idea what she'd say when he brought it up and she wished she could have her words back.

'Catherine? Are you still there?'

She hoped her voice wouldn't convey her nerves. She reminded herself that he was the one who adopted an assumed name when it suited. Let him justify his behaviour.

'Yes, sorry. Momentarily distracted. So why did you call me?'

'Because I would love to see you again. If you would like to. I'm sorry, I'm a bit nervous. Out of practice at this.'

She smiled an involuntary smile to herself. If only he knew how out of practice she was. Or how nervous. She hoped her mobile couldn't convey the sound of her heart racing. And he still hadn't referred to her Max comment. Maybe he expected her to.

'You don't sound nervous, and I'm flattered you want to see me again, especially after my outburst as I left. Although it can hardly have surprised you.'

'It totally surprised me. And confused me. I had no idea you even knew of Max's existence. But let's leave that for another time. Would you like to have dinner on Friday? Please, say yes. I feel like a schoolboy asking a girl out for the first time. Put me out of my misery please.'

In spite of her nerves she laughed. Something about this man completely drew her in. She couldn't imagine ever saying no to him about anything, and his reaction to her Max remark intrigued her. Had he forgotten their Tinder encounter? Meeting up with him would at least give her the chance to find out.

'I wouldn't want you messing up your homework waiting for an answer, so it's a yes.'

'Thank god for that. It's a geography assignment. I usually flunk those.' He paused as she giggled. 'I like that sound. Let me book something and message you. Italian OK for you? At around eight? There's a great place near my university building if it's not too far for you.'

Too far? His voice and the fact that he liked her giggle were making her melt. She'd take an Uber to the North Pole to meet him if he suggested it.

'Sounds perfect. I look forward to your message, and to seeing you. Thank you, Dr Mortimer.' She paused. 'Clayton.'

He laughed. 'I'm glad we got that straight. I look forward to seeing you too. Enjoy the rest of your day, Catherine and take care.'

After he rang off, she hugged her phone, imagining him still on the other end of the line. Three days till she would see him. And three days till she found out what the hell he'd tell her about Max.

. . .

When George called her an hour later, her irritation at him passing on her number without warning her had completely evaporated, obliterated by her giddy excitement after Clayton's call. As soon as she answered the phone, she pre-empted his explanation.

'It's OK, you don't need to tell me. You gave him my number. He called earlier. I should be mad at you, but I'm not.'

George whistled down the line. 'He phoned you already? The man's keen. Since you're not mad at me I'm guessing the conversation went well.'

'We're having dinner on Friday.' She hoped he didn't notice the excitement in her voice as she rushed out the words.

'That's great. I have a good feeling about you two.'

She raised her eyebrows at him. 'It's just dinner George.'

'Hey, everything starts with just dinner. So, is this purely social, or will you be fact finding at the same time? Great opportunity to hear the inside track on his research, and see what he says about the break-in.'

She asked herself the same question, then felt guilty. Guilty towards Adam that this dinner was more about her attraction to Clayton than discovering anything that might help their investigation, or guilt towards Clayton for hoping he might tell her something that would.

George interrupted her thoughts. 'I'm kidding by the way. Step away from all this for a couple of days. Take a break, you need it. Buy a hot dress, enjoy the dinner, enjoy the man. You hear me? Doctor George's orders.'

She smiled. She could certainly use a break from the trauma of recent events. She'd always trusted her journalistic instincts, but the Adam investigation was uniquely personal.

Some time away from it might give her some perspective.

She needed to be sure she wasn't letting herself see things that weren't there.

CHAPTER THIRTY-FOUR

Clayton sat at a candle-lit corner table at the back of the restaurant. He'd specifically requested it, so they'd have privacy to talk. Now he hoped it wouldn't look like some unsubtle seduction scene. Not that the idea of seducing the woman who had invaded his thoughts constantly for three days was anything other than appealing, but he didn't want to come across as crass and obvious. He looked at his watch. Ten to eight, time for a quick drink to settle his nerves before she arrived. He had a feeling Catherine Preston didn't do late.

He ordered himself a beer and a bottle of Prosecco, hoping she liked it. He was nursing his glass and trying to look interested in the menu when she arrived. As he watched her walk towards the table his nerves went into overdrive. All his senses were under assault. When she smiled the same nervous smile that had melted his insides at the conference, she dazzled him. She looked breathtakingly gorgeous. Blonde hair tumbling softly to her shoulders, eyes sparkling with that intelligence he'd been instantly drawn to, but with a vulnerability behind them that made him want to leap out of his seat and envelop her.

And the dress she wore. Black, definitely her colour, short but elegant. It hugged her curves, emphasised her slim figure and showcased long shapely legs, He wondered if she'd bought it with tonight, and him, in mind. He dismissed the thought as presumptuous, but the possibility irrationally pleased him.

He stood to greet her, and she held out her hand. He shook it, feeling ridiculously formal, but reluctant to let go of it. He imagined a time when the formality would be replaced by him sweeping her into his arms. For now though, he sensed he should let her set the pace and not rush her.

'Clayton, how lovely to see you again. What a delightful place you chose.'

He returned her smile as the waiter seated her, then discreetly stepped away, giving him a conspiratorial look. Was it so obvious why they were there?

As he sat down, he leaned over to Catherine and whispered. 'Think he knows we're on our first date? I must have looked nervous.'

She grinned at him. 'I'm sure he's seen a few. I'm pretty nervous myself.'

'You look great. Fabulous dress.' She smiled her nervous smile again, as if she found personal compliments awkward. He couldn't imagine why. 'It's lovely to see you again and I'm glad you like the place. The food here is great.'

'Thank you. The dress is new, a friend convinced me to buy it. It's not terribly forgiving though I'm afraid, so I'd better go easy on the pasta. Which I love by the way.'

He laughed, totally at ease with her. His nerves disappeared, as if he'd always known her. But he sensed that whenever he saw her, he'd be filled with the excitement of seeing her for the first time. He imagined that's how life with Catherine would be, then told himself to slow down. He smiled at her. 'I passed the first test then, chose the right cuisine?'

'You passed with flying colours. You chose the right wine too. I rarely drink but I love Prosecco.'

On cue their waiter returned, poured her a glass and discreetly backed off again. This guy was good. He'd better reflect that in the tip.

He raised his glass in a toast. 'To you, for agreeing to join me and looking wonderful.'

She chinked his glass and her eyes met his. 'To new friendships. And to getting it right.'

They were still holding each other's gaze when the waiter returned to take their order.

For the past two mornings Catherine had woken to find Adam's face wasn't the first image that came into her mind. Instead she saw Clayton, and her stomach had fizzed with anticipation at the thought of seeing him.

She'd called the one person she knew could calm her down. Nina answered the call immediately. 'Catherine, it's so good to hear from you. I'm dashing a bit though. Everything ok? Tell me.'

Speaking to Nina was so refreshingly normal. She was obviously running late as usual, so Catherine rushed out her news. 'Won't keep you then but had to tell you. I'm pretty involved work-wise, but I have a date on Friday. I'm ridiculously nervous and I wish you were here to sort me out.'

'That's my girl. I told you it wouldn't take long. So, is he hot? I need details. A pic when you can please. Do a selfie with him.'

'I think he's pretty hot, yes. I'll tell you more after Friday. There's a work connection too.'

'You and work. Take at least a night off and enjoy the

man. And quit being nervous. You'll look great and you are great. Wear the hair down, whack on that black dress you bought, add the heels and job done. Trust me, he'll be a goner.'

Catherine laughed. 'Nina, I do miss you. You have to come down here and stay as soon as I've got a place sorted.'

'Try keeping me away. I need to give this guy the once over and make sure he's good enough for you. You have to call me Saturday and tell all. Sorry I have to dash now; I'm running late for a meeting at the school. You know me. I'm even worse since you left.'

'Go. Give my love to Jack. I'll speak to you at the weekend.'

As the call ended Catherine had realised she was excited for herself for the first time in ages. She'd been excited for Will about Cambridge, and for Nina about her divorce. But she'd barely had one night to indulge her own excitement about the prospect of a new life in London before she'd been catapulted into the Adam investigation. Now she felt guilty about stepping away from it for an evening, but she tried to tell herself not to.

By the time she walked into the restaurant on Friday, the nerves that had disappeared after her conversation with Nina had returned and she took some deep breaths to compose herself. The restaurant was lovely, he'd made a perfect choice, and she was right on time. She had a feeling he'd expect that from her.

As the waiter escorted her to their table, she saw Clayton and the butterflies in her stomach went into overdrive. She couldn't imagine a time that wouldn't happen. She got to the table and held out her hand, feeling stupidly formal. When he smiled and took it in his, a jolt surged through her entire body and she wondered if he'd felt it too. She spoke with no idea of what she said as the waiter seated her.

Then Clayton leaned across the table and confessed he was nervous. When she heard his voice and looked at him, her own nervousness lifted. It felt so right to be sitting opposite this man. She wanted to know everything about him.

Choosing their food took no time. Catherine happily went with Clayton's recommendations. Conversation and laughter flowed between them as if they were an established couple updating each other on their respective days. They compared notes on life with a teenager and he listened intently to the story of Will's adoption, her move North to focus on her role as a mother and how she'd single-handedly parented him through to his Cambridge acceptance. He told her Will sounded like an exceptional young man of whom she should be rightly proud.

The more they spoke about her son the more Catherine realised how much she missed him, and tears threatened to well up in her despite her efforts to blink them back. She stared down at the table. Clayton reached over and placed his hand on hers.

'I understand Catherine, you must miss him. I can see he's been the centre of your life for so long.'

The gentle touch of his hand made her feel better. She looked up at him and smiled. 'He has, but I know this will get easier. No more tears, they play havoc with the mascara. Anyway, I want to hear more about you. Tell me how an Australian wound up as the top genetics professor in London.'

'My story is uncannily like Will's. I'm adopted too. Brought up in Sydney by an incredible single Mum, and any success people think I've had I owe to her. The reason for London is I came over here to do my postgrad study after my first degree in Sydney, and I stayed. I met my now ex-wife here. Which is a whole other story, best left for another time.'

His look suggested his marriage was definitely a subject he wanted to avoid so Catherine asked about his mother. He told he she'd died ten years earlier and then paused. His face assumed the enigmatic expression Catherine had noticed before. As if he was wrestling with something he wanted to talk about, but couldn't bring himself to. Before she could try to coax it out of him, he changed the subject.

'So, what about the men in your life Ms Preston? Looking the way that you do I have to think there have been plenty of suitors. But I have the impression you never married?'

'Thank you for the compliment. No, I've never been married. The right person never came along, I suppose. Nothing ever quite worked out.' She hesitated and looked down at her hands, choosing her next words carefully. 'And I had my career, then Will, plenty to occupy me. So not having a partner never bothered me.'

She looked up to find him scrutinising her and waited for the question she was sure he was about to ask.

'Does it still not bother you? Now that your son is going to be more independent?'

She looked at him, hoping she wasn't blushing, but fearing she was. Sitting opposite this man it did bother her. It bothered her a lot.

'I suppose it would be nice if someone did come along. But I've got so used to doing things my way I'd probably be a nightmare. To most people anyway.' She felt an involuntary smile forming and hoped he hadn't noticed. He'd think she was flirting with him.

He answered with a grin. 'I'll bear it I mind. And I believe there's a soul mate for everybody.'

'You're lucky, you found yours, even if it didn't last forever. Sorry, I'm being presumptuous.'

'No need to be sorry. You're not being presumptuous, but you are inaccurate. I assume you mean my wife and no, she wasn't my soulmate.'

His expression told her she shouldn't respond to his admission. Instead she decided to steer the conversation towards the elephant in the room. Max.

'My best friend is convinced I'll find Mr Right here in London. But Nina's a born romantic. She says I haven't been looking hard enough.'

'Did Nina help you choose that dress?' She raised her eyebrows and nodded to him. 'Then you should listen to her. Nina knows what she's doing.'

'She's a big advocate of online dating. Told me to try it. I'm a little suspicious of it to be honest.'

'She sounds like my friend David. He's a Tinder regular, in fact he's all over it. I'm suspicious of it like you, not especially my scene either to be honest.'

She almost choked on her food, then stared at him in disbelief. Everything had been going so well, but now what the hell was he playing at? Not only was he not acknowledging their Tinder encounter, he was acting as if he'd completely forgotten about it. Perhaps he'd been drunk when he saw her profile. Something didn't make sense here, and she wanted an explanation.

'Clayton, this has gone on long enough. The joke's over so tell me the truth please. What the hell is the Max story? Were you drunk and messing around with your friend when you saw me on Tinder? Because it seems out of character. Or do you have a double somewhere?'

To her surprise he started to laugh. 'As a matter of fact, I do. And I'm sorry for laughing, but I see what's happened now. I should have guessed something like this.'

'I'm glad you find this funny but forgive me for not quite

seeing the joke. And what does "as a matter of fact you do" mean?'

He put his hand on hers again and didn't let go despite her attempt to pull away. 'It means I have a twin brother. An identical twin. And I shouldn't have laughed and I'm sorry. But it seems we have a very simple case of mistaken identity here.'

She opened her mouth to speak but couldn't find the words. All her senses were focused on the touch of his hand. She looked into his eyes, and knew he'd told her the truth. This was not a man who would lie to her.

A smile started deep inside her, where she knew something else.

In that instant, as he held her hand and his eyes looked desperate for her to believe him, she fell in love with Clayton Mortimer.

CHAPTER THIRTY-FIVE

Once again, her smile enraptured him. It started in her eyes then lit up her entire face. If she ever asked him the exact moment he knew he'd fallen in love with her, his answer would be now. He had never seen anyone so beautiful and he couldn't imagine he would ever tire of looking at her.

Her eyes held something else too. He dared to hope she felt what he did. That they were at the beginning of something. Something that less than a week ago neither of them could have contemplated. Something that would change irrevocably the landscape of both their lives.

Then the image of Becca crashed into those thoughts and ran them off the road. Reality hit with its usual impact and reminded him he still had a job to do. He might be close to finding the Huntington's cure he'd worked day and night for, but he still wasn't there. Ten years ago, he'd vowed that nothing, and nobody, would distract him from that. Unfortunately, he'd reckoned without the woman opposite entering his life unannounced.

That woman now looked at him expectantly. Of course she did. The Max genie was out of the bottle and he couldn't put him back. He needed to tell her the truth. The watered-down version he'd given everybody else about his twin brother would sound hollow and stupid to her and he doubted she'd buy it. Those eyes held a piercing intelligence he'd never encountered before, and half- truths would never be an option with her.

As he started to speak, he knew he wouldn't stop until he told her everything. He'd finally found the person he could share the last ten years with and there was only one place to start. At the beginning.

Two hours later Clayton felt a weight had lifted from his shoulders. He'd shared it all with her. His mother's death, her letter, his Huntington's diagnosis with its potential conse-quences and his discovery of his twin. As he knew she would, she let him tell it his way and in his own time, with scarcely an interruption. When he stumbled mid-sentence, she reached for his hand and gently encouraged him to continue. She smiled her support when he needed it and squeezed his hand when he needed that.

For better or worse she now knew his story and he hoped she could deal with it. For a few seconds she stayed silent. Then she picked up his hand and gripped it with both of hers.

'Clayton. I can't believe you've carried the burden of all this on your own for ten years. And I'm honoured you chose me to tell.' She lowered her gaze, staring at her hands on his. 'I'm a little taken aback that you did. I mean, since we only just met. You've put so much trust in me.'

When she looked back up at him her eyes were moist with tears.

His hesitated before replying as his own feelings threat-ened to overwhelm him. 'Catherine, I'll be honest. I never imagined telling anybody this, apart from the stuff that I told my friend Malcolm when he was alive. But suddenly, tonight, looking across at you, it felt right. I needed you to know.' Then he looked directly at her. He had to confront the obvious question. 'But it hardly makes me the ideal catch does it? A man who could develop uncontrollable limb movements at any moment...you should run a mile. Most women would.'

Without taking her eyes off him her answer was immediate. 'I'm not going anywhere. Not a mile, not even an inch. Not now and...' She hesitated before continuing. 'For as long as you don't want me to, not ever.'

He held her gaze then he beckoned to the waiter, gesturing that he'd like the bill. He needed to take Catherine Preston into his arms, and he needed to do it now. She smiled her nervous smile at him as the waiter brought the bill and the credit card machine. He added a generous tip which the waiter keyed in, then he punched in his pin. He and Catherine had still not spoken. He couldn't, and it seemed neither could she. Words were unnecessary. Only one thing mattered now. Holding each other.

As soon as they were outside the restaurant, he took her hand, surprised how small and delicate it felt in his. He pulled her into the first shop doorway they passed, took her in his arms and whispered into her hair as he hands caressed her back.

'Catherine...I...My God. I've never before felt such a connection with somebody. You overwhelm me.'

Her body quivered as his hands continued to move down her back and he pulled her closer to him. She gasped as their bodies pressed against each other and he knew she felt his arousal, which had been immediate and urgent. Her hands gripped his back and she pulled him even more tightly against her as if she was desperate for his body to invade hers.

As her breathing quickened, he moved his hands to lift

her head and stared into her eyes. They glowed with passion and desire, yet they held the same vulnerability and confusion he'd seen earlier, as if she didn't comprehend what was happening to her. Perhaps things were moving too fast and he should slow the pace down, although he had no idea if his body would allow him to do that. He'd never wanted a woman as badly as he wanted this one. He wanted to possess her, in every possible way.

'Clayton.' As she said his name those glowing eyes burned into his. Her pale skin was flushed, and he glanced down at her lips which trembled as they parted. As he looked into her eyes again her gaze dropped to his mouth. He pulled her closer to him, lowered his head and started to kiss her.

Later, neither of them would be able to remember how long that first kiss lasted but within seconds of their mouths meeting they were devouring each other with a hunger they both confessed they had never experienced before.

Eventually Catherine pulled back and spoke, her voice shaking. 'I...I don't know what's happening to me. This is not what I do. I feel like I'm spiralling out of control.'

He smiled and took her face in both his hands. 'Then we're both spiralling, and you should get used to it. This will be happening a lot.'

He bent to kiss her again, but she put her finger on his mouth and pulled back from him.

'Clayton, wait. I'm...I'm sorry. But this...you...it overwhelms me. I don't want to stop, but we should. I need to think. Please understand. This intensity, it's...it's something I didn't expect.'

His hand stroked her face. 'Me neither, although I should have done. I wanted this...you...from the moment I first saw you at the conference. You hit me like a tidal wave. I thought you were special then Catherine, now I know you are. As special as it gets.'

'I feel the same, but it's scary. And I've got so much else going on in my life at the moment that I haven't even begun to explain to you. Give me some thinking time please.'

'I will, but I can't promise how long. I'll be desperate to call you.' He grinned at her then bent his head to give her a brief kiss. 'And you must promise me something. Don't over-think this, please.'

She clasped her hands around the back of his neck and leaned into his shoulder as she spoke. 'I won't. I promise I won't. And I'll call you.'

'OK. Then let's find you a taxi, before my body insists I change my mind.'

He took her hand as they walked to the next junction and he hailed the first yellow light.

As he opened the door for her to climb into the back of the black cab, he raised her hand to his mouth and kissed it.

'Goodnight Catherine. Sleep well.'

She gave the driver her hotel address then turned to close the door and wish Clayton goodnight, but he'd disappeared into the Friday night crowds.

Thirty minutes later Clayton lay on his bed. For a few seconds he wondered if he'd crashed out before going to meet her, and just woken up. Maybe this had all been a fantasy and tonight hadn't actually happened yet. But the taste and the touch of her were all too real. Catherine Preston had invaded all of his senses.

He knew he had to give her some time, although how long he could hold out before calling her he had no idea. He couldn't have found this woman to let her go without a fight. He glanced down as he felt his arousal return, remembering the taste and feel of her mouth. He wanted that mouth everywhere. If it was up to his body, he clearly wasn't going to be able to hold out very long.

He set his alarm and switched off the light. In the darkness he could still feel her body pressed against his, and images of her face flooded his mind. Despite his exhaustion after a long week, he suspected he wouldn't sleep.

Twenty minutes west of him, lying in her hotel bed and staring at the flickering light bulb in its cheap garish fitting, neither could Catherine.

CHAPTER THIRTY-SIX

Clayton woke with a pounding headache to the sound of his phone alarm ringing way too loud. He had no recall of setting it and no idea how long he'd slept, but he guessed not long. Images of Catherine, interspersed with those of Becca and Max, had dominated his night and they were still there, competing for centre stage in his head. The beautiful but vulnerable woman he knew for certain he was in love with, the carefree smile of the daughter he adored, and the sneering smile of his twin.

Max. How could Catherine have confused them? He hoped he was nothing like his brother. At least not where it mattered - beneath the surface. Telling Catherine about him had brought back memories from ten years ago. That first meeting in the prison, when Max had taken no time at all to tell him their mother was dead and good riddance to her. How she deserved the horribly undignified end she had endured, limbs out of control and her mind even more addled than it had always been. He left Clayton in no doubt that he'd felt no love for her, calling her a waste of space who should never have been a mother. According to Max, whatever he had become, she'd made him that way.

When Clayton had suggested, to his own surprise, that maybe he was being too tough on her - surely giving birth to them counted for something - Max had slammed one fist on the table and held the other one up to Clayton. Two prison officers appeared within seconds, but Clayton waved them away.

'It's OK. It's my fault. I brought up a sensitive subject, but we're fine now.'

With a warning to Max that a repetition would end the visit, the officers walked away. As soon as they were gone, he assumed the sneering expression Clayton was to see so often in the subsequent ten years.

'Hey bro, she dumped you without a backward glance, didn't she? So why the fuck are you defending her? Mind you, trust me, she did you a favour mate. Looks like you got the best deal. Bet you got all the things a kid could want right? I wound up with her shit. So if you've come here feeling sorry for yourself and expecting me to apologise for being the one she chose, forget it. Remember which one of us is banged up in here.'

And so it had begun. A relationship - if it could be called that - where Clayton never stopped feeling guilty for the opportunities he'd had, that Max hadn't. A relationship where he constantly felt he owed his brother some payback.

He assumed responsibility for him when he left prison, setting him up in a decent flat that he paid for, in a different part of town where nobody knew his twin's history. With that, a makeover, and new clothes, he'd hoped Max would make a fresh start. He messaged him weekly and they met monthly for a meal. They were never pleasant evenings and the atmosphere was always strained. Max was unpredictable. Sometimes he would spend the entire evening giving monosyllabic answers to Clayton's questions, or simply shrugging his responses. Other times he would talk non-stop about himself, obviously high from his latest addiction, and dressed in an outfit Clayton doubted the monthly allowance he paid could run to. Eventually he decided not to delve into how Max found the money for his more expensive indulgences. As long as the law didn't catch up with his brother's activities he didn't want or need to know. Over the past ten years he'd regularly expected a call from the police to tell him his brother was in custody, but the call never came. Max had presumably learned a few extra tricks about playing the system from his prison buddies.

For Clayton no news was good news. He kept a watching eye, which his self-imposed guilt and a sense of duty compelled him to do, but he kept Max at arms' length. Apart from Malcolm nobody had even met him. And that had only happened once. Ironically, given why he'd set out to find his twin in the first place, Max had refused point blank to help him with his research or even to discuss Huntington's disease.

Clayton told Becca only that he'd discovered his brother's existence and they kept in occasional touch by letter but had decided never to meet. He hated lying to her, but he didn't want his daughter dragged into the murky pool of Max's world.

She was disappointed, telling him how cool it was to have an uncle who was her father's identical twin. Clayton smiled whenever she said it, but privately found it anything but cool. In ten years he'd never got used to looking at Max and seeing a man who could be him.

Now he faced the fact that Catherine had initially thought he was. Last night he'd seen the funny side of that, but in the cold light of day, underslept and with a pounding headache, it made him uncomfortable.

He glanced at his watch. Time for his morning call to

Becca. He needed a black coffee and a paracetamol first. He wondered how Catherine felt this morning. He was desperate to call her but knew he shouldn't. Her message had been clear that he should wait for her to call him.

Fortified with caffeine he picked up his phone. He'd talk to Becca then take a quick shower before driving to the lab. Hopefully work would distract him and give him the extra willpower he needed not to call Catherine. In the few short rings it only ever took for his daughter to answer his calls, he made another decision.

He didn't want Catherine to meet Max. The thought made him uneasy. Maybe because Max had seen her beautiful face first, through the most ironic of online coincidences. Maybe because he'd always kept his brother in a separate compartment from the rest of his life. Whatever the reason, he was determined to keep him away from her.

She was still in his mind thirty minutes later as he reversed out of his parking bay to drive to the lab. He needed to connect with her. If he couldn't call her, he would at least message her.

He stopped mid-manoeuvre, picked up his phone and started typing.

CHAPTER THIRTY-SEVEN

Catherine opened her eyes and squinted against the flickering overhead light. She must have fallen asleep with it still on. She hugged the pillow to herself, wishing it was Clayton Mortimer. If she hadn't called a halt to things last night, she imagined it would have been. Now she regretted that decision and couldn't think of anything she wanted more than to wake up next to him.

She reached for her phone to check if he'd messaged and was surprised to see she'd slept till just past 10 a.m. She had a list of notifications but nothing from him. She swallowed down the disappointment that rose up in her, then told herself to stop being stupid and unfair. '*You asked him to give you some time. You can hardly blame him when he respects that.*'

And she had an investigation to get back to. Hopefully George would be calling later to let her know he'd made progress on the CCTV footage they were anxious to examine, and she planned to call Lizzie to ask what, if anything, she knew about Richard Cameron's connection with Adam.

But first she needed to wake herself up and get Clayton

Mortimer out of her head. She decided to go into the west end. The anonymity of blending in with the Saturday crowds might make filing him away for another day easier than the solitude of her room would, and she could make her calls there before meeting up with George.

After shivering through a quick shower in the cold bathroom she threw on jeans and a sweatshirt. She looked round the spartan hotel room, telling herself again she should find somewhere else to live. She needed more comfort and this place was hardly ideal for entertaining Clayton. There he was again, invading her thoughts. She grabbed her bag, keys and both phones. She needed to get out.

As she stood in line at the nearest coffee shop her phone pinged a message alert and she smiled when his name came up on screen. She found an empty table and opened the message.

Hi. Hope I'm not breaking the rules,
but I wanted to check in and see how you are.
Sleep OK?'

Breaking the rules? This man could break as many as he liked. She typed a reply.

'I'm fine thanks.
Having first caffeine fix.
Slept so so.
Bit preoccupied...can't imagine why...
something to do with shop doorways...
How about you?'

'Much the same.
I promise to do better than a
shop doorway next time.'

'Really know how to show
a girl a good time huh?
Assuming there'll be a next time?'

'There has to be.
But I won't rush you.
You're worth waiting for.'

'Your homework won't suffer will it?'

'Can't promise that.
Teacher won't be pleased.'

'Tell her I'll write a letter.'

'Lol. Gtg...sorry.
Early meeting. Laters....baby.
(Well that worked for the
50 Shades bloke...so I'm told).'

'You'll be telling me
you've got a red room next!!!....
Have a good mtg'.

'Nope. More of a neutrals man.
Hope that doesn't disappoint!
Have a great day xxxx'

'You too Mr Neutrals. Cxxxx'

She was still smiling about their exchange ten minutes later as she walked down the steps of the tube station. Their connection was so powerful, so why had she backed off last night? For a moment he'd looked hurt and she hated that thought.

She heard the echoing roar of the train approaching, ran down the steps of the escalator and jumped onto it before the doors closed. She grabbed a hand rail as the train quickly picked up speed and tried to distract herself with the adverts which lined the carriage walls.

She got off at Trafalgar Square, sat beside one of the fountains, and reflected on how much she had missed London over the years - its perpetual motion, its pulsating heartbeat. She hated the tragic circumstances that had brought her back, but it felt right being part of it again. And now she had another reason to love it. It was Clayton's city. How different life might have been if she'd never left. Maybe she would have found him sooner. Instead, she'd found the perfect man at the most imperfect time. She could only hope he'd give her the space to finish what she'd started for Adam and be there for her when this was over.

She moved to a quiet spot where she wouldn't be overheard. Before she called Lizzie, she decided to do some more research on Richard Cameron, and googled his name. There were several entries about him. She thought he looked smug in all his photographs, which reminded her again why she hadn't liked him, but he was undeniably regarded as a leading authority in his field. He was an established adviser to the pharmaceutical industry, but details were sketchy, which surprised her.

Lizzie answered her call almost immediately, with a hesitant 'Hello?'

'Lizzie, hi, it's me.'

'Sorry, took me a moment to realise it was you calling from the new number. How are you?'

She was tempted to tell Lizzie about her meeting with

Clayton, but immediately dismissed the idea. 'Had a late start but I'm fine thanks. How are you feeling today?'

'I'm OK. Some days are better than others, but it helps that you're here, and I know I have to get on with life. Adam would expect that of me, and I can't let him down.'

'You won't, and you never did. You two had something so special together.'

'We did, I was lucky. Remember there's someone special out there for you too Catherine, and you have to find him.'

Catherine smiled into her phone. 'Actually, I might have some news for you on that front. But now's not the time.'

'Yes! At last, I knew it. I could hear it in your voice. Hearing that makes me feel better. Tell me about him, please. I want to know everything.'

Catherine laughed at Lizzie's excited reaction. It seemed she had been right to tell her. 'You will, although it's early days and I'm still getting to know him myself. I'll tell you more when I see you, but... he's a great guy, I really like him and I keep thinking about him...and... shit, I'm gabbling. This gushing girly stuff is so not me is it?'

'Never has been, and maybe it's about time it was. Let's have some good news alongside all the bad, and don't over-think this Catherine. Nothing wrong with letting your heart rule your head for once. He must be quite a guy to have caused this reaction.'

'He is, but it's complicated. I met him at the genetics conference, which gave George and I a couple of leads which I need to tell you about. Which also means I have to put him out of my head for the moment.' She paused. 'Right man, wrong time, I guess. Anyway, change of subject. I need your help on something to do with Adam.'

'Ask me anything but promise me something too. Don't lose the right man because of all this, please. Adam wouldn't want that, and you're entitled to some time off to live your life, Catherine.'

'I know, and I won't, because if he's the right man he'll understand and wait for me, Lizzie. Now, back to business. Does the name Richard Cameron ring a bell? He's a top cardiologist. I met him briefly at the conference and I recognised him from somewhere. I'm actually fairly certain I saw him at the funeral, but didn't meet him, which is odd because you pretty much introduced me to everybody who was there. My recall is he stayed in the background. I wondered what you knew about him and his connection with Adam?'

'Richard Cameron. The name doesn't ring any bells, but then Adam came into contact with so many people, and I only met a fraction of them, most of those briefly. Describe him for me.'

'Tall, slim, supercilious-looking type. Arrogant as soon as he speaks. I'll send you some online photos of him. If inspiration strikes, call me on this number, or email me from that family account Adam set up. Let me know anywhere else you might have seen him with Adam too.'

'I will. You think he's connected with all this in some way?'

'I've nothing concrete to go on. In fact, to be honest George and I are going round in circles, but I had a feeling about this guy when I saw him. It may be nothing, but I want to check him out.'

'Your feelings about people and situations have a track record of hitting the spot. Let me see what I can come up with. Dammit, the office phone's ringing, better take it. I'll get back to you soon, OK?'

'Good. Go. Catch you later.'

Catherine closed her eyes and thought about Richard Cameron, forcing his image to block out Clayton's. Why did she suspect he was involved in all this? She hoped Lizzie would be able to throw some light Adam's connection with him, and that George might discover something if he could get close to him via Susie.

As if on cue her phone rang. It was George.

'Hi. How's my partner in crime?'

She laughed. 'Don't you mean your partner against crime? Did you get hold of the CCTV footage?'

'I called in a few favours, and I'll have something early evening. Why don't you come over to my place around 7-ish?'

'Sure, message me the address. By the way, I spoke with Lizzie. Richard Cameron's name means nothing to her, but I've sent her some photos of him and we'll see if they trigger anything.'

'Not much more we can do at the moment then.'

'I guess not. It frustrates me though.'

'Why don't you play tourist for a while? Change of scene can focus the mind. Or pay your hot professor a surprise visit. How was dinner by the way? Actually...no, save that update for this evening. Incoming phone call from my mother; better take it.'

Catherine laughed, 'Go. See you later and tell you all then.'

As soon as she rang off, she felt at a loose end and frustrated. The truth about Adam was out there, somewhere. Why was it proving so difficult to get any closer to finding it?

It was almost lunchtime. She wasn't hungry but decided she'd grab something light then head to the British Library, sign up as a reader, and use the time to research recent articles about genetics research and Galen.

She emerged from the library as the weak winter sun finally

dipped, the street lights took over, and London began its transformation from workday frenzy to evening party capital. Her research had been interesting but produced nothing concrete and her feet ached from her long day as she walked down towards the Embankment, wanting to lose herself in the energy of the Thames, London's aorta and lifeblood.

She shivered against more than the evening chilliness as she relived the previous night's encounter with Clayton. The chemistry and desire had been instant, mutual, overpowering and impossible to deny.

She knew that's why she'd hesitated. She was shocked by the intensity of her reaction to him. She'd never felt anything like it before. She remembered her conversation with Nina only weeks ago, and her admission that the thought of intimacy after all these years alone scared her. Now here she was on the brink of it.

Lizzie had encouraged her to embrace and enjoy it, and as she thought about Clayton and the vulnerability he'd shown her, she knew she mustn't allow herself to hesitate any longer. She had fallen instantly in love with him and she couldn't lose him, even if the circumstances might not make this easy. She'd waited long enough to find him, and she wasn't going to wait any longer. He deserved the same honesty he'd shown her, and to know how she felt. She reached the Strand and paused as she typed a message to him.

> *'Hi. Thinking time over.*
> *I don't know what exactly this is between us,*
> *but it feels important.*
> *You're already important to me.*
> *Can we pick up where we left off please?*
> *Tomorrow? Cx'*

Within minutes he messaged back.

'Good. You're important to me too.
I need to show you how much.
But what's with tomorrow?
How about now?
Tell me where you are &
I'll pick you up.'

She grinned at her screen. In this outfit? He had to be kidding. Even if she wasn't committed to seeing George, she'd be passing on tonight. She started to think of a humorous reply when a TV screen in a shop window caught her eye. *Breaking News* it said, then the headline

CABINET SHOCK - HEALTH SECRETARY KILLED IN FREAK ACCIDENT

Her finger still hovered over her phone screen. She typed a quick reply to Clayton.

'So sorry, would love to, but can't tonight.
Something urgent to attend to.
Nothing to do with us but need to go.
Will message later. Cxxx

Then, in disbelief, she tried to google the full story as she hailed a taxi. Clayton messaged again as she gave the driver her hotel details.

'Let me know you're OK Catherine.
Call if you need me.
Talk later.'

As she settled in the taxi and, in spite of the shock news, smiled at his concern, her phone rang. Not surprisingly, it was George.

CHAPTER THIRTY-EIGHT

'Catherine, where are you? Have you heard the news about Charles Sedgwick?'

'A few minutes ago. I saw the TV headline, but I haven't read any of the details yet.'

'Jump in a cab and come to my place. I just got in. I'm sending you the exact address now.'

Her phone pinged. 'Got it, and I'm in one. I'll call you back.' She changed her instructions to the cabbie who executed a perfect, if illegal, U-turn at the next lights and headed towards Docklands. She skim-read the BBC news report on her phone then rang George back. 'On my way. Should be there in about twenty minutes. I've read the BBC story. So, it was a car accident?'

'Yes. No more details released yet, only that he and his driver are believed to have died instantly and that no other vehicles seem to have been involved. Until there's anything more to say the news channels are focussing on Sedgwick's career and his family. Apparently he remarried two years ago and had twins a year old who both have health problems.'

'God, how awful. His wife must be devastated.'

'I know. They've mentioned Adam a few times of course.'

'Saying what?'

'That it's a tragic coincidence. For both families obviously, but politically too. The Deputy PM's being interviewed now, saying what a blow this is to the PM and to the health agenda, losing two key players in such rapid succession.'

'You know how I feel about coincidences George.'

'I certainly do. I'm glad you're coming over Catherine. You shouldn't be on your own. This will be difficult for you, seeing all the Adam stuff replayed.'

'Even more awful for Lizzie. When I spoke to her this morning about Richard Cameron she sounded so much brighter, but I don't know what this news will do to her. I'll see you shortly.'

She sat back, closed her eyes and thought about Adam. She missed him so much. What a loss he had been to so many people. Ironically, the death of his boss would have created an opportunity for him, but not the way Adam would have wanted it. He had never spoken to her much about his relationship with the Secretary of State, but she sensed he liked him as a man. She was less sure how he'd regarded him professionally. The email he sent her before his death had told her to trust nobody. Had that comment extended to his boss? Yet again she wondered who the 'Not even my' at the end referred to. The PS he'd started to type, before he felt ill and hit send. Had he been about to type 'my boss'?

Her thoughts were interrupted by the driver telling her they'd arrived and as the cab pulled up outside George's building she also wondered if the two of them would ever solve this puzzle.

The apartment was everything she had expected it to be. Modern, minimalist but comfortable, masculine but homely with every possible gadget and appliance, and the perfect home for George. Occupying one corner of the 32nd floor, the views from its floor-to-ceiling windows were stunning. It looked directly over Canary Wharf and the O2, which always reminded her of a giant birthday cake with candles around its edges, but tonight was the first time she'd seen the candles lit. George led her out to the balcony and smiled at her sharp intake of breath as she looked out over the City's lights.

'Wow George, it's mesmerising, and hypnotic. How do you ever stop looking at it?'

'It is and I love it. I know London's frantic, but I always feel peaceful looking out over this.'

'I can see what you mean. Down on the ground it is frantic, but up here it feels different, like another world.'

'Let's take our drinks outside to talk then. I'll whack the patio heater on.'

'That would be lovely.'

Warmed by hot coffee and enjoying the heater's glow, she accessed the news report on her phone again. 'Have there been any further updates on the accident since we spoke? The BBC are saying that, according to the police, the car went out of control on a bad bend.'

'Apparently the driver was very experienced. Maybe it's one of those tragic freak accidents.'

Catherine raised her eyebrows at him. 'Do you believe that?'

He shrugged. 'Not sure I know what to believe to be honest.'

'That's the frustration. We've got so many random strands here but we've no idea what links them, assuming that something does. Did you manage to get the CCTV footage? Let's hope that's some help.'

'I did, and I've taken a quick look, but nothing jumped out at me I'm afraid. It doesn't help that we don't know what we're looking for, and there was hardly anything to look at from the cameras in your Professor's building. Seems most of them weren't even working the day of the incident Susie told me about.'

Catherine raised her eyebrows. 'Not having much luck, are we? What about the Edinburgh fire?'

'Nothing I didn't expect to see. A bunch of demonstrators who turned up outside the place while the emergency services were dealing with the fire. There was some suspicion at the time that the whole thing was a sabotage attempt that went horribly wrong. Nothing concrete though and the police dropped their investigation. It got filed under accident.'

'Like the Secretary of State's death probably will too.'

George poured her another coffee and gave her a questioning look. 'So where do we go from here? What do we know about Adam's relationship with his boss by the way?'

'The answer to your second question is not a lot. I never got a chance to talk to him about work that much. On the first, I'll take a look at the CCTV before I leave. Worth another pair of eyes. And I'd like to know where Sedgwick stood on these NHS so-called advisory payments. The Telegraph haven't mentioned him much. How good are your contacts there?'

'There's a female reporter I sort of went out with once. I'll call her and make nice. See what I can find out.' He winked at her.

'Work the George charm again huh? Make sure you keep most of that for Susie. We need to keep close to her dad remember?'

'Seeing her tomorrow. I'm sure I can wangle an invite to the house. And talking of charm... How did your date go with Professor Charming?'

Catherine's cheeks tingled and she realised she must be blushing like a lovesick schoolgirl. 'He's extremely charming and he wants to meet up again. I told him I'd think about it. I like him. Rather a lot actually. But I'm worried about rushing into something too fast.' She looked up at him. 'And stop grinning like that. It probably won't go anywhere...'

He gave her a serious look. 'But I have a feeling you want it to. Give it a chance Catherine. Fast, slow, it doesn't matter. I think you're perfect for each other. I watched you at the conference and you seemed so right together.'

It was her turn to grin. 'Since when did you become such a romantic?'

'Don't laugh it off, I'm being serious. If this man can make you happy, go for it, don't fight it.'

She got up and gave him a hug. 'I'm so lucky to have you as a friend.' She released her hold and looked him in the eye. 'And you're right. I've been thinking about him all day but trying not to. This is hardly the time for romance, is it? I'm acting like some lovestruck idiot and it needs to stop, but truth is he's totally bloody perfect. But after waiting so long for somebody, I'm scared, and he's complicated. What if it all comes crashing down around me?'

He held her by the shoulders. 'Somehow I don't think it will, but it's a risk you've got to run. We all do, otherwise none of us would ever go into a relationship. Running away from something isn't your style, so don't run away from this. Whatever the complications are, and however bad the timing may seem, you'll deal with it.' He stood up to clear away their cups. 'Right. Now we've decided our next steps and got your love life sorted I'm going to fix you something to eat.'

'You mean you actually cook with those shiny appliances? I assumed they were purely there to impress.'

'You'll be pleasantly surprised at my culinary talents. Go and relax for five minutes and enjoy the view.' As he went inside, he turned around to her. 'And message the Professor. Pronto.'

She smiled as he headed towards his kitchen. She walked to the corner of the balcony and marvelled again at the magic of the city, which sprawled as if to infinity in front of her. The view was intoxicating, and it made her think of Adam, how much he loved London, and how much she missed him.

But it was Clayton she wanted to be drinking in the view with her.

She reached into her pocket, pulled out her phone and started typing a message to him.

Then she went inside, hit play and sat down to view the CCTV tape.

CHAPTER THIRTY-NINE

The shock news about Charles Sedgwick continued to dominate the news channels the following morning. Although she
and George were frustrated at the lack of concrete progress
they had made in their investigation, the more they'd talked
on his balcony the more they believed it was only a matter of
time until they did. They were convinced they were on to
something and the deaths of Sedgwick and Adam were
connected. George had called his Telegraph contact and
arranged to take her to lunch. They hoped she could provide
some background on the Health Secretary which might give
them a lead.

Like George, she'd seen nothing in the Edinburgh fire
footage that helped them, and with nothing available from
Clayton's lab they couldn't even try to spot connections. It
seemed they kept hitting dead ends.

The thought of Clayton lifted her spirits. He'd rung her
again and she was meeting him for lunch. She'd spent the last
hour with one eye on the TV news and the other assessing
her limited wardrobe trying to decide what to wear. Eventually she settled on the pencil-slim skirt and white blouse she'd

worn to her first Guardian meeting. It had earned her a few admiring glances that day and she hoped he would like it. When she'd bought it on their shopping trip, Nina had called it 'sexy without being too obvious.'

She pulled out the black heels that Nina had also insisted she buy. She'd been tempted to dismiss the stilettos as impractical when Nina suggested them, but she knew they emphasised the shape of her legs. Her gaze shifted to the bed and her nerves went into overdrive as she imagined inviting Clayton back here and the two of them being in it. There was only one person who could calm her down. She called Nina who answered on the second ring.

'Well, about time! I've been dying to phone you and ask how it went the other night, but I thought you might still be loved-up with Mr Perfect. So, tell all please. Was he hot?'

Catherine laughed at Nina's excitement which immediately helped her nerves. 'Yes, he's hot, but a lot more besides. I like him Nina. I mean, I really like him. He's in my head, all the time, and it's ridiculous. This is so not like me, and I need to focus on work.'

'Sounds to me like you've fallen for him. Talk about going from nought to sixty in record time. He must have been good.' She laughed, then paused. 'But seriously, how was it? I mean, after what you told me...after all this time? Were you nervous? What did you wear? Sorry, lots of questions, but I'm excited for you.'

'Me too. And a bit shocked and overwhelmed. Still can't quite believe this is all happening. I wore the black dress to answer that question. And if by "it" you mean sex, we didn't. I didn't want to rush into it, and he respected that.'

'With you in that black dress? Surprised he could keep his hands off. Not gay, is he?'

'He's very definitely not that. No, I was the one who

pulled back. God knows why, I feel bloody stupid now, but I did.'

'You weren't thinking this no-sex-on-the-first-date nonsense, were you? We're in the twenty-first century Catherine. That waiting crap is old-think. Especially at our age.'

'Thank you for that reminder. I don't know what I was thinking. Truth is I got scared about the whole thing and freaked out a bit. I suppose that sounds ridiculous to you.'

Nina's tone softened. 'No, it doesn't, not given your history. Did you tell him how long you've been hibernating? He sounds like the kind of guy you can be honest with.'

'Not in so many words, but I did tell him I've never been seriously involved with anyone. And I was all over him like a rash one minute and backing off the next, so I think he guessed. He's smart, maybe the smartest person I've ever met. Brilliant sense of humour too.'

'It sounds like you found your Mr Perfect Catherine. I hear it in your voice. What did I tell you? I didn't expect it to happen quite this fast, but I'm thrilled for you, you deserve this, it's been long enough arriving. But you need to stop being scared of it. When are you seeing him again?'

'Today. We're meeting for lunch.'

'Wow, Sunday lunch! It could lead anywhere with the whole of the rest of the day at your disposal. This could be showtime. Do you feel more ready for it now? Don't deny yourself what you want Catherine and don't let your head get in the way of what the rest of you is telling you. Please. You're ready for this, and you're ready for this man.'

'Of course I'm not ready. He'll think I'm a naïve idiot. I won't know what the hell I'm doing, I'll be a disappointment to him and...'

'You'll be no such thing so stop being stupid. You obviously want this man, so go with the flow and enjoy it. Enjoy him.'

'I do want him, but...'

Nina cut across her. 'No buts. If he's the man you say he is he'll understand you're nervous, so don't be afraid to tell him. I'm not the person who needs to know what you're feeling, he is. When it happens it'll be great, trust me, but...'

'So much for no buts. And but what?'

'There might be some practical issues. At least the first time.'

'What the hell are you talking about? What sort of practical issues? You got me calmer and now you're freaking me out again.'

'Don't freak out. I mean he'll need to take his time with you, which is why you should tell him.'

Catherine remembered the look on his face when he'd shared his secrets with her. How vulnerable he'd looked. She wasn't the only one with some demons to lay to rest here. Nina was right. She had to be honest with him, about everything. As he had been with her.

'You're right. And I will tell him. I think he's a man I can say anything to. Thank you.'

'Then you're lucky. He's special, and today will be special, I know it will. I want news later, OK? I'll give you till tomorrow, but don't you dare not message me in the morning.'

'As if. You have to come down here as soon as I've got a proper place sorted. I miss you.'

'Same here. Now go and get ready. Knock his socks off kiddo. I know you will.'

'Bye Nina.' Catherine smiled as they ended the call. Life was bittersweet. She'd lost such a good friend in Adam, but she told herself how lucky she was. A wonderful son in Will, the best friend possible in Nina and now, she hoped, after so long, the most amazing man in Clayton.

She took a look round the hotel room. Perhaps not the best place to invite him back to, but it would have to do. She looked at her watch. Enough time to go out and stock up the mini fridge, which just about functioned, with some wine and food before she got ready.

She typed him a quick message telling him she couldn't wait to see him, then grabbed her bag and headed for the door.

CHAPTER FORTY

Clayton was waiting for her when she arrived at the restaurant two hours later. He'd chosen a small French bistro in Kensington and she loved it the moment she walked in. Intimate and quirky, she imagined it becoming their go to place. She irrationally hoped he hadn't brought lots of other women here.

He stood the instant he saw her. This time she didn't shake hands but threw her arms around him. Their kiss was tender but brief as the waiter hovered to seat her. Their table at the back was quiet and intimate, as if they had the place to themselves.

'This is lovely Clayton. Have you been here a lot?'

He smiled at her. She suspected he knew the real meaning behind her question. 'First time, and I like it too. A colleague recommended it. And talking of lovely, so are you.'

She smiled back as the waiter returned with menus, water and the house wine Clayton had ordered. As they both decided on the chef's recommendation of the day, she relaxed into her seat, feeling the same intimate connection with the man sitting opposite that she had the other night. Nina was right, he was special.

'Thank you for the compliment. Looking good yourself Professor. So how was your morning? How's the research going?'

He paused briefly and glanced around. His fingers twirled the stem of his glass, as if he needed the reassurance of a familiar object while he considered his answer. When he spoke, it was almost a whisper. 'I can hardly believe I'm saying these words…after all this time…but I think I'm on the verge of a breakthrough Catherine.' He paused, still watching his own fingers on the glass, then looked up at her, his face serious but expressionless.

She didn't speak. Instead she nodded encouragingly at him.

His fingers steadied on the glass. 'You know how long I've been working on this. How very…personal it is.' He paused again and looked straight at her. 'But at last I think I might be on to something.'

She smiled at him and touched his hand as his fingers made contact with hers. 'This sounds like wonderful news. I had a feeling you were further ahead than you implied at the conference.'

He raised his eyebrows at her. 'How could you possibly know that?'

'I don't know. Something in the way you looked and how you spoke. As if you were choosing your words carefully. Not wanting to give too much away.'

His seriousness gave way to a broad grin. 'Sometimes I think you can see right into my head. Yes, I'm working in a sensitive area, on lots of levels. And as I say to my team, in research there are a lot of false dawns. You think something might work then it goes nowhere. This might go nowhere.'

'But you don't think that do you?'

'There you go again. No, this time I don't. And if I'm right this could be the game changer we all thought was years away.'

She almost whispered her next question. 'Are you talking about finding a cure for Huntington's Disease?'

'Cure is a brave word, but effectively yes, that's where this new discovery would eventually lead us. Without giving you the whole technical speech, we may have found the way we can silence the faulty gene which causes Huntington's. Effectively stop it in its tracks before it leads to disease symptoms. We've known for some time how that should be done theoretically, but the problem has been how to deliver the solution practically. We may have solved that. And more.'

'Clayton that's incredible, you must be so excited. What a leap forward. Please, tell me more about how it works. I can cope with some of the science bit, or I'll try to, if you're happy to share it with me.'

'I'm happy to share everything with you. I'm not used to having someone I can share any of this with.' He looked directly into her eyes. 'But I'm pleased I do now and talking about it makes it come more alive somehow. Makes me stop feeling like a lab rat.'

'You don't look remotely like any kind of rat. So, tell me more about gene silencing.'

'It effectively means we intervene between DNA and RNA. RNA is like DNA's messenger. It sends signals to cells to produce proteins. Good and bad. When it sends a message to produce the protein that leads to Huntington's it's bad obviously.'

'So, you silence the messenger? Sorry, that makes it sound easy.'

'Don't apologise. Conceptually so many things in science are easy. In this case the challenge is in delivering the silencing treatment, but I hope we're on our way to nailing it. Time will tell as we keep testing the theories.'

'And what did you mean earlier when you said there was more?'

'The more is the real game changer. Editing the faulty gene out completely. I think this development will also lead us to that, and quite soon.'

'You mean the brave new world stuff you were talking about. Editing the genome. Yes?'

'Precisely that. You see, with gene silencing the DNA mutation is still there. We simply limit what it can do by stopping RNA sending the bad protein message. But with editing we tackle the DNA directly. We cut out the faulty parts and insert good ones. Like you cutting and pasting when you're writing.'

'Except rather more challenging.'

'The challenge has been the cutting part. We've known how to paste DNA into a strand for some time, but the cutting always eluded us. And that's the breakthrough leap, if we can keep making this method work, and I think maybe we can.'

'My God, Clayton. If you're right, then this is...I'm not sure what word to use... monumental in its significance. What an achievement for you and your team. They must all be thrilled to be part of it.'

'Actually, apart from Susie none of them knows how close we are.'

Catherine gave him a puzzled look. 'I don't understand. I thought you had several researchers. Why don't the others know?'

'Sorry, I didn't explain properly how we work.' He paused as the waiter returned with their starter, a sharing platter, then nodded his thanks and told Catherine to eat. 'Our area is so specialised, everybody tends to focus on one particular aspect, and I pull it all together. Susie's the only one I've shared the totality with, and that was by accident. She was helping me with my conference prep, and in the process I told her what the latest computer model showed. I suppose I needed to share it with somebody.' He looked at her and smiled. 'I didn't have you then. Or I might never have told Susie.'

Catherine smiled back at him. 'I'm flattered by that and flattered that you've shared it with me now. Now eat please, before I demolish this entire starter single-handedly. I assume you need to keep the possibility of this breakthrough under wraps until you're sure. I really liked Susie by the way.'

'Yes, she's great. A real asset. And I do have to keep this confidential, for a whole host of reasons. When...if...the time comes it will cause a major stir in the genetics world. And I have to protect the interests of my sponsors.'

'ANZ Pharmaceuticals yes?

'Yes. They have a massive amount riding on this, and they're not one of the biggest players. You probably picked up on that at the conference.'

'Yes, I know there's a group of three companies who are way out there as the market leaders and I know they have huge investments at stake in research. But very much geared to a treatment solutions strategy as I understood from the Galen pitch. What you're talking about would change that whole landscape wouldn't it?' She paused as she realised the significance of that question.

'If a cure starts to look viable then yes, it would. I doubt I'd be on Paul Naylor's Christmas card list, put it that way. Or the other two corporate giants in the gang of three.'

'I have some idea of the amounts at stake. And the lead time for the development of drugs before the investment pays off. Any change in direction that cuts across that would have major financial consequences. Especially for the gang of three as you call them.'

'You're very well-informed Catherine, and absolutely right. I've been so involved in the science of all this, and my personal agenda, I never stopped to think what the consequences of success would be. Now I'm this close I guess I have to think about it. I realise a lot of people will be hostile, and not only the ones with a vested financial interest. The ethics brigade will be all over it too; telling me I'm tampering with the natural order of things no doubt.' His hand clenched beneath hers. 'Even when the natural order sucks.'

As she had before when she knew he was struggling with his thoughts and emotions, she squeezed his hand before she spoke. 'I'm not sure that as a scientist you should worry about the consequences of success Clayton. Your job is to find solutions to problems. Society has to decide how to deal with the options you give it. Surely that's been the case with every scientific or medical advancement.'

'Yes, but people are especially sensitive about interventions in genetics, I understand that. DNA makes us what we are. It's at our core. They don't trust scientists with it.'

'They're distrustful because they don't understand it. I felt the same way until I heard you and others, but especially you, talking at the conference. Ignorance always breeds fear and you can't let others' fears stand in your way.'

She felt his hand relax, then he grinned at her. 'As ever you say the right thing. Anyway, you're up to date now, so enough work talk. At least, enough talk about my work. I want to hear about yours.'

CHAPTER FORTY-ONE

Catherine looked away from his expectant expression, took a sip of water and twiddled with her napkin. The time had come to tell him the truth about how and why their two worlds had collided.

She began with Adam's death, hardly believing how recent and raw it still was. An hour later he knew everything, from Adam's email on the morning he died and the investigation it had led her into, to her conviction that his death was linked to that of the Health Secretary. She paused before she mentioned Cerberus, then decided she shouldn't withhold anything from this man, including her suspicions about the group she was convinced were behind the name.

Like her, he was a good listener and he let her speak without interruption. When she'd finished, he put his hand over hers and spoke quietly. 'Catherine, that's... quite a story. I guess our worlds really have collided. And fairly dramatically.'

She gave him a questioning look. 'You're not sure you agree with my suspicions though, are you? You think I'm getting carried away.'

'Catherine, I don't think you're remotely the type to get carried away, you're way too intelligent and analytical. But you've hit me with a lot here. I'm still processing what you told me. I am certain of one thing though. You need to be careful. This payments issue is one thing. I suspected it went on even before I saw the Telegraph article and I don't like it. I can't be too precious about it though because I'm a researcher and we all need funding. But I'm a purist too. I also want a level playing field and I don't like anything that compromises impartiality. It needs to be looked into and sorted out.' He paused, looked directly at her and his tone became more serious. 'But this other stuff's in a different league. Deaths, sabotage, break-ins. It scares me to think you're running risks getting involved in it all. Leave it to the authorities. Please.'

'And let it all go unchecked? With everything filed under accident and unfortunate coincidences? How can I do that after what Adam asked me to do?'

His hand clenched on the table. 'Maybe he shouldn't have asked you. If his suspicions ran as deep as you're suggesting he must have known the risks this would expose you to.'

'It's not something he would have done lightly Clayton, so he obviously believed he had no choice. And remember he felt unwell as he wrote that message. Hardly surprising as it turned out.' Her eyes filled up as she imagined those last few minutes of Adam's life. 'I have to live with the fact that one of my closest friends, who I loved dearly, died as he tried to send me an email. It's an image that haunts me, and maybe it always will. But maybe finishing what he started might help me deal with it. So please don't have a go at him. Or me.'

'I'm sorry. Maybe I went too far, but only because I'm concerned. I can tell how important he was to you. Incidentally I heard him in action a few times and he impressed me a lot, as a scientist and as a politician. I think he would've gone on to great things.' He put his hand on hers. 'He's a real loss, and I understand how much this must hurt you.'

Her voice softened as she replied. 'Thank you for saying all that. You would have liked him as a man too...' She smiled, imagining these two men together. '...and he would have liked you. I wish you could have met.'

He clasped both her hands between his. 'I do too. I'm sorry I lost it a bit there, but I don't want you running risks. I need you to promise me something. That you'll tell me every-thing you're planning to do on any of this from now on, before you do it. You don't go it alone; you've got me now.'

She gave him a mock salute. 'Aye aye Sir.'

'I'm serious Catherine. If Adam was the man I think he was, he'd expect nothing less of me than to say that.'

'I promise I'll be careful. But you have to promise me you'll be careful too. If I'm right, and Cerberus are behind this, then they're going to try and derail you if they sense how close you are to threatening their interests.'

'There's no way they could know. Only Susie knows and I trust her totally.'

'I would trust her too, but I have to ask this. Is it possible she said something to her father? Innocently maybe, but to grab his attention and make him proud of her? She seems desperate for his approval.'

'She is, but I'd bet my life that she hasn't said anything to him. She wouldn't, she knows what's at stake. Which means, unless your mysterious Cerberus are hacking my system, they can't know.'

'But you did have an incident shortly before the confer-ence I understand. Unauthorised access to your computer?'

'Let me guess. Susie mentioned it to George.' Catherine nodded. 'Then you also know I concluded it was an oversight by one of the team, which is still the most likely explanation.'

'Despite everything else I've told you?' Catherine felt irritation rising within her. Why did he not see the dangers lurking that she did? Or was she seeing demons in the shadows? Part of her hoped so, but she was certain she wasn't. 'I think you're in danger Clayton. You have to be on your guard. Please.'

He reached for her hand again. 'Catherine. You know how I'm starting to feel about you. More than that, I've never respected anybody's intellect as much as I respect yours and if you're concerned, I'm concerned. So I'll be on my guard. For both of us.' He smiled at her. 'But now let's take a break from all this. I can think of things I'd far rather be doing with you than talking about death and corporate espionage.'

Her stomach somersaulted at the way he looked at her. She remembered Nina's words earlier. She deserved to enjoy this man. Nothing should get in the way of that. Somehow she managed a shaky 'I agree.'

He paid the bill as she freshened up in the restroom and checked her appearance in its ornate mirrored walls. She emerged to find him waiting at the door and he took her hand. 'Let's have half an hour in the park. Walk lunch off. Sound OK?'

With his hand enveloping hers it sounded more than OK. As they walked, he let go of her hand, put his arm around her shoulder and pulled her in closer to him. She slipped her hand around his waist and felt the tautness of his muscles. His masculinity overwhelmed her. She wanted to abandon herself to this man in every possible way.

As if he read her thoughts, the moment they entered the park through its ornate iron gates he took her in his arms and whispered into her hair. 'What are you doing to me? I know you want to take this slowly, but I'm not sure I can. I want you and I need you.'

She tightened her grip around his waist and nestled into

his body. 'I thought I wanted slow Clayton, but not anymore. I want you too, so much. And I don't want to wait.'

He bent to kiss her, and her body moulded into his like molten metal as his gentleness became a frenzied exploration of her mouth. Her passion matched his and she clung on to him for support, weak and oblivious to anything but him. She barely heard his phone ringing until his body tensed as he reached into his pocket to try and shut it off. It refused to stop, and she pulled back from him. 'Clayton. You need to check that. It might be important.'

With one arm still around her he checked the caller. 'Damn it's the lab number. I'd better call back.'

He punched his phone to return the call as Catherine rested her head on his shoulder. He spoke quickly but she heard concern in his voice and felt his shoulders tense as he listened then replied with a short 'I'm on my way.' She lifted her head and gave him a questioning look.

'University security, telling me that somebody unautho-rised got into the lab and assaulted one of my researchers, Anna. Her phone and bag were taken. The medics have seen her and she's OK but shaken up. I need to go and see her.' He stroked her hair. 'I'm sorry.'

'Don't apologise. You must go, and I'm coming with you.' As he started to speak, she put her hand to his mouth. 'No arguments Clayton. Don't you see? It's beginning.'

As he drove, Catherine turned to him, frowning. 'It's a strange day and time to break in. High risk I'd have thought.'

'Not in a research college like ours. Even on a Sunday it's a busy building, people are coming and going all the time. A diverse bunch of people too. It would be easy for somebody to blend in, and I'm not sure our security's all it should be.'

She nodded. 'It doesn't sound it, but something else is

niggling me. Whoever broke in banked on this girl Anna being alone. Is that usual?'

'Not usual, no, but at certain times of the day it can happen. She's my only full-time team member. Everybody else is combining research with their study commitments. Susie said she'd be in this afternoon. Of course, normally I'd have been there. It's rare for me not to have lunch working in the lab, even on a Sunday.' He gave her his warm smile.

'So someone knows what the general pattern is. And they also knew you wouldn't be there. Who did you tell?'

He looked at her briefly as he turned into the university car park. 'Nobody. I only told Anna thirty minutes before I left to meet you.'

'Too late for somebody to have planned this. Whoever broke in had to have known your plans earlier and there's only one logical conclusion.'

'Then share the logic with me please. Like I said, I didn't speak to anybody earlier this morning about my plans. Apart from you.'

'That's the point. You spoke to me, Clayton. And somebody else knows exactly what we talked about.'

CHAPTER FORTY-TWO

They arrived at Clayton's lab to find Susie comforting Anna. Although the younger of the two women by several years, with much less work experience, it was clear she'd become used to taking charge in Clayton's absence and she had today. As she had been when they met at the conference, Catherine was impressed by her.

With her arm around Anna's shoulders she smiled a hello at Catherine then quickly brought Clayton up to date with the events of the last hour. She had arrived to find Anna slumped over her desk and confused about what had happened. She'd refused to be taken to hospital, but the university's on-site medical department had examined her, declared her shaken and groggy from her ordeal, but otherwise fine. Security had no evidence of suspicious activity on CCTV, and in response to Catherine's questions they'd been forced to admit it wasn't functioning as it should. Her handbag had been taken, along with her phone which had been on her desk. Apart from that nothing else appeared to have been disturbed, and Anna's recollection of events and her attacker was hazy.

Clayton nodded and mouthed his thanks to Susie, then moved to sit alongside Anna. He took both her hands in his. 'Anna, I'm so sorry about this, but we'll do everything we can to find the person responsible. I'm also going to insist security is beefed up around here. It's ridiculous there's no record of what happened.' He shot a glance at Catherine who nodded her agreement back.

Watching Anna become calmer as Clayton continued to hold her hands, Catherine smiled to herself. He seemed to have no idea of his effect on women. The young researcher already sounded more composed when she replied.

'I feel so stupid that I can't remember more. I poured myself a coffee, went out to the vending machine for chocolate, came back and ate it but...after that...nothing. Next thing I knew Susie had her arm round me. I think it must all have happened very quickly.'

Catherine walked over to Susie and spoke in a low voice. 'Do we know where the coffee cup is?'

The younger woman's eyes turned towards the coffee machine before she replied, keeping her tone low. 'I don't remember seeing a cup on Anna's desk. And there are only five over there. We have six.' She turned back to Catherine with a questioning look. 'Do you think...?'

'Maybe.' As Catherine replied she moved towards Anna and Clayton. She had to ask Anna the obvious question without frightening the girl any more than she already was. She took the chair on the other side of her and put her hand gently on her shoulder.

'Anna. I have to ask you this. The coffee. Did you finish it?'

'I don't remember. I ate my chocolate so I must have drunk some of it. I like them together. I don't remember putting my cup back though. Isn't it on the desk?'

Catherine gave Clayton a quick glance as she answered.

'No, it isn't, it seems to be missing. Anna, I think we have to assume someone tampered with your drink, which explains why you can't remember anything.'

'You mean drugged me? But I'd know surely? And I feel fine now. Wouldn't I still feel weird?'

'Not necessarily. There are some fast-acting substances around now. They knock you out quickly, but they leave your system quickly too and the newer ones are virtually untraceable.' She looked away from Anna, saw Clayton and Susie looking surprised, and grinned at them both. 'Research. I wrote an article on this recently.'

She turned back to Anna and clasped her hand again, not surprised the girl looked on the verge of tears, realising how vulnerable she'd been earlier. Catherine looked over at Clayton. 'It's time Anna went home. Sleep will help.'

Before he could reply, the laboratory phone rang. Susie answered it, turned to them and mouthed 'It's Security.' After listening for a few minutes, she thanked the caller, hung up and turned back to them. 'Apparently the police called with an update. They traced Anna's phone to a refuse bin, twenty minutes from here. SIM card still in it, which is kind of weird. They're testing for fingerprints.'

'They won't find any.' Catherine got up and walked to the coffee machine as she spoke. 'I don't know about anybody else, but I need one of these.'

Anna looked over at her. 'But it's not safe surely?'

Catherine smiled. 'Don't worry. This person knew what they were doing. The rest of this coffee will be perfectly safe.'

'I could use some of that myself.' Susie joined Catherine at the machine. 'And I'm interested in your theory about all this Catherine. You talk as if you don't think this was the work of some amateur opportunist thief. So, what do you think?'

'Susie.' It was Clayton. 'Let's leave this to the authorities for a while longer, please. I think Anna's had enough for the moment. I'm going to drive her home. I suggest we secure the lab and you go home too. Tomorrow's another day.'

He walked over to Catherine and put his arms round her as Anna slipped on her jacket.

'Will you be OK? Why don't you take a cab back to your hotel and I'll call you after I've dropped Anna off and spoken to her parents. She lives with them, so she won't be on her own.'

She gave him a brief kiss before answering. 'I'll be fine. You drive Anna home and we'll talk later.' She lowered her voice to a whisper. 'You do know we have to, don't you? You can't ignore what's happened here Clayton.'

'I know, and I won't ignore it. But do me a favour and make sure you both leave soon please.'

As soon as Clayton and Anna were gone, Susie turned to Catherine. 'I know Clayton wanted us to stop speculating in front of Anna, but you have a theory about all this don't you? What do you know that the rest of us don't?'

Catherine chose her words carefully. She didn't want to lie to this girl, but she didn't want to launch into a series of vague suspicions either. 'Nothing of any real substance about what's happened today. Trust me, I don't. Maybe it's the journalist in me, always looking for an angle.' She laughed as she looked at Susie. The sceptical face that looked back told her she hadn't fooled this girl for a second. She was way too smart for platitudes.

But the sceptical look became a smile. 'I've a feeling you and I are destined to become friends. I think we can read each other's minds. No, I'm not entirely convinced by that speech. But you figured that out already, right?'

'You got me. And yes, I want us to be friends too. Apart from anything else we share a joint purpose. We both want to protect Clayton and the work you're doing here. I know you guys are in the verge of some great things.'

'Yes, it seems we might be. He's a special man, but from the way you look when you talk about him, I don't need to tell you that. And if he's told you about these recent developments, he thinks you're special too. He's always so private. He never shares what we're doing here with anybody.'

'I know. I'm flattered he told me.'

'You think this break-in is connected with our work, don't you? Nothing to do with a mobile phone and a handbag. But nothing's been disturbed. No machines seem to have been tampered with. No papers moved or taken. If someone's spying on us, which I assume is what you're suggesting, then it doesn't look like they learned very much. Frankly most of our stuff would look like gobbledegook to anybody other than an expert in our field.'

'I understand that. Whoever did this isn't giving us much to go on, so let's see what the next couple of days bring. Perhaps the police investigation will uncover something, or Anna will remember more when she's had chance to rest.' Catherine glanced at her watch. 'Enough speculating for now. I promised Clayton I'd get you out of here, so we'd better be gone by the time he calls me.'

'OK. I'll start packing up. Let me print a couple of things quickly to take home. Are you happy to wait?'

'No problem. I'll put the wait to good use. Lock the door behind me and I'll go and have a quick word with the guy on security.'

Susie groaned. 'The lovely John. A man of few words, and most of those not terribly polite. Good luck getting anything out of him. Mind you, I think he has a thing for blondes so maybe you will. Give me fifteen minutes OK? Knock and I'll let you back in.'

CHAPTER FORTY-THREE

John looked up from his desk as he sensed someone approaching. Probably more bloody questions about this lunchtime incident and another bollocking coming his way. Like it was his fault the shitty CCTV hadn't been working properly. If the powers that be weren't so stuck up their own clever backsides they'd have upgraded it by now. He and his mates had told them enough times. Sunday should have been a quiet time. Just his luck his weekend rota had turned out to be this one.

But it was her, the blonde from earlier. He'd given her a good look up and down when she'd walked in with the professor. She'd even given him a smile. He wasn't used to that from the usual arrogant twerps here and he liked it. She had a great smile; it lit her whole face up. Mortimer was a lucky sod; she was hot too. Not like the young babes he usually watched on his phone. He knew most of them were all fake tits and ass and they wouldn't give him the time of day anyway. This woman was real, and in bloody good nick. Long blonde hair, slim but curvy, with killer legs. Shit, he wouldn't say no.

He felt a familiar stirring as she walked towards him,

imagining himself undressing her. He moved uncomfortably in his seat and hoped his face wasn't betraying where his mind was going. If his frigging wife would put out now and then he wouldn't have this problem.

The blonde was smiling again as she extended her hand to shake his. Unusually he smiled back.

'Hi. John isn't it? I'm Catherine. You may have seen me arrive earlier with Professor Mortimer.'

He shook her hand back, self-conscious that his was probably clammy. What the hell was he thinking? A woman like this wouldn't look twice at him. As if he could compete with a professor who all the women in the place seemed to have the hots for. But at least she was friendly. He decided he liked her. 'Yes, I saw you walk in. Sorry about what happened. How's the young researcher? Anna, I think she's called. Quiet girl. Must be a bit shaken up.'

'Yes. Anna. She was shaken up when we arrived but she's a lot better now and on her way home. She can't remember too much about what happened though, and I gather the cameras aren't giving us any clues about who might have done this. Clayton ...Professor Mortimer...tells me there are lots of people in and out of the building, even on a Sunday and especially around lunchtime, so I'm sure it's tough for you to keep track.'

John nodded. At last, somebody who got it and treated him with some respect. 'It is.' He leaned towards her, keeping his voice low. 'And between you and me the surveillance system's bloody crap. Only works when it wants to, and any images are usually too grainy to be useful. Needs a complete upgrade. But they won't pay for it. I'm sorry about the young woman but maybe now this has happened they'll get their arses in gear.' Despite himself he blushed. 'Sorry for the language Miss. But it's not right. I hope the professor will have a thing or two to say about it.'

'You can be certain of that John. He cares a great deal about his staff.'

'I can tell. Decent bloke I've always thought. Some right up themselves types here I can tell you, but he's one of the good ones.'

Catherine laughed. 'I won't argue with you on that one. So, you didn't notice anything odd or different about today? Nobody hanging around who you maybe barely noticed at the time but now you wonder about? Anything at all John. Sometimes these things strike us later so please...tell me anything that comes to mind. However daft it sounds.'

'You sound like a policeman Miss. Bloody hell, you're not, are you? That stuff about the cameras...I mean...I was only sounding off. Wouldn't want any of it getting back to the big knobs. Sorry, I mean the managers.'

She grinned at him. 'Don't worry. I'm not the police. I am an investigative journalist though, so questions are my job. But...' She leaned forward and whispered. 'I never reveal my sources.'

John felt the stirring return, worse than before. She was even hotter this close up. A sharp pang of jealousy hit him deep in his gut as he imagined her naked and romping with the professor. He'd have to take a crack at his wife tonight. If there was nothing doing as usual, he'd have a late night with the porn channels and a few chat sites. Maybe he'd get lucky for once and find a woman to talk to. He needed something to help him finish what Mortimer's girlfriend had started.

But for now, he wanted to help her. As she stepped back and looked at him, he went over everything that had happened earlier. Surely he'd noticed something.

Then it came to him. Why the hell hadn't he remembered sooner? Probably because he couldn't be bothered. But he could be bothered now, for her. She'd asked nicely.

'There was someone. I've seen the bloke before, but I've

no idea who he is. Never got a chance to ask, but he was here today. Right impatient bastard he is. Rushed right past me like he did last time I saw him, without a fucking...sorry... without even a backward glance.'

'So, what made you remember him from last time John? I mean, if you barely saw him, and you see so many people, something must have stuck in your mind about him.'

'Yeah it did. I got the same feeling I got last time, like I knew him from somewhere, but I've no idea where. Especially because his face was hidden, which is the other thing that made me recognise him from before. He was wearing the same baseball cap again. Pulled low over his face. Always think that makes blokes look shifty.'

'Lots of people wear baseball caps. What made you remember this one particularly?'

'It was unusual. Had some sort of fancy metal logo on it. An animal I think.'

He gave her a triumphant look. He felt good he'd remembered and expected to see her smile. But her expression had changed in an instant.

What the hell had he said? And why had it bothered her so much?

CHAPTER FORTY-FOUR

Fifteen minutes after she'd left Susie, Catherine was back, knocking on the lab door, still processing what John had told her. She knew her instant reaction and inability to speak for a minute had disconcerted him, but his words had triggered a memory. She'd stared at him without seeing him. Instead she'd seen a baseball cap, exactly like the one he'd described. Baseball caps were everywhere, but not like this one. She'd only ever seen anything like it once before. Now she had to figure out its significance.

Susie opened the door straightaway. Her agitated expression suggested she had something important to tell her and Catherine gave her a questioning look.

'I have news. Anna called and she's remembered something. She's still a bit hazy, but she thinks while she was out of it somebody logged onto one of the machines. She can't remember which one, but she heard some tapping and the odd ping.'

'Like the ping when you make a wrong input? Someone trying different passwords perhaps?'

'Yes, exactly that sound, but I've done another check on

all the computers and I don't see anything to suggest anybody's tried to access any of them since before lunchtime. In fact I'm certain I was the last person to log out.'

Catherine looked directly at her. 'Then if Anna's right we're dealing with someone who seriously knows what they're doing. And knows how to cover their tracks. I need to talk to Clayton about this. You all have to be really careful from now on. I mean it Susie. You need to convince him of it too. I'm afraid he'll play the erudite professor and dismiss this as my over-active journalistic imagination.'

'Sounds to me like your journalistic instincts were right. This doesn't feel like your average bag snatcher to me either.'

Catherine shook her head. 'No, I don't think it is. What sort of amateur opportunistic thief works on a computer before leaving the scene? This guy isn't average or an amateur. He's smart, he was looking for something, and we'd better figure out what. But for now, we should get out of here. Going over and over this is leading us nowhere. We need some distance to help us think straight.'

Susie nodded, grabbed her bag, then hit a keypad which Catherine assumed set the laboratory's internal alarm. The two women left in silence, both lost in their own thoughts as they took the stairs to the ground floor and walked to the main exit. They each took a deep breath as fresh air hit them, then Susie broke the silence.

'I'm not sure I want to go straight home yet. Can we grab a quick drink somewhere first? I need something to bring me down from all the drama of today. I'm guessing you might too.'

Catherine grinned at her. 'Must be our mutual telepathy again. I was about to suggest the same thing. You pick the place. I'm still a stranger in town.'

'There's plenty to choose from round here, but we'll head for one of the quieter ones. Can't say I'm in the mood for the raucous student vibe tonight and I don't suppose you are either.'

'Not exactly, no. And Susie.' She stopped walking and reached for Susie's arm. The younger woman turned to face her.

'What is it? You're looking very serious.'

'I am serious. I want you to promise me something. Please say nothing to anybody about what we talked about earlier. I don't want our suspicions out there. Not yet.'

Susie's reply was hesitant. 'OK. I'll say nothing for the moment but only because it's you asking. It all seems a bit weird if I'm honest. Surely we should be telling the police? I mean...'

Catherine cut across her. 'No, not at the moment. Their wheels will grind too slowly, and in the meantime whoever did this will know we're on to them. I need that not to happen until I've had time to figure this out. Please, trust me.'

'OK. I'll give you some time, but not too long. And you have to promise to tell me the minute there's something I should know. Otherwise no deal.'

'You have my word. Now let's go for that drink.'

As they walked, she wondered how much of what she suspected she should share with Susie. For the moment probably nothing, not until she'd talked to George. She felt certain this girl could be a trusted and useful ally in their investigations, but her father was a different issue entirely. Catherine was convinced Richard Cameron was not to be trusted. That meant this could become complicated and uncomfortable and she feared Susie might become collateral damage. She shot a glance at her and made a silent promise that she'd do everything in her power to protect this young woman who reminded her so much of her younger self.

Then another young woman came into her thoughts.

Clara. And the question that had refused to go away since her conversation with John earlier.

Who was the tall man she'd seen with Clara in Muswell Hill? The man who'd been wearing a baseball cap identical to the one John had described.

CHAPTER FORTY-FIVE

Clayton messaged as Catherine and Susie walked into a bar. He'd spent an hour with Anna and her parents, doing his best to convince them the incident was most likely the work of an opportunistic amateur. He'd also assured them he'd have security immediately stepped up in response. Now he was anxious to know how she and Susie were and asked her to call him.

As Susie headed to the bar to top up their drinks, Catherine hit his number. As soon as he answered she felt the excitement she always did when she heard his voice. She couldn't imagine the day would ever come when her insides didn't melt at the sound of it, or when she would ever not smile at the uniquely Australian upward lilt at the end of his sentences. She was still getting used to the fact that not every statement was a question.

'Hi Mr Professor. It sounds like Anna was relieved to be home.'

'Very. She's obviously close to her parents so it helped seeing them. She needs to relax for the evening, and I think she will, but she's desperate to remember more about what happened. Maybe more will come back to her now she's home. How are you and Susie?'

'We're fine. Still together actually. Neither of us wanted to go straight home so we're having a drink. I like her a lot.'

'It doesn't surprise me the two of you have clicked. You're very similar in lots of ways. Thank you for looking after her. She was obviously shaken up, much as she didn't want to show it.'

'I imagine that's typical Susie. Good at coping with whatever life throws at her, at least on the surface. But I think she has a soft centre and she deserves her father to treat her better than he seems to. The way he dismissed her at the genetics conference clearly hurt.'

'I know, I hated seeing that. Anna's father is the exact opposite. So warm and affectionate with her.'

'Which has clearly helped to relax her. She's remembering more. She called Susie.'

'That's good news. Can she recall more about her attacker now? I so want to nail this bastard, but we need something to go on.'

The molten warmth that was her body's automatic reaction to hearing him was replaced by a shiver. She didn't want him anywhere near Anna's attacker, who she suspected was more than a match for anybody, even someone of Clayton's physique.

'No, she still can't describe him, but she's convinced he worked on one of the computers while she was semiconscious. This is definitely no amateur mugger Clayton. You have to be seriously on your guard. Susie understands that.' She regretted her words the moment she said them. He paused before replying and she sensed an unspoken tension between them for the first time, even through the filter of the mobile phone network.

'Dammit Catherine. Let's not go making leaps of logic here. We don't know what happened.'

'No, we don't, but something did. Susie accepts the need for vigilance, so why can't you?'

'Does it not occur to you that she accepts it because you told her to? It's hero worship. Or in this case heroine worship. She's young, and although she's smart, she's still impressionable. Let's not scare her prematurely please.'

'No. You're absolutely right. Why not bury your academic head in the sand instead and pretend nothing happened? Good idea Professor.'

'Don't be silly, I'm not suggesting that. And don't let's argue. Please.'

She looked up from her phone as Susie approached the table with their drinks. The younger woman took in her exasperated expression, raised her eyebrows and mouthed 'Men.'

Catherine smiled, lifted a finger and mouthed back 'One minute...' before she replied to him, her tone softer.

'No, you're right, let's not argue about it. Susie's back with our drinks so I should go. Let's talk again later.'

'I want to see you. Call me when you leave Susie. Please?'

'I will. Safe rest of journey.'

Susie gave her a questioning look as she put her phone down. 'Do I sense trouble in paradise?'

'He's being exasperating. I'm certain he thinks I'm seeing demons lurking where they may not exist.'

'Hope you told him I agree with you.'

'Unfortunately I did, and that backfired a bit. He thinks I've scared the shit out of you prematurely. I haven't, have I?'

'Good God no. I'm quite capable of reaching my own conclusions and this whole thing definitely feels odd to me too. And now, Catherine, I think you should share whatever else you know with me.' She paused and looked down at the table, squeezing her fingers uncomfortably. 'Which I suspect might help to explain some of the odd questions George has been asking me.' Catherine guessed what she was about to be asked next and waited for the question. 'Oh God. Please tell me that's not the only reason he wants to keep seeing me. As an information source for the two of you.'

Catherine put her hand on hers. 'Don't be silly. He couldn't take his eyes off you at the conference. Don't you dare tell him I said this, but he's totally smitten.'

'But you are working together on this right? And that's why you were at the conference in the first place?'

'Yes, and yes. But we also both got more than we bargained for. Him with you, me with Clayton. Some weird double twist of fate I suppose. Now we have to keep those feelings separate from the job we have to do, which isn't going to be easy. As that conversation with Clayton proved.'

'Then you really do have to tell me what you know and suspect. I'm involved in this whether you like it or not. I want to help Clayton too Catherine, but I can only do that if I know what's going on. Talk to me.'

Catherine barely paused. Susie's intellect was second to none, they could use her insight, and she sensed she could trust her. Maybe she and George were at a point where they needed a new perspective.

She decided to tell her everything. She took a deep breath and began at the beginning.

Two hours later she was back in her room. She'd stopped the taxi ten minutes from the hotel and walked the rest of the way. After telling Susie the whole story she wanted to clear her head. Reliving the events of Adam's death and everything that had happened since for the second time that day had been difficult.

Susie's reaction had been logical and analytical. She listened but asked lots of questions. The more they talked, the more she agreed with Catherine's certainty that Adam's suspicions had been correct and that he had been killed because of them. Charles Sedgwick's death and Anna's attack convinced them this was a high stakes game, and it was moving faster.

Now Catherine lay on her bed wondering where she went from here. She had to figure out the connections between the events of the past year, piece all this together and assemble some proof of her suspicions. She needed to know more about the lab fire of a year ago. If it was arson, then it confirmed she was up against an enemy prepared to kill without conscience.

She tried not to, but her thoughts turned to Clayton. If Cerberus were conspiring to manipulate the progress of key research, then he faced real danger. Not only had they probably killed her best friend but now they threatened the life of the man she loved.

She messaged George, told him of the events of the day and asked him not to contact Susie until she'd had a chance to update him. He reluctantly agreed and suggested they meet in the morning to compare notes. She messaged back with a thumbs up sign.

Tonight, she needed Clayton, and a break from all this. She'd called him when she left Susie and he told her he'd be with her soon. She wanted him so badly, in every possible way.

CHAPTER FORTY-SIX

Clayton messaged as he'd told her he would when he was on his way. She glanced around the room for the umpteenth time wishing it could be more fit for purpose, then checked herself in the mirror, hoping at least she looked the part. Here she was again, anticipating him, but somehow this time felt different. This time she wouldn't let anything get in the way.

When she'd called Nina this morning, she'd had no room in her stomach for anything but nerves. Now they were competing with a throbbing ache she'd never experienced before. As the minutes ticked by it grew stronger and the thought of him pervaded her with warmth as if her blood was at simmering point.

Lying on the bed, freshly showered, her body still slightly damp and glistening with her favourite body lotion, she touched herself through the sheer black fabric of the lace thong she'd chosen to wear. With its matching bra and negligée, she knew it would signal to him exactly what she wanted. Nina's words rang in her ears. 'Enjoy him.' The throbbing inside her intensified as she imagined his hand touching the brief triangle of lace before he slipped it inside and slid his fingers into her. She felt herself getting moist and her breathing quickened as her phone rang. She knew it was him.

'Clayton.' She heard her own breathlessness as she tried to speak. 'Please say you're here. I...' She couldn't get the words out. The tension of waiting for him was unbearable.

'I know. I'm on my way up. Two minutes. I want you too.'

He'd read her mind. It amazed her how he could already do that. She got up and walked towards the door. She didn't want to waste a second when he arrived. Hearing his voice made her want him more and she took a deep breath of anticipation. Tonight, nothing mattered but this man. She wanted to abandon herself to him, in every possible way.

She'd forgotten she was still holding her phone when it rang again. Lizzie's name flashed up. She must be calling with news about Richard Cameron. Catherine hesitated before letting the call go to voicemail. She turned to put the phone on the bedside table as Clayton knocked on the door, and she made a silent plea to Lizzie to forgive her for putting him first.

They smiled and stared at each other, with no need for words, as he walked in. She closed the door without taking her eyes off him. She whispered 'Hi' and the room became a blur as she threw herself into his arms, her hands clinging to his neck. Their mouths and tongues were hungry for each other and his hands moved down her body to pull her in closer as she pressed into him and felt his hardness against her. His 'Hi' was smothered by her moaning into his mouth. He broke away from the kiss, pushed her gently away by the shoulders and stood back to look at her.

She didn't move. Watching his expression aroused her even more. She was aware of nothing but his eyes burning into her body as her other senses abandoned her. He muttered something she couldn't hear and pulled her back towards him. His thumbs traced the line of her cleavage as he pushed aside the half-cups of the bra that had barely covered her breasts. The throbbing ache of earlier became waves of pleasure at him touching her for the first time.

He whispered 'I need to taste these' as he bent his head, his mouth and tongue teasing her until her breasts swelled and her nipples stiffened. She moved closer to him and wrapped one leg around him, opening herself up to him, wanting his fingers to explore her. He responded instantly to her invitation and she gasped at the feel of him sliding a finger into her as his thumb circled and caressed her. Her back arched and she wrapped her leg tighter around him, pressing down on his thrusting finger. He lifted his head and she pulled him towards her mouth and kissed him deeply. Suddenly he withdrew his finger and she felt him smile through the kiss as she tightened her grip on him, desperate for him to replace it.

'Clayton ...please...don't stop.'

He responded instantly to her breathless plea, and she gasped as something thicker plunged into her tight wetness. He murmured 'Do you like my thumb inside you? Sounds like you do.'

She moaned her 'yes' into his mouth and shock became pleasure as he varied the direction and rhythm and she felt herself opening up more to him. She started to unbutton his shirt, hungry to touch him. As her fingers made contact with the thick, dark hair that covered his chest he increased the pressure from his thumb until she was on the edge of climaxing on to it. She shuddered and gripped on to him as she heard her moans of raw desire grow louder. She wanted more. She wanted him taking her, invading her. She wanted everything.

His other hand grabbed hers and guided it down his chest and stomach. She buried her face in his chest hair and felt his heartbeat as she began slowly stroking the length of his hardness. Now it was her turn to look, and her stroking became firmer and more urgent at the sight and feel of his arousal.

When she lifted her head, his expression told her he knew she was ready for more. He pushed her towards the bed and she sank onto it, overwhelmed with desire. She wanted his powerful naked maleness on top of her, she wanted his hard thickness inside her. Every part of her wanted to surrender to him completely.

He towered over her and she reached for his belt. As her frantic fingers fumbled with the buckle, he took her hands and pushed her back on to the bed. She watched him undo it with one hand as his other hand moved to push her legs aside and pull the thong down. She heard herself begging him to rip it off her. He tore off the rest of his clothes as she removed the negligée. His bare masculinity towered over before he straddled her and wordlessly pushed her legs further apart.

This was the moment. A moment she'd never allowed herself total abandonment to before. Not like this, with a raw passion and desire she'd never imagined she could feel. Now she wanted it more than anything, as the fear she'd harboured for so long was finally obliterated. It was the moment she invited this man to take total possession of her.

She locked her gaze with his as he moved to enter her. Her back arched as he paused, making her wait a few seconds longer before he slid into her. She gasped at the sudden fullness of him, as he lifted her hips to drive deeper into her. She moaned his name as waves of pleasure washed over her, growing more powerful with each thrust of his body.

He reached for her breasts and squeezed them in turn as his thrusting became harder and faster. His breathing quickened and his eyes widened as she squeezed her muscles to grip him more tightly inside her.

She saw him smile as her moans got louder, her body spasmed and her hands gripped the bed. She heard his breathless 'Catherine' as his expression changed. His body shuddered and she sensed his release was close. She watched him, watching her, as he edged her once again towards a climax.

She closed her eyes and cried out as exquisite spasms rocked her entire body. His hands gripped her hips and she opened her eyes to see his face contort. He groaned 'Yes' as his moment got closer. She felt his spasms start and lifted herself towards him, gripping his back until his release was over and she felt full of him.

Then he collapsed on top of her and she gently held him to her. Her fingers caressed his back with feather light strokes as his breathing calmed. She buried her face in his chest and luxuriated in the intimacy of this moment with this man. She hugged him tightly to her and heard him sigh with satisfaction as he hugged her back.

She smiled and continued to hold him. She couldn't imagine ever wanting to let go.

CHAPTER FORTY-SEVEN

She watched him walk to the shower the following morning as she stretched out in contented satisfaction.

'Nice view.'

He turned his head and smiled. 'I'm glad the lady's satisfied.'

She ran her hand down her body as she continued to stare at him. 'The lady's very satisfied thank you. She'll be calling on Sir's services again, if Sir's happy with that?'

She watched his eyes follow her hand then glance down at his body before he replied. 'I assure you Sir's very happy with that. Now stop trying to tempt me back into that bed and make me even later. I'll see you in five.'

As she hugged the pillow where his head had been, and heard the water running, she was tempted to join him, but she resisted. She really should let him get to work. But when he emerged, wrapped in a towel, his mass of dark hair still damp, her willpower evaporated. She got up and walked towards him. Wordlessly she wrenched the towel away and pulled him onto the bed. She ran her hands over his chest, then trailed her fingers and kissed her way lightly down his stomach. She paused and looked up at him, as his hands moved to stroke her hair and grip her head. His grip tightened as she took him into her mouth. He lay back on the bed, his breathing quickening as his hands grabbed her head and pulled her further down onto him.

Catherine abandoned herself to his pleasure. Nothing mattered more than satisfying him. As she felt his body spasm and he shuddered into her mouth she doubted anything would ever matter more to her again.

The minute he left she was already anticipating seeing him again. She didn't have long to wait. His daughter and her boyfriend were having dinner with him later and he'd insisted she join them.

She lay on the bed that was still damp from his barely towel-dried body and breathed him in. The room felt full of him, and so did she. Reluctantly she dragged herself out of bed to make herself another drink and smiled at the sight of the mug he'd had to leave half-full as he'd kissed her and raced out of the door, throwing his jacket on as he did. It was still warm, and she finished it for him, tasting him and the coffee as she remembered how his mouth had felt on hers.

She picked up her phone, feeling a pang of guilt at ignoring Lizzie last night. She hoped her friend would understand. She needed to call her and Nina, then agree a time to meet George later. She wanted another look at the Edinburgh lab fire CCTV.

She sat on the bed, hit voicemail and played Lizzie's message.

> *'Hi, I hope the fact you're not picking up's a good sign. Graphic details when you call me back please. Don't you dare hold out on me.*

And we need to talk about RC.
I remembered something.
Sent you an email but call me.
Love for now.'

She smiled then flipped to her email account and opened Lizzie's message.

Remembered where I saw Richard C. It was the day of Clara's 21st party but before you arrived. So much was happening that day with caterers and everything else, so I didn't get involved with him. Adam took him into his study for about 30 minutes then showed him out. I'm certain about the time because the musicians were due at 12 and he pitched up out of the blue around 11.30 and I thought he might be them arriving horribly early before I was ready. Then he left in a hurry as their van drew up. He'd brought a gift for Clara but I'm certain there was no gift tag. I can't even remember what it was, and I doubt she would if I asked her. She got so much stuff that day. I think it was a book but I'm not sure. Anyway, that's the only time I recall seeing him apart from the funeral. Now I wish I'd asked Adam more about him, but at the time it didn't seem important. Sorry if this isn't much help. Call me when you can and let's meet for that drink. L.

PS I also remember Adam's Government line rang while the guy was with him. He took the call after a couple of rings but I've no idea who it was. Never got chance to ask. Sorry.

Catherine leaned back on the bed. At last they had a connection between Cameron and Adam. Thirty minutes was a long time to hand over a birthday gift. What else had they talked about? And who had that call been from?

She emailed a quick thank you to Lizzie, apologised for missing her call which she punctuated with an emoji wink, and promised to speak with her later. Then she messaged George and agreed to meet him in a couple of hours. She needed a shower, she wanted some air, and she owed Nina a call.

When she was ready to leave, she picked up her phone and scrolled to Nina's number. Her friend would never forgive her if she didn't call soon. She smiled, remembering how much she'd freaked out in their conversation before her encounter with Clayton. Why had she been so nervous? It seemed ridiculous now.

She looked at herself in the mirror, seeing an involuntary blush spread across her cheeks as she thought about everything they'd done. She wondered if she looked different as she glanced at the reflection of the bed behind her. She wanted him back in it, making her feel the way she had all over again.

She sat on the edge of it, her hand reaching out to where his body had been earlier, then she hit call. She wasn't surprised when Nina answered straightaway.

'Hi. I hope this is my morning report. Tell me all.'

Catherine laughed. 'That was quick. Not that you were waiting for my call or anything right?'

'You bet. So how was last night? You sound pretty good on it.'

Catherine laughed. 'I'm feeling pretty good on it. Nina it was fantastic. He's fantastic. I can't believe now how nervous I was when we spoke yesterday. I'm sorry I put you through all that now because I really needn't have worried.'

'I'm so pleased for you Catherine. Did you talk to him and explain things?'

'I didn't need to, and once he was here, I didn't even want to. It all just... happened, and he knew exactly what I wanted and when. Sorry, too much information maybe.'

'No, not between friends like us. It sounds like he knew how to make everything feel right, and I'm so happy for you. My turn to be a bit envious now we're adding great in bed to this man's list of attributes. Don't suppose he's got a twin brother by any chance?'

Catherine spluttered with laughter at the question. 'Oh Nina, if only you knew what you'd asked.'

CHAPTER FORTY-EIGHT

She and George sat hunched in adjacent chairs, in the office which had briefly been hers, as he loaded the Edinburgh CCTV footage again.

'This is a longshot Catherine. How many times have we been through this?'

'Well sometimes longshots pay off. And this time I know what I'm looking for.'

'Care to enlighten me?'

'Let's see if I spot it first. And before I look, tell me the meeting with your ex at The Telegraph gave us something...please.'

His frown gave her the answer which his words confirmed. 'I wish I could, or at least something concrete. They aren't planning on making a big deal out of the payments story. They don't see anything more significant at play, nor do they appear to be looking.'

'What about Charles Sedgwick's death? Are they linking it with Adam's? And what do we know about his position on the payments issue?'

'No to the first question. Their editor doesn't want to go

there. He's not prepared to intrude on the private grief of two families by suggesting a connection or floating conspiracy theories. As far as he's concerned it's a tragic coincidence, nothing more. He's satisfied to have got government agreement to a public inquiry and intends to leave it at that. It sucks in my opinion, and it also means I'm running out of road as far as my assignment for Sam is concerned. Until the inquiry is launched the momentum of the whole thing's gone, so there's hardly much for me to report on.'

'I know, and yes, I guess he will move you on to something else soon. He'll have to, he's got a business to run. I'll hate losing your time and support on this, but you need to go wherever he sends you. If I have to, I'll go this alone.' She clenched her fist. 'I can't give up on it, not yet.' As she said the words her conversation with Clayton came back to her. She'd promised not to run risks by going it alone, but she might have no alternative. She turned to look out of the window, thinking how good it would feel to hold and be held by him later. She turned back as George spoke again.

'You're not going it alone Catherine. I'm sticking with you on this, unless or until we decide there's nowhere to go with it, and we're not at that point yet. You haven't heard my answer to your second question. Sedgwick's position on the payments issue before he died.'

She raised her eyebrows as she looked at him. 'Tell me.'

'It may be nothing. But my friend was there when Sedgwick was interviewed, and apparently he tried to downplay the entire thing. He said he trusted that most of these payments would be shown to be entirely appropriate for services rendered.'

'He would, wouldn't he? It's a typical political answer. This government were elected on the back of a commitment to transparency and a promise to clean up politics and public services. The last thing they need is for this to blow up in their faces. If he was confident the inquiry wouldn't throw up much, what does your 'It may be nothing' mean? So far it sounds like the interview did amount to nothing.'

'There's the thing. Yes, he sounded confident, but my ex is a trained psychologist, an expert in human communication, body language, all that stuff. She spots things the rest of us wouldn't. It used to freak me out when I was with her to be honest.'

Catherine smiled and gave him a nudge. 'Would you stop digressing and get to the point please?'

'The point is she thought he looked uncomfortable through most of the interview. He said all the right things, gave all the typical politician's answers, but she sensed some personal discomfort behind the words. As if he had some agenda of his own and wanted to tell them something else, but he couldn't. Her colleague dismissed the idea, thought she imagined it, but she convinced me. I've never known her reading of somebody to be wrong. Ever.'

Catherine frowned. 'So, what was it I wonder? Did Sedgwick know about Adam's suspicions or did Adam suspect something about him? Remember his 'not even' comment at the end of his email to me when he told me not to trust anybody? Maybe he meant Charles Sedgwick.'

'It's possible and it would be a logical way to say it. If this guy was involved in financial manipulation, or anything else untoward, that would really elevate this whole thing.'

'That's an understatement. It could hardly get much more elevated, since Sedgwick's boss was the PM. Not that I'd have any suspicions there. I never heard Adam say much about Sedgwick, but he did discuss the PM a lot. He was a big fan, and I trust his judgment.'

'Same here, I'm a fan too. I think the PM's a breath of fresh air and who will effect some real changes for the good in this country.'

Catherine clasped her hands behind her head and nodded. 'Which brings us back to the recently departed Mr Sedgwick. We know he was under a lot of stress and family pressure, especially with his twins' health issues.'

'Which would make him more vulnerable to being got at. Not to mention a younger wife, and an ex who by all accounts likes to make things difficult.'

'So the offer of money to turn a blind eye to things might have been impossible to resist. I must say I always rather liked him when I watched him being interviewed, but I guess everybody has their tipping point.'

George nodded. 'And their price. But if he was being complicit and going along with some sort of conspiracy...'

'Our alleged conspiracy.'

'OK Your Honour, alleged, if it makes you happier. But if he was keeping quiet about whatever was going on, why kill him and lose a major asset?'

'It would only make sense if he was about to become more of a liability than an asset. Maybe he started to grow uncomfortable with whatever he knew. That would be consistent with your friend's assessment. God knows how we find out, but we'll need to try. Meanwhile let's focus on our other name in the frame. Richard Cameron. I spoke to Lizzie about him.'

'And?'

'We have a connection with Adam, from a year ago. Cameron brought a twenty-first birthday gift for their daughter Clara to the house. Lizzie didn't speak to him, Adam handled it, but apparently they spent about thirty minutes in his study. That's all she knows, but they might have met on other occasions.'

'And thirty minutes is a long time to discuss twenty-first birthday celebrations, so what the hell else did they talk about I wonder?'

'I've been asking myself the same thing. That was a big

day for Adam. He always put Lizzie and Clara first, so it must've been something important for him to take so much time out for Richard Cameron. Otherwise I suspect he'd have dealt with it at the door.'

'It's an odd day for the guy to show up, if he wasn't invited to the party. We definitely need to know more about him. I'll put a call into Susie and firm up our arrangement to meet. I'll agree to pick her up at her house then arrive unfashionably early. See what I can find out.'

'How do you propose to do that Mr Intrepid?'

'I've absolutely no idea, I'm hardly a practised sleuth. I guess I'll play it by ear.'

Catherine put her hand on his arm. 'George, I know we both use humour as a coping mechanism, but let's be serious for a moment. We need to be careful. We don't know who or what we're dealing with here, so don't take any risks, please.'

He put his hand on hers and gave her a reassuring smile. 'I won't, I promise. I may make jokes, but I know when to be serious, and when to be careful. Which applies to you too incidentally.'

'I know. We've been talking about two recent deaths. Let's not add a third.' She nodded in the direction of the screen monitor. 'Now let's hit play and take another look at this.'

He gave her a sceptical look and shrugged his shoulders as she leaned forward in her chair, her eyes scanning the screen intently.

'What exactly are we hoping to see, Catherine?'

She didn't take her eyes off the screen as she replied. 'Somebody who doesn't fit. Someone who's trying to blend in but...something about them doesn't. Let's focus on the demonstrators. If we're going to spot somebody that's where they'll be, trying to fade into the crowd. If you'd set the fire isn't that where you'd take cover while you watched the results of your handiwork? We should take a closer look at them again.'

He zoomed in on the protest group which had become larger and more vocal as the fire had taken increasing hold of the building and as the activist leaders had used social media to draw in more support. George slowed the footage down and Catherine leaned in further to the screen. There had to be something here, she was convinced of it.

And then she saw it or thought she did. She turned to George, telling herself not to get her hopes up yet.

'Can we go back a few seconds please. Then slow it as much as you can.'

He pressed the control button and the action slowed until it was moving frame by frame. Catherine watched and waited, hoping she hadn't been wrong.

And suddenly she saw him. She grabbed the control pad from George, hit pause and pointed excitedly to the screen.

'There. I knew it.'

George moved closer to the paused image. 'Tell me what I'm looking at.'

'The guy to the left pulling his cap down and starting to move away. I've seen him before. And I think he was at Clayton's lab the day of the break-in. The security guard saw him.'

'Forgive me if I'm being slow here Catherine, but he looks like any number of guys in a baseball cap. How can you be so sure you've seen this one before?'

She hit the zoom button. 'Look at the logo on the cap. You can make out it's a red and black dragon, and it's shiny. It must be metal, and it looks custom made. Have you ever seen one like it before?'

George peered at the screen. 'No, I haven't. These custom-made logos are expensive, but they're cool and on trend at the moment. One-off exclusives.'

'Precisely, and I've seen that particular one-off before, but

I only just made the connection.' She turned to see George's puzzled expression. Of course, he didn't know about her recent encounter with Clara.

She told him about how concerned Lizzie had been about her daughter's behaviour during Catherine's last visit, and her suspicion that a man was involved. She described Clara's aggression towards her personally and how uncomfortable the girl had seemed later when she'd seen her from the back of her taxi, with a man. A man who immediately pulled down a baseball cap to hide his face. A cap with a shiny animal logo that had glinted under the street lights, and identical to the one they were now seeing on screen.

George let out a whistle. 'Wow. Now there's a connection. And you think he was involved in the assault on Clayton's researcher?'

She shrugged her shoulders. 'That's more of a leap on my part. But the security guard told me he'd seen a guy he didn't know entering the building a couple of times, including that day. And it was the baseball cap he remembered. That and the fact the guy completely blanked him. But he said the weird animal logo stuck in his mind. That triggered the memory of that night I saw Clara. I thought it might be a coincidence and I was clutching at straws. I'm certain now that I'm not.'

'Me too. That dragon fits his weird animal description. Look, let me figure out how to copy this CCTV image on to both our phones. Then we need to decide where we go from here. We have to find out who the hell this guy is.'

'Yes, to all of that.' She leaned back in her seat and gave a sigh of relief. 'At last we have a link between Adam and both these lab incidents. And Mr Baseball Cap's it. Play the tape on a bit further, let's see if there's another image of him.'

George hit play, but the man continued to turn away from the camera and disappeared from view, masked by the crowd of protesters. As Catherine watched him in profile, his head down and obscured, she knew beyond doubt he was the man she'd seen with Clara.

She also had an alarming suspicion that she'd seen him somewhere else. She had no idea where, and she decided not to share the thought with George.

At George's insistence, and on his account, she took a taxi back to her hotel. Five minutes into the trip her phone pinged with a message from him.

'I've copied the image of our man.
I'll message it to your phone later.
Well done for not giving up. Gx
PS You holding out on me?
You forgot to tell me how your
encounter with the
hot prof went.'

She smiled as she typed her reply.

'You didn't ask.
But you have now & the answer's simple'

She followed up with a line of thumbs up emojis and smiled as George replied with a matching number of winks.

She sat back in the rear seat, closed her eyes and thought about Clayton, then turned her attention to what she should wear to meet his daughter later.

CHAPTER FORTY-NINE

Catherine couldn't believe how alike Clayton and his daughter were. She'd never seen a father and daughter so in tune with each other.

Ironically, they were complete opposites in appearance. Becca was the archetypal English Rose - diminutive and blonde, with porcelain skin and delicate feminine features, in contrast to Clayton's towering height, mop of dark hair and the rugged masculinity and skin tone that reflected a healthy childhood spent outdoors in the sunshine of Sydney.

Yet their mannerisms were virtually identical and their emotional closeness immediately apparent. They moved the same way, they ate and drank in unison, they frequently finished each other's sentences. Despite being born and brought up in England, Becca had even assumed her father's characteristic Australian upward lilt at the end of her sentences.

Their relationship reminded Catherine of hers with Will. Despite their different ethnicities nobody ever doubted they were mother and son. Thinking about him brought a lump to her throat. He was never far from her thoughts and seeing

Clayton with his daughter made her realise how much she missed him.

They were sitting round the glass table in Clayton's St John's Wood apartment. She'd loved his home from the moment she walked in. It was stylish but comfortable, elegant but understated, and his boyish pride at its view over the iconic pedestrian crossing of Abbey Road made her smile.

Dinner was relaxed and fun and she warmed to Becca and her boyfriend Tim instantly. As she watched them interact with Clayton, she could see the three of them had a strong bond, yet the warmth of their welcome made it seem entirely natural she should be there. Becca seemed genuinely happy to meet her. Tim was cook for the evening and the food was delicious. Catherine realised how much she'd missed the warm atmosphere of a home and vowed to double her efforts to escape the impersonal sterility of hotel life.

She and Becca made eye contact as the two men got into football conversation. The younger woman raised her eyebrows as she spoke.

'If you two are going to start this usual debate I think we'll leave you to it and take our coffee on to the balcony. OK with you Catherine?'

Catherine nodded as she stood up. 'More than OK. I have a reputation for having something to say on most subjects, but football isn't one of them.' She put her hand on Clayton's shoulder. 'And it's a chance for your daughter to tell me all your deep dark secrets.'

He laughed as he slipped her hand round her waist. 'Enjoy discovering them. Maybe you'll let me know what they are when you find out. I think I missed them.'

By the time the two women re-joined the men, when huddling up against the balcony heater in two of Clayton's heavy jackets couldn't protect them from the late-night London chill, Catherine felt a genuine bond with Becca. They talked non-stop for over an hour about her career as a journalist. It was a path the younger woman planned to follow after university, and she listened intently as Catherine spoke about the stories she had worked on. She was fascinated by the story of Will's adoption and his plans to become a surgeon. Catherine laughed at the questions she fired at her and suggested she was a natural for journalism.

Finally, they discussed their feelings for their respective men. It was clear to Catherine that Becca was serious about Tim, and equally clear she was delighted that her father had found someone. She squeezed Catherine's hand as she smiled and announced she was even more delighted it was her.

She learned that Clayton's ex-wife, who he'd been so reluctant to talk about, was called Angela, but she barely featured in Becca's conversation. She referred to her mother in passing, but with none of the warmth which radiated from her whenever she talked about her father. The relationship sounded more functional than loving. And when she talked about her Australian grandmother, who'd died when she was eight, the love on her face told Catherine that this was the woman who occupied the place in Becca's heart where her mother should live. She remembered how the same look of devotion had filled Clayton's expression when he'd talked about his mother, and Catherine wished she could have met her.

As they stood to go in Becca caught Catherine's arm and whispered to her.

'Before we go in, do you know about Max, my dad's twin? He never talks to me about him. Acts like he's a mad, bad uncle, but I don't know why.'

Catherine decided the less she said about Max the better as she followed Becca's lead and whispered back. 'I don't know much, Becca. He told me had a twin but wouldn't tell me any more. I guess he must have his reasons and I didn't want to push him on what they were.'

'I suppose you're right, and I shouldn't either. All the same, I'm curious, and I bet you are too. So now I don't feel so alone with this mystery. Will you see if you can work on Dad to at least let us meet Uncle Max?'

She looked at Becca's pleading expression and couldn't think of anything she wanted to do less, but as they stepped back into the warmth of Clayton's living room, she hoped her conspiratorial smile and nod were convincing.

After a final hot nightcap Clayton ordered a taxi for Becca and Tim. Catherine began to feel excitement building in her at the prospect of being alone with him. He shot her a reassuring smile as if, yet again, he'd read her thoughts.

She and Becca hugged each other as if they'd known each other for years and promised to message each other the following day to fix up a girly lunch and a shopping trip. Tim returned with their coats and held Becca's out to her. She reached for it but didn't grasp it in time and it fell to the floor. Becca and Tim laughed at her clumsiness and their joint lack of coordination as Catherine bent down to pick it up.

As she stood to hand it to Becca, she caught Clayton's reflection in the mirror. His face was expressionless, like a blank piece of paper. She reached out to touch his arm, willing Becca not to look round and see it too. She wondered how many times over the years he'd reacted like this to normal everyday clumsiness on his daughter's part, because of his condition.

She squeezed his arm and he turned to look at her. She hoped her smile told him he wasn't alone with this any longer.

Once Becca and Tim left, she took his hand and led him to the sofa.

'Sit down Clayton. We need to talk.'

He looked down at his hands. 'I know what you're going to say. That I'm overreacting. That it was only a jacket. You're right, and I need to stop doing this, but it's so difficult. I worry that one day she'll notice how I'm reacting to stuff like that and I can't deal with telling her about the Huntington's risk. I can't handle the thought of her having to live with the fear of it.'

Catherine squeezed his clenched hand, willing the tension to leave it as she replied. 'I can only imagine how difficult this has been over the years and your reaction is entirely under-standable in the circumstances. But you're a scientist, you know you need data before you draw any conclusions. You have to have Becca tested so you know what you're dealing with and whether you're overreacting or not.'

He was about to respond but she squeezed his hand again and continued. 'I know you don't want to Clayton, but you don't have a choice. One of these days she's going to notice how you react to things, and you'll be forced to tell her something anyway, but with no information to give her. Why not be sure you have the complete picture before that happens?'

He lifted his head and looked at her. 'Because I'm scared of finding out for certain she has it, Catherine. The odds are she does, as I explained, but at least this way I can tell myself maybe she beat them, and she doesn't.'

'That's you being Clayton the father not the scientist. I know you're scared, but you have to do this. You need to know, and you also have to be fair to Becca. She has a right to know too, and to decide how she copes with this.' She gripped his hand more tightly. 'She and Tim seem a serious item. She deserves to know how this would affect a possible future pregnancy, Clayton. You owe that to her.'

He nodded without speaking and she put her arms round him, pulled him closer until her cheek brushed against his, and whispered into his ear. 'And remember, you're not on your own with this now. I'll be with you every step of the way and we'll deal with whatever this throws at us together, starting tomorrow. But this is tonight, and tonight we both need something else.'

Then she stood, took his hand and led him wordlessly towards the bedroom.

CHAPTER FIFTY

He pulled his cap down as he walked into the empty office. If he couldn't see them, he'd make it more difficult for the bastards to see him. He sat down, put his feet on the desk and sneered at the phone, waiting for it to ring. He glanced up at the camera on the wall. It was blinking, so they knew he was here.

As usual they'd summoned him to the small unmarked building in a City side-street at short notice. That always pissed him off, but with luck he'd be free of them soon. He had a feeling he was about to be instructed to bring the whole timeframe forward, and that suited him fine. His new life beckoned and he'd soon be out of that poky flat he was supposed to be grateful for and into somewhere a lot flashier. And he liked flashy, it suited him.

The phone rang and after its third insistent ring he punched the loudspeaker button and waited for the familiar disembodied voice to speak to him. As usual there were no pleasantries. The voice always cut straight to business.

'You were late. We don't like being kept waiting. It's time to step things up. Those last pieces of data you brought us were interesting, but your assault on the girl was messy. Were you late that day too?'

He shifted uneasily in his chair. He had got his times wrong that day. He hadn't expected her to be there and he'd been forced to improvise. Easy for these guys to criticise, they weren't the ones out there doing this stuff. They just sat on their pin-stripe suited arses and barked instructions at him. He clenched his jaw and his fist in unison as he stared at the phone, waiting for the voice to continue.

'We want more aggressive action now. Mortimer has to be slowed down. He's getting too close.'

He smiled, hoping they could see it. Sometimes he wondered if they credited him with even half the knowledge he had. He knew how much investment they had on the line and how close his brother was to threatening their interests. He knew they were about to launch new treatment drugs, and he'd done his homework. They spent billions in research and testing to bring products to market and these latest developments had been particularly costly. Costs they needed to recoup over the next few years.

The stakes were high for them and this was his opportunity. There'd be no better time to renegotiate his fee.

He leaned back lazily in the reclining office chair. He looked up and gave the blinking camera a challenging stare. He kept his voice flat and expressionless.

'I know what's at stake. Your shares will take a nosedive as soon as anybody gets wind of how close to a result my dear twin is. Which means my stock's currently trading a little higher. Time to take another look at our deal boys. Another twenty-five per cent works for me.'

The speaker crackled as he heard the mutterings of three voices. Then the faceless voice that always did the talking for them replied. 'Get your feet off the furniture, listen, and lose the cocky attitude. Cocky leads to sloppy, like last weekend.

If you're as smart as you think you are, you'll remember who calls the shots here.'

He pointedly re-crossed his legs on the desk. 'Like you ever let me forget it.'

'Shut the fuck up and pay attention. As of now you've got two weeks and no more. You do whatever it takes to stop or delay Mortimer's research. No arguments, no sloppiness and no renegotiation. Get this done.'

'Would that include taking him out? You guys happy to go that far?'

'You heard what I said. Whatever it takes.'

He moved closer to the phone. 'Then the price has definitely gone up, and you guys can afford it. You stand to gain enough, and I run the risks.' He spat the rest of the words out. 'More than you wimps in your posh suits and fancy offices could ever do. You moan about shit, but it's people like me who sort the shit for you. And the price of shit sorting just went up.'

CHAPTER FIFTY-ONE

Catherine had decided the next step she would take in her investigation on Monday, but before then she could indulge herself over the coming weekend. Clayton had insisted she invite Nina to stay, and now Catherine glowed with excitement as she waited for her best friend to emerge from the train at Euston.

Despite the short notice Nina had wasted no time in accepting when Catherine called her.

'Are you kidding me? Try keeping me away. I meet Mr Perfect and have a weekend in your posh new abode. Wild horses wouldn't stop me saying yes. Got to hand it to you Catherine, when you go for it, you really go for it.'

Catherine giggled. 'I know. To think that a matter of weeks ago we were sitting in our café and I felt so jealous of everybody. I can't quite believe all this myself.'

'That boot's on the other foot now, believe me. In fact, several other feet. Everybody at home is envious but pleased for you at the same time. Who knew?'

Catherine laughed through her reply. 'Who indeed. Now make your train reservation and I'll meet you at Euston later.'

Clayton had driven her to her hotel the morning after their dinner with Becca and Tim and waited while she packed her solitary suitcase, after insisting she move out and into his apartment. She'd wavered at first, telling him it was too soon, but he'd refused to accept it.

He held her and told her he wouldn't let her go until she agreed. 'Catherine, everything about us feels right. We both know that, so why should we wait?

His voice dropped to a whisper. 'And I need you. I can't deal with what Becca's test might throw up without you. Please, don't say no.'

She'd looked at him and knew she couldn't refuse, and now here she was, about to welcome her friend to spend the weekend with them in St John's Wood.

She moved closer to the barrier as the train from Manchester Piccadilly drew in. As soon as the doors opened Nina emerged from the nearest carriage. Her face lit up when she spotted Catherine's excited wave and both women kept smiling as she rushed towards the exit.

They hugged each other with the uninhibited joy of friends reunited. Catherine couldn't believe how much she'd missed the woman who'd been such a big part of her life for so long, or how much had happened since she'd last seen her.

As they let each other go and looked at each other, Nina spoke first.

'Wow Catherine. As the saying goes...I'll have what you're having! You look fantastic. Is this all down to Mr Perfect?'

Catherine grinned and winked at her. 'He might have something to do with it, yes. But you look pretty good yourself. Anything you want to tell me?'

Nina laughed and linked arms with her as they moved away from the barrier into the station concourse. 'Nothing as exciting as I suspect you're going to be telling me. If I'm looking well it's purely the result of clean living.'

'Let's change that. I'm in the mood for some disgustingly unhealthy calorie-laden cake.'

'Lead me to it. Then I want all the details about this man of yours before I meet him.'

An hour later they were in St John's Wood. Nina loved the area from the moment they drove into it. Catherine had loved it on sight too when Clayton brought her here only days earlier. Despite being so close to the centre of London, it combined architectural grandeur with an aura of tranquillity that created an atmosphere all of its own which its residents were proud to call home. She'd immediately felt part of it.

Nina's eyes widened with approval when they walked into Clayton's flat. Now she was unpacking and changing in the guest bedroom while Catherine made tea and prepared some pre-dinner appetisers. Clayton was due back in an hour and bringing his friend David with him. He'd booked dinner for the four of them at an intimate French bistro in the High Street.

'So, what's this guy like I'm going to be meeting? Is he hot? How much trouble should I go to?'

Catherine turned to see Nina in the kitchen doorway, her hair still damp from the shower. As always, she smiled at her directness.

'You'd blow his socks off if you wore a bin bag. But to answer your question, I've never met him. Apparently he's quite a hit with the women though. Or at least so he tells Clayton.'

'Good enough for me, I'm on it. You know I always like a challenge. Do you need some help first though?'

'Absolutely not, I'm almost finished. You go and get ready. You've got thirty minutes.'

Catherine giggled as her friend turned, gave her a mock wiggle and a thumbs up and left her to her preparations.

She heard Clayton arrive home minutes before she emerged from their room wearing her favourite pair of black sparkly jeans and leather ankle boots. When she walked into the living room, he gave her a look of approval and she felt the familiar instant chemistry rush between them as she threw her arms round him and kissed him. A voice in the background reminded her he wasn't alone.

'I'd tell you two to get a room, except you've already got one.'

One arm still round Clayton's waist she spun round and held out her hand to greet David.

'Hi. Clayton's told me so much about you. I'm pleased to meet you at last.'

David clasped her hand with both of his. 'The feeling's mutual Catherine.' He nodded in Clayton's direction. 'He's talked about nothing else since he met you. Now I can understand why.'

Catherine blushed with slight discomfort from the intensity of his gaze. Clayton had told her David had been single for a long time and was now a committed online dater. She hoped he'd never come across her profile during his searches and told herself she should delete the account she'd only kept open to keep Max in view. Clayton's twin no longer seemed important.

'No flirting with my girlfriend please.' Clayton smiled at his friend, then down at her as he squeezed her waist and pulled her closer to him in a gesture of mock possession. 'Time I opened some champagne, I think. We need to celebrate your first weekend in residence darling.'

She reached up to brush her mouth briefly against his. It

was the first time he'd called her that, and her insides melted with pleasure at how good it sounded.

'Did I hear the word champagne?'

As Nina swept into the room Catherine let go of Clayton and moved to take her hand. Her friend looked stunning. Her long black hair was swept up into an elegant crystal clip and the fitted red dress she wore emphasised her athletic build and was the perfect complement to her olive skin.

Catherine introduced her to Clayton first and smiled as they hugged each other warmly. It was important that these two people who meant so much to her should be friends.

Clayton gave Nina a grin. 'So, this is the lady responsible for the mesmerising outfits that reeled me in is it?'

Nina laughed. 'Guilty as charged. I told her they'd be effective. I didn't expect things to move quite this fast though, but I'm delighted they have.' She turned to look at Catherine, then back at Clayton, and her voice softened. 'She's more than my best friend. She's a special lady and she deserves to be happy. But I have a feeling I don't need to tell you that.'

Clayton grinned as he pulled Catherine back to him, slid his arm round her and looked into her face. 'That obvious I'm smitten huh? Don't worry, I intend to make this lady very happy.'

Catherine pressed her head into his neck, then realised she hadn't introduced David to Nina.

'David, I'm so sorry. Where are my manners? Let me introduce you. This, as you've gathered, is my dearest friend, Nina. She generally likes to make an entrance.'

As Nina turned towards David and he stepped forward to shake her hand, Catherine noticed it trembling, and smiled inwardly at the look on his face. She could tell Nina's entrance had knocked him sideways. Their handshake lasted long enough for her to suspect their approval of each other was mutual.

She and Clayton shot each other a conspiratorial look and headed to the kitchen. He leaned into her and whispered into her ear. 'Think David's a little overwhelmed. Did you see the look on his face? What is it about you northern women?'

She gave him a playful dig in the ribs, then assembled the plate of appetizers while he organised champagne flutes and opened a perfectly chilled bottle of Moet & Chandon. As they worked in harmony, she wanted to pinch herself to be certain she wasn't dreaming.

Was she really the same person who, only weeks ago, had been so dissatisfied with everything in her life apart from her son and best friend? The usual pang of sadness hit her that Adam hadn't lived to share in this new phase of her life, but as she turned and looked at Clayton, she knew Adam would have liked him.

She smiled as he popped the champagne cork, and knew she'd remember this moment. Nothing would interfere with tonight's celebration of the new life she'd begun with this man she adored.

CHAPTER FIFTY-TWO

By the time they were all choosing from the restaurant's delicious array of desserts, it was clear that Nina and David were attracted to each other.

He hardly took his eyes off her, and her face wore a permanent smile as he kept them entertained with his seemingly endless supply of stories. Catherine had warmed to him more as she got to know him better. He reminded her of someone, but she couldn't think who.

There had been an awkward moment at the table earlier when one of his stories had involved him and Clayton at a party with their ex-wives. Catherine saw him hesitate and glance at his friend as he started to tell it. David's flustered reaction and immediate change of subject prompted her to turn towards Clayton. For a few seconds his face was devoid of expression until he seemed to become aware of her looking at him and gave her a weak smile. The moment passed, but she wondered why he hated any discussion of his wife, and why Becca rarely referred to her.

It was a part of his life story Catherine felt excluded from, and she wondered if he'd ever let her in.

He'd been quieter than usual throughout dinner, but she knew he felt nervous about Becca's Huntington's test. After the jacket incident, he'd followed Catherine's advice. He'd told his daughter he needed to conduct more research into the DNA of children born to a parent who was one of a set of identical twins and would like to anonymously include her profile. Knowing the limited sample size he had to work with, she had accepted willingly.

Clayton's assistant Ian, unaware of whose blood he was testing, rushed through the genetic analysis his boss had requested. The results were imminent, and he'd promised to email them the instant they were ready. Despite his efforts to act naturally, Clayton's glance continually flickered to his phone. Catherine knew how anxious he was, and how much he dreaded the prospect of telling his daughter the news he'd convinced himself he was about to receive.

David was midway through another of his anecdotes, and she and Nina were giggling, when Clayton stood abruptly. David and Nina were still absorbed in each other as she swung round and put her hand on Clayton's arm.

'What is it? A message from the lab?'

'Yes. Excuse me for five minutes, Ian's emailed. I'll go outside and take a quick look at it.'

'Everything OK mate?' It was David. 'You're about to miss the punchline, one of my better ones. Work problem?'

Clayton gave a weak smile. 'Nothing I can't deal with.' He turned back to Catherine. 'I'll leave you to organise coffee. Don't wait for me.'

He moved away from the table and she started to walk towards the restaurant exit with him.

'Do you want me to come out with you?'

'No Catherine, I don't want you to come with me.'

She took a step back at his abrupt response as he spun round to face her, and his tone softened.

'I'm sorry, I didn't mean to sound so sharp, but I'm on edge. Let me go and look at this.'

'Of course.' She put her hand on his arm. 'I hope the news is good.'

She wasn't sure her comment had registered as she looked at his blank expression and felt the tension in him before he walked out.

Nina and David both gave her questioning looks when she returned to the table and she shrugged at them.

'Sorry he's dashed off. Urgent email he needs to look at. We should order coffee.'

David grinned at her. 'Life with a mad professor. Hope you know what you've signed up for.'

She gave her best attempt at a grin back, but her insides were lurching with nerves as she beckoned the waiter.

Five minutes later her phone rang. She answered on the second ring. 'Clayton? What's the news?'

'I'm heading into the lab. Ask David to pick up the tab and I'll sort it with him. I'll see you later. I've no idea when.'

He ended the call before she could reply. She muttered 'Give me a minute guys.' and half ran towards the door.

She gasped from the cold night air which assaulted her as she walked out to see Clayton about to climb into a taxi.

'Clayton.'

He jerked his head in her direction. 'I must go. Finish your evening.'

She wasn't sure he heard her 'Please message me.' competing with the taxi's engine as he closed the taxi door and leaned forward to speak to the driver.

She shivered and waved as the black cab moved away from the kerb. She prayed he would turn and look at her as he drove past, but he didn't. Something was wrong. The news had clearly been bad, and she wished he'd shared it with her. For the second time that night she felt excluded.

And it hurt.

CHAPTER FIFTY-THREE

Catherine forced herself to smile as she and Nina walked home from the restaurant. She'd heard nothing from Clayton since he'd driven past without acknowledging her. He hadn't replied to the two messages she'd sent asking him to call her.

Nina almost danced as they walked, a little giddy from the champagne and from meeting David. They'd exchanged numbers and arranged to meet for a drink the following evening. He'd messaged her twice on his way home which made Catherine more hurt at hearing nothing from Clayton.

'Catherine? You're miles away. Is everything OK? Sorry, I've been so wrapped up with talking about David I didn't ask if you've heard from Clayton yet. It's such a pity he had to leave early.'

She hoped her attempt at a light-hearted response would fool Nina into thinking she was alright. Thankfully her friend was so high with excitement that she probably wouldn't notice that Catherine's heart felt anything but light.

'Everything's fine. It's like David said, an occupational hazard of falling for a mad scientist. I guess I need to get used to it. Clayton's research is potentially ground-breaking, and he's committed to it. It's one of the things that draws me to him.'

Nina grinned. 'That and the fact the man's hot as hell. And besotted with you. It's obvious how much he adores you.'

She smiled at Nina's certainty. She wanted those words to be true, but the smile on her face masked the frown in her head. She wanted him to adore her, and she wanted to feel the contentment she'd felt when they were giggling in the kitchen earlier, but instead contentment had been replaced by rejection.

He'd turned in on himself, and away from her, and she couldn't understand why.

She woke up in darkness and shivered, despite slowly realising she was fully dressed. For a moment she couldn't remember why, or even where she was. She had no idea how long she'd slept. She fumbled for her phone to check the time. Barely 3 a.m. She involuntarily turned and reached out to the other side of the bed. A narrow shaft of moonlight from the half-open curtains eerily illuminated the pillow. She stared at its emptiness as her aching head started to focus. Clayton should be alongside her, but she was alone with the moonlight. Her body shivered again, not only against the cold of the night but against the cold numbness inside her. Where the hell was he?

She looked at her phone again. Still no response from him, although he had read one of her messages. Why was he ignoring her? Did she not know him as well as she thought she did?

She should stop tormenting herself with questions. Being alone and cold in the darkness made it all feel worse. She needed warmth and light. She got up and walked to the kitchen to make herself some hot tea as quietly as she could. She didn't want to wake Nina who she heard breathing in contented sleep as she walked past the spare room door. Perhaps she was dreaming about David and their next meeting later today. She hoped Nina could find the happiness she deserved. The happiness she thought she'd found with Clayton.

She took her mug into the lounge and, with a table-lamp lit and the gas fire's dancing flames warming the room, she began to feel more like herself, at least physically.

Her emotions were a different story. Her head was all over the place. Twice tonight she'd felt excluded from Clayton's life. She knew nothing about his first wife and now he'd rebuffed her offer of support as he faced Becca's results, despite only days ago saying he needed her.

Perhaps she really didn't know him as well as she thought she did. Had she rushed into this relationship? She wished she had more experience of men and knew better how to navigate this particularly complex man's emotions. Maybe she'd given too much of herself to him too quickly. For the first time in her life she'd made herself vulnerable to a man and the only thing she knew for certain was how much she hurt from his apparent rejection of her.

Her hand hovered over her phone as she contemplated sending him another message. She decided against it. Damn him. She'd tried, he'd ignored her, she wouldn't try again.

Instead she turned her thoughts to her investigation. She should throw all her attention at that and not allow her emotions to distract her. Especially not after this treatment from him. She owed it to Adam, Lizzie and George to keep up the momentum. Their only concrete lead was Mr Baseball Cap. She needed to track him down, and her best route to him was Clara.

She planned to call Lizzie in the morning, steer the

conversation around to her daughter, and get an idea of the girl's plans for the next couple of days. She half-smiled at what she was planning to do. She'd never followed anybody before. She wondered if she should ask George along but dismissed the idea. She'd be less conspicuous on her own, and with a hoodie pulled low across her face Clara wouldn't recognise her.

She remembered her promise to Clayton, that she wouldn't do anything without telling him first. But that was then, and this was now. If he could keep things to himself, then so could she.

She'd take this next step alone.

She was contemplating trying to attempt an hour's sleep when she heard a key in the door. She glanced at the kitchen's digital clock as it clicked its way to 5 a.m. She walked into the hallway as Clayton half-stumbled through the door. He looked at her with a glazed expression as if he'd encountered a stranger in his home, and she realised he was drunk.

Wordlessly she grabbed his hand, pulled him into the lounge and pushed him onto a chair. She didn't want Nina hearing whatever was to come. He was too drunk to argue, and his arms flopped uncontrollably on either side of the seat.

She stood in front of him, arms crossed. 'Where the hell have you been Clayton? Do you have any idea how worried I've been?'

'Told you where I was going Miss Crossed Arms. My lab. Scientists do that. We love our labs.' He reached out to her. 'Anyway, I'm back now. So, come here. Let me show you how much I love you too baby. That aggressive pose is a mega turn on.'

She took a step back. 'Don't even think about it. Tell me

what's happened. Unless your lab's moonlighting as a whisky distillery I doubt you've been there till this time.'

He looked down at the floor then back up at her. Confusion was etched on his face like contours on a map.

The anger and hurt that had flooded her for the past few hours disappeared the moment she looked into that face. This strong masculine man, who had overwhelmed her with desire, had an inner vulnerability that overwhelmed her too. She couldn't imagine ever being mad at him for long.

She knelt in front of him and took both his hands in hers.

'I'm going to make you some strong black coffee, and you're going to tell me what happened to get you into this state. Then you're going to sleep it off and tomorrow we deal with whatever we have to, together. And do not argue Clayton.'

His hands gripped hers. 'I don't deserve you.'

She put her fingers to his mouth to silence him and smiled. 'After this performance probably not, but you've got me. I'm not going anywhere, apart from the kitchen, and I'll be right back.'

When she put his coffee next to him, she half expected to find he'd fallen asleep, but he was staring into space. She sat on the arm of the chair and squeezed his hand.

'Now talk to me. You can't avoid it any longer. What were Becca's results?'

He gave her an odd half-laugh before he replied. 'What you might call good news and bad news. The all-time mixed blessing.'

'Stop talking in riddles and answer the question. Does she have Huntington's?'

'Well here's the good part. She's all clear. Not a triple repeat in sight. Dancing mania will never be a problem for Becca.'

She leaned forward to hug him. 'Clayton, this is fantastic.

She's beaten the odds, what a relief.' Then she sat back and looked at his expression. 'So, what's the bad news? Have the tests shown up something else? Tell me, please.'

'Nope. She's genetically perfect. Should live to a ripe old age barring accidents.'

'Then what's the issue?'

'Ah...issue. The old biblical term for offspring. A perfect way for you to ask the question Catherine.'

'This isn't the time for silly jokes Clayton, please.'

'You're right, it isn't. The bad news, at least for me, is that her DNA doesn't remotely resemble mine. So, the issue is... she's not my issue. Maybe now you can see why I got drunk. I didn't see that one coming.'

For a moment she wondered if she'd misheard him. She stared at him, trying to find the right words to respond. Was he really saying what she thought he was?

With his knack for reading her mind he reached for his coffee, took a gulp of it and turned back to her.

'Yes, you heard me right. The result is unequivocal. Becca is not my child.'

CHAPTER FIFTY-FOUR

Catherine propped herself up on one elbow, looked at the sleeping man beside her and stroked his face. Perhaps he'd been right to get drunk last night. It had made it easy for him to fall into an oblivious sleep.

After he told her the news she'd got him into bed and held him to her until his breathing told her he'd fallen asleep. At least for a few hours he'd escape the shock of Becca's test results. He'd struggled to tell her, but saying the words had made it real, and he'd broken down as the whisky-induced denial disappeared.

She'd said very little to him. Instinct told her he needed her touch to comfort him and not words. She'd keep her words until later today when he'd slept off the initial shock and the alcohol.

Surprisingly, despite so little sleep herself, she didn't feel tired. It was still only 8 a.m. but she'd heard Nina up and about. She needed to go and fix her some breakfast and decide what she would tell her. She quickly changed into a different pair of jeans and a warmer sweater and headed towards the kitchen.

Ten minutes later Nina bounded in and gave her a hug. 'I thought I smelled your speciality pancakes. I could eat the whole stack. Fancying the backside off someone gives me an appetite in more ways than one.'

Catherine laughed in spite of herself. Her friend's energy was irrepressible, and she swung round to grin at her.

'I can satisfy the hunger part, but I'll leave the rest of the satisfying to David. What time are you meeting him?'

Nina gave her a sheepish look. 'Ah...we need to talk about that.'

'Why? Not a problem is there?'

'Not with him, no. He's already messaged this morning...and this is a bit awkward. I feel awful even thinking about saying yes, but he's asked me to spend the day with him. Because of our distance we're going to have limited opportunities to meet and...'

Catherine interrupted her. 'Don't think twice about it. You have to spend it with him. Remember what you told me? Go for it? Now you have to follow your own advice Nina. If you haven't told him yes yet, go and do it, right now.'

'But I came here to see you Catherine. I mean I want to see him, but...'

'No buts, do it. We'll have lots of opportunities to meet. Even more if David turns out to be Mr Right. Go and message him and say yes or I'll eat all the pancakes and I've no eggs left to make more with.'

'Don't you dare. I'll go and grab my phone. Keep my stack warm.' She started to bound out but stopped and turned as she reached the doorway. 'Shit I nearly forgot. He's anti-smoking so I've decided I'll follow your example and quit. Can I leave this with you? It's the fancy new lighter I bought on one of our shopping trips and if I keep it I'll be tempted to light up.'

Catherine laughed. 'I'll keep it in case you lapse. I know you and your willpower.'

She took the lighter and tucked it into the pocket of her jeans.

Clayton didn't surface until early afternoon. Standing in the kitchen, preparing some food, she sensed him in the doorway and turned to see him still looking bleary-eyed and hungover, watching her. He gave her a sheepish smile and her insides melted. She ran to him, threw her arms round him and hugged him. She felt his body relax into her as she rested her head on his shoulder.

For a moment neither of them spoke. Then he cupped her face in his hands and tilted her head back.

'I'm sorry. Am I forgiven for being a prat? I didn't know what to do when I read those results last night. Staring into a glass seemed like the best option.'

She nuzzled her face into his neck, wanting to breathe him in, and caressed his chest through the shirt he still wore from dinner. It was creased and he was unshaven, but desire ran through her like a lightning rod. The top two shirt buttons were undone, and she was desperate to rip open the rest, but for now she had to focus on helping him deal with the events of last night.

'I understand, you've had a terrible shock to the system, and of course I forgive you. Don't you ever quote this back at me, but I'm sure I could forgive you anything. By the way you're ridiculously hot when you're all dishevelled and hungover.'

'Even smelling of beer and whisky and needing a shower?'

She smiled into his neck. 'Yes, to both, but you should go and have one. It'll make you feel better. Then come and eat and we'll talk.'

'I don't deserve you.'

She poked him in the ribs. 'Probably not, but you've got me. Now do as you're told. You've got ten minutes.'

He gave her a mock salute. 'Doesn't feel like a good time to argue. I'm on it. By the way, where's Nina? I suppose I've screwed her weekend up too.'

'I wouldn't worry about Nina. Right now you're the furthest thing from her mind.'

'Ah, David?'

She nodded. 'They're spending the day with each other. She's smitten, I think. They've been messaging like lovesick teenagers all morning, so it seems they both are. I'm so pleased for her. She's had a rough time.'

He met her smile with a frown. 'I'm not sure how keen David is on serious involvement. Maybe you should warn her.'

'I'm not sure Nina needs serious at the moment either, her divorce is still so recent. But she does deserve some fun, and maybe he's it. Let's see what happens. Now go and have that shower. You've got eight minutes of your ten left.'

'You're a hard taskmaster. I'm gone.'

She watched his retreating back and turned back to her lunch preparations. Something wasn't right. They'd spent the last ten minutes behaving as though nothing had happened. As soon as they'd eaten, she had to make him talk about Becca.

Last night's temporary alcohol-induced denial was one thing, but for it to continue was dangerous. He had to confront this, and she had to help him. As she assembled plates and cutlery, she wondered what she could say to him that would make dealing with this any easier.

CHAPTER FIFTY-FIVE

As Catherine lay in bed on Sunday night, with Clayton finally in a deep sleep, she reflected on the events of the last forty-eight hours.

Nina had spent Saturday night at David's flat. Clayton's warning about his friend not looking for a serious relationship rang in Catherine's ears. She still wasn't sure she trusted him, but Nina was so excited she couldn't bring herself to be anything other than supportive, as her friend had been with her. Now she realised how the speed at which her relationship with Clayton progressed had probably alarmed Nina, but she'd never said so, and now neither must she.

David was due to leave on a business trip on Sunday afternoon and drove Nina back to St John's Wood for lunch before Catherine took her to Euston. Clayton went into work briefly, so she and Nina got some more time alone. They clung on to each other at Euston as they said their goodbyes. Both were excited about the men in their lives, but their friendship had a special place in both their hearts.

Catherine turned in bed to look at the man beside her and stroked his cheek gently. She didn't want to wake him, but she couldn't resist touching him as his face wore the relaxed expression of someone sleeping calmly. She'd hardly dared to contemplate that when he'd first given her the news about Becca, or on the several occasions he'd broken down over the weekend. But several long talks as he lay on the sofa with his head in her lap seemed to have helped. As had the intimacy of their love-making. Their connection was like nothing she'd experienced before and had never dared to hope she would. Sometimes raw, urgent and passionate. At other times, like tonight, slow and gentle, as if nobody existed but the two of them.

The more she'd encouraged him to talk about Becca, the more she knew he was seeing the discovery that she was not biologically his for what it was. The haunted look he'd worn on Saturday was overshadowed when he talked of the first moment he'd held her within seconds of her birth. He'd loved her instantly then, and he'd loved her through every second since. The fear he'd harboured for ten years that she may have Huntington's Disease had so often felt like too much to bear. Now, thankfully he was released from that fear. More importantly, his daughter was healthy.

Catherine held him tightly to her when he broke down with relief that Becca had escaped the ticking clock of a genetic defect. She repeated the message she'd delivered throughout the weekend.

'Clayton. You're Becca's father in every way that matters, and in the only way she's ever known. You always have been, and you always will be. You know better than anyone how much more important that is than biological parentage.'

He clung to her and whispered, 'I know'.

She lifted his head and looked directly into his eyes. 'I understand how difficult this has been for you, but you're coming to terms with it. She's still your daughter and nothing has changed, except for one thing. You can stop worrying that you've passed a defective gene on to her. I know how guilty you've felt about that. Not that you should have done, your genetics are hardly your fault. But at least you've been saved having to face the result you feared. Feeling the way you do now is a huge price to pay for that, but...'

'But I'm still her Dad, and I would willingly have paid any price for her to escape this disease, including feeling like this. Thank you for helping me see that.'

Then he pulled her into his arms and kissed her slowly and intimately as if he never wanted to release her from it. When his phone rang, Catherine reluctantly broke away from his exploring mouth. She hoped the call was from Becca. He needed to hear the bubbling normality of his daughter's voice.

He grabbed his phone from the charger and gave her a smiling thumbs up. She breathed an inner sigh of relief. He would still face some demons about all this, but she would help him deal with them. She'd suggested he tell Becca nothing about the test outcome, and when she heard him laughing down the phone at something his daughter had said, she knew for certain this would be OK.

Now she lay in bed desperate for sleep herself, praying that his research efforts would pay off. They'd talked so often about his daughter's risk of Huntington's that she'd scarcely thought of the consequences of it lying dormant in him.

She switched off the light and lay motionless in the dark. The realisation that she might have to face losing him to it, when she'd only just found him, cut through her like a dagger.

Please God let it not happen.

CHAPTER FIFTY-SIX

Clayton left early for work on Monday, more positive than Catherine had hoped for. His commitment to his research appeared undiminished. She'd feared it might be, now that Becca no longer faced the threat that had motivated him for so long.

She clung to him when he kissed her goodbye. She didn't want to let go.

'Clayton. You will keep going, won't you? Please. I know it's not for Becca any more, but I need you to do this for you. And for me.' Tears pricked at her eyes. 'I can't lose you to this cruel disease.'

He tilted her face and brushed her tears aside. 'I will keep going. We're so close, I can feel it. Becca is spared this, but I've known that fear for her for so long, like an ache that never goes away. If I can stop others having to go through that, then I must. And I'm doing it for you too now. I love you and I have no intention of leaving you.' He pulled her closer, as if he wanted to absorb her into him. 'Don't worry baby. I can do this.'

She stepped back and smiled. 'Then go to it Mr Scientist. I'll see you later.'

By midday Catherine was on her way to Lizzie's. She felt a pang of guilt at not telling Clayton about her plan to follow Clara, but she knew he'd try to stop her. And she had to do this. Although she couldn't convince him, she continued to feel he was at risk given how close he was to a game-changing breakthrough. Now her investigation was about more than Adam's death. It was about protecting the man she loved.

Over the weekend she'd again considered taking her suspicions to the authorities, but she didn't know who she could trust. In any case she didn't have enough firm evidence to present to them, only her conviction that a series of random events were connected. She couldn't expect officialdom to reach the same conclusion without something more concrete.

She'd called Lizzie earlier on the pretext of a catch-up chat to tell her about Nina's weekend, and to apologise they hadn't had a chance to all meet up. She learned Clara was still at home and being difficult. Lizzie suspected she was still seeing the man she knew nothing about, but who she feared was completely unsuitable for her daughter. Clara had announced she was going out for lunch and Lizzie presumed she might be meeting him.

Catherine hadn't expected the opportunity to follow Clara to come this quickly, but she couldn't let it pass.

As she sat in the back of a taxi making its way towards Muswell Hill, she asked herself what the hell she thought she was doing. She was making this up as she went along and she knew she should tell George what she was up to, but she also knew he'd try to stop her.

Instead she looked down at her outfit, quickly purchased that morning, and very un-her. She doubted anybody would recognise her in it. Certainly not Clara, who had grown up knowing a very different looking Catherine to the person she'd become after Nina's makeover. The girl had only seen her twice since then, and on neither occasion had she taken much notice of her appearance.

Although rush hour had passed, the cab driver cursed under his breath as he tried to snake his way through another traffic hold-up. Catherine stared out of the window, barely aware of it; her mind was back on Friday's dinner. Thinking about her own appearance had brought somebody else's to mind. David. Why did he seem so familiar? And an uncomfortable realisation hit her. She tried to dismiss the idea, but it had taken root.

He reminded her of Becca.

She stood at the end of Lizzie's street where she had a clear view of the house. Her hair was pulled back under the hoodie she'd bought, and she frowned as she stared down at the new mock camouflage trousers. The horrible combo almost made her giggle, and under any other circumstances it would be totally inappropriate, but it suited her purpose today.

She looked at her watch. 12.30. She hoped she hadn't missed Clara, and doubted she had. According to Lizzie her daughter was rarely an early riser and took ages to get ready. Apparently today had been no exception. Catherine tucked her hands into the hoodie's oversized pockets against the cold. As she jogged on the spot to stay warm, she thought again about David. She couldn't dislodge her growing suspicion that he might be Becca's father, but she vowed never to hint at it to Clayton.

He'd opened up more to her about his ex-wife over the weekend. It seemed she'd never shown any of the normal female delight at being pregnant, and from the minute she gave birth it was clear she regretted motherhood. Her doctor diagnosed temporary baby-blues and assured Clayton she would change, but it didn't happen. She never embraced her maternal feelings or responsibilities and had instead been cold towards both him and their daughter. He'd been sole parent to Becca, and her grandmother, despite her long distance, had become the mother-figure she'd needed.

He confessed his marriage had been a mistake from the beginning. He'd rushed into it when Angela told him she was pregnant, and Becca was the only good thing to have come out of the relationship. From the moment his wife recovered from the birth he doubted her fidelity, until eventually he announced he wanted a divorce.

As he spoke neither he nor Catherine acknowledged the now glaringly obvious. That his wife hadn't been faithful before they married either.

Catherine wondered why he'd never been struck by the similarity between his daughter and his best friend. Maybe she was jumping to a stupid conclusion, but something in the way David had talked about Angela on Friday night before Clayton had shot him a look that shut the story down made her wonder about his relationship with her.

Her thoughts were interrupted by the sight of Lizzie's door opening. Clara emerged and gave a dismissive wave to her mother standing in the doorway. Catherine shrank back behind the cover of a tree and pulled the hoodie closer to herself. As she watched Lizzie go back inside, and wishing she knew what the hell she was doing, she started to follow Clara at a discreet distance.

She realised her legs were shaking as she walked. She had no idea who or what Clara would lead her to.

CHAPTER FIFTY-SEVEN

When they finally reached the Broadway the crowd of lunch time shoppers gave Catherine some cover, as she merged into their anonymity, but they also made it more difficult to keep Clara in her sights, so she took the risk of closing the distance between them.

With her head down she almost collided with another hoodie-clad figure who emerged from a doorway straight into her path. He cursed without seeming to notice her and she glanced up as he turned his back to her to walk on. Her heart skipped a beat and her insides somersaulted at the sight of the now familiar baseball cap.

It was him. He barged through a group of girls huddled in conversation on the pavement, then caught up with Clara and threw his arm over her shoulder. As the girl looked round Catherine dropped her gaze, but she caught him in profile, seemingly sniggering at the fact he'd made Clara jump. She caught the same sneering expression she remembered from the blurred CCTV footage, and it was frustratingly familiar. She needed to see his full face.

She followed them until they turned into a café. She

walked past it and glanced in through the window. Clara stood in the queue to order but she couldn't see her companion. He must have found a table. She had no choice but to follow them in. She decided to wait until enough people were in line behind Clara for her not to be spotted, then she'd order and wait to see which table Clara headed to with the drinks.

Five minutes later, waiting to collect the skinny flat white she'd ordered, she still hadn't seen the man's full face. From her sideways view of their table she saw him typing into his phone. Clara appeared to be arguing with him as he ignored her, apart from occasionally raising his hand to silence her. The speed of the gesture sent a shiver through Catherine. She imagined that same hand would have no reservations about making direct body contact. Suddenly she felt frightened for Clara. What was she doing with this man? Had he played some part in her father's death? Instinct told Catherine he was dangerous.

She contemplated running but Adam's face flashed into her mind. If this man had been involved in his death she needed to find out. She had him in her sights and she had to see this through.

She shifted in her seat, feeling uncomfortably warm and wishing she could take the hoodie off. A few glances from her fellow customers suggested she looked conspicuous in it.

She risked looking directly at Clara to check the girl hadn't noticed her, but she was pointing her finger at Mr Baseball Cap, her face twisted with anger as she mouthed something at him. He raised his hand to silence her as his mobile ring.

From what she could see, he listened then ended the call without replying. He stood abruptly, threw some money towards Clara and turned to walk out. Catherine lifted her coffee cup and dipped her head as low as she could. She didn't want to make eye contact with this man, but she needed to see what he looked like. Before she caught a glimpse of his face, he span back round to Clara who'd stood to follow him. He towered above her in an aggressive stance, grabbed her by the shoulders and pushed her back into her seat. She looked visibly shaken and on the verge of tears. Catherine wished she could intervene. She shared Lizzie's concern about this guy. He was a nasty piece of work and wherever he was going he clearly didn't want company.

The cup shook in Catherine's trembling hands and she put it down. With her hands tucked into the hoodie's pockets she tried to shrink down into it, wanting it to swallow her up. She should grab Clara and run, but she'd come this far, and she had to stay focused on this man. He approached her table, heading for the exit, clearly in a hurry. She lowered her head, still keeping him in sight, ready to follow him as soon it was safe.

As he passed, looking straight ahead without seeming to notice her, she got her first glimpse of his face. She let out an involuntary gasp and a shiver ran through her.

She was looking directly at the face she'd woken up next to this morning.

CHAPTER FIFTY-EIGHT

Catherine recovered from the initial shock of the face she'd seen, jumped out of her seat and ran to the exit, determined not to let the man that face belonged to out of her sight. It could only be one person. Clayton's twin brother, Max. Her stomach lurched and she felt sick. If he was involved in all this, then it was about more than a plot to derail scientific research. It was also personal.

She reached the street in time to see him on the other side of it, about to turn the first corner. The traffic lights were against her but fortunately the traffic was moving slowly. She darted her way through blaring horns, her hands up in a gesture of apology, and caught up with him in time to see him take the next left.

She pulled the hoodie further down over her face. Away from the busy Broadway these streets were quiet. She guessed this man would not be so easily fooled as Clara and she told herself to be extra careful. Now she regretted not telling George her plan. She contemplated calling him, but Max was moving too quickly. She couldn't risk taking her eyes off him and losing him.

At the next corner he stopped abruptly and pulled his phone from his pocket. He turned to look across the street and Catherine took her phone out and pretended to be texting in case he turned further in her direction. She was close enough to see that he looked agitated as he put the phone back in his pocket and crossed the road. She sensed he'd been summoned somewhere, and whoever was summoning him was growing impatient. She hoped she was right. This might give her another link in the chain.

Five minutes later he stopped outside a pub which looked like it had seen better days. If he was meeting someone here, she'd need to figure out what to do. On her own and dressed as she was, she knew she'd look conspicuous. When he went inside, she stayed where she was and decided on her plan. She'd give him five minutes to meet his companion, then go in herself on the pretext of feeling unwell and asking to use their bathroom. She hoped the pub would be more crowded than its shabby exterior gave it any right to be, to give her some cover while she tried to spot him.

She decided to use the five minutes to message George and tell him what she was doing. It was about time she did. But before she could complete and send it a black cab drew up outside the pub entrance. When the passenger door opened, she had her second shock of the day. Even in profile she recognised the man who stepped out of it. Susie's father.

She knew from George that the family lived in North London, although she struggled to imagine this being Richard Cameron's local. But it was too much of a coincidence to contemplate that he wasn't here to meet Max. He'd clearly chosen a venue where he was unlikely to be spotted.

She waited until he went in, then gave it a few minutes before she followed him. She had to be extra diligent now. She was about to spy on two men who had both seen her very recently. Max in a photograph and Richard Cameron at the conference. She hoped they were at a table where she might be able to see their interaction without the risk of being noticed, and not at the bar.

She walked in, conscious that her legs were shaking. The pub was quiet, and most of the tables were empty. Not what she'd hoped for. From a quick glance she couldn't see either of them. Thankfully there was nobody at the bar. She had to stick to her plan, find the ladies, and hopefully spot these guys somewhere without them spotting her.

The bartender was bald, covered in tattoos and spoke with a broad cockney accent. He gave her a wink and a smile when she apologised and asked if she could use their facilities.

'Be my guest darlin'. You look pale under that hood. You alright? Need me to fetch the wife?'

She gave him a weak smile back. She must look even worse than she felt. Undercover surveillance obviously didn't agree with her. He pointed in the direction of the ladies' room and told her he'd have a glass of water waiting for when she got back. 'On the house. You look like you need it love. Don't want you collapsing on us.'

She thanked him and moved towards the back of the small pub. Where the hell were these two? She realised there were more tables tucked around the corner. They must be there. Huddled into the jacket she was confident she'd be unrecognisable to them, but she decided her best vantage point would be when she emerged from the ladies'.

She half-ran to the restroom door, noting that the table next to it was occupied. Safely inside she took some deep breaths, leaned over the sink and splashed her face with cold water. Despite the fleecy hoodie and the warmth of the pub she shivered. Every part of her was cold and she yearned to be back in the safe haven of Clayton's apartment. She considered running away again, but the idea that they'd had some part in the death of one man she'd loved, and posed a threat to the man she now adored, meant she had to keep going.

She waited a couple of minutes to calm her nerves then opened the door back to the bar. She was aware of raised voices from the table immediately to her right. She recognised the arrogant tone of Richard Cameron. It was one of the things about him that she'd detested when she met him. With the door conveniently hiding her from them she strained to listen to what they were saying.

She heard a chair being scraped back against the pub's wooden floor. Perhaps one of them was leaving. If so, their exchange had been short. Then she heard a voice she didn't recognise speaking. Was it Max?

'And I don't like you bastards treating me like a piece of shit who comes running when you click your fingers. Like any of you have got the stomach to do what I do. Haven't got the balls any of you.'

Then she heard Cameron again. 'Shut the fuck up. We pay, you do what we tell you to. Let's get this over with so I never have to listen to your crap again. You've got your extra money, so now deal with that pain in the ass brother of yours. Deliver what Cerberus want and get what you want. And the rest of your money. From now on no more stupid mistakes, or you get replaced. Permanently.'

She clasped her hand to her mouth to stifle her gasp. Cerberus. So, Adam had made that connection, and maybe not long before his death. She tried to blank out the image of the vibrant friend she'd loved and lost to these people. The first voice, which she now knew to be Max's, was speaking again. It sounded so different to the lilting softness of Clayton's. This voice was hard, aggressive and unfeeling. How could they be twins and share the same DNA?

'Oh they'll get what they want, and so will I. It'll be a pleasure to take out that dear brother of mine. Two days from now; it's all planned. So, run along and tell them that, messenger boy. I'm having another drink.'

Catherine shrank back into the safety of the ladies' room. She didn't wait to hear Cameron's reply. She'd heard everything she needed to, and she felt tainted by her proximity to these two men. She was desperate to escape the stifling atmosphere of this place, breathe some air and decide what to do next. She needed to get to Clayton, and she needed to warn him.

She flung open the door, keeping her head down. Their table was empty. She looked at the bar where Max was downing a beer. Thank God he had his back to her. She couldn't bear to look at his face. A face that was identical to the face of the man she loved. But on this man it was the face of true evil. How could twin brothers be so different?

She ran to the door, gasping for the fresh air on the other side of it. As she pulled it open, she heard the bartender calling to her.

She didn't look back.

CHAPTER FIFTY-NINE

She ran until she reached the Broadway, eager to be back in the safe anonymity of its crowds and walked into the first coffee shop she saw. She glanced round briefly to check neither Lizzie or Clara were here. God, she was jumpy. She found a table at the back and unzipped the hoodie with relief. The café was warm, and she could afford a temporary respite from her disguise. She took a few grateful sips of her coffee and began to feel more like herself. The last couple of hours had been like a crazy rollercoaster ride with a madman at the controls and she was glad she'd stepped off it, but now it was time to come to grips with what she'd discovered and decide what to do next. She only had two days to stop Max.

Surely Clayton would take her fears more seriously after what she'd learned today. She suspected he'd seen her warnings to him so far as the product of her journalistic overactive imagination. Now she had to convince him he was in real danger and it was imminent. The fact it was from his twin would be a difficult message for her to deliver, and for him to hear, especially since he was already dealing with the shock about Becca.

She would have to convince the authorities to take action too. She switched her phone back on to call George. It was time they took what they had now to the police. Max had to be stopped, and the clock was ticking.

Her phone sprang into life and bombarded her with notifications. A missed message from Will, one from Clayton and three missed calls from George. Maternal instinct made her click on Will's name first. She needed to know he was OK, and she smiled in spite of everything as she read his message.

'Hi Mum.
Got an A in big Anatomy test,
had to tell u.
U ok? Can't wait to c u at
Xmas!!!! xxxxxxxxxx

Christmas. She'd given it no thought since she'd joked with the taxi driver about it. She'd stopped noticing the festive displays that were now everywhere, or hearing the familiar music. But her son had no idea of the turmoil in her life. She kept their daily messages light and upbeat, and now the normality of him looking forward to them spending Christmas together had butted right up against the strangeness of this morning. Her phone screen was a blur as tears stung her eyes. She blinked them away and typed a reply.

'You're a star!! I'm so proud of you.
Can't wait to see you at the end of term either.
Not long now!
Let's video chat at the weekend
and agree the plan.
Love. Mum xxxx'

The weekend, the other side of Max's deadline. The tears

disappeared as she refocused on what she had to do. For her son, for the man she loved, for Adam and Lizzie. And for herself.

She had to make this right, whatever it took.

She opened Clayton's message. It was typical of him.

'Hi. You ok? All fine here.
I couldn't be going
through this without you.
See you later. Dinner?
Let's make up for the weekend we lost.'

She replied with a simple *'I love you.'* There was nothing else she could say until they were face to face.

She hit George's number and he answered on the second ring. 'Catherine, thank God. Where the hell are you? I've been calling you all morning. Your phone kept going straight to voicemail.'

'I'm sorry. I started a message to you, but I had to switch the phone off and...'

His concern was immediate as she broke off, feeling overcome again by the events of the morning. 'What's happened? Are you OK?'

She took a deep breath. She knew he wouldn't be happy to hear she'd gone it alone this morning. 'I'm OK. I have news to share but you have to promise not to yell at me.'

'That depends. What have you done and why do I have a bad feeling about it?'

'I followed Clara. And she led me straight to our man. To two men actually.'

'Bloody hell, Catherine. We agreed...'

She cut across him. She understood his indignation, but she didn't have time to indulge it. 'I know what we agreed, George, but it felt the right thing to do. It's been a weird weekend to be honest, but I'll tell you more about that another time, because right now time's something we don't have. I need to tell you what I've discovered. It was impulsive of me but at least now I know what we're up against. The clock's ticking before there's another attempt on Clayton's life so we've got to move fast. There's no time for recriminations.'

His tone softened. 'I understand. Tell me, but let me sit down first.'

Ten minutes later she'd shared everything with him. The identity of Mr Baseball Cap, his meeting with Richard Cameron, the mention of Cerberus, and the planned move on Clayton in two days' time.

She heard his occasional sharp intake of breath as she spoke, but he let her talk without interruption. When she was finished his response was instant.

'Wow, Adam was right all along. This is as big as he suspected. And you think Cerberus is the codename for the unholy trio of Galen and the other two big corporates? No wonder Cameron was brown-nosing around Paul Naylor. You never mentioned this name Cerberus before though. Why not?'

'Because I didn't know what it might mean. It was just a word among Adam's doodling on the spreadsheets, but I had a feeling about it, and something made me destroy it. Now we know he was on to them.' She paused for a moment as her voice trembled. 'I so wish he'd shared more of this with me before that morning. He might still be alive now if he had.'

'We'll never know that Catherine, so don't punish either yourself or him by going there. What we do know is his suspicions were correct and it's up to us to deal with them for him. That validates him in some extra way. I know it doesn't bring him back, but...as you've said...we have to make his death mean something.'

'Thank you for saying all that, and yes, we do. Somehow Cerberus must have suspected he was getting too close to comfort. Maybe Richard Cameron overheard something when Adam took that call the day of Clara's party. It's a pity Lizzie doesn't know who it was from. Maybe it was Sedgwick, and after that he and Adam were both marked men and these guys decided to keep closer tabs on them. Or maybe they got to Sedgwick and bought his silence for a while. The police will be able to trace that call. And remember Adam was being tipped for Cabinet promotion only weeks before his death.'

'Which would have put him in a more powerful position to nail them, especially if they were about to lose the cover of Charles Sedgwick.'

'Exactly. So, we have to finish what Adam started and make sure this group are exposed and stopped. And we have to stop Max before he gets to Clayton in two days.'

'So Cameron's the middle man and Max is the hitman? Doesn't surprise me about Cameron. I didn't have chance to tell you I went to Susie's for dinner last night and he was there, and very jumpy. Kept looking at his phone all evening and disappearing.'

'He was being summoned by Galen and Co presumably.'

'It sounds probable, and it all fits. This guy Max is a shock though. I didn't know Clayton had a twin.'

'He hardly talks about him, so I don't know much either. They were separated at birth. Their biological mother kept Max and Clayton was adopted. Max has been in and out of institutions and prison since he was a kid. Clayton looked him up ten years ago and has supported him ever since. That's about all I know.'

'The guy's got a strange way of saying thank you. I wonder how he got involved in all this corporate stuff? It's a long way from petty crime.'

'Presumably Cerberus wanted to get at Clayton, and they traced Max and recruited him. I suppose an identical twin seemed like a lucky asset and finding out they could manipulate the guy because of his personal vendetta against his brother must have been music to their ears. But it makes him more dangerous George. He has to be stopped.'

'We need to take all this to the police fast, Catherine. Let's involve Sam too. Having his voice alongside us will help, and we know we can trust him completely.'

'I had the same thought. I feel better already talking to you, George. Now we need the authorities to move on this right away.'

'They won't have a choice once they hear all this. Jump in a taxi and get here as soon as you can. I'll line Sam up. I'll feel better once I can keep an eye on you. This has become a very dangerous game Catherine and I don't want you going off on your own again. That boyfriend of yours would never forgive me if I did, and he's bigger than me.'

Catherine laughed. 'Aye aye Sir. Only you could manage to make me half-smile in the midst of all this.'

'All part of the service. Message me when you're in the taxi, OK? See you soon.'

She walked out onto the Broadway and hailed a taxi. She leaned back in the seat with relief, messaged George, then hit Clayton's number. His phone went to voicemail and she left a quick message before calling the lab phone. Unusually it rang out with no reply. Frowning she sent him a text message and her frown deepened when she didn't see the usual message received indicator, as if his phone was either out of range or off.

Her heart started to thump in her chest. Something didn't feel right. Clayton never switched his phone off. She tapped on the driver's partition and asked him to change direction.

She had to get to the university as quickly as possible.

CHAPTER SIXTY

Fifteen minutes later Catherine found Clayton's lab locked. It appeared to be empty. There were no lights on, and she could hear no activity through the door. The ball of fear in her stomach grew bigger. It moved its way towards her throat, and she thought it might choke her. She leaned against the lab door, breathed herself calm again, then ran to John.

The security guard looked up from his phone and smiled as he sensed her approaching.

'Hi lovely lady. How are you?'

Her voice was breathless and jerky. 'John, I need your help. I'm worried about Professor Mortimer. Did you see him leave today?'

'No, I didn't. I thought he was still in his lab. He sent the others home early a couple of hours ago. Study time or something. They lead a charmed life these bloody students. Should try working for a bleedin' living. See how much time they get off then.'

Catherine barely heard him. Nothing mattered but finding Clayton. Max's plan was still two days away, but she was already uneasy.

She looked back at John, who was clearly expecting some response to his anti-student rant, but she ignored it. 'Did you by any chance see that guy with the weird baseball cap around today?'

He gave her a puzzled look. 'Can't say I did, and I'd remember that cocky bastard. What's he got to do with the Prof anyway?'

'Oh, probably nothing. And if you're sure you haven't seen him...'

'Well I can't be absolutely certain. There's a lot of them coming and going through here and sometimes I get a bit distracted I suppose.' He coughed nervously. 'Listen love, what's wrong? I can tell something is. Do you want me to fix you a brew? You look a bit peaky if you don't mind me saying.' He put his hand on hers. 'Look, I'm sure the Professor's alright. More than likely disappeared for a walk. He does that sometimes. When he needs to think, that's what he tells me.'

She remembered. Clayton had told her about the park he liked to sit in sometimes. She should check it out before she started jumping to conclusions. She leaned over the desk and kissed John on the cheek.

She stepped back and smiled into his shocked face. 'Thank you. You're probably right. Can you give me directions to this park? I'll take a walk round there.'

She sat alone on the bench Clayton had described to her, and wished he was there. She shivered and pulled the hoodie tightly against her. She understood why he found it peaceful, but she sat, sick with worry, her head in her hands as she wondered what to do next.

Her spirits had lifted as she ran here, convinced she would find him. But now they'd sunk even lower than before. She called him again and left another voice message. There was still no indication he'd received her earlier text messages. Her fingers trembled as she sent another one.

Panic rose in her stomach again and she tried breathing through it. Somehow, she knew he needed her, and falling apart was not an option. If he wasn't reading or responding to her messages, it could only mean one thing. He wasn't able to.

She jumped up from the bench. The action made her dizzy and she grabbed on to the wrought iron arm for support. She'd eaten nothing all day and felt sick with emptiness and panic. She tightened her grip on the bench. She mustn't give in to this, she had to get moving.

After some gulps of fresh air, the nausea passed, and she set off back towards the university. She would hail a cab back to the flat. She had to track down Max, and for that she needed access to Clayton's files.

Her phone bleeped with messages, then it rang. She prayed it was Clayton, but it was George. He must be wondering where the hell she was. Feeling guilty she declined the call, with a silent promise to message him from the taxi and suggest he go ahead and make the initial contact with the police without her.

He'd tell her to get to his office straightaway and she knew that was the sensible option, but she was being overtaken by some temporary madness. She had to find Clayton, and she had to do it now. If she waited for the wheels of officialdom to get in motion it might be too late.

She jumped into the first black cab with its light on and pleaded with the driver to get her to St John's Wood as quickly as he could. He shrugged as he gestured to the line of cars in front of him but told her to jump in. She stared at her phone throughout the journey, willing Clayton to call. When she looked away from it briefly to silently curse the slow-moving traffic it rang. It was George again.

'Catherine, where are you? You should be here by now.

I've got Sam lined up. He thinks we should talk and decide how best to proceed.'

'I'm not sure there's time for talking. I'm on my way back to the flat. Clayton's gone missing. I need to find him and there may be some clues there.'

'Missing since when?'

'This morning.' As she said the words, she knew he'd say she was panicking prematurely. She hoped she was, but her intuition told her she wasn't. 'And I know what you're about to say, but don't.'

'I'm about to say I think you've had a bloody awful day and you should stick with the plan and come over here. Right now. Let's figure this out between us. And yes, I do have to say Clayton's hardly been missing long enough for you to panic. I doubt the police would launch an investigation this early. And you heard Max's timing. Two days from now. So, let's stop him, but let's do it properly. There's a lot at stake here.'

'Tell me about it. Starting with Clayton's life. I'm not sure there's time for properly.' She glanced up as the taxi pulled up outside her building. 'I need to go. I'll call you back.'

'Catherine...' The rest of his sentence was lost. She hit call end, switched the phone to silent, reached in her pocket to pay the fare and ran into the building.

She leaned against the familiarity of the apartment door with relief. She sensed Clayton all around her and imagined she could smell his cologne. She dared to hope he might be here waiting for her and called his name, but she was met with a silence that hung heavily, as if she'd walked into an airless vacuum. The apartment was exactly as she left it earlier. The mail and several circulars sat on the hall table where she'd put them, undisturbed. The normality of junk mail made her wonder if the abnormality of the last few hours had really happened.

Her stomach churned with a sick emptiness. She went into the kitchen, poured herself a glass of milk and drank it in one go. She needed energy to cope with whatever she did next. A glance at her phone showed two missed calls from George but no news from Clayton. Putting it on fast charge, she ran into the bathroom and splashed her face with warm water. She tore off the camouflage trousers and hoodie and threw them on the bed, grabbed the first pair of jeans she found and added a thick black jumper.

In familiar clothes, and with the milk taking effect against the empty nausea, she began to feel more herself, and checked her watch. It had been ten minutes well spent.

Now it was time to decide what to do next.

CHAPTER SIXTY-ONE

If she didn't call George back soon, she suspected he'd come and find her, so she had to move quickly. Catherine went into Clayton's study, feeling guilty at what she was planning and not even sure what she'd do if she found what she was looking for. She pulled open the first drawer of the wooden filing cabinet. The files were in neat alphabetical order but stopped at K. She slammed it shut, pulled open the second one and pulled out the section marked M. She hoped it would tell her more about Max, but it held nothing on him.

She turned to the desk. It was locked, which suggested Clayton kept sensitive information in it. She had no idea where the key might be, and no time to look, so she ran to the kitchen and grabbed a knife.

As she tried to prise the lock open, she looked around the empty study furtively, imagining she was being watched. She gripped the knife between the drawer and the frame with both hands, until her knuckles turned white, then shrieked a triumphant 'Yes' into the air when the wood splintered, and the top drawer flew open. As she stared at stationery, she wrenched the drawer out and flung it to the floor. Now she had access to the bottom drawer, and there it was. A thick unmarked folder, its contents starting to spill out, including a photograph.

It was full of information on Max and she rifled through it until she found what

she wanted, his address. He'd had several over the past ten years, all at Clayton's expense, but this one appeared to be current. The latest rental payment had been processed barely three weeks ago and she did a double-take at the amount. Clayton had clearly been generous with his twin. She memorised the address and put the file back.

Repeating the address in her head, she walked back into the kitchen. She had a decision to make. She knew the sensible move was to grab her phone, take what she had to George and do what they'd agreed, but the same madness that had assaulted her all along told her to go and confront Max directly.

She jumped as her phone rang. She didn't remember switching the sound back on. It must be George again and she owed him at least some response. She yanked the phone from the charger and stared at the caller name in relieved disbelief. It was Clayton.

She barely recognised her own voice as she hit reply and yelled at his picture on screen.

'Where the hell have you been? Do you have any idea what I've gone through in the last few hours worrying about you?'

He paused before replying, then his tone was factual and unemotional, almost cold. 'I went to the library to do some research then for a long walk. I wanted to clear my head and think. You know what about. I left my phone in the lab, which shows I wasn't thinking straight. I'm sorry if you were worried, but I don't quite see where this attack's coming from. The security guy told me you turned up here earlier in a bit of a panic, that's why I'm calling you.'

'In a bit of a panic? That's a bloody understatement even by laid-back Australian standards. Didn't you read my messages?'

'No, I didn't, I prioritised calling you. Listen, there's nothing to worry about. We'll talk about this when I'm back.'

'We need to talk about a lot of things when you're home Clayton, trust me. You're in real danger and this time I need you to take it seriously. Please get out of there and come home.'

'I will as soon as I finish something up. Please don't argue Catherine, it's important.'

She shrieked into the phone in exasperation. 'Clayton... no...I...'

He didn't let her finish. 'I have to go. I'll be back as soon as I can, and I'll tell the security guard to stop worrying about you.'

She stared at the silent phone and her eyes filled with tears of relief mixed with anger. Anger was winning and her legs shook with it. He'd been almost dismissive of her concerns, which surprised her after their weekend closeness when she'd got him to open up about his feelings. He hadn't sounded like the loving Clayton who'd left for work this morning. She sank down onto a kitchen stool, her head in her hands.

The loving Clayton. She thought about those words again, and about the conversation he'd abruptly ended. Something didn't feel right. He hadn't sounded himself, but there was something else that was niggling her.

Of course, it was the way he talked about John. She'd never heard Clayton refer to him as the security guard. He always used his name, and she knew John liked to joke that he was the only member of the academic staff who did. Why hadn't he now? This was more than him not feeling himself.

Something was all wrong about that call.

CHAPTER SIXTY-TWO

Catherine stared into space, in a state of suspended animation, seeing nothing apart from Clayton's face. She'd lost
count how many times she'd had this sensation today, as if she
was a detached observer, watching a movie unfold on screen.

Her head started to pound, and she poured herself a glass
of water and rummaged in her bag for a paracetamol. Her
hands shook as she tried to press the capsule through its
blister pack. The sound of a phone ringing in the apartment
made her jump again and she swore as the painkiller flew out
of its pack and fell on the floor. It was the landline in Clayton's study. She'd never heard it ring before.

She ran to it and lifted the handset which flashed private
caller. Before she could speak, she was assaulted by a voice
she'd heard for the first time only hours earlier.

'So, we meet at last, in a manner of speaking. You know
who this is don't you?'

Her clammy fingers almost lost their grip on the handset.
Somehow she managed to put it on the desk, hit speaker-
phone and mumble a monotone reply.

'Yes Max. I know it's you.'

He sniggered down the phone. 'Not sounding quite your self. But then you've been busy today. Quite the little amateur detective, with the emphasis on amateur. Didn't think you'd get the better of a pro like me, did you?'

How did he know about her morning? She tried to focus and ignore the pounding in her head. She couldn't afford to fold now, there was too much at stake. She was certain he hadn't spotted her following him, in which case he must be monitoring her phone in some way and heard her updating George. Had he listened in to her conversation with Clayton too? How many others had he heard? Nausea hit her like a tsunami.

He was speaking again. 'Getting this now, are you? Yes, I do have your phone monitored. Your newspaper really should upgrade their security firm, the current crowd's pathetic. You're wondering if I listened in to your conversation with Mr Professor too aren't you? Or have you figured that one out?'

Her stomach lurched, and she tasted the semi-digested bitterness of milk. No wonder the call hadn't felt right, and Clayton hadn't sounded like himself. Now she understood why.

Max was right. She was up against a pro, and he was good. But she was angry, and that was good too. Anger had replaced the paralysis of fear, and it would make her focus. This man was dangerous, and he was clever. She'd need to match that cleverness to stop him and save Clayton.

She took a deep breath and summoned the strongest voice she could. 'I've figured it out. You didn't need to listen in did you? Because I was talking to you. You're good, I'll grant you that. But whatever you're planning you won't get away with it. Are you forgetting how much I know? And not just me.'

'I never forget, and I don't leave loose ends. Don't

threaten me with your sidekick, I'll sort him out. You see, you're ignoring the power dynamic here. Let me spell it out for you. I've got it, you don't, and I suggest you stop acting the smart bitch for once and listen. Especially if you want that clever little son of yours to ever take the Hippocratic oath. See? It's not only you and lover-boy who know some long words.'

She gripped the desk for support as her shaking legs gave way. Will. This bastard had Will.

She spat down the phone at him. 'If you lay one finger on my son...'

'And you'll what? See there you go again, imagining you're in a position to make threats. You're not. So be a good girl and sit your pretty little smart ass down at that posh desk you broke into, and listen to brother Max. Then do exactly what I tell you to do.'

She glanced behind her at the broken desk drawer on the floor where she'd left it. Fear struck at her again. He'd seen the entire thing.

Max didn't just listen. He watched too.

CHAPTER SIXTY-THREE

Ten minutes later Catherine was in the back of a minicab that Max had sent to collect her. She had no idea where she was going, and the driver refused to tell her. He caught her eye in the rear-view mirror, his face expressionless, his voice monotone.

'Mr Smith told us the destination's a surprise. Not the sort of bloke you argue with.'

Before she could respond he turned his attention back to the road and made a U-turn. From the direction they were heading in he was clearly not taking her to the address she'd found in Clayton's papers. Where the hell were they going?

She had no idea to what extent the driver was in Max's pocket, but she decided to risk a question and leaned forward to speak to him.

'I wonder if I could ask you a big favour. I really need to send Max...Mr Smith that is...a quick message. Unfortunately my phone's died on me. Is there any way I might borrow yours for two minutes? It'll be a very quick message I promise. I'd be so grateful.'

He half-turned to her and the expressionless face had

assumed a sneering smile. 'Sorry love no can do. Another of his requests. No using your phone, or mine. I guess he knew you'd ask. I suggest you sit back and enjoy the ride. It won't be long till you see him.'

Damn. She'd half guessed Max would have that one covered. This guy didn't seem to make mistakes. She leaned back in her seat and tried not to feel defeated. She couldn't afford to fold. She owed it to Will and Clayton to keep going, but she was up against a tough adversary and it would take every ounce of strength and ingenuity she possessed to get the better of him.

She had nothing to defend herself with apart from her wits. His instructions to her had been clear. She was to bring her phone with her, with her GPS switched on, but she mustn't use it. If she made contact with anybody he would know, and he would hurt her son. As long as he had Will she had no choice but to do what he said. She couldn't risk gambling that he might be bluffing.

He'd given her minimal thinking time, but she'd used the ten minutes she had to consider what she might take with her that could help her. She had no idea how much of Clayton's apartment he was watching and when she walked into their bedroom her stomach lurched at the thought he may have seen them in bed. She leaned against the wall for support against the wave of nausea that washed over her.

She forced herself to erase the image and focus on some means of defending herself, or at least making contact with someone who could help. She remembered her previous mobile phone which she now barely used since Sam had provided her and George with new ones. She frowned at the irony of how easily Max had hacked into their apparent security.

But maybe he was unaware of her old one. She rummaged for the handbag in the wardrobe where she knew she'd put it after she last checked it only days before. Hoping she was hidden from Max's prying eyes, she prayed it still had battery strength as she found it and tucked it into the pocket of her jeans.

She touched the phone through the thick denim as she stared out of the taxi's windows with unseeing eyes. If only she could use it. She didn't know where she was going or what Max had planned for her when she got there, but the prospect of being face to face with him scared her. She could taste her fear, like the aftertaste of a bitter pill.

She shook herself back into awareness as she recognised her surroundings. They were approaching Clayton's university building. Was Max waiting for her there? With Clayton? Her question was answered as the driver continued past it and made a left. She forced herself to concentrate on the route he took. She suspected Max was nearby, as her mobile rang.

'Nice try asking the driver for his phone. You did ask, didn't you? I'll let you off with that one for now. I'll look forward to punishing you for it later.' Her blood ran cold at Max's suggestive laugh as the taxi took a sharp right turn. She tried to ignore the image of his hands on her and concentrate on imprinting a mental map in her memory.

She didn't reply. She wanted to blank out his voice, but he continued. 'Disturbing your concentration am I? I wouldn't bother. You won't be seeing those streets again, but you will be seeing me soon. Within minutes in fact. The driver will give you more details when he drops you off. Do what he tells you. You know what happens if you don't.'

As the phone went silent the car slowed down and pulled in alongside a narrow building. It was grey and nondescript and the scaffolding outside it told her it was about to receive the same overdue facelift its neighbours had. The driver turned to her.

'Been a pleasure, but out you get. Hit 2487 on the keypad of that black door and head for the first floor. Mr Smith will meet you.'

She stepped out of the car and stared up at the building in front of her, then turned as the driver sped off. She was alone in the quiet street. This was it.

She took a deep breath and told her legs to stop shaking as she walked towards the unmarked black door.

CHAPTER SIXTY-FOUR

When Catherine emerged from the stairwell through the heavy fire door on the first floor, Max was leaning lazily in the doorway opposite. She walked towards him, feeling naked under his gaze, then stopped, unable to move. His eyes seemed to penetrate her body, and hatred for him burned in every inch of her.

She thought of the man with an identical face, who with one glance made every inch of her tingle. And now this man in front of her threatened him.

She remembered the excitement on her son's face the morning he'd received his Cambridge acceptance. This man threatened him too.

And the fear that had taken root inside her disappeared, overwhelmed by the two faces she loved. The odds were stacked against her, but she wasn't going to give in without a fight. Max was arrogant enough to assume that she would fold, and underestimating her might be his one mistake, and her only advantage. That and the fact she was certain he liked to sexually dominate women and planned to satisfy those urges with her before he disposed of her in some way.

However vile the prospect, she would play up to that and maybe he would let his guard down. She swallowed down the nausea that threatened to engulf her, tossed her hair back and walked towards him.

He stood to one side as he beckoned her in, but his breath was hot on her neck as she walked past him. The narrow hallway was dark and empty apart from a threadbare carpet. Max nudged her in the back and propelled her forward.

'Straight ahead. Living room. Sorry it's not quite up to my dear brother's posh gaff, but the place serves its purpose.'

She walked into another almost bare space. It held a ripped leather sofa, a coffee table and a large storage box. It smelled musty and dust particles hung in the air. She imagined them settling on her and she felt dirty. Max clearly wasn't here often, and she wondered what he did when he was, and who else had been in this room.

She turned around to face him. He gave her a twisted smile and his eyes glinted with evil. Despite the identical features he didn't look like Clayton at all, he was like an identical stranger. She stared him out but didn't speak. She saw disappointment flash across his face.

'Trying to be tough, are we? Thinking it might faze me?' He yanked her arm behind her back and she tried not to wince at the pain that shot through her shoulder. 'Maybe that'll make me enjoy you even more, when I sample that body my brother's been playing with. I've seen you in action with him, but then you figured that out, didn't you? I was quite impressed with your...skills shall we say? And you can be sure you'll be impressed with mine. It's about time you found out what the more talented twin can do, but that's for later. I need to take care of business first so give me your phone and sit down.' He held out his hand.

With her free hand she passed him her phone. He put it in his pocket, shoved her forward, and jerked his head in the direction of the sofa as he walked towards the storage box and lifted the lid. She stopped, unable to take another step towards the shabby piece of furniture. She was certain this room was about to become her prison cell, and that ripped leather sofa her deathbed, after whatever physical violation he had planned for her.

He swung round to look at her, his face still wearing that twisted smile. 'What are you waiting for? Sit, now.'

Her gaze dropped to his hands. He was holding a length of thick rope and behind him she saw the open chest was full. She tried not to imagine what its contents were or how he might be intending to use them on her.

She took a step towards the sofa and stopped again. This might be her last opportunity to try and get help and she had to take it.

She forced herself to give him a shy smile before she spoke. 'If you're going to hold me here, can you let me use your bathroom first? Please, I really need to.' She looked down at her feet, wringing her hands, hoping he'd believe an embarrassment she didn't feel.

Her performance was met with a sneer. 'If you must. You might be here for a while. And you are playing nicely now, good girl.' Her insides churned as his eyes glinted and roamed over her again before he gestured towards the door. 'Back to the hall and turn right. Bathroom's off the bedroom. You've got five minutes, and don't try anything clever.'

She turned and made her way to the bedroom, pushing the door closed as much as she could without him hearing. She had five minutes to make contact with the outside world, to think of some way of stalling him, and to find something to defend herself with.

She reached into her pocket for her spare phone, thanking God Max hadn't spotted it in his scrutiny of her. She switched it on, praying it was on silent, had some charge

and enough signal for her to message out. As it sprang sound-
lessly into life she walked towards the bathroom.

She stopped when she noticed the wardrobe door was
slightly ajar. Her phone was asking for her passcode and she
typed it in as she opened the door and looked for anything
that might help her. The cheap wire hangers held nothing
apart from two black hoodies and two baseball caps identical
to the ones she'd seen Max in. This was clearly his working
uniform. She glanced down at a cardboard box hidden behind
a pair of trainers. She looked at her watch. She had two
minutes before he'd come looking for her. Time to check out
the box and type her message.

She bent down, pushed the lid aside and found herself
staring at a gun. As she saw bullets lying next to it in the box,
she heard Max's footsteps. Damn, it was probably empty, and
she didn't have time to load it before he reached her. She
replaced the lid, pushed the door almost closed as she'd found
it and ran into the bathroom. It had no lock, so she ran the
tap. Hopefully he'd assume she was freshening up and not
walk in on her.

Her phone battery was low, but it should be enough to get
a message to George. She typed '*Held by Max. Help.*' and hit
send. Then she switched on GPS again, ready to send her
location.

'Well aren't we the smart arse. Now put that phone the
fuck down.'

She turned as the door flew open. The phone shook in her
hand as she saw her location flash up on the map.

There was no time to hit send.

CHAPTER SIXTY-FIVE

The excited glint Max's eyes held earlier had been replaced with a look of pure evil. Catherine stared into pools of black, with no hint of colour. She took a step back as he snatched the phone from her, smashed it against the sink and tossed it on the floor where it landed in pieces.

He grabbed her hair and she winced as he dragged her out of the bathroom and threw her on to the bed. He towered over her, then pushed her back, pinning her hands above her head. The violence of his grip made her shoulders ache. She tried to lift her knee to push him off her, but her legs refused to move.

His face was virtually on hers and she smelled the excitement on his warm breath. She turned her head away to escape it, but he gripped her under the chin and jerked her back, forcing her to look at him as he spoke.

'I love it when a woman gets that look on her face. Scared, wondering what I'm going to do next, but secretly turned on. Sorry to disappoint you but I'm not about to take you. Not yet anyway. There's the rather pressing matter of taking care of my dear twin brother first. But I'll be back before you know it, and I'll have you then.'

He released his grip, looked at his watch, and smiled. 'In fact, before too long I'll have everything that was his. Everything that should've been mine in the first place.'

He glanced towards the wardrobe. 'Thanks for noticing the caps by the way. I assume you opened that door and had a look. Cool, aren't they? Not my dear brother's style unfortunately, so I'll miss them. Must take one of them with me now. A good plan always relies on detail don't you think?'

Fear rose again in her stomach and chest as she shrank back from the manic look on his face and began to comprehend the full horror and madness of his plan. She ached with tiredness and shock, and her head hurt from the violent way he'd dragged her from the bathroom. She sank back on the bed, exhausted and defeated. There was nothing she could do to stop this man and for a moment she prayed she could drift into a deep sleep and let semi-consciousness deaden the pain of whatever Max had planned for her.

Her eyes closed and images of Clayton and Will appeared. A rush of energy hit her like a lightning bolt and forced her upright. She stared back at Max. She wouldn't give up. She had to find a way to stop his madness.

'What have you done with him Max? Whatever you're planning you won't get away with it.'

'I rather think I will. You see I'm just as smart as my brother, but his trouble is he's burdened with morals. Me? I got the don't give a shit gene.' He leaned closer to her again. 'So much for identical. But we're identical enough for this to work.'

She spat her words out. 'You're forgetting something. I'm not the only one who's on to you.'

He laughed into her face. 'Oh right, the poncey sidekick. That suits me fine. I hope he tells everybody what an evil bastard Max is. Or rather was, because Max is about to be history. You see that's the beauty of this whole plan. Started to figure it out now haven't you?'

She lunged at him. 'Where is he? And where's my son? I won't let you get away with this.'

He grabbed her wrists. 'And what the hell do you think you can do to stop me? You're way too late for that. I've got your Mr Wonderful in a safe place and there isn't a damn thing you can do to help him, but if you want to save your son I suggest you cooperate. Or trust me, I really will hurt you and him.'

She backed away. If she went along with him, she might learn some valuable information. Instinct told her his ego was desperate to brag about his masterplan. 'Please at least tell me where they both are. No harm in that surely.'

He sneered at her. 'See how nice you can be when you try. OK, I'll tell you. Your son's where you'd expect him to be, doing his normal stuff. I've got no interest in him anymore. You needn't worry about him, providing you behave.'

Thank god. At least her son was safe. 'And Clayton?'

He smiled his self-satisfied twisted smile. 'He's about to be where you'd expect him to be too. In his precious laboratory. But not for much longer.'

He leaned in towards her, his eyes flashing with excitement. 'I know he was planning to set the world on fire with his scientific brilliance. Now he's about to get his wish.' He threw back his head and laughed as she shrank back from him. 'Who says you shouldn't laugh at your own jokes? That's a bloody good one.'

CHAPTER SIXTY-SIX

Catherine swallowed the bitter taste of shock that rose like bile from her stomach and threatened to choke her words.

'You're going to set another fire.'

His face flashed with demonic pride. 'You bet I am. And this one will be spectacular. It'll make my others look like amateur night, but then practice does make perfect. It's my last job for Cerberus, so I should go out with a bang, don't you think? Between you and me I'm pretty pissed off with those bastards, but they've paid plenty, so I'll give them a good final show.'

He paused and looked at her, but she said nothing. The less she reacted the more she was sure he'd tell her.

'Anyway, this time it's personal. You see I get everything my brother had that should've been mine in the first place, and the Cerberus assholes off my back...all in one fell swoop. It's perfect symmetry and the perfect plan.'

Catherine shrank back from the evil insanity etched into his features and echoed in his voice. He tightened his grip on her shoulders and his manic smile told her how much he was enjoying exposing his plan.

'By the time I come back to sort you out there won't be a trace left of your Mr Wonderful or his laboratory. This fire will take out everything. Then all the bad guys come out on top. Cerberus get rid of Professor Clayton Mortimer and his research. And I get his life. A different version of it of course. The new Clayton will be way too shell-shocked to work. Especially when he finds out his girlfriend's vanished too.' He leaned closer and spoke directly into her ear. 'I'm looking forward to acting the grieving lover. It'll be such fun.'

She jerked her head away from him, sick from the warmth and smell of his excited breath on her neck. 'This can't possibly work Max, you're insane. You'll never pull it off. Nobody will believe you're him.'

'No? I've got away with it all so far. Taking out that inter-fering politician friend of yours for starters. Not a bad bloke as it happens, but he had to go. Now I need to shake off that horny but way too clingy little daughter of his. She's long past her sell-by date, and she's served her purpose. Then there was his smug, arrogant boss Sedgwick. Typical lying politician, it was a pleasure getting rid of him. Almost a public service you might say.'

Her insides screamed with pain and nausea. She wanted to lash out at the insane evil in front of her, but she stayed silent.

'Cat got your tongue? Trying to be Ms Cool, are we? Well Ms Cool's wrong, I will pull this off. I fooled you on the phone, didn't I? And you've slept with him, so everybody else should be a piece of cake. And remember I'll be a traumatised Clayton after the fire.' He pulled a mock grieving face. 'A fire that tragically claimed the life of his twin, despite his...or should I say my...efforts to save him. Poor Max, dying in his own arson attack. Gets a bit confusing while we're both still around doesn't it? It'll be so much easier when we're minus one twin. Even you must admit it's perfect.'

She shook her head at him. 'Perfect? No, it's not perfect Max. It's evil. You're evil. I wish you would burn in your own fire.'

He slapped her across the face and laughed. 'Sorry to disappoint you, but the genie ain't granting you that wish. He'll be too busy granting all mine. Swanky apartment, status, money, respect. Everything my brother got, and I didn't, because I got the shitty rap from our dear departed mother. What a pity she can't see me now. I won't have to work of course. Not after a nice big payoff from the university to help me deal with my trauma. And I'll have women all over me like a rash. You gullible bitches love a hero, don't you?'

He got up from the bed and stood in front of her. She stayed motionless, absorbing everything he'd said and wondering what he was going to do next. She started to speak but he cut her words off with a smug wink.

'And before you give me the dental records speech, I've got that handled too. Turns out our teeth are the one area where we're not identical. He went to fancy dentists, I didn't. But that cute little dental receptionist was so obliging. I'll keep her sweet long enough to make sure the authorities see what I want them to see, then I'll dispense with her. Pity, she was bloody hot in the sack, but there you go. Can't have any loose ends.' He leaned over her, his voice dropped, and he ran his eyes and hands over her body until her skin prickled and bile rose into her mouth again. 'I'll have to get rid of you too eventually. But all in good time, and not before I sample what my dear twin has already.'

As he moved away, she forced her legs to lift her from the bed and rushed at him. She rained punches down on him, but they had no effect against his strong body. He turned, laughed and grabbed her wrists, shaking her as if he was playing with a rag doll. Then he tightened his grip and banged her head against the wall.

She heard her cry of pain mixed with the sound of her head hitting the hard unforgiving surface, and she got one of her wishes.

She finally lost consciousness.

CHAPTER SIXTY-SEVEN

Catherine blinked against the dark unfamiliarity of her surroundings. Her mouth felt dry and her lips were stuck together like parchment. Her head ached and she was desperate for water and a painkiller. Automatically she turned to switch on the bedside lamp, but her arm refused to move. She tried to swing her leg out of bed but was met with the same refusal. She was immobile.

Why was her brain not communicating with her limbs? Panic rose up in her, on a collision course towards the pain radiating down from her head. She took a deep breath before they hit each other straight on. She squeezed her eyes tight shut, preferring the familiar darkness of her own eyelids to the disorientating darkness of the room.

She told herself to stay calm and think. If she was ill why wasn't she lying comfortably in a bed with Clayton and Will talking to her as she woke up? Instead she was upright, cold and uncomfortable. Alone in a black, airless and soundless vacuum where none of her senses worked properly.

She tried to cough but her mouth wouldn't move. The strange noise of its strangled escape echoed into the vacuum.

At least she could hear, so she was alive. Images of Clayton, Will, and Nina swam across her eyelids. Then, like a monster rising from the deep, another face appeared and obliterated them all. A twisted face, familiar but distorted by anger. And she remembered.

Max. She winced as she relived the force of the blow he'd dealt her. It had obviously knocked her unconscious. She wondered how long she'd been out for, and how and where he'd restrained her. She guessed she was gagged. That explained her inability to move her lips more than a fraction, and the muffled sound her cough had made.

She forced her eyes open to escape the image of Max. The horror of his plan replayed in her head and shook her back to her senses. She had to escape. She was the only person who could stop him.

She told herself to think logically. Her intelligence was the only thing on her side, and she had to use it. She focused on her arms and hands which she could barely feel. If she was in a chair, they must be bound behind her back to it. She had to move before her circulation slowed down beyond a point where she could manage movement. She wiggled her fingers. Slowly and stiffly they came back to life and as they gained strength, she felt them make contact with something. It was the rope she'd seen earlier. She scraped her nails against it until they hurt. It was thick and heavy duty and she had no hope of untying it.

She dropped her head in defeat as a wave of exhaustion washed over her. She was powerless. Max had beaten her. Then her son's words crashed through the oblivion she was about to slip into. He'd told her she rocked. He believed she could do anything. She forced her head up. She couldn't give in. Not yet.

She took some deep breaths then tried moving her feet, but she couldn't. She assumed they were bound with the same rope. She shifted her lower body in the chair as much as her restraints allowed. Even the most minor movement might keep her alert.

As she wriggled against the frustration of her incarceration, she felt something digging into her through the fabric of her jeans. She moved again and it was still there. Whatever it was, it was small, and it was inside one of the rear pockets.

She was puzzled. The only thing she'd slipped into the jeans was her old phone, and Max had taken that. Then she remembered the last time she'd worn these jeans. Of course, Nina's first night in London. The night they'd met David. And the night her friend had asked her to look after her lighter. That's what was tucked it into her pocket. So much had happened that weekend because of the Becca news that she'd completely forgotten it was there.

Thank God it was. It was all she had. Now she had to stay calm and figure out how to use it.

CHAPTER SIXTY-EIGHT

It seemed to take forever for Catherine to use her lower body to force the lighter up towards the top of her pocket until she could press two of her fingers against it. She kept pausing for breath. If she made one clumsy move and it fell to the floor, she'd lose her only potential means of escape.

When she finally got a grip on it, she waited a moment. She knew what she had to do, and she knew it was going to hurt. She used one finger to stretch the opening of her jeans pocket, and the other one to flick the lighter. She braced herself against the pain. After three attempts the flame burned into her skin. She could smell her own flesh. Her eyes watered and she cried out as the pain intensified, but the tape on her mouth stifled the sound. She arched her body and clenched her muscles as much as her restraints would allow.

She'd never felt pain like it, and she prayed she wouldn't pass out. Then another smell began to compete with the unfamiliar smell of her charring skin. She recognised the aroma of singed fabric. The lighter's flame had made contact with the rope.

She had no idea how long it would take for the rope to

weaken enough for her to loosen it, or how she would endure the pain until it did. She held the lighter as steadily as she could while she wiggled her opposite wrist against the rope. She told herself to focus on that movement and think past the pain. She bent her head and tried to bite her lip in concentration through the mouth tape. Then she moved her wrist again. There was less resistance against it, the lighter was doing its job. She turned her wrist with more force as she felt the rope's grip against it continue to weaken.

Her finger quivered with the effort of pressing the lighter and she lost her hold on it. As it fell to the floor, she twisted her wrist sharply against the rope in angry desperation, and it worked itself free. She put her hand to her mouth, ripped off the tape and screamed with anger, frustration and pain.

She stretched her arm out to see what she came into contact with. The rough fabric she felt told her she was next to the shabby sofa in Max's living room. If she shuffled the chair forward, she could maybe get to the light switch, then at least she'd escape this darkness and be able to see how to untie the other ropes. She took a deep breath and started to move.

Her journey across the room, dragging herself in the chair, was slow and laboured, but as her feet hit a hard surface, she knew she'd made it to the other side. She was certain she'd moved in a straight line, so she guessed the light switch was immediately above her. Trying to ignore the agonising pain in her wrist and hand she reached up, her fingers desperately searching the wall until she found it.

After the strange unfamiliar darkness, now her eyes hurt as they struggled to readjust to the familiarity of light. She told herself not to look at her wrist, but the pain radiating from it drew her like a magnet. She wished she hadn't. It was charred, red and oozing with blisters. The sight made her feel sick and tears threatened to engulf her, but she blinked them back. She'd come this far, she was still alive, and she was part way to being free. She had to stay strong.

She glanced at her watch, but the heat of the lighter had melted the face. There was no sign of a clock in the room. She had no idea of the time or how long Max had been gone, but she needed to move fast.

Her other wrist was still tied to the chair. She reached behind her with her free hand, and within seconds both her hands were free of the still smouldering rope. She bent over to untie her feet which were bound together to the support bar between the chair's legs, but the knots were too tight. She turned herself and the chair round and saw the lighter on the floor across the room. She needed to get to it. Her progress back was quicker with both her arms to lift the chair. She picked up the lighter and shook it. It was almost out of gas, but at least now she knew where to focus whatever flame it had left.

When she flicked it on it died on her in moments. She swore and gave it a violent shake. It came back to life and she held it close to her feet as the rope started to blacken. When her ankles could no longer stand the pain, she flicked the lighter off and her hands tugged at the rope. She moved her feet in unison, trying to pull them away from the chair as she felt the rope weaken.

She paused for breath, then a guttural yell rose up from the pit of her stomach and gave her the strength for another attempt. The rope started to give way, but not enough. She needed something else to help her. Max's storage box was two feet away. Why hadn't she looked in there sooner? She bounced herself and the chair over to it and opened the lid. It was full of sexual devices and equipment and she shuddered as she imagined the depravity Max had in mind for her later.

She threw things on to the floor in frenzied disgust until she found what she needed.

She tried not to imagine what Max used the hammer for as she aimed it against the chair. It made light work of breaking the cheap wooden strut she was tied to, and within seconds her feet were free. She threw the hammer across the room in disgust, wriggled her legs to get her circulation going again, then ran into the narrow hallway and headed for the door.

As she flung it open, she remembered the gun. It might still be in the wardrobe, and Max had no idea she'd seen it.

She rushed to the bedroom and prayed it was still there.

CHAPTER SIXTY-NINE

Catherine ran into the street and took a deep breath. She was desperate to replace the rancid dust-laden atmosphere she'd been held in with different air, but she kept moving. She was relieved it was still daylight. Maybe she wasn't too late.

She touched the back pocket of her jeans, comforted by the feel of the gun. She'd found it and loaded it, a skill she remembered from researching an article on firearms as a junior reporter. She hated guns and had never fired one, but as she thought of Max's evil face she knew she was prepared to shoot him if she had to.

She estimated she was ten minutes running time from the university and she concentrated on the route she'd memorised earlier, forming her plan as she ran and trying to ignore the pain in her ankles. She'd tell John to call the police before she confronted Max. She dismissed the voice in her head telling her it was foolhardy to face him alone. For once, she had an advantage over him. She had the element of surprise, and she was armed.

Breathless when she reached the university's automatic glass entrance doors, she ran in as they slid open. Everything looked normal. Max had clearly not put his plan in motion yet. She saw John's shocked expression as she approached him. She couldn't imagine what she must look like.

Without stopping, she yelled her instruction. 'John, call the police. Now.'

As she ran for the stairs he started to speak, but she cut him off. 'No time to explain John. Trust me, and do it. Please. Fire brigade too.'

She took the stairs to the basement two at a time. When she reached Clayton's laboratory its lights were on, but the door was locked. She punched it with her fist and screamed Max's name. The door flew open and he grabbed her by the arm and dragged her in.

The smell of petrol assaulted her nostrils, but before she could look round he jerked her head towards him and sneered at her. 'Well, aren't you full of surprises Miss Smart Ass. Looks like I underestimated you. Still, I can cope with an unexpected guest. I'll improvise.' His eyes swept over her body. 'Pity I won't get to sample your delights after all, but I'm afraid you're going to have to be collateral damage of evil Max's handiwork. Suppose it saves me a messy job later.' He smirked at her. 'And this way you'll have a front row seat as Loverboy goes up in flames. Before you do.' He shoved her roughly to the floor. 'Sorry about the petrol fumes but it's nearly showtime. Now stay there while I think. Don't move or I really will hurt you.'

She shrank back against the wall and looked across the room. Her heart raced and she thought it might explode in her chest. Clayton was slumped in a chair. He seemed barely conscious, as if he was drugged. She called his name and saw his fingers move. Thank God he was still alive.

Max walked towards him, stood behind the chair, and whispered something she couldn't hear. She reached into her back pocket for the gun. She tried to focus her aim, but it shook in her hand. She shouted across the room. She needed Max to move away from Clayton. She couldn't trust herself to take a shot while the two men were so close.

'Leave him alone Max. Hurt him and I'll kill you.'

Max jerked his head up and sneered as he looked at the gun in her trembling hand.

'Here we go again. You really don't give up do you? But I don't think you're going to try and shoot me while he's in between me and that gun, do you? Not the way you're shaking. You probably haven't even taken the safety off.'

He stared her out, but didn't move, and neither could she. She heard a murmur from Clayton and glanced down at him. In the split second she took her eyes off Max he flew across the room, made a grab for the gun and punched her. She fell back against the wall and the gun slipped out of her hand.

She watched it fall to the floor in slow motion as she felt herself slide down the wall, and everything went black.

CHAPTER SEVENTY

Catherine's eyes flickered open. In the half-light two men were struggling in front of her. Two identical men, dressed in identical jeans and sweatshirts, trying to overpower each other. Where was she? Maybe she was dreaming. Her head was muddled, and it hurt. She shook it, wanting to shake away the confusion. Her eyes closed again. She wanted to sleep, but she was breathing in sickly air. She knew that smell, it was petrol. And she started to remember.

This wasn't a dream. She was in Clayton's lab and she'd come here to save him. She had to protect him from Max. She'd brought a gun, she remembered that too, but where was it? She opened her eyes, looked around her and saw it on the floor, about six feet away. She crawled over and picked it up.

She sat, clutching the gun tightly, as both men turned and stared at her. They held each other by the shoulders, frozen in a motionless tableau. She glanced down at the gun, and checked the safety was off.

She could hear her heart pound and the blood raced to her head. She felt dizzy as she struggled to stay conscious.

She looked up again, straining her eyes to focus on the two men in front of her. The identical twins.

She had to make a decision, and she had to get it right. For her. And for Clayton.

Then a voice emerged from the silent tableau. 'Catherine. Please. Do it.'

Pain ripped through her head and the words were barely audible, but she was sure it was Clayton. Max had almost fooled her once, but she knew the voice of the man she loved. She looked at the two motionless men who were staring back at her. She didn't know which one had spoken. She felt herself slipping into darkness again and tried to hold the gun steady, but it shook as she pointed it at them each in turn.

The twin tableau moved closer to her and the overhead light illuminated two identical faces. Then she stared directly into both sets of eyes. And instantly, she knew.

Just as she'd known when she'd first seen him. His eyes jolted her back into consciousness now and told her the decision she must make. She steadied her hand and directed her aim. She took a deep breath, closed her eyes and fired.

She fell backwards from the force of the shot and felt herself sink into a pair of strong arms as a voice started to speak. She couldn't hear the words, but the voice was soft and familiar.

The strong arms held her more tightly, the voice spoke again, and she smiled.

She was still smiling as she slipped back into the darkness.

EPILOGUE

HIM

Clayton turned over, propped himself up on one elbow and stared at her in the half-light. Her face wore a faint smile, and her breathing was steady with the contentment of sleep. He thanked his mother's God, as he had so often in the past two weeks, that the painkillers were working, and she was finally free of the agony she'd endured.

An agony she'd endured to save his life.

He reached out and gently stroked her cheek, anxious not to wake her, but unable to resist touching this stunning woman who he adored. She'd walked into his life unannounced so recently, but now he couldn't imagine a life without her. He rolled onto his back and stared at the ceiling. He moved his hand to make contact with the small of her back, desperate to reassure himself that this wasn't a dream and that she really was here, back home, and in their bed. His stomach lurched when he thought back to how close he'd come to losing her on that fateful day in his lab, and to everything that had happened since.

In that agonising first week after the shooting, when he almost didn't dare to think about her lying beside him again, he'd hardly left her hospital room. But expert medical attention, heavy-duty painkillers and antibiotics, combined with her fighting spirit, had set her on the road to recovery. The doctors assured them that, with treatment, the scars she'd been forced to inflict on herself would eventually be barely visible.

Whenever he looked at the dressings on both her wrists and her ankles, his hatred for his twin threatened to overwhelm him. As it had when he'd cradled her fall when she collapsed into oblivion after she fired that fatal shot. He'd looked at her battered and bruised body and the pain etched on her face as he held her. In the brief minutes before the police had arrived, he'd looked at Max's still body, and into his face. He felt nothing but contempt at the twisted smile it wore, even in death. A twisted smile of pure evil which his brother would now take to his grave.

Later, when Catherine regained consciousness in hospital, he'd touched her face gently to reassure her as she opened her eyes.

They filled with tears of relief as she gave a weak smile and muttered, 'Clayton, you're here.'

His finger pressed a soft kiss against her mouth. 'Welcome back, darling. Of course, I'm here, thanks to you. And I'm not going anywhere. Do you remember everything that happened?'

She nodded. 'I remember every second.' Her voice was sounding stronger, but it dropped to a whisper. 'Max...is he...?'

He caressed her fingers with his. 'Yes, he's gone. He'll never hurt anybody again. You saved my life, Catherine.'

She smiled at him. 'I saved my own too. How would I have lived without you?'

Their initial interview with the police had been short. They were in no doubt that she'd had no choice but to pull the trigger that fired the fatal shot. Max's history and their search of his flat and the building where he held her captive had told their own story.

When the police had left, he placed his hands lightly on hers to reassure her as she looked at her bandaged wrists and a tremor of panic rocked her body. 'They're going to be fine baby; I promise. The doctors have told me that.' He paused as his voice faltered. 'When I think what you went through... the pain he caused you. Yet you never gave up.'

She moved her hand slowly and pressed a finger to his mouth as she sat up. Her voice was barely a whisper. 'How could I have given up? When that would've meant losing you?'

He looked up at her. 'Thank God you made the right choice. How did you know?'

She lifted her hand slowly to touch his face. 'Your eyes told me. I fell in love with you when I looked into them the first night we had dinner. I knew then, and I knew when I fired the shot. Max may have shared your DNA. He may have looked identical. He might have been able to fool the world. But he could never fool the woman who loves you.'

Then he'd held her, unable to take his eyes off her, until she closed hers and fell into a deep sleep.

Now, in the early morning half-light of the apartment, he

watched her in deep sleep again, and listened to the sound of her breathing. He would never grow tired of waking up next to her.

He glanced at his watch. It was still only 6.30 a.m. He could use some more sleep, then he'd go out to buy them breakfast. Will was arriving at noon, and the two of them had a welcome home dinner planned for Catherine. Becca and Tim were coming, Lizzie and Clara too, and he was collecting Nina from Euston later as a surprise guest. Will had told him how much Christmas meant to his Mum. This one had been spent in hospital, overshadowed by events, and they hoped tonight might be some compensation.

He moved closer to her, put his arm gently around her waist and she murmured. He smiled at the sound, and at how good he finally knew life could be.

The woman he loved and had waited for all his life, but had almost lost, was lying beside him. Together they could face anything.

He was free from the fear that had haunted him for ten years that his daughter was a victim of Huntington's disease. He hadn't told Becca yet that he wasn't her biological father, or about his personal genetic flaw, but when the time was right, he would. And with Catherine by his side, he knew they could deal with it; they were a family now.

His research had been thrust into the public arena after the shooting and the dramatic events that followed, as a result of Catherine's investigation. It had become the talk of the scientific community and set the genetics world alight. The opinion of other experts in his field was that he had made the most significant breakthrough since the genome project itself.

He and his team were about to start work with the in-house researchers at ANZ on final rigorous testing of his theories before clinical trials began, and the Chief Executive had already gone public to confirm his confidence that they would be in a position to announce more details within six months. Susie and the team were teasing him with the rumours he was being considered as a potential Nobel prize winner.

With his head against Catherine's, he smiled at that thought and closed his eyes. The rhythm of his breathing quickly matched hers, and within minutes he was asleep himself.

HER

Catherine turned over to stare at him. He was wearing the frown he often wore when he was asleep. It always made her smile and was one of the many things she loved about him. So many that she'd lost count.

It was a frown of concentration. It seemed he dreamed as a scientist, his mind refusing to abandon the facts and formulae that dominated his days, even in sleep. He hadn't realised he did it, until she confessed to her early morning scrutiny of him and teased him about it.

She reached out and ran her fingers across his mouth and down his neck until they settled in the thick dark hair of his chest. The frown became a slow smile as he lifted a hand to clasp hers tightly against him and opened one eye.

'The morning frown?'

She lay her head on his shoulder and smiled into it. 'I missed it while I was in hospital. I love watching your face when you sleep.' She pressed her body more tightly against him. She wanted every inch of her skin in contact with him. 'When I think how close I came to never seeing it again.'

Her voice faltered and tailed off. He wrapped his arm around her, pulled her closer and kissed the top of her head. He gently caressed her hands against his chest. She glanced down at the dressings on both her wrists.

He bent to kiss her, and she abandoned herself to him. When he held her, she could bury the memory of what Max had subjected them to, but she knew it would never leave her. Neither would the image of the moment she'd fired the shot that killed him, but she knew she would face it all again to be in the arms of this man.

She smiled and propped herself up on one elbow as she watched him throw on jeans and a t-shirt. She hadn't wanted to let go of him as they held each other in satisfied contentment, but he had insisted on going out to buy them breakfast.

He kissed her and promised he wouldn't be long. She sank back into the pillows that still bore the imprint of his head and reflected on how much had happened in the space of a fortnight.

Apparently, she'd been unconscious for twenty-four hours, her body's mechanism for dealing with the trauma it had endured. Will had rushed to the hospital as soon as Clayton called him. For two days they both refused to leave her side until eventually she regained strength, reassured them she'd be fine, and insisted that Will should get back to Cambridge for the end of term events. When he had reluctantly agreed and left, the two men in her life hugged each other like father and son, and she knew they'd formed an unbreakable bond.

Becca had visited the hospital daily. She and Will had become instant siblings, united by the shared relief that they hadn't lost their beloved parents. She lay on Catherine's chest, crying her thanks for her father's life, and she hugged

Clayton as if she couldn't bear to let him go when she learned the full horror of what Max had intended.

George joined her when they gave the police the details of their investigation. His anger at her for facing Max alone disappeared when he saw her in hospital for the first time, replaced with clear emotion for the friend he'd so nearly lost.

Things moved quickly after the dramatic events in Clayton's lab. Max had kept detailed notes and secret recordings of his meetings and conversations with Richard Cameron and the members of Cerberus. Within hours the police had swooped on their homes and offices. Paul Naylor and his associates were on remand facing trial for fraud and conspiracy to murder. A number of senior government officials were under investigation.

Richard Cameron disappeared before the police could arrest and charge him. A day later he was found dead in his car, his body slumped over the steering wheel and an empty pill bottle on the passenger seat. His wife fled to Scotland to escape the press furore and Susie moved in with George, at his insistence. He told Catherine he was certain he loved her and was committed to helping her through the grief of losing her father within two days of discovering his role in the conspiracy.

'The Cerberus Affair,' as the media had christened it, had dominated the press and news channels daily in the immediate aftermath of its exposure. The evolving love affair between her and Clayton, against which such dramatic events had unfolded, had captured the imagination of the nation. As had the personal story behind his research, and the fact that it had so nearly cost both of them their lives.

The Guardian's circulation shot up, to the delight of Sam, who gave her and George front page coverage for the story, told from their uniquely personal perspectives. He'd also given George the opportunity to work with the science editor in reporting Clayton's breakthrough, hailed as one of the most significant game-changing medical advancements of all time.

Catherine sank further into the pillow, smiling at being back in their bed, and as she always did when she thought about him. Her phone pinged on the bedside table and she turned to check it. His message told her he loved her and was on his way back with breakfast. He added a P.S. to tell her that David had confirmed he would join them for dinner and was looking forward to catching up with her.

She messaged back a kiss emoji as she thought about David. Clayton didn't know, and she could never tell him, but she'd seen him last week. He'd visited her in hospital, and she'd confronted him with her suspicions about his relationship with Becca's mother. He broke down as he confessed to spending a drunken night with her two months before she and Clayton announced she was pregnant. He'd never asked Angela if he was the father, and the first time he watched Clayton holding Becca he'd told himself to bury his curiosity and simply love her as Uncle David.

Catherine had held his hand after he finished his story. Neither of them needed to acknowledge what they both knew was a silent understanding. Instead, they hugged each other, and agreed never to discuss it again.

She sat up as she heard Clayton's key in the door, then the sound of movement in the kitchen. Minutes later he walked into the bedroom with a tray and turned to give her a grin. She watched him stride across the room towards her. Was it only a few short months ago that she'd woken up wishing away the tedium and predictability of her life? Then she'd been faced with the news of Adam's death. She'd got more than she bargained for, but she'd done what Adam had asked her to do.

And as she looked at the man in front of her now, she knew she wanted nothing more than to spend the rest of her life with him.

If waking up every morning with him became her new predictability, she was happy to take it. She gave him an inviting look and he put the tray down, leaned towards her and took her in his arms. His smile told her he knew exactly what she wanted. She reached for her phone and switched it off.

Google headlines could wait today.

A NOTE FROM CHARLOTTE

I hope you enjoyed reading **THE CERBERUS AFFAIR** and meeting Catherine and Clayton.

Their story continues in my next novel **THEY,** available later in the year, which will also see Catherine's investigative skills called upon once again.

To hear more about that and other releases, please visit my website -

www.charlottevalentinewriter.com

Building a relationship with my readers is important to me, so please hit the link on the website to join my reader community - for updates on my writing, to receive exclusive free reading content, and to contact me.

Finally, please consider sharing your thoughts with others about **THE CERBERUS AFFAIR** by leaving a review, and thank you again for reading my debut novel.

ABOUT THE AUTHOR

Charlotte Valentine was born and grew up in the north of England then studied law in London. She worked in investment banking before deciding to pursue her love of literature and study for her MA with the Open University. This inspired her to write. After completing a Creative Writing course, *The Cerberus Affair* is her first novel. She splits her time between London and southern Spain and shares her home with her teenage son, 9 rescued cats and a dog.

For more information:
www.charlottevalentinewriter.com

ACKNOWLEDGEMENTS

Few things in life are achieved without the contribution, support and encouragement of others, and the writing and publication of *The Cerberus Affair* has been no exception. I owe heartfelt thanks to many people who helped me along the way:

Everybody at the Faber Academy, especially Julia Crouch, who introduced me to the art of writing and, most importantly, brought my writer buddies Amanda Campbell and Bridget Guzek into my life. This novel would never have been finished without their unwavering support, advice and friendship.

My editors Eve Seymour and Janet Laurence; the book is so much better for your input.

Professor Julian Blow in Dundee for his initial invaluable advice on the science of gene editing. Any errors are mine alone.

My cover designer Tim Barber, whose graphics brought the essence of the story to life.

And to Anna; technical guru to me (an unenviable task),

marketing consultant, and - above all - friend. Without her constant support and expertise, the book might never have been transformed from a file on my laptop to its published format, or found its audience. I am indebted to her.

I am grateful to everybody in my advanced reader group for their comments - but especially Barbara, Louise and Nadia. They were the first to read the completed book when I knew it still needed work, but by telling me they liked it, they encouraged me to believe it could be good enough to publish.

And I thank all my friends offline and online, who knew when to ask about my writing progress, and just as importantly when not to, and for being there when I needed a break to recharge the batteries.

And some especially personal thank you messages: -

To my stepfather Pat for never letting me doubt my ability to get this done.

To Stewart for his wise counsel, for his patience in listening to my updates on progress, and for the innumerable cups of Spanish coffee while I told him.

To my son Alex, for telling me he was proud when the book was finished. Without him it would have been finished a lot sooner, but life would be a lot less fun.

And, almost finally, to my cats and dog who were by my side throughout, tolerated my frequently erratic work schedule, and who could probably recite the entire novel backwards!

Above all, to my mother, who was my biggest supporter from the day I wrote the opening lines of *The Cerberus Affair*. Sadly, I lost her before it was finished, but her voice has always been in my head, telling me I could do this. And somehow, she knows - I did it!

Made in the USA
Coppell, TX
10 September 2020